kaleidoscope

Kaleidoscope

A Novel
by
Elliott B. Oppenheim

ATOM Press
316 SE Pioneer Way
Oak Harbor, WA 98277

ISBN 978-1-942426-19-6

Printed on Acid-free paper
Cover by Ravi - Designer

Preface

Kaleidoscope is a coming of age novel set in 1964-1965, in the form of fictional memoir. It is based upon my facts, my life. Chaim Goldberg is a part of me that I will let you see through the eyes of someone looking though a twirling kaleidoscope. There is a lot of drugs, sex, and rock and roll.

Kaleidoscope required five years to write and is the first in a series of five novels, a pentalogy I call Waiting for Winter, similar to the Five Books of Moses, the ultimate coming of age tale. There are few, if any, other literary pentalogies which trace an entire life. I can do this now that I am seventy-two and have the ability to critically look back.

In *Kaleidoscope*, Chaim Goldberg searches for meaning as he tosses around in the lives of Nedda Boudreaux and Stella O'Shannahan. He is a lonely boy, misunderstood by himself and others, seeking love in all of the wrong ways and places. He seeks acceptance and understanding. Is that too much to ask?

The next book is *Medicine Man*, continuing with Goldberg's misconstrued life and commences in September of 1977, when he is practicing medicine and makes some wrong decisions bringing about calamitous consequences to him and to his family and to his profession.

The next three novels will detail Goldberg's early life, on becoming a doctor, and on becoming a person, in his perpetual search for meaning.

I dedicate *Kaleidoscope* to:

    Lester Sauvage, MD- a doctor's doctor
    Anthony Russo, Attorney at Law
    Leonard Schroeter, Attorney at Law
    Peter Chatard, MD
    Longtime friend and personal magician, Steffan Soule, ATOM Press.
    My children, David and Laura and to my grandson, Jack

-Elliott Oppenheim, Florence, MT and Jerusalem, Israel

The pool thermometer looked as if it were about to burst, like hirsute Karen's zits, with the mercury meniscus, swollen in the heat, nearing the top of its column. It was only eleven, and southeast Pennsylvania sizzled in its summer. *Never know how much I love you, never know how much I care...Fever!*

The lyrics filled his mind like a hose gushing water...*when it sizzles,* and his radio played beneath the tube-steel guard seat. Perspiration trickled from his armpits as he daydreamed of the protected dunes on the New Jersey shore when, just a few days before, he'd snuggled between the nubile breasts of his ophthalmologist's daughter, Joanie Hoffmann-Willberger, a Willberger, of the Trenton landed gentry. His mother was in ecstasy with that liaison. She was Jewish.

Kissing Joanie was like licking an ashtray, but he endured that because she gave him what he wanted—what every teenaged boy wants—sex... ungarnished sex. She let him linger between her breasts, and he dared to suckle until she pushed him away with, "Hurry, my mother'll miss us." She pulled her padded bikini top back into place and stubbed out her cigarette in the hot sand. He drew satisfaction knowing that his mother would never know what had happened on the date she'd arranged.

He'd had some fun with girls: a few fervent, quick, surreptitious hand jobs at the movies and assorted bj's in cars or in other dark, secluded places. One time, he slithered his fingers into Joanie's moistness, and she shuddered, and then he tried to enter her, but she snapped shut like a clam shell diving for safety.

Her lips accepted him like the petals of an hibiscus flower. "Don't get me messy," she warned as she pulled off him just as he spurted. Zingo! He laughed at how wonderfully offended she was when he splatted her bouffant. She slapped him. "You're a dirty, mean boy," she'd said, and he loved it. He thrilled at her pretextual annoyance with his bad-boyness.

1

Clandestiny

August 1963, Yardley, Pennsylvania

Flipping open the worn paperback, he bent the cover around the spine and skipped through the first few lines. "Indian summer is like a woman. Ripe, hotly passionate, fickle, she comes and goes as she pleases, so that one is never sure if she comes at all, nor for how long she will stay." He knew that he shouldn't read on the guard stand, but this was hot stuff, and D.H. was meant to be read on a hot summer day. A pup tent grew in his swimsuit. This was his second time through the book.

He had to appear attentive as he scanned the golf course with heavy, black, Zeiss 7 x 80 binoculars. Out at the rough, just to the side of the fourth green, he spotted Poe, a shiny raven, the size of a football, which he'd watched all the dry summer. He pecked the eyes out of a dead rabbit, and the long ears wiggled in the dried grass each time the bird nipped at it.

Poe was a *Corvus corax*, distinguishing it from *Corvus brachyrhynchos*, the common, smaller, crow. He liked Latin taxonomy and enjoyed watching it flap its wings and take flight with its earned rabbit morsel.

3

He regarded girls as a sexual commodity, like McDonald's cheeseburgers, whom he could consume at his whim and as often as possible.

Sweat dribbled down his sculpted *latissimi dorsi* into his swim shorts, drenching his red, Yardley Country Club lifeguard shirt. *Fever, when it sizzles.* His controlling mother vexed him but, despite her admonitions, one goal remained paramount. He wanted another cheeseburger. He had to get laid. He'd had enough of reading and vicarious experience; he could not go to college in such a defective condition. Henry Miller was vicarious; this was real.

Virginity would be worse than low SAT's. Every guy, so it seemed, had already gotten laid, and his time had come...and he laughed at the pun...come. *O tempore, O mores*, to hell with Cicero.

A devoted academic, he'd done his exhaustive research masturbating to *Playboy, Lady Chatterley's Lover, Memoirs of Hecate County, Peyton Place,* both *Tropics*, and looking at French pictures he'd found in his dad's books in the bookshelf in his room. "No one goes to college a virgin," Zubarsky said. His friend huffed and puffed as if he'd already been a big, bad wolf.

His band mates laughed at his ineptitude with girls, not that any of them were any better at it. Then, there was that other smarmy threat: pregnancy. In her high-pitched hysteria, she threatened. "One sperm, and you can forget about medicine."

"Mom!" he answered, aghast and embarrassed. She transgressed with impunity his most intimate areas. He'd been slow to physically mature, so pubic and axillary hair were recent additions to his lithe and muscular swimmer's body. He *was* shy with girls, but to have her articulate such things was like catching him jerking off.

Cobblestone Karen, one of Johnny Calamari's nieces, teased him at the Club, "Hey Red, do you shave?" Ravaged by acne, Chaim nicknamed her that because of her cobblestone complexion.

"Go grow your mustache," he replied, and she shut up. She looked like a catfish, complete with an odd wiry hair sticking out from a facial mole on her left cheek. He wondered if she had hairy tits.

At the beginning of the summer, he'd taken over the family's 1955 Buick, tattered, green, and bug-eyed, and his friends quickly hectored him about that, seeing its resemblance to a bullfrog. The Frog, they called his key to freedom. The best part about the car was that it had a massive V-8. He would soon learn that it had another great benefit: an hospitable back seat.

Wet vapors steamed as he lifted his pith helmet, and the moist, hot air ventilated his soaked, copper hair, cooling him, but in the swelter, daydreams spun. Lifeguarding was boring. No one will ever drown here, he thought, but then he heard commotion, splashing, thrashing, a shrill "help, help!"

A snappy looking woman wearing a yellow-polka-dot bikini pretended to struggle in the three feet. "Hey! Lifeguard! Yoohoo! Are you awake up there?" She called out to him, laughing, bouncing up and down, gyrating, then arching and flopping like a porpoise back into the water, all the while holding her hands high. She was a mixture between Marilyn Monroe in *Some Like it Hot* and Eva Marie Saint in *North By Northwest*.

"Yeah, well I am!" he barked, unable to rescue his eyes from her cleavage. Sexual urges commandeered his brain as he felt he could do a back flip into her itsy-bitsy, teeny-weeny, yellow, polka-dot bikini. Beneath the suit fabric, her erect full-button nipples yearned for freedom. Insouciant, in response to his scolding, she puckered her lips and blew a defiant kiss. "Tonight, Tonight," from *West Side Story*, emanated from his D-battery-powered, red, GE transistor radio, stowed beneath his seat, which Uncle Elijah sent for his sixteenth birthday gift.

Men took refuge in seersucker and women wore their hair up to let any breeze cool them. It was the time of year when sunflowers drooped in the heat and dandelions whined. All of Lower Bucks County lay as limp as corn tassels. Women in linen with a moist perspiration layer appeared as juicy as tomatoes in the field, and they needed a good plucking.

When he taught the women lessons, he focused on the beads of sweat that formed on their upper lips and in their cleavages. Just before jumping off his lifeguard stand, Chaim empathized with a praying mantis, praying for a breeze on an acacia twig, pressing asthenic push-ups.

Dipping his helmet into the pool, he sloshed water over his head, replaced it, and jumped onto his seat. He settled until a prod in his side disturbed him, and he looked down into gracefully conical breasts in a yellow polka-dot top, beautifully gift-packaged like two Fuji apples, alluringly wet.

Seductive and flamboyant, she was. Club rumors murmured about her and her husband. He was rich and powerful, and she was lonely. This was the first time he'd had any real contact with her other than setting before her drinks. "Extra rum," she commanded at each service, and her bevy of friends chuckled as she exerted her authority, bossing around the boy. When he deferentially bowed and served her, he smiled. She smiled. There was no tipping, but he could tell she'd like to give him a little something more.

In the hot sun that day, when she taxed him, he looked down at her, and she said, "Here. We went to Atlantic City. It's full of niggers, but my girlfriends and I liked the rides." She handed him a rectangular box. There was a hand- calligraphied label, stating "handsomely hand-crafted in New Hampshire," with a thin, blue, silk ribbon bow around its middle.

"Open it," she said, and he pulled the ribbon. Her eyes lit on DH. "Nice summer reading?" she teased. "…it's a kaleidoscope."

He never called Negroes *niggers*, though his mother did, but not his father, and he knew how humiliating and wounded he felt when *goyim* ridiculed him for being who he was. He looked down at her from his perch on the guard stand, embarrassed that she'd seen *Lady Chatterley*, which he'd borrowed from his father's nightstand.

Her fabulous teeth stood as brilliant soldiers at attention. Her long uvula dangled and flailed as she laughed. He would become a doctor someday, and her anatomy, in its totality, fascinated him. "It's made of rosewood," she said with purchaser-pride.

She watched him pet the cylindrical instrument, rubbing its shaft. "It's beautiful!"

"Look into it," she offered, licking her lips, and he did.

"Open it. Take it out." She chortled, encouraging him, delighting in her naughty double entendre. He liked her tessitura and musical laugh. Branded into the barrel, in small letters, was *Gunk Kaleidoscopes, Acworth, New Hampshire.* He thought: V= πr2h, the formula to calculate the volume of the cylinder, base times height, as he peered into the kaleidoscope, twirled the cylinder, and watched the tumbling beads.

As the glass pieces spun around, he marveled at the arrangements. "It's like a geode! These permutations are endless," he said, admiring the symmetrical rays and sparkles in all of their optical complexity. "Infinity. It's infinity inside," he said, turning the drum, marveling, captivated by the images.

The colors were vivid, deep purple, reds, blues, greens, yellows, some heliotrope. "It's great! It's like an aaaaartist's palette." He stuttered when he got enthusiastic. He liked art, liked colors, and was tickled by this instrument's complexity, yet enthralled with its simplicity.

"It's got four mirrors. Most have three."

He handed it back to her. "It's really great!"

"No, no. Keep it! It's for you!" she insisted as she returned the cylinder. "It's my gift to you." Pursing her lips, she kissed through the air. "Mmmmwaaah." Evidently pleased with herself, she went on. "I got it for you. You've been so nice to me all summer. All those delicious extra-rum drinks...and you didn't even charge me."

"Thanks!" he said, astounded at her generosity yet squirming a bit. He'd trespassed into the YCC forbidden zone: speaking to a member. Karen appeared in the corner of his eye. She was always watching him, which was the reason he had to look busy.

The new friends took refuge in the shade. "No one's ever said 'thank you,'" he told her.

"All of us like you. You're so polite and, uh, well built," she replied, giggling. Ordinarily, the members treated the worker bees like their Adirondack chaises, arranging them, beckoning them, ordering his services with arbitrary, nonchalant will. Her consideration and notice touched him.

Fearing discovery, he tucked the favor into his towel, concealing it from Karen who would soon relieve him on the stand. He saw her on the other side of the pool and, as she approached, biceps rippling, she scowled.

Barry Campbell, a dumpling of a man in his sixties, the manager, rounded the corner from the pool pump house building, nailing him with his gaze. Snapping his fingers loudly three times, his cigar oscillating in his lips, he quacked, "You got a lesson to teach or something?"

"Yeah, in ten minutes. I *have* to *get* something to eat," he said, correcting his superior's grammar error.

"Red, we don't pay you ninety-cents an hour fer you to sit aroun' and entertain members. Get to it. Chop, chop." Chaim hated his condescension and commonness, but the money was better than no job. He liked money.

She ended their forbidden meeting by announcing coquettishly, "I'm in your lesson at noon. Surprise!" Teeth flashed, and she took off towards the snack bar, twitching her hot crossed buns. The D. H. Lawrence flopped onto the pool deck, and he stared at the cover art, portraying a woman in a wanton pose who, he felt, personally, teased him, then pleased that Itsy-Bitsy had seen his secret.

The Club's new money snobbery mimicked the venerated, old money, Philadelphia Cricket Club in Chestnut Hill. Yardley Country Club, while lacking the PCC's trapshooting range, had its own distinctive Tartan crest: green with a red and purple plaid pattern that created a gagging sense of pomp and circumstance. When he started at the Club, Chaim noticed the logarithmic geometric relationships between these plaid lines. Excited about his observation, he mentioned that fact to Karen who sneered, "So?"

"So you're a dolt," was her reposte, and they'd been enemies ever since then, she teasing him about his lack of body hair and he goading her about her manly physique, especially her prominent moustache.

When he pointed out this mathematic, plaid relationship to Barry, he looked at him, incredulous that anyone would care about such a thing, and commanded, "Stop thinking, genius; just work."

Chaim's brain sopped up life's gravies and sauces like Jewish rye in brisket, and he couldn't stop thinking and mulling and rearranging all that he saw and felt. To stop thinking was *unthinkable, absurd,* as Tevye would say.

The Club's social facade, robed in Christianity, with its arcane rules and boundaries, was, to Chaim, foreign. Members were to wear "appropriate attire" at all times. That rule translated to donning color-coordinated, traditional golf togs and meant that all golf carts bore an YCC chevron with the Tartan plaid logo in its crest. Players had pretentious golf carts, agleam with their name emblazoned on the back, emulating the mode on the sterns of their great mahogany Chris Crafts, moored at exclusive Atlantic City marinas.

What annoyed Chaim so much was their smug air of...of... respectability. Yes, the *goyim* were so goddamned... respectable. But over that summer, Chaim had learned the truth about their pervasive respectability. It was all a charade. They refined hypocrisy to an art form, even unto death. Yet, there was one person who was better at it than them: his mother.

While the doors to the locker room opened wide for Chaim to remove cigar butts, as a Jew, in off hours, the Club excluded him from the lush course he watered and manicured, and he was forbidden to relax in *his* pool. His job was delicate, "like walking on eggshells," his mother empathized, "as we have to do with Daddy."

A brilliant boy, he resented that members viewed him as a piece of furniture. Observant, he quickly learned that their veneer of propriety was paper thin. Beneath it seethed all the Dickensian dishevelments, spanning debt, social climbing, spouse abuse, profound hypocrisy, ghastly hidden secrets, replete with pairings of lecherous men molesting pubescent lassies and sun-wrinkled women indulging themselves with smooth lads.

Barry explained the anti-Jew situation with a fatalistic "jus' is" and turned up his palms. "You unnerstan'," he summed, as if this should make sense and that anyone would willingly endorse these fundamental human transgressions.

He learned to materialize with poolside drinks and food. His truest test, though, was to be invisible, to be seen, not heard or, even better, not seen unless absolutely necessary, like maids behind the scenes emptying chamber pots in Victorian manses. He fretted over what Barry would do if he found out about this clandestine gift. He wanted this job, he needed the job, and he wanted the gift, and he worried that Karen would rat him out.

Chaim remembered his dad telling him, "People hate Jews. Fact of life...read Faulkner." His father's answers to all questions came from books. Maybe Dad and Barry Campbell were right, but this angered Chaim. In *The Sound and the Fury* he learned of the cruel, pre-War anti-Semitism, and he'd experienced plenty of it at the Club.

Club members were the thin-nosed golfers, mostly Catholics, who bounced big cigars in their taut lips as they puffed about their big deals, while simultaneously huffing down leonine servings of porterhouse steaks and swilling Rob Roys. On their women, the men adorned the fourth finger on every left hand with ostentatious, large-carat diamond rings, hooking diamond earrings in their earlobes the way a rancher identifies his cows with ear tags, all of this finery ablaze like klieg lights in the summer sun.

A dutiful gardener, he watered these aromatic poolside flowers, delivering sweating glasses and dumping their heaped ashtrays containing the filtered ends, butts colored by vivid lipstick stains, looking like pots of misshapen, grotesque African violets.

He and his mother had a major battle over her cigarette butts. "Clean the ashtrays," was the way it started. He dumped her ashtray on the living room carpet and yelled, "Clean it yourself!" She beat him. He was eight.

The swans preened in the late morning sun, fortifying before the heat of the day before they coiffed, shaved, painted, and plucked, only then to congregate at tasty bistros. Their scat were lip marks on the glasses and cigarette butts after guzzling martinis, whiskey sours, Manhattans, vintage champagnes. Then, when luncheon-time arrived, they genteelly nipped but the smallest bites, like mice, into massive, juicy burgers with thick slices of beefsteak tomatoes, accompanied by the crispiest, salted French fries, or from baskets of fried, heavily battered, *traif* catfish and more stacks of French fries: no mayo, please.

Their puny lips curled as they specified *no onions*, twittering over their nourishments like hummingbirds, ever diligent not to muss their lipstick. The scented bouillabaisse of their intimate perfumes dizzied him. Most of the food wound up not in their gizzards but in the garbage.

His mother would not have approved of the waste, sliding avalanches of nutritious leftovers into the waste bins, right past the gaping mouths of children starving in China. There was nothing lacking in the food. All was perfectly prepared, brought to the table steaming, flavorful. They just didn't eat it.

This was *goyishe kopf,* nauseating and excessive. His mother warned him, but he wanted to taste what they had. Once, furtively, he purloined a piece of catfish from a barely molested platter. He was disappointed, finding it soggy, the fish slimy, and not as tasty as his family's smoked sturgeon, whitefish, or salmon.

By the end of the summer, he saw that these *goyim* were like their catfish: breaded and fried on the outside, slimy and tasteless on the inside. The gaggle beckoned him by simply raising an empty glass, the more subtle the gesture, the more *chi chi*. They often teased around him, making sly comments about what they would do with him during their *private lessons*.

Drunk by that time, they called out for drinks inspired by visits to their tribal watering holes in New York, London, Paris, Brussels, Berlin, Helsinki, Frankfurt, and Rome. Their one-upsmanship conversations about their husbands' *big* business deals in the world's great capitals and lavish vacations in Europe or Africa whet his appetite for the faraway while simultaneously disgusting him.

For these people, everything was "the best." Their kids went to the best schools, they wore the best clothes, and they had the best cars. On Saturday morning, when he and his family prayed at Temple Beth El, these men played golf. The parking lot looked like the *Grande Concourse de Elegance* at the Madison Square Garden car show with its long line-up of gleaming, new and antique Rolls Royces, Bentleys, Mercedes, and Caddys. On one occasion, he'd seen a sparkling Hispano-Suiza J12, a 1933 model. Only a king could own such a vehicle, he imagined... only a king.

On his way to teach his lesson, he bit into a BLT, eating from behind the grill, the cost for which, one dollar, they shamelessly deducted from his paycheck; the cheap gentile pricks. Then they deducted for the uniforms, the YCC guard jackets, even his pith helmet...and they call Jews cheap. By the end of a week, he netted about twenty-bucks: *bubkas*, his mother said. There was no overtime pay. His mother ridiculed his first real job with, "They treat you like a nigger. Why work for *goyim*?"

13

"Jews pay less," was his rejoinder. He cringed at her racial reference. Fact was that he was glad for the work and envied the *goyim*. He was ashamed of being who *he* was and felt like an ugly Jew, as pictured in the Dutch woodcuts. He was kosher but wanted *traif.*

All these inconsistencies swirled in his head as he returned to poolside. On the way, he snatched another piece of breaded catfish from a returning plate. Fresher was this bite, but it was bland. Wading into the water he looked up, "I booked a private," she announced, pleased with herself, clasping her hands behind her head, expanding her chest, nipples at attention, stretching the bikini fabric across her torso... Eva Marie Saint.

"Goldberg...*Chaim* Goldberg," he said, parodying the James Bond style in *Dr. No*, all the rage then.

"Boudreaux, Mrs. Boudreaux," she said, picking up on his fun, giggling, "I loved that movie." She extended her hand, and they shook. "I'm scared of water," she announced.

Karen scrutinized from the guard stand.

"You have to wear your cap. It's the rules. I'll get in trouble," he said. His student tugged on her rubber cap, cramming her blond hair beneath the band, but one errant lock remained free over her right ear. It screamed for his adjustment. He wanted to tuck it in under her cap, to touch her, but he didn't dare. He wanted to tease her about her itsy, bitsy, teeny-weeny, yellow, polka-dot bikini. Is this first time you wore this? he wanted to provoke, but didn't dare.

She had lovely ears, and her neck was poetic in its curve. She was stunning, and he thought of Constance Reid, who married poor, crippled Sir Clifford Chatterley. He envisioned that Constance would've looked like Mrs. Boudreaux and that he could be Oliver Mellors.

In the pool, she levitated above his hands in standard American Red Cross Water Safety Instructor teaching technique. Nervous, he felt the warmth of her buttocks as she quivered into his palms, jiggling like pools of mercury. "I'm scared of water," she repeated, trembling.

"I can fix that," he told her and balanced her buttocks on one hand, then supported her back with the other hand. "It's okay, Mrs. Boudreaux. Yes. Relax against my hands," he soothed. He let go and, like a lily pad, she floated effortlessly in the cool water.

"Am I pretty?" She crossed into unexpected intimacy, and the lifeguard, off guard, smiled. His penis responded. It was impossible not to caress her buttocks as she became unsteady and quivered.

As she wriggled to rebalance, his finger slipped into her soft area. "Ohh!" she cooed. And again, "Ohh," she squeaked, startled. "I'll take that as a 'yes.' I guess I am," she said, evidently pleased with the accident. He hadn't done that on purpose. Both were embarrassed. This was only the second time he'd ever touched a woman there.

Karen was Big Tommy's only daughter. He owned the Club, and she was a churlish tattletale. Nature scarified her evil body with boils. Her face and back were pock marked, and she looked like a basset hound, not pretty, mannish, and all summer she spied upon him.

"A leaf on a still pond," he coached. "Good, Missus Boudreaux," he complimented, and then "Wwwwe're done, Mrs. Boudreaux," he said, at last, ignoring his errant fingers, but then he realized that he still had a javelin in his pants. "Ffffreestyle stroke next week," he stuttered.

"I'll have another private...tomorrow if you can make it as fun as this one," she murmured, lightly drawing her right index finger from his left ear, down the curve of his left shoulder, to his bicep and again blowing him a kiss. "You have such big muscles," she complimented him, looking directly into his crotch, his erection apparent. She was coy and alluring, impudently trampling the social and cultural mores like a child in a pansy garden. Chaim couldn't speak.

"Red?" she entreated.

"I hate that. I don't let anyone call me Red, but I have no choice here. They do it anyway. They give everyone nicknames."

"Well, Whateevertheycallyou, do you like ping-pong? I have a nice *ping-pong* table," she emphasized. "Wanna play *ping-pong* with me?" She stressed the words and shook her torso.

He withdrew, again feeling his social place. "Missus Boudreaux, I'm not allowed to talk to you."

"Sure you are. We're talking, aren't we?"

"You're not really afraid of water, are you?" he summed.

"I was a *breast stroker* at college," she retorted, intentionally articulating, and then she twitched away, tantalized him with her dancing cantaloupes.

Turning, he said, "You must have been the *best* breast stroker...on the team." He thought, Marilyn Monroe.

***

Cleaning the locker rooms later that day, he disarticulated his mind from these banal struggles, from silly Mrs. Boudreaux, and daydreamed. With strains from 77 Sunset Strip and Route 66 playing in his mind he dreamed of California and, barehanded, he cleaned the mens' urinals by brushing out toilets and extracting their cigar and cigarette butts. How he hated smokers. Aristocrats attained YCC membership—goyishe kopf, but Jews could not—yiddishe kopf.

...and piss...the amoniacal smell of piss.

Big Tommy, an irascible cur, tapped him on the shoulder and handed him a very nice leather satchel. That's how they talked: very nice. "Jus' put it in dere," the Cro-Magnon grunted. "Dat dere's real pig skin, Jew-boy," he said. "So don't touch it too much." Then, like a Jules Verne creature from

Journey to the Center of the Earth, he dematerialized ahead of a cloud of aromatic cigar smoke.

A bottle of *nice* Scotch rolled out from the satchel, clinking onto the tile floor: Glenfiddich. Then followed another *nice gift*: a 9 mm clip, full; with gleaming copper-tipped, hollow-points. Why didn't Mr. Phillippo, himself, just put the satchel into the locker?

Badda-boom, badda-bing...security...he mumbled to himself, imitating their language. He tried to snap shut the locker door but, shiiit, the dilapidated satchel handle broke, and the rest of the contents, an M1911A1 Remington, splatted out, nearly amputating his toe, and several tightly bundled bricks of cash. Grabbing the handle, impressed at its heft, he stuffed it back into the satchel, and neatly arranged the bricks of cash.

An abrupt shoulder tap interrupted his ministrations. He looked up. "Mmmmister Calamari!" he said, pulling his hand from the till.

The goon pawed his shoulder with bear-like claws, squeezing, then compressing him, preventing him from standing up. Chaim was terrified. It was Friday, about 1:55 PM. Mr. Calamari, the size of a stuffed grizzly he'd seen at the New York Natural History Museum, appeared from behind his cloud of cigar smoke, his slicked, Brylcreamed black pompadour reflecting the overhead light. "Whazzup, Putz?" he sneered, smoke billowing. "You woikin' for Chubby dese days?" This man smelled of death.

Chaim hated it when Mr. Calamari called him Putz. He also called him Skippy, and he hated that, too, though he wished he could have a nickname. That summer, for Chubby, he learned to operate a green John Deere, a serious, ten-thousand pound tractor. He was "diggin' holes." He was not a putz. The job began innocuously as "yard work." Chubby told him "we can't hire no moron union guys," when he hired him. He needed the money.

He learned quickly, and soon expertly dug nine-and-a-half foot deep holes, "as deep as you can go." Mr. Calamari's nickname was, aptly, The Squid, and he specified. "The size of a... garbage pit," he directed, tossing his cigar butt into the loam. But soon, as the Jacksons and Grants fluttered in like autumn leaves into the cigar box he kept beneath his bed, these dainty moral objections vanished. He liked "da'money." He was digging graves.

"Yyyyes, sir. Sssst-sstill working for Mmmmister Golondrino. Hey, don't call me Putz," he said losing the last part under his breath, hating that he stuttered so when stressed.

"Hey, jus' fun, kid."

He tried to rise from his squat, but Calamari's counter-weight prevented him. He looked at his imprisoner's dark, malevolent orbits. Calamari missed shaving a tuft of beard beneath his right nostril. Must be right handed, Chaim concluded. Chaim was a lefty.

"You're Anna Zubarsky's kid. Yeah, I know zactly who you are." And squeezed. His hands were like vices. He felt like a trapped muskrat in a body trap and dared not to correct Don Calamari's misperception.

All delicious thoughts about Mrs. Boudreaux vanished. He *fanfaed*, as his mother would have said. "Tttthe satchel fell open, Mr. Calamari. Honest, Mmmmister Calamari," he managed apologetically against the painfully increasing two-finger pincer squeeze into his neck muscles. "Iiiit wasn't my fault." He was nauseated. He could wind up like that rabbit out on the golf course, with crows biting out his eyes. The "they" and "them" were Mafia, as deadly as African black mambas, *Dendroaspis polylepis*, aggressive and unhesitating to strike.

He needed the money.

Calamari was a three-hundred pound swine who adorned his kielbasa-like fingers with gaudy gold rings and wore cologne, *eau d'embalming fluid*, reminding him of Bratstein's mother. The Squid's right pinky was adorned with a gold coin bearing an 1865 American Double Eagle gold piece. Another ring, with a prominent, centered, round, brilliant cut diamond, flashed from his left pinky. He wore no wedding ring.

Chaim heard him fan the cash and, for a moment, he felt he would pass out. "You didn't look in dere, dija', kid?" asked Mr. Calamari in his distinctive antagonistic tone. He released his hold. Chaim remained at ground level but saw him re-light his cigar and admire his jewelry.

Chaim knew this man, wearing a gold Rolex on his left wrist, could crush a human skull with those bare hands. Calamari crunched his knuckles, which sounded like crumbling, dry bones. He methodically pared his fingernails with a small red Swiss Army knife.

Chaim shook his head as an answer. "Nnnno, Mister Calamari, I didn't see nuttin'," he said, voice quavering, unconsciously mimicking his captor's Sout' Jersey accent. "Sweah." He said nothing about the maternal misattribution. He wasn't a Zubarsky.

Mr. Calamari chuckled, ridiculing, mocking him, "Oooo, not exceptionally grammatically correct, my monosyllabic, smart-ass Jew-boy."

"Get up," commanded The Squid as he extended a chilly tentacle. "Youse okay, Skippy. Here's sumptin'. Dis is for doin' good." Mr. Calamari held out a green bill.

"Thank you, Mr. Calamari," he said deferentially, but feeling anointed, as if winning an award, but not looking at the bill. "But do you hafta' call me Skippy?"

"Okay, Putz ...look at it." Calamari showed him the bill face.

Chaim looked. "It's a hundred dollars, Sir."

"Yeah, Skippy. Oh, I'm sorry. Yeah, I can count, too. I ain't da' ice cream man, so's I don't carry change, Putz," Mr. Calamari let the bill flutter to the floor. "Ooooh. I shouldn't do dat wit money, Skippy. Pick it up."

Bending over to grasp the bill, Calamari moved his shoe onto his fingers, pinning him to the floor. "Mr. Calamari, that hurts."

"Yeah, it does, don't it?"

He applied pressure until his tissues gave way, until Chaim writhed in anguish, until blood oozed out from beneath his purple fingernails on his left hand. "So's you done a good job wit dem toilets? Get all the butts out?" Calamari thought a moment. "Not much ever happens in here, does it, Snow White?"

He felt the tissues give way, and there was more blood from beneath his fingernails. Chaim managed to shake his head "no." Tears flowed. "Take the bill," said the big man, moving his foot from his fingers. From the pool of his blood, Chaim grubbed the blood-stained bill with his crushed left index finger and thumb.

"Chubby says youse doin' good buryin' dat garbage out dere. I'll be in touch," he said, and the bully slithered from the locker room, hissing, shrouded by puffs of gray cigar smoke. "I own you, Skippy."

Shaken, in pain, glad that these digits were not as important as those on his right hand for playing his trumpet, Chaim plunged his throbbing hand into a nearby bucket of ice intended for the urinals. He hated Calamari demeaning him with Snow White, or Skippy, or Putz, but it was worth da' money. He had a hundred bucks. He liked the money.

At sixteen, he'd learned his street lessons well. "You do not fuck wit' deese guys," was one rule. These wise guys could shake his hand and crush his skull, and they traded short on allegiance, like hog belly futures. When he left that afternoon, he knew he'd passed an important loyalty test and felt spared, as if the Angel of Death had passed by him.

Chaim's work day commenced at dawn, six-thirty, but even at six PM, there remained more to do. Where Poe nibbled that rabbit, he had to spray the brown grass splotches with green paint, a primping club affectation.

On the mower, he mulched the rabbit carcass and ran over a hornet's nest, and the varmints chased him to the next hole. In his flurry, he demolished an expensive hose, and water shot all over.

Frustrated, fatigued, dusty, and hot, he coiled up the munched hose, and then he dipped his bleeding fingers into a melting ice bucket at the pool. He threw the coiled hose into a trash bin and hoped that the Puerto Rican caretaker, whom everyone called Spic though his name was Rinaldo, wouldn't notice. If they tagged him, at ninety cents an hour, it would take him the rest of the summer to pay it off.

Into the pump house hopped a hapless frog. Without thought, Chaim picked it up and tossed it into a two-hundred gallon vat of liquid pool chlorine. As the frog fizzled, he smelled the liberated chlorine gas. From chemistry class he knew that one can discern chlorine with as little as one part per million. The halogenic smell reminded him of the Clorox fumes when his mother would go on her cleaning binges. He'd nicknamed her Chlorine.

In the curtainless shower in the pool house, next to the chlorine vats, he thought of his mother, whom everyone said resembled sexy Dolores Del Rio, the Mexican chanteuse...chica, chica, boom, boom. He undulated, thinking about sexy Mrs. Boudreaux. Stirred by Mrs. Boudreaux's cleavage, he stroked himself hard. A familiar, but unwelcome girl's voice horrified him. "Jeez, catch a mouse in your hand?"

It was his muscle-bound nemesis, Karen Phillippo standing right there, square in front of him, smirking, Brownie camera in hand, snapping away, catching him *en flagrante*, as exposed as that rabbit. She cackled diabolically, wickedly. Karen was the embodiment of the Club's Catholic, anti-Semitic contingent. "What are you going to do with that *little* thing?" she derided him, looking at him fully hard, foamed and frothed. He stared at her wiry hairy facial mole on her chin point. "I can't wait to develop *this*," she squealed maliciously and ran off. "Nice shampoo job!"

He burned with shame, dreading what she may do with the photos.

In the employee parking lot, by contrast to club members' sparkling rides, his car had a tattered paint job with rust rash that looked like Karen's face. From beneath the frayed driver's side windshield wiper peaked an envelope. Shit! He fumed. Yet another YCC ticket.

He looked at the embossed envelope, held it, felt it. It was crisp and cool, so clean. The flap was wax sealed in deep red with the initials "MB," and there was a red lipstick imprint above the seal.

This was not a ticket. He hesitated to open it because he didn't want to spoil its artistic beauty. Unaddressed, it must have been misplaced, meant for another. He looked around to see if Karen was still lurking. This could be one of her sadistic ploys. He tore open the envelope through the side crease, not wanting to disturb the glossy sealing wax. At the bottom of the note was a flamboyant signature in peacock blue ink:

The Duchess of Yardley, Mrs. Nedda Boudreaux.

He read the note, done in black calligraphy:

From the desk of Her Majesty,

The Duchess of Yardley,
Mrs. Nedda Boudreaux:

The Duchess requests the honoure of thine company at a formal ping-pong and pool party this eve, 8:30 PM, sharp Manor Boudreaux

Dress optional

The Duchess of Yardley, he laughed. Then he paused, hesitating briefly, chastened by the Club's strict rule about fraternizing with its members, and slid into his car looking around for the lurking Kat-Fish Karen. A genie appeared on his shoulder and whispered, "Do it!"

He overlooked a precipice into his future and realized that what was about to unfold could forever change his life. He knew that he should return home and practice his trumpet...but, again, the devil genie tap-danced on his shoulder. *"Putz,* practice later, play now."

He looked into her kaleidoscope, marveling at the stunning patterns, and made his decision.

***

Guarding the gate into Manor Boudreaux stood Cerberus, Monster of Hades, in three poses in richly patinaed cast-bronze figures. Steel gates, with vicious hunting hounds in bas relief divided her world from his. The self-appointed Duchess of Yardley lived in the *auld* section of Yardley, near Langhorne, ensconced in Revolutionary War tradition and history, hidden from view, and eons away in culture from his home.

Levittown, his neighborhood, was new and plebian, springing from potato fields in a post-war, proletarian burst of twenty thousand uniform seedlings. It was the commune of Pete Seeger's song about the ticky-tacky houses on the hillside.

On the middle pilaster, he paused to read the brass plate:

Manor Boudreaux*exitus acta probat*

1791

Dominici Foundry 1960

The weighty plaque was one foot by three feet, one inch thick, of solid brass. Beneath the letters was a detailed coat-of-arms, featuring a horse with trailing hounds and a hunting crop overhead. Like Tevye, the plaque shouted T-R-A-D-I-T-I-O-N: status quo; stature. The Latin legend was pragmatic: the end justifies the means. He could not know at that moment how this expression presaged what would unfold in the next year.

A massive oak dominated the landscape. He inspected its harsh, time-ancient vertical eight-foot gash in the trunk, with tophi of congealing sap.

Years later, as a surgeon, when he amputated a man's lower leg, he suffered from chronic osteomyelitis, he would return to thoughts of that tree and this, his first visit to Nedda Boudreaux's manor.

The home befitted a true duchess. Centered in the driveway was a massive, stone, circular fountain that rhythmically ejaculated spray. The pattern began with a series of lower pulsations, then escalating and, finally, ahhhhh, a dramatic climax. To the east, a glass pool house with white gazebo punctuated the weed-free verdant lawns, all bathed in yellow eventide sunlight. There were six swans and six geese in the pool. Strains from her piano reverberated.

"Welcome to Manor Boudreaux," she said, magnanimously. *"Enchanté*, so glad you've come."

"You like piano?"

"Play some more," he asked, and she did.

"The Last Romantic 6/12 Chopin, Scherzo No. 1 in B Minor?"

She smiled, amazed. "I studied with Horowitz." She stood there in a flimsy chemise that blew behind her in the door draft with the auric evening light painting her breasts. As when she touched his shoulder at the Club, she stroked his chin lightly with her right index finger, then kissed the end, blowing a kiss back to him. Her home was wonderfully air-conditioned and so pleasant.

She terrified him. Was this...it? Could it be? "Am I eeeearly? Where is... is...everybody, Mrs. Boudreaux? There is a ping-pong tournament?"

"Ohh, please, please, please...Nedda, Neddy." Pausing, then, "Silly boy! Why would I waste your succulent talents on such mundane activity as ping-pong? I can play with...myself." She chortled. "I'm going to make valuable use of your natural... endowments."

"You have work for me?" he asked naively, still missing her drift.

"Oh, yeees. I have work for you. You'll work very hard," she laughed. "Very hard."

Chaim, child that he was, gawked at the numerous ornate Venetian mirrors and French Rococo scrolls with intricate leaf designs, many gilded and framed in plush satin. Mirrors, mirrors, everywhere, with candles aglow, bounced kaleidoscopic reflections everywhere.

"You...you...tricked me! Bbbbut you said it... iiit... iiiit wwwwas a party."

"It is a party."

Tripping over his tongue, he stuttered, overwhelmed, nervous, but intensely excited. His mind swirled, and his lion stirred as he began to consider that her deception, though objectionable, was well worth his anxiety.

"Calm down, calm down. It's a party...you and I. Unless..." She stopped there.

"Unless?"

"Unless you need to breast feed with your mommie, or have to return a library book, or tend to your pimples." Her sarcasm scalded him. "Here, come along. Nice doggie," she teased, taking his hand. He liked her softness. "You were such an adroit swim teacher, and this *is* a party. It's my thank you... to... celebrate... my... husband's departure and, of course, our first lesson. Relaaaaaax." Clasping his hand, confident, she led them into the ornately furnished sitting room, then, turning on him, she kissed him full on the mouth, biting his upper lip, exactly the part he needed to play his trumpet.

"Oh," he managed and returned her luscious kiss.

"This is your first time?"

"Yes," he answered, beginning to understand what she meant.

"You kiss like a man. How did you learn?"

"I rrread a lot, I guess. I read *Lady Chatterley's*... and Henry Miller."

"You must be an assiduous reader," she said. He liked her vocabulary but enjoyed it more as she directed his hand between her legs.

"Wwwwwhat about your husband? I've heard about him. What would hhhhhhe do?

"What have you heard?"

"Ttttthh... that... he's a pretty ttttough character... a wwwwwise guy... friends with Calamari."

She didn't laugh at his stuttering. "Nervous? Him? It's okay. He's off in China, on one of his little boats," she explained, derisive, then filling his free hand with a crystal champagne flute. "See if you like this." She pulled the dense green bottle from an ice bucket and poured clear, bubbling wine into two glasses, monogrammed with the **MB** escutcheon. Chaim thought about how he inscribed his initials on his mother's tea pot. Some day, he mused, he'd have monogrammed glasses.

"You like champagne?" she questioned, letting the last syllable trail out, as if drinking champagne were as mundane in his world as in hers. He tried to be suave and smiled, but this was his first taste.

From reading Jansen's art book, many of the paintings seemed familiar: Renaissance triptychs, Madonnas and child. "Sip. It's okay," Mrs. Boudreaux urged, her lips vermillion, like the Queen in Disney's *Snow White*.

"Are those Dutch Masters?" he asked, pointing to a grouping of paintings in heavily gilded frames.

"Rembrandt," she answered, "and Pieter Bruegel the Elder. *The Connoisseur*, his self-portrait. Flemish."

Timorously slurping, Chaim guzzled, and she filled it anew. The art collection was the sort of assemblage only seen in the world's finest museums. It was... Sardanapalian, exactly what the Assyrian king would have adored, a word from the last weekend's *New York Times* crossword puzzle.

Woozy, the alcohol made it hard for him to form words as she led him on a tour, hand-in-hand. "You do *like* champagne!" she exclaimed, filling his empty flute.

On a resplendent stand, he eyed a jeweled box, cigar box sized, which he held and inspected. Encrusted with amber and mother of pearl, there was an emerald the size of a quarter on its top.

To one side of the table, on a small couch, set a dressage whip, a set of reins, and her riding gloves. "We rode in the arena this morning," she said. "You do have a taste for fine things," she observed as he turned the box over in his hands. She removed the whip and reins and explained, "That was Henry the VIII's box, the exact one he used for chocolates while courting Anne Boleyn."

Chaim said, "1536. Executed."

"You know your history," she complimented. "I like smart boys." Then, like a museum docent, she continued. "In the painting by Hans Holbein the Younger, in the library, you can see the box, that precise box, next to his throne. It's historic."

"Mrs. Boudreaux, this is the most amazing home I've ever seen... the most amazing museum." He was effervescent, admiring her worldly treasures while peering into her cleavage.

"Mrs. Boudreaux, I love your vocabulary," he burbled and felt self-conscious knowing that would not have been what Hemingway would have said... or John Wayne.

She howled. "No one has ever complimented me on my vocabulary! But, Neddy, Neddy, Neddy... puhleeease!" she cooed, glissading from piano to mezzo forte, chiding him breathlessly and pecking his cheek. "If you make that mistake again, I'll have to spank you." They laughed. "My daddy named me for the diva in the opera Il Pagliacci. I hope I am not too much of a diva for you," she toyed.

She played the first few bars of the Rach II as if they were an unconscious thought. "He called me his little swan and gave it to me when I was such a girl," she said. Her carmine colored lips mesmerized him as he eyed the full, concert grand. "This's Vladi's 1898 model C. He played his farewell concert on it when he came to America. I have no idea how he got it out of Berlin."

"C. Bechstein Pianofortefabrik AG," he read. "Aktiengesellschaft."

"You know your German," she complimented, then played Chopin.

"That's gorgeous," he said. "You play spectacularly." The windows resonated throughout the home.

"Oh, c'mon. That's just a little ditty. I gave up Vladimir Horowitz and the piano when I married Harry."

There was a minor lilt, like the last bars she played. "I want to become friends." She slurred, "You need a friend?" She clinked his glass, oozing, "My frieeends call me Neddy." She was a bit shiker, dropping words and syllables.

At every tidbit in her tour and at every turn in their walk, at every opportunity, she pulled him to her and kissed him, each time escalating their intimacy. As if revealing a guarded secret, she whispered in his ear, "*My* family, the Robesons are diamonds, old money. The Boudreauxs," with snooty disdain, "are... coal."

"Old money's better than new money?"

Mrs. Boudreaux laughed. "How charmant. What a chiiiild you are!" Pouring him more champagne, draining down another glass herself, in her best pedantic, Socratic tone, she answered, "Money's everything. Old money's always better...sooo comforting."

She went on, "Old money's better, because it's like that oak out front. There's always more, and the roots are deeper." She laughed and kissed him again, rubbing his crotch as she said roots.

Then she became somber. "But with aaaall the money and aaaall these art pieces, I live alone. Every morning, I eat my Cheerios alone. I am verrry sad and verrry lonely, m'boy. You have to give me a special back rub. Can you come and eat my Cheerios? Are you a big breakfast eater?"

Her intoxicated soliloquy continued. "Here I am, uncared-for, thirty-two, no children, ten starved, craving years into a disappointing marriage... giving up music. I haven't been touched by a man in months," she lamented, slipping her hand into his shorts, compressing him, sighing, "any man."

Chaim gasped and felt he was about to spurt, like the fountain.

"My life is like that piano... a very nice mahogany case but no one to hear my music. I ache. Touch me, darlin'," she slurred, positioning his right hand onto her breasts. "Puh-leeze, touch me."

"You nnnneed love," he managed. He took the initiative, cradling her face and, as Mellors would have done, he kissed her deeply.

"I need to be fucked!" she groaned adamantly, exasperated. "Love is okay, like new money, but I need your oak tree, a deeeep root. My peonies are wilting!" She kissed him voraciously. "I need to be surrounded by flowers and art and all beautiful things and perfumes. Can't you doooo me that one favor, Chaim?" She wrapped around him like a wisteria vine.

That was the first time she'd said his name, pronouncing the guttural perfectly. "You make my name sound soooo llllovely," he complimented her, he, too, intoxicated.

"Make music with me now." Her voice texture was creamy, smooth, sweet, like the *mille-feuille* that his mother made. "You can. I know you can."

On her scholarly art tour, they reached the staircase landing and, melodramatically, she spread her bedroom doors wide. "See this?" she asked him. Another champagne bottle in an ice bucket awaited them at the foot of her bed. "I've been waiting for you."

He recited the bottle label. *"Krug, Clos du Mesnil* 1957."

"Your French is good! This is *your* champagne."

Popping the cork, she delighted as the champagne bubbled onto his Connies. She wiped her wet hands on his shorts, briefly clinging to his hardness. They sipped. "This is the *tête du tête*, best of the best, from my husband's prized collection. He's such a snob, going on about how 'it comes from one small-walled vineyard of just four-and-a-half acres.' I brush my teeth in it. Fish fuck in water."

Her wanton vulgarity excited him, but he worried, "Neddy, your husband..."

"Vapor? That's what I call him," with a thespian flourish. "He's in Hong Kong, so he says, but really, who knows? I'm Rapunzel in his fortress," she said, rustling and arranging her silky, long strawberry blonde tresses.

Her graceful pianist's fingers undressed two Hershey Kisses and pressed them into his mouth, and she kissed him. Her lips were succulent, warm; her mouth soft, luxurious, and chocolaty. He melted along with her Kisses. Her perfume was like Ilona's, French and intense. Her overt fecundity blew his embers into a conflagration he'd only imagined from D.H. Lawrence and French playing cards. She'd become his Lady Chatterley.

"Don't get ahead of yourself. Drink more." She held the champagne glass to his lips. He was ready to explode but she knew when to stop. "Don't worry. I'll take good care of you," she whispered on his ear.

Excusing himself to her bathroom, he bent over and asked, "What's this?"

"Oh, silly boy. It's a *bidet*. Verrry European. To clean a woman..."

"I thought it was a drinking fountain!"

She howled, laughing. "This is your tutorial..."

"I've never done *this* before."

She laughed. "That's the attraction." She splashed him from the bidet.

"Just bring that cute blush along, Mr. Cutey-pie," she tantalized, following him to the toilet and watched.

"Iiii've never... ggggone in front of anyone," he said. She laughed.

"Just leave your shorts off."

Embarrassingly erect, he joined her on a small, buttery, tan, Italian leather couch in the bay window. Dressed in her peignoir, she placed her feet into her pupil's lap and motioned him to rub her feet. "Now, I'll put you to work," she instructed. He began. "Verrrry good," she purred. "Verrrry, verrry good."

He watched her through the sheer material: gorgeous, gently contoured, caramel buttons, like candies. He rubbed her legs, which were smoother and more arousing than Ilona's *haute couture* lambskin jacket. Then, without further permission, he ascended into her plush places. "Verrry, verrrrry good," she responded, so wet. "Oh, you are an exceptionally naughty boy! I love it!"

As luscious as were her nipples, her adjectives were equally sumptuous, but with the alcohol, his brain had become molasses. She removed his red YCC lifeguard shirt with the Tartan shield and he, not shy and naked for the first time before a woman, delighted as her silky hands toured his skin.

They intertwined fingers, then she rubbed her carefully French polished, soft hands, on his torso. "This *is* your first time?" Her breaths quickened. "with a woman? Sixteen years, isn't it? It's time." She licked and squeezed his nipples between her teeth. "It's been too long for me, too, but I can't wait sixteen years." He liked her nipple bites.

As her gossamer negligee floated away, he'd reached that moment in which his chaste Victorian period novels left off. Nothing further was left to his imagination. She moaned a deep guttural sound and took him in to his hilt. He wanted to hold back, to wait. Dare he? What was he supposed to do? Choice left him, and biology took over as he shuddered, then weakened, and then he felt sweat on his back and in the nape of his neck. She captured his mouth, returning all that he'd given her and, without thinking, he gulped.

"Oh, you incorrigible. You *do* like this. I knew you would. And you're good at it. You're a natural. I won't have to teach you a thing!" She giggled. He delighted with her debauchery.

He lapped up the praise like a puppy at a milk dish and was embarrassed and speechless. He was so accustomed to being brow-beaten and criticized that this adoration satisfied his insecurities. "You have to talk to me. I want you to say everything."

Vermeer, Frans Hals, Jan Steen, Pieter de Hooch, and Rembrandt looked on, smirking jealously as the lovers drained the bottle of the obscenely expensive, rare champagne and uncorked another. "It's just like you," she teased as the champagne foamed out of its bottle.

Erubescent, Nedda led him to her canopy bed done in large, Laura Ashley, fluffy goose-down pillows. "Now, it's my turn, *young* man. Don't worry about your beauty sleep! You're going to suck me and lick me and don't stop... no matter what. Promise? And I'll show you how to give me my back rub."

He shivered at all his forbidden thoughts.

"Oh, youth!" she sighed as she buried him into the loft of the twelve-hundred thread count Egyptian cotton comforter. "The dirtier the better. You must tell me what you want to do to me." He was taken with her obvious desires, that a woman sought sex as much as he did, as he encircled her petite form with his legs.

She wrapped her arms around his shoulders, and he inhaled her perfumes. "*L'Heure Bleue* by Guerlain. Remember that. It's me, my scent. For the rest of your life you'll remember my fragrance." He looked into her blue eyes, and she tantalized him with, "Talk to me now."

"But what do I say?"

"Say what you want... what you want to say," she instructed.

So, he spoke. "I like the way you hold me."

"That's a good start," she said and turned over onto her tummy, and she showed him how to rub her back, "but not yet," she said.

After a while, there came a surprise turn of events in her tutelage. She reached over to a side table, into a shallow drawer. "It's a 3032 Tomcat. Beretta, of course. I like it!"

"Yeah, it's gggreat." This scared him but he realized that part of her thrill, like a Black Mamba, was her unpredictability. *EDIT

"Hold it," she ordered and, from a few inches, she dropped the gun into his palm. "I use 60-grain, .32 ACP, 7.65 mm, hollow-point bullets. It'll stop anything."

"Yes. Yes!" He chilled, his body stiffened with the rush of flight or fight. "What's it for?" he questioned, returning it to her.

"In case you come up short, I just kill you," she joshed. He blanched. She almost sounded serious. "Oh, c'mon. I'm just showing off. But there *are* wild animals around here." She rubbed the gun-metal gray barrel into her cleavage and set out on a *tour de force* passing it between her legs, cocking it, then caressing his chest with the cold steel, then took the whole barrel deep into her mouth, sucking it, then passed it, with her wetness, slowly across her moist velvet, then across his lips and, finally, pointing it directly at his heart.

He was terrified it would fire. "Wwwwhat are you doing?"

"Do I scare you? You don't trust me?"

"Yes. Yes!"

"I'm snapping off the safety. You will do what I want."

It was then that he noticed a stick of butter in a butter dish, but no breads or jams. Seeing sweat on his upper lip, she teased. "I really had you going!

33

There're no bullets... see?" Then, she fired... and she blew out the mirror in her bathroom wall. She laughed. "Seven years of bad luck!" she cachinated.

"Oh, my god," he yowled and wanted to leave.

"Oh, calm down, calm down," she cajoled as if nothing had happened. "Anyone can make such a mistake." Dust settled all over the room. "Ping'll clean it up," she said and pulled out a pink, silk purse, chortling, oblivious as to how serious firing the gun had been. "Now it's unloaded. There was only one bullet in there."

She pressed the barrel right at his heart.

"No," he said, adamantly, and pushed her armed hand away.

From the pink purse she withdrew a hand-rolled cigarette and offered it to him. The smell of gunpowder hung in the air.

"I don't smoke," he said, guarded, wondering what caprice would follow.

"You didn't drink champagne, either." She kindled the joint with a sterling silver lighter coiled in the shape of a snake with incandescent, red opal eyes and she sucked in deeply, mocking his naiveté. "Or," inhaling, "play with guns. Incroyable!" she chirped, exhaling. Sweet, acrid smoke filled the room as she puffed, and she held the joint to his lips. "Marijuana... try it."

With his family's devotion to the reprehensible habit, he hesitated, but inhaled. He felt a pleasing sensation, a unique relaxation.

"Harold brings," inhale, inhale, "this from Thailand." Exhale. "This is the best. Thai-stick," she laughed.

She placed the joint into his lips, and he copied what he'd seen his mother do: inhale. Upon exhaling, sputtering with some coughs, floating, he said, "It's marvelous," he giggled. She moved her well-proportioned arms onto his shoulders. He felt an heightened tactile sensation.

"Feel better?" she asked, and then he noticed nasty, symmetrical, purple-yellowing bruises on the inside of her arms, just above the elbows. "It's a rope burn," she said.

Languid, they sat naked in her nest. Unlike Joanie Willberger's Sherwood Forest, Neddy was smoothly shaved. "You like?" she asked as he pet her absentmindedly. He reached for an idea, to formulate something. "Henry Miller," he sputtered but the thought sailed out of grasp... like the fluff of the summer's end. "Periwinkle," came to mind.

"Oh, you are stoned."

Her smoothness drove him wild, and he was unable to remember what Henry Miller thought.

"Oh, yes," he replied. "To shave or not to shave? that was the question," he said. "Shakespeare."

The gunshot became a dream and vanished with his other anxieties. Her biology came alive. "Now," she said, grasping his soft youthful face as if he were a sex appliance, and centered him on her muff. She purred as he licked away, taking full advantage of all of his trumpet tonguing lessons. "You're a natural," she sighed.

Frank Sinatra crooned in the background on her Orthophonic Victrola. *Fly me to the moon.* He needed no further instructions as they fox-trotted, tangoed, and cha-chaed against each other, dancing their conjoined rhythms and then, from deep within her she began, subtly at first, a low ahhhhh. Then louder. She climaxed with "Oooh, ooooh." She soughed, suspiring. "I'm commmmming! Ohhh."

It was miraculous. He'd only read about this. Her body quaked and seized, her muscles rhythmically contracted, her voice echoed through the candlelit passages, up the main staircases, down to the kitchen, into the library, caroming off the marble floors and glass mirrors. The Dutch

Masters chuckled in full appreciation, nodding to one another in approval. It had been a while for those wanton voyeurs.

Into the wine cellar, her celebration went, off the Baroque and Rococo mirrors, their gildings fluttered, and the Madonnas and children smirked. It had been such a long time since they'd heard real passion in these dank foyers. Yes, they'd heard her screams of pain and penance with that monster Harry, but this was joy, the most concentrated distillate of pleasure.

In her, riding her, he, too, came... but for him, Neddy's outcry was the most exhilarating experience. Then stillness. Drenched in sweat, from above, her raindrops pooled on his chest. Exhausted, they alloyed like longtime, convenient lovers, hugging each other so closely, melting into each other like crayons in the hot sun, and collapsed into an expansive, champagne-pot-opium-induced sleep.

At daylight he awoke, feeling something strange. She'd tied that blue, silk ribbon from the kaleidoscope around his cock. "You won first prize!" she said, gleefully. The dawn's early light invaded the room, and there came a rap, rap, rapping at the chamber door.

Chaim startled as he pulled away the ribbon. "Oh, my God, it's your husband."

"Probably not," she answered, in condescension, while pulling on her carmine peignoir that previously had matched her lipstick, which they smudged away by their lovemaking. She spun her flowing tresses and secured them with a sterling silver barrette, signed by Georgia O'Keeffe, then she opened the door just a crack.

"Will Madame and... uh, guest... enjoy breakfast?" asked a pleasant male in a Chinese accent.

"It's Ping, my houseboy," she said to Chaim, swaddled in the comforters. He delivered Eggs Benedict and, as they ate, Nedda dipped her fingers into the sauce and offered morsels from her plate into Chaim's mouth. "I want *you* in my mouth again... soon," she said.

He felt painfully self-conscious as he realized he'd transgressed all of his mother's sensibilities and values. What was such a nice Jewish boy doing, staying the night in a married woman's bed? As he stirred, the pistol thudded from the bedclothes onto the oak floor.

"I better put that little plaything away," she admonished herself, "but it's always here if you want to dabble with it again," she said stroking her thigh with the barrel.

Feeling guilty, he pulled on his shorts and t-shirt. Somehow, in their doings they'd dumped the better part of the bottle of champagne into his clothes.

"Oh my God!" he exclaimed. "My mother'll kill me!"

She watched him dress. "Come back for a swim sometime?" she cajoled and blew him a kiss.

"Do you even *have* a ping-pong table?" he asked. She smiled.

Running past Ping, through the kitchen, on a maple chopping block, he saw a commercial-sized meat cleaver resting next to a goose, its body severed from its head. Out the front door he ran as the Dutch Masters gave him a round of applause for the great show it had all been.

Ordinarily, the great works of art just hung around. "Great theater," Vermeer complimented, nodding to the paintings, all of them clapping as he ran through the study. Rembrandt's helmeted night watchman, ruffled from his duties, looked up briefly at the hullabaloo, perturbed at the disturbance of his vigil, but ceremoniously tipping his helmet to the conqueror.

As he exited Manor Boudreaux, he thought of... his clandestine... destiny...his clandestiny. There was Nedda Robeson Boudreaux, of the privileged class, of Vassar, as a pedigreed woman, looking at her life alone, who was as empty a personage as those drained champagne bottles.

He was of Poland, Hungary, Rumania, by way of Toronto and New York. His father was a Polish immigrant. Mother? She was from a family who had a horse-drawn vegetable cart, one of ten kids born in Cincinnati, the family of Rumanian and Hungarian roots. He was an unpapered Polack mongrel.

The yellow morning sun shone, and the graceful vines glowed as they meandered along the stone perimeter wall; a deep purple clematis, a white wisteria, a yellow trumpet vine, a pearlescent silver lace, a golden honeysuckle. There were only five geese in the pool as he drove away.

Nedda was like a succulent cherry atop a delicious ice cream sundae. Tall and tan and like a samba, ecstatic, he was wonderfully shaken and stirred and ready for college.

2

The Restrictive Covenant

On the way home, he passed Saint Joseph the Worker Church. Slaphappy tired, the sight evoked Hemingway's expression: Hope to Christ. He needed to be ever vigilant to defend against his mother's sarcasms and his father's belittling. He kept the offensive expression as an arrow in his wordsmith's quiver, ready to fire it at just the right time. It would drive his mother nuts, and he'd savor that.

His Cinderella evening was over and, like the coachman's transformation at dawn, he had reverted to a dingy, dirt-spotted frog, like his car. The gate to Estate Goldberg was a standard Levitt, flimsy aluminum storm door, monogrammed with an Old English font G, in the center. Unlike Manor Boudreaux, there was no brass plate, no Rococo, no "décor," no architecture, no mirrors, no foyer, no swans ejaculating, no beheaded goose on their chopping block.

Turgid with rebuke in her muzzle, she stood in the driveway, smoking, wearing a stained apron with her brunette hair bound by a red, cowboy kerchief; a do-rag. He could see the bulges caused by curlers. "Where the hell have you been?" she yodeled, smacking at him with the morning *Levittown*

Times. "Your father and I have been dying all night. We called everywhere; the police, the hospital." She cried, and her tears wet her cigarette. Seeing his mashed fingers, she exclaimed, "What did you do?"

Arthur, his father, the Groundhog was his moniker, scared of his own shadow, far less than a king, poked at his thick, black-framed glasses positioned on his snout. He'd wriggled out of his hole, wearing deep blue, almost violet, Bermuda shorts held aloft over his pot belly by a tattered frayed woven hemp belt with a frayed leather end. A sleeveless t-shirt with black knee-high socks, open-toed, filigreed leather, black, Italian sandals completed his gardening costume. He clutched a handful of fresh-cut gladiolas, held upright. Suffering from the subterranean shock contrast into daylight, he squinted.

A ribbed, white, sleeveless tee shirt covered his father's barrel chest, and his sternum was sweat-soaked. Chaim had to laugh. His dad looked like a self-portrait of one of his garden grown eggplants. "Sonofabitch," he cursed, shaking the gladiolas at him, his forehead veins popping, and then looking away in consternation.

He viewed his father as a failure. He was a low level government factotum, a clerk at the Veteran's Administration, a post-war paper-pusher, an ordinary beige disappointment. Chaim compared him to the mastodons at the Club, the capitalistic warriors, and he sought that sort of success, to achieve money, power, and prestige. He wanted an Hispano-Suiza.

In the eyes of the community, anyone would see Arthur as an ideal father, appearing to be doting, devoted, loving, soft, and gentle, but the truth was different. He was a sad and harsh man. Gardening defined his taciturn soul. He related better to nasturtiums than to his family.

In summer, he planted. In summer, he snipped here, tied there, and dug gentlemanly holes. In winter, he turned inward, pursuing his true excitement, nurturing orchids, tending his variegated dieffenbachia, pinching his coleus, and then he interred himself in his bedroom with his books.

He was cruel to his children and withheld affection. He was a *Ragesaurus Rex*, often with explosive fits and tantrums, in which he would almost crap his pants, like a four year-old. These outbursts he blamed on his family. "Look at what you made me do," he would rant. They would cower in fear.

"I had to clean up after a party at the Club. Iiiii got ten dollars in tips," he told them but he couldn't tell them that he'd gotten drunk and stoned and then lost his virginity by fucking the richest woman in the county, whose husband was Mafiosi... although he wanted to tell them... very much.

"You did what!" she hollered in her most piercing glissando. "My God, you smell like a god-dammned whorehouse!" She chased him into his bedroom, pounding on him with the folded paper. He nearly escaped. In the struggle, his new kaleidoscope, his precious gift, bounced onto the black-and-white speckled linoleum tile.

"What's that?"

"I... I... fffound it... ssss... someone lllleft it at the Club."

"When you *fanfa*, you're lying. Where did you get that?" she challenged, so antagonistic. She pinched her lips together tightly, and a nimbus cloud formed on her mustachioed upper lip.

"Ssss... someone left it," he hissed, realizing that he was within a praying mantis whisker's width from blurting out a full confession. With all the booze and dope, he was about to puke, too.

Gears grinding in confusion, he whirled, slamming the door, partially sealing her yowling on the other side, but she huffed and puffed and forced the door open and came at him. "What happened to your hand, your fingers?"

"I... I... a horse stepped on it."

She sniffed. "Have you been smoking?"

41

"No, no, of course not."

"Take off your clothes, and I'll wash them. You stink." She stood there. "Give me your clothes," she decreed, meaning then and there. "I'm your mother. Give them to me."

He rose from his bed, shed his clothes. "Underpants!"

He complied. She gazed at him and, seeing his pubic matted hair, sneered, "Hmmm… I guess you have grown up." After Karen, this ignominy was too much, and tears scalded his sunburned cheeks. The wound was as deep as Karen Phillippo's humiliation, as severe as that gash in the oak tree.

Wanting to keep Nedda's aroma, he vowed he'd never shower again or wipe his face, but that promise changed quickly. His chest burned. The acid taste was awful, so he scurried to the toilet, puked his guts out a few times and died, waking some hours later that morning, still captivated by Nedda's odor and scents, but extremely nauseous.

Cold water. He needed cool, clear, water.

What were the names of those perfumes? *L'Heure Bleue* by Guerlain. *Un Jardin Sur le Nile* by Hermes, "my other favorite" she'd said, and then *24 Faubourg* by Hermes.

Face in the toilet, he felt as if he were being turned inside out when the barf wave heaved again. He felt as if he'd yakked out his sneakers, it was that violent, and some vomitus cauterized his nose. From a cabinet above the toilet he saw red… a red rubber pouch of some sort, a bag connected to a long red rubber tube culminating in a black nozzle, which looked like that goose's nose on Nedda's kitchen counter. Another powerful green torrent left him, and then a few moments passed, and after a glass of chilled seltzer water from the fridge, his stomach settled down.

He loved and hated his bedroom. On the other side of his bedroom was a single bed, a steel-framed rollaway, where Jeffrey, his cousin from his mother's side, coerced him to suck his dick. He'd been only eight. That was the part he hated.

Idly, he peered through the kaleidoscope, turning it, focusing, imagining his past, present, and future. Then he held out his right index finger, closed an eye, and noticed the viewpoint shift. He'd seen that on Mr. Wizard. It was called parallax.

Nedda was recreation, but what he wanted was a girlfriend, someone his age, someone to watch over him, to love him, like the words in the Gershwin song... and then he fell asleep. An hour later, he showered, despite his vow, and when he returned from the bathroom, he saw that an envelope lay on his desk. It was from the Philadelphia Symphony. Herr Knauss, the Hungarian principal trumpet, had accepted him as a student. He slid the letter beneath his desk blotter, a *naches* ace to be played later.

She intercepted him. "Where do you think you're going? What was in that letter? Your father wants you to cut the lawn!" screamed Chlorine, dragging on her Raleigh while ambushing him at the bathroom. He zipped quickly. "I made *mamaligga* for you!" Her exhaled acrid smoke swirled through her nostrils into the morning light in the kitchen.

"You should work for the Katzenellenbogens at the dry cleaners. They're Jews at least."

"*Mom*. It's a job." She annoyed him so, trying to control every aspect of his life. "I'm leaving for college in a year!" he retorted. "I'd rather die than work in that concentration camp, Chlorine." He slipped!

Glowering, "What did you call me?"

"Nnnothing... I ..."

She cut him off. "You have no idea what a concentration camp is like."

"Neither do you. Have you been to one?"

She swung. He ducked. "So you're a Jewish nigger? You work for *goyim*, like niggers?"

43

"Band practice!" he answered in a *non-sequitur.*

"The Rintalas are coming to dinner! It's an early dinner," she yelled as she whacked up a chicken with a black-handled Henckels meat-cleaver, like Nedda's, but not that hefty. He fled to his beloved '55 Buick but realized that she'd so distracted him that he'd forgotten his trumpet and music folio.

Retrieving these from his room, he bolted back to the car, again calling out, "Band practice." The *non-sequitor* distraction had indeed worked. Backing down the driveway, he demolished Jackie Kennedy, one of his dad's prized rosebushes.

Would he ever see her again? As he drove, he sifted through the rubble on the passenger side of the floor of the Buick, where, hidden by two brown-glass Hires Root Beer bottles and one Dad's, lay Mrs. Boudreaux's— Nedda's— Neddy's—invitation. Like a bear in huckleberries, he pulled it to his face, whiffing her scents again. Her handwriting danced off the page as if penned by a ballerina with pens on her toe shoes. His lion twirled in a mating jig.

Dare he call her? But how? The Goldberg phone, and there was only one, was jet black, shiny Bake-Lite plastic stuck up on the kitchen wall next to the dining table. To attain a sense of privacy, he'd have to stretch the tightly coiled, springy cord, with its wad of knots, into the entry vestibule and close the front door over the cord. "Why do you need privacy?" his mother would complain. This conversation had to be private, fer Chris' sake. He experimented with that expression.

Pelligrini's Bowling Alley was his next stop, and he stuffed a dime into the phone's crotch, dialed, then he writhed in anticipation for her answer. He fixated on Roosevelt's profile on another coin and read the motto: In God We Trust. God, please help me. Neddy, answer! Bowling pins crashed in the background and then, finally, he heard the receiver lift. He gingerly spoke. "Tttthis is Chaim."

"My sweeeet, sweeeeeet lover boy," she intoned. He got a boner. "You're gonna come see me again, aren't you?" she cooed, lamenting like a mourning dove. "Come now," she instructed.

"I can't. I have band practice."

"Come over here, and I'll make your trumpet sound," she coquetted, then they settled for his visit the next day.

Loose lips would sink ships, and three could keep his secret if two were dead, he said to himself, trying to make sense of this. And her husband, what *if* he found out? Chaim liked the idea of a woman with a gun; threateningly dangerous... but no one, no one, must know what I am thinking, he thought. No one can know my truths.

Once at band practice, his pucker was barely able to manage quarter notes. He composed melodies with her name, whispered her name, replacing Maria's name in the West Side story song with Neddy. Imprisoned by his mother's example of secrecy, he contorted in his conflicting impulse to tell.

Sexual rushes tumbled inside of him like the glass shards in his twisting kaleidoscope as he fumbled through the intricate trumpet parts, which ordinarily, he could play with ease. By the time band practice concluded, Chaim was unsure if he'd played John Phillips Sousa or Percy Grainger.

As he drove along, he thought about how much he despised his name; both names; both Chaim and Goldberg. Could it be worse? There was that song, *The Name Game. I say now let's now play a game; I bet you I can make a rhyme, out of anybody's name,* except mine. How could anyone put his name into that song? It would sound like an animal in its last moments, he told himself.

Why couldn't he have a plain, unisyllabic, name, like Jim? Jim Smith? He hated "being" Jewish. He felt marked, like wearing the Jude star, the yellow armband: Chaim the Jew. He hated being different, and he was convinced that no one would ever like him or love him because of his name and religion.

Nedda was *goyishly* thin-nosed, and that appealed to him, and she liked his "pretty cock," once clasping him and singing to it as if it were a microphone. She'd bestowed upon him her gift of penis-optimism, of penis-pride, and when he was with her, he could be a *goy*, feeling the way he thought *they* must feel: confident, sturdy, as indestructible and as permanent as that brass plaque at the stalwart gates at Manor Boudreaux.

By the time he arrived home, the Rintalas' land yacht berthed in the street. He hated these drunken bacchanals, often ending badly like Albee's play, which he'd seen on Broadway, *Who's Afraid of Virginia Woolf.*

These gluttonous, Kraut-hating Kikes, the Rintalas, retold deprivation war stories while driving around in their ostentatious German car. Theirs was *der Grosste Mercedes:* fearsome gangster model; big, black, Mercedes 500, windows, opaque black, like their lives. *Hoschstaplerin*! Frauds!

"Turn up the air conditioner," his mother dictated to Chaim the instant he entered the sweltering home. "Ya' could *plotz* from this heat!"

"If you didn't smoke so much, it wouldn't be this bad," he replied.

"Don't get fresh. You're not at college yet," she returned. He winced at this endless banter between them.

After visiting Manor Boudreaux, seeing real wealth, lusting after the YCC lifestyle all summer, and hearing about such unthinkable indulgences as going to Europe to buy a rug, he knew how the other half lived. The Rintalas were the other half. He hated *them*, rich bastards, but he loved their lifestyle.

His father saved soap chips, and his mother lusted after a new toaster, which she planned to buy through amassing sufficient Raleigh coupons. His mother told him that his father worked for the President, and Artie would chime in, adding, "and he doesn't pay all that well." His father persistently portrayed the wolf scraping at their door and made Chaim feel as if he were a burden rather than a blessing. To waste one bite of turnip would constitute a morsel sin.

A solid crystal bowl he did find elegant. It was a family prize from Rumania, which he could tap and make it sing. "Your Bubbie brought it when she came to America," said Eva. He escaped into the world that bowl evoked by tapping its lip, releasing its high A. That single tone transformed his spirits towards optimism and hope, delivering him from the mundane, the barren, the sparse, away from that drab, pre-fabricated Levittown world of asbestos siding, which Aku's company attached to every home.

Aku handed Chaim a gift, and he pulled apart the wrapper, staring at *The Conscience of a Conservative,* with its red, white, and blue striped cover with white stars. Aku, jowls bouncing, preached, "Chaimy...this should be *your* Bible!" There he went again, *your* this, *your* that... *your* Bible. His father and Aku exasperated him as they directed him about how and what to do at every turn in his life.

The book felt *traif,* foreign, offensive in his Democrat home, and he hated it when Aku called him *Chaimy.* The nickname was his playground death sentence. Kids at school teased him: Hymie Chaimy...and when they learned about the hymen in sixth grade in health class, everyone looked at him and smirked. Zalingus mouthed "pussy."

But Martha Hymen did not laugh. Her predicament was worse. The boys were savage. They called her, "Hymen, hymen."

Obligated to endure, to be grateful, ever polite, Chaim managed, "Uncle Aku, thanks," but his tone, while polite as his mother taught, lacked true enthusiasm or genuine gratitude.

"So, you don't believe that this is *your* Bible? Chaimy, this is America's future! That guy Kennedy's not going to be able to stop it!"

Out of respect, but a concocted sign of familial connection, Eva instructed her children to title the Rintalas with Aunt and Uncle. This confection confused him because he had a hard time discerning who really *was* a blood relative. What is true about my family?

Arthur, ever sullen, arranged a bite of roast on his fork, then daintily daubed on some horseradish sauce, his lacquered fingernails reflecting the light from the Levitt-style, one-bulb chandelier. Loading the morsel into his mouth, he coughed. *"Oy vey, Eva, this is hot!"*

"I just said that, Artie," she answered, inconvenienced by the repetition... and on they twaddled. They'd been through three dry martinis before the *entré*, and Finnish, Aku was going on about American patriotism.

Artie, besotted, let loose. "I served ten years in that war. Where were you? You made millions on minks in Moscow while I buried bodies in Burma." Then, Artie continued. *"Your* Nazi-loving Joe Kennedy's a gambler, and he's got that affair with Gloria Swanson to explain. That's your style of hero..."

Eva interjected. "Artie..."

"Philanderer... adulterer... like..."

"Artie!" Eva cautioned.

Chaim inwardly applauded. This was great family theater.

Ilona, humiliated, drunk, blathered, "Never mix, never worry!" She tried to stand. "Let's go," she said to Aku, but she was too boozed to budge. Hearing Honey's line from *Virginia Woolf*, Chaim lurched.

Chaim thought Aku needed a good punch in the chops, and he was gratified that his father had the balls to take on this man. Gossip, booze, hilarity and neurotic, narcissistic self-indulgences, arrogance, with no sense of propriety or vulnerabilities, with more than hints of adultery, that was the glue that united these couples in, as Chaim saw it, a defective illusion of camaraderie and friendship. Following the War's deprivations, social hedonism was pandemic. After famine came these dark chocolates.

"Did you hear what happened over in Dogwood Hollow?" asked Eva, breaking the uneasy mastication. Chaim listened. "The mailman went to the door at Wechslers looking for the Meyers family, and a *Schwartze* answered! Well, it wasn't their maid. She said she *was* Dixie Meyers and that she lived there!"

The Rintalas gasped.

"There're *Schwartzes* in Levittown!" Eva exclaimed.

"That's what happens when you elect a nigger-lover for President!" Aku spoke through a mouthful of horseradish-slathered pot roast, juice dripping onto his chin. He sucked his Gordon's and Schweppes. "Ahhh, Nixon shoulda won."

Interrupting this insufferable gaggle, the phone rang. Chaim grabbed it. "Yeah. Oh, yes. I'll ask," he said. "Mom, can I go up to Zubarsky's? Some kids are there..."

"It's 'may I,' and okay...but get back early."

"At least he asks permission," Aku groaned. To Chaim, whom he genuinely liked, he invited, "Come see my new car. It's a BMW 503."

Chaim smiled, thought a moment, pretending to be nonchalant, "Mom, did I mention that Herr Knauss accepted me to study with him?"

"*Schoene punum*, what wonderful news!" She turned to the guests. "Chaim auditioned for Herr Knauss. He's the Principal Trumpet for the Philadelphia Symphony."

"A good Hungarian," said Ilona.

He was their trained intellectual seal in the imaginary family circus. He announced, appreciating the notice, "He accepts only two students a year." His mother *kvelled*.

"Such a genius," Aku added, but his notice was always condescending sarcasm, not heartfelt praise.

Arthur derided the boy, shaking his head. "I never hear him practice. They must be deaf at that symphony." Everyone, except Chaim, chuckled.

***

Not even a houseplant could grow inside Zubarsky's home at 353 Thornridge Drive, but looks could deceive. This home had nothing like his father's sunlit collection of delphinium, ficus, and variegated dieffenbachia. Yet, despite the apparent darkness, an inner light shone, which Chaim never experienced at his home. Those controversial kids got Mad Magazine, which was their form of King James.

His mother discounted Zubarsky's reading matter and prohibited him from getting his own subscription. "That's *goyische chazerei*," she maintained. The boys loved Alfred E. Neuman's juvenile antics, *Spy vs. Spy*, the lampooned TV shows, and celebrity parodies. Chaim lapped it up like a thirsty intellectual puppy. 25:13 *begin

The Zubarskys saw life and light differently than the Goldberg family. "We hate fuckin' snoops," Anna once explained about her louvered shutters. "Youse boys need to know not to take no shit from no fuckin' idiots." That's how she said it. "And with Mr. Zubarsky gone, these boys are the only thing I have. So, 'fuck 'em!'" "'Em" were the neighborhood rumormongers.

When Chaim entered the home, Steve, nicknamed Zube, played a Coltrane riff on his Selmer tenor sax and called out, "Pizza's comin'!" Uncle Milty, after Milton Berle, and Dave Chernikov, Cherni, the trombonist, completed the gathering. Zube was friends with the Jews.

The bell rang, and the Gambino's Pizza guy, Charley "Chaz" Ghilarducci, Calamari's nephew and one of their high school chums, appeared. The kids looked at one another. "Money? Anybody got money? Pizza's here," Zube, wrinkling his brow, stated. "I'm busted."

"I got it," said Chaim, emulating Calamari's swagger, and he donated a bill from his YCC pay envelope, handing it to Chaz. The Country Club, mercifully, hadn't charged him for the cut-up hose, so he netted some money after his long week.

"A fiver, a Lincoln!" Zube announced. "I knew you'd have some money," he joked, and everyone joined in ovation. Steve was a handsome, dashing lad, said the girls. He had a heavy beard, jet black hair inherited from his mom, and long fingers, thick eyebrows, but he evinced a brooding manner, like his mother. He was two inches taller than Chaim, athletic, with generous shoulders. "I told them you'd have some dough." Zube continued. "Someday, we're gonna visit your mansion."

Chaim smiled and looked at the pepperoni, sausage, and cheese pizza on the coffee table, which made him think about using a pizza cutter to partition discordant pieces of his life's puzzle... pizza cutter, ziiip, ziiiip, ziiiip... and ugliness would be gone.

As the boys attacked the pizza, Chaim looked across the coffee table, past the pepperoni and sausage, realizing that he'd missed a figure. "Want some pizza?" he asked, offering her a wedge.

Quiet, protected by the *Take Five* record album cover like a Japanese woman concealed bashfully behind a fan, she twittered, "I'm Estelle O'Shannahan." She gingerly stretched her hand across the table. Smiling, she held a hand over her mouth, concealing her glistening, stainless steel braces. "Heinous, aren't they? They're coming off soon."

"Pizza," he offered, handing her a slice. He could think of nothing else to say, she was that lovely. She peeked out from beneath the Dave Brubeck cover as the LP went into *Blue Rondo à la Turk*, took the piece, covered her mouth again with her left hand, and bit into it as marinara sauce and a piece of pepperoni slid onto her chin. Mortified, she excused herself with "I hate these braces," while awkwardly licking the debris from the wires, her freckles dancing on her cheeks as she whipped her tongue around.

"I think they're cute," he said, and she smiled, covering her mouth. Thick, wire-rimmed, academic-looking glasses, similar to his, framed her delicate face. Freckle-speckled on her arms and face, she had dark, chocolate-red, curly hair. As he looked at her, she clasped her hands over her ears and giggled.

"What?" he queried.

"My ears are so *biiig*!" she chortled, and a dainty gold cross dangled in her supra-sternal notch, bouncing in unison to her nervous breaths. "My brothers call me Dumbo."

That crucifix would enrage his mother. These new feelings at finding a girl in his school class overshadowed Nedda's lactescent thoughts. He'd never had a real girlfriend, and he was ready. In the background, Paul Desmond's trio played *Pick Up Sticks*, and the two nervously giggled in the way that teens do when nothing they want to say makes sense. He forgot about Joanie and, for the moment, about Nedda.

Soon they chomped pizza in synchrony with *Unsquare Dance* and laughed again. "You're left-handed," he said as she picked up her slice.

"That's a compliment," she said. "A left-handed compliment. My Mom always says that." She smiled, and another chunk of pizza slipped out onto her chin, but this time he wiped it away with his finger. Electricity sparked between them. This was the first time he'd touched her. "You're left-handed, too."

"Yes, and thanks for the compliment." He wiggled his fingers on his left hand.

When the Desmond record ended, Estelle played an album with *Blue Moon*. Chaim ascended, extending his hand and, as she took it, she looked into his eyes, rising into an imaginary ballroom. This was their second touching.

"I like your red hair," she complimented, her shy eyes averting his.

"We're hair twins," he said, wanting to giggle, enjoying her enthusiasm, but he restrained himself because he thought that such silliness was faggy. He wore Bermudas and a tee shirt, but she made him feel like James Bond in a tux. Her scent excited him, and he thought of Bogart's line about a great beginning.

Then, out of the corner of her eye she must have seen his crushed fingers. "What happened?" she asked.

"Horse stepped on it."

"That must hurt."

"It's okay now," he said, not wanting to go into Mr. Calamari and the Club scene... or Karen, the hag.

She stuttered. "I...I...hhh...heard you play the other day. You play well."

Her stuttering made him feel cozy. "Thanks," he said and, chancing it, he pulled her closer as they swayed to the music.

"That's the first time I've danced with a real boy," she said, again dodging his eyes, "besides my brothers." She snuggled into his rhythmic hips. "They're boys... but, you know."

"You play piccolo? You're in my third period English class," he said. She was gorgeous, splendid, even if she wasn't Jewish. Her boobs barely pooched out her shirtfront, though he felt something on his chest.

"Eat up, gang. Let's go," Zube directed while bending over and tying his Converse tennis shoes.

"Where?" Chaim asked, as he and Estelle sat down. Her name was awkward, but not as cumbersome as was his.

"Over to Dogwood. There's a riot," said Zube. "Let's go see it."

"A riot? A real riot!" exclaimed Chaim, in disbelief. "What's it about?"

"Something about a Negro family moving in," Zube said. "It's these restrictive covenants... no Negroes," he said, showing the *Levittown Times* front page.

Out they went on the Falls-Tullytown Road, down Penn Valley Road, then Mill Creek Parkway, then, left on Dogwood Drive. As they drove, with a Catholic girl at his side, he recalled his mother screaming about Jules Bratstein, his classmate, whose story the synagogue *yentas* blabbed, who had gotten involved with *goyishe kopf*, a *shiksa*. "Don't you ever do that to me," she castigated, punctuating her threat by snapping a match and lighting up.

Again, for the umpteenth time, she brandished Mrs. Bratstein's sorrowful rendition heard in open court at Rosenberg's about her son breaking his mother's heart over his *shiksa* girlfriend. "They turned off the hair dryers just to listen! It was that bad...Oh, Honey don't do it!"

His mother whispered, "She died the next day, and she'd just gotten her hair done!" Eva was in a full-blown hysteria by then. Chaim found something comical in her snot and dishevelment. He laughed.

"You'll kill me. Why can't you find a nice girl... like Martha... Martha," sob, sob, "Hymen?" More tears. "Why are you laughing? You think causing my death is funny?" She swung at him, he ducked.

"She makes me puke!" were his last words when he bolted. "How can I go out with a girl with a name like that?"

"It's a good Jewish name."

"How about if her name was Vagina? Would that be a good Jewish name?"

"You'll be a murderer if you go with *goyishe* girls!" she oathed. "You'll kill me!" And so it went with her.

They'd arrived. Screaming, seething people filled the lawns and streets. "Let's get out of here," Chernikov warned. "This is scary!" his voice, deep, like the trombone Mahler notes in his second symphony.

Estelle squeezed Chaim's hand. "I'm scared," she said. "What's going on?"

"It's a riot!" Chaim said, curious about the scene. In the confusion he took up her sweaty hand. By nature, he, in some ways, was a bull in a china shop, a risk-taker, and he wanted to see what would happen.

"I want to see what's going on," he said, looking at Estelle. Then, confidently, "C'mon, this is our first adventure. I'll protect you."

She laughed.

"What?" he asked.

"I thought it would be fun for you to call me Estelle, but it makes me feel as if I've done something wrong. That's what my mother always calls me. She says I should introduce myself as Estelle, but everyone calls me Stella… like in *Streetcar Named Desire*."

"So, I'm Stanley Kowalski?" he teased, and they gripped hands and ran towards the melee, with change and car keys jangling in his pockets.

Everyone except Cherni advanced. "I'm not going," he said.

"Meeee-yow! C'mon, you… dipthong," Stella chided, emboldened by her prince. The guys laughed.

Cherni blanched, humiliated. "Okay, let's go!" he said, yielding to peer pressure, and the six entered the roiling mob foray at 43 Deepgreen Lane.

"You've got *chutzpah*!" Chaim complimented Stella as the throng jeered.

"What?" she asked. The crowd was loud.

"*Chutzpah!*" he said over the noise but that was interrupted with the crowd taunting, "Kill the niggers!" Epithets flew along with a hail of rocks. Lower Bucks County Sheriff cars made their way through the piceous crowd, lights flashing, their sirens at full volume in the pandemonium. *Levittown Times* photographers popped flashbulbs and those bursts further incited the crowd.

"Blow da niggers ta bits," one rioter railed. The chant took hold as another screamed, "Dynamite," and he waved a handful of red dynamite sticks, his arthritic knuckles bulging white against the red cylinders. Twelve sheriffs, with backs like oxen, jumped upon the miscreant and slammed him to the ground, then sitting on his back, they snapped on glistening stainless steel cuffs. Sweat poured from the sheriffs' brow bands onto the man's torso, leaving large wet spots on his shirt back.

Stella cringed. "These people are crazy!"

"Hold my hand." Chaim quelled her fears. "There's no danger in just watching."

"Nigger-lovers!" the crowd screamed at the police who vainly tried to calm things. "Kill the niggers," came the chants.

Chaim recognized trouble as he saw Zalingus, an irascible football player well known for having the biggest dick in school. He and his jock cronies eyed the band kids, who, fearfully, sought safety in one another.

"Nigger-lovers!" hollered Zalingus, extending his middle fingers to the band cadre. "Kikes! Nigger-lovers! Zubarsky, you fag!" he screeched, and this spark ignited the crowd's flash powder. Outflanked, jocks twice of the musicians' sizes surrounded them.

"Fucking faggot cocksucker!" Zalingus yelled as he launched a beer bottle, hitting Steve in mid-chest, who buckled at the blow.

Chaim's protective instincts detonated as he saw the bandersnatches advance to Steve, his beloved friend. "Stop! Stop!" Chaim screamed and tripped Zalingus, who, in attacking stride, fell hard into the roadway, his head bouncing on the hot, black asphalt. Blood spurted. Zube, like a fullback, ran past Chaim's block.

"Stella!" Chaim called out, fearing for her, and instinctively he grabbed her hand. He started to panic. The world went out of control as flashbulbs burst, bricks and stones flew, crazed rioters turned on them, beating them with sticks, clubs, hoses, and bicycle chains.

"Nigger-lovers!" the mob railed, throwing more rocks. The centrifugal forces tore the crowd apart.

"Run, Stella," he yelled, grabbing his thick glasses from the road as he warded off blows coming from every side. He began to panic as he felt that visceral fear, prescient of death, similar to what soldiers must feel as he'd seen portrayed in John Wayne movies where all hell breaks loose and things take a turn for the worst. His heart ratted and tatted like a regimental snare drum.

Chaim tried to run with her as she screamed, but bodies obstructed them and they fell to the ground. A police flank waded in with batons, throwing tear gas grenades and extricated them from the savages. Another cop phalanx wedged in and doused the rioters with fire hoses. Stella and Chaim fled with dissenters pursuing them more fervently than that cloud of hornets that chased Chaim on the golf course only a day before.

Chaim pulled open the Frog's passenger door, and she slid in. Safe. Chaim revved the engine, and the stock V-8 launched them down Dewberry Lane. They zoomed out Mill Creek Parkway. Doors locked, sequestered in the Frog, a tank of a car, they quaked and trembled in the summer heat, their clothes sweat-soaked.

He'd torn his shirt when freeing himself from the crowd and lost the buttons. "My mother'll kill me," he said.

"Oh, my God, look at you!" she said. She had blood and road dirt all over her pinafore, and her knees were badly scraped.

Blood spotted his right shoulder, and he had sanguine smears on his glasses. "I have to stop," he told her. "I can't see." He nosed into a cornfield near the Fairless Hills Shopping Center and halted, the two clinging to each other in the aftermath.

Stella, terrified, overwhelmed, sobbed. Forlorn, she asked, "Oh, what are we going to do? Oh, Chaim," she cried and hugged him for security. "Look at you." Then she laughed. "*You* told me that this would be safe." She punched his arm.

"I'll tell you one place we can't go... my house. My mother'll kill me."

"*You* have to get fixed up. You're a mess. Let's go to the emergency room."

"My father'd kill me! He hates to spend money and besides, they'd call my parents." As he pondered what to do, looking for her bleeding sources, Chaim ran his fingers through her soiled red hair, and rubbed her back and arms, soothing her. He liked the way she felt.

"It's amazing you've been able to live so long with both parents so ready to kill you all the time." Again she joked, and he laughed.

"I think that's my blood," he said while laughing more. In her eccrine state of terror she was like a wild animal, and her mammalian scents stirred him. "I don't see any injuries on you."

Stella smiled. "You're so kind," she said, wiping hair from her face, licking her lips. Her cheeks were road-sand crusted, spackled with tears and blood. She was fabulous, he thought, even when dirty. She managed a modest grin. "Thanks for saving me!" she said and hugged him tightly, "but you have to get some treatment."

"I have an idea." He paused a moment. "So you don't like *Estelle*? I think it sounds glamorous."

"I like it, but I just feel... like a toddler," she said, "as if I am about to get spanked."

He laughed. "Okay. My mother shortens my name and I hate it. She calls me Chaimala. I hate it. I hate my whole name...all of it. I don't know the origin of my name other than it's Jewish. Anyone hearing my name thinks, 'He's a Jew.'"

"You don't like being Jewish? But that's what you are. I think it's a nice name… an interesting name, Chaim Goldberg. No one else has it. I can pronounce it, too. What's so bad about being Jewish? We're Catholic."

They laughed well together.

Stella said, "Ahhh!" and reached into the seat. "This is cool! Where did this come from?"

"It's my kaleidoscope."

She peered into it, holding it up to the fading sun as they drove. Then, with her delicate fingers, she twirled the barrel and concentrated intently. "I've never seen one of these. I'm amazed. It's so beautiful. So complex." She sighed, catching her breath. "That was so exciting. Do you *always* get into so much trouble?"

"Stella, I've never seen anything like that riot."

"So, you're Jewish?" Stella summed. She gazed into the kaleidoscope, avoiding a direct look at Chaim. "We don't know too many."

"*You're* an Irish Catholic, a *shiksa, a goy*. That's what we call you."

"We don't go to church," she said. "You're nice. *Shiksa*, a *goy*, huh? Jews aren't so bad…at least we're not black. She paused a moment, thinking. "What was that word you used when we went towards the riot?"

"I don't remember. I used a lot of them."

"It sounded like your name, almost, the first part." she said.

"Oh, *chutzpah!*"

"Yeah, that's it. What's that?"

"It's Yiddish for," then laughing, "for balls!"

"I'll have to learn Yiddish." She laughed.

"If you visit my family, you'll hear a lot of Yiddish. My mother and father speak Yiddish all the time. It was my mother's first language."

She squeezed his hand. "I *like* you. You're so brave! You saved poor Zubarsky."

"I just tripped Zalingus. It wasn't anything more than that."

"But you saved him." Stella chortled. "My brothers would save me. I have three... I mean, two." She looked at the next corner as they drove. "I live out here. But not really here, because this is Upper Yardley... in Lower Yardley, though, not here," she meandered in small talk. He made another turn up a dirt road.

Then Stella said, "Chaim, you have *chutzpah*!" She nailed the guttural.

"Oh, Stella. You're wonderful!"

"Hey, where're we going?" she asked.

"You'll see," he answered. "Stella, you really put Chernikov in his place!"

She oscillated her crucifix up and down on her gold necklace. He'd have to take on his mother for Stella, but he was ready. He liked her. She'd be worth his mother's tirades.

"This is an amazing place," she said, referring to the massive hardwoods in full summer foliage as they followed along on the crushed-stone driveway. "We just moved here from San Diego... Look at the clematis and the silver lace. I like plants. Those roses are Mrs. Lincolns."

He knew he was taking a big chance, but where else could he go? "That play, *Streetcar*, opened only two days after I was born," he told her, "with Brando." The impressive bluestone pilaster gates welcomed them to the safety of Manor Boudreaux.

3

Cloisonné

"This is *your* house... home?" she asked.

"Oh, no. We live way over in the poor part, in Levittown, near Zubarsky's."

"But you *know* these people?" Stella asked in disbelief.

"I just work at their club. I'm their summer slave," he half-joked. A stunning Hispano-Suiza J12, white, convertible, sparkled at the main entrance. In the remaining evening light, the elliptical, chrome-plated headlamps shone.

"Have you ever seen one of those?" asked Stella, referring to the car.

"Only in *Life*. I've never seen *anything* like this... maybe at the New York auto show." He'd forgotten that he'd seen this very car in the Club parking lot. "I've only heard about people living like this... kings."

"Or a queen? Queen Elizabeth," Stella bantered.

He considered throwing the Frog into reverse as he wondered if this was a good idea but Nedda foreclosed that possibility when she sprang like a Jackie-In-the Box onto the front steps.

"Is that *Vesti La Giuba from Il Pagliacci*?" Stella asked hearing the music from inside the mansion.

Nedda dazzled in the gold evening light, as if she'd stepped out of the L. L. Bean catalogue, wearing summer-traditional khaki Bermudas, creased, and a pinstriped seersucker shirt, pink, crinklingly crisp. Bass Weejuns completed her outfit with shiny new pennies in the arch bands.

At first she reacted as if this were merely a surprise social visit but then, she became empathetic. "Oh, my God! What happened to you two?" She hugged Chaim and kissed his cheek.

Stella blurted, "We were in a riot!"

Nedda's *L'Heure Bleue* scent wafted delicately, and like a well-trained Pavlovian dog, inwardly he salivated, wanting her again. This Hispano-Suiza, he sensed, could only be a harbinger of trouble and, in dread, Chaim's stomach knotted. As radiant as she appeared, he detected her facial tension.

"Come in, come in," Nedda invited, waving her hands too dramatically; a contrivance. A man descended the main staircase, and Chaim knew that secrets were about to unfold. When he'd bitten of her forbidden apple, he'd seen those arm bruises. Stella stared at the dashingly handsome, angular, elderly gentleman.

He was much older, maybe twice her age; her father? Above him Chaim saw a dark cloud, eyes, deep-sunk, lean, an intense man with a white, sea captain's beard, a Partaga in his mouth. His facial skin on the sun-exposed areas had become corrugated and leathery. His cheeks were pocked and cobbled, ruddy. He stood deeply tanned, dapper, in a summer, well-pressed linen business suit, blue shirt, print tie with striped tigers, and sported a white, rakish, Panama hat. He could have been Central Casting's Hemingway figure, an old man in from the sea.

Fingers long and thin, his jaw receding, he carried a drink in a crystal tumbler in his large left hand and, on the dorsum, veins lifted his bronzed skin. The sweating crystal tumbler bore the MB monogram.

Had he noticed his wife's greeting embrace? The air was spongy wet, and beads of sweat shone on Ernest's upper lip with rivulets coursing down his woolly beard. Chaim drew the obvious conclusion.

The Old Man admired his French cuffs, also monogrammed, and he wore ostentatious hammer-and-sickle-shaped links dangling, unfastened, through the outside buttonholes. "Like these?" the master fawned. Pleased at the attention, with studied joviality, he switched his cigar from right to left, to the one holding the drink, dropping ashes onto the marble tiles, and he extended his right hand. "Captain of the new Russian freighter, Gdansk, gave these to me. Gold. Nice? Huh?"

His hands, his dress, his manner, all reflected a poseur. "*Mister* Boudreaux," he introduced himself, speaking in an aureate manner, as if playing to movie cameras. "Welcome to our home. Got in from the Orient on Pan Am night flight... Hong Kong... cost a fortune... already heard so *much* about you."

He was so conceited, like Aku, Chaim thought as the two shook. Where did the articles, pronouns, *and* conjunctions go? "Damn long flight. Refueled on Sakhalin, got stuck." Sucking his drink, clinking the ice, "Russkies took forever; three martinis before takeoff. Ahh, yes, Boudreaux ships all exceed eighty-thousand tons," adding a gratuitous fact in between sips but without connection to other thoughts, puffing his cigar, then dropping more parts of speech. "Permafrost melted... tires mired," he said, posing with his cigar and drink.

Hemingway's apocalyptic *basso profundo* was so deep that nearby leaves quaked, and he was so physically impressive that the earth trembled as his feet hit the ground. Though a poseur, a fop with deficient grammar, he was a Black Mambo of a man to be feared.

But what did he know? And from which novel had he stepped? It didn't seem as if he knew about them. If he knew, he'd be irate. Yes, that was it. He wasn't irate; he didn't know.

And Stella, what did she sense? *No one must know what I am thinking,* he said to himself in the instant in which Boudreaux held his hand. Chaim imagined the director's call: Quiet on the set, lights, camera, and... action. "New freighter's *The Neddy Bee.* Missus Boudreaux must have mentioned that in your *swim* lesson," he sneered, emphasizing *swim,* and then, with his ten-fingered vise, he crunched Chaim's hand hard as they shook. "I love her so," he proffered. "Losing her would be like losing a ship," he wandered.

Hemingway's hands lacked the callosities of a stevedore, detected Chaim. Hemingway was a ship'sman who had done no physical work.

"*Mister Boudreaux* jjjjust arrived," said Nedda.

Chaim eyed Hemingway's ivory fangs. He was Lieutenant Henry Barkley from *Farewell to Arms...* but not such an honorable figure. What if something slipped out? Such a predator would not miss a subtle facial wrinkle from Neddy's usual, an eyebrow awry from everyday, a giggle at the wrong pitch. But, if he knew her, he would read her betrayal the way a hunter would interpret a subtle change in wind direction or a bent leaf when stalking a kudu.

"Eighty-thousand tons," he repeated, then eyeing Chaim, who acknowledged, trying to appear fascinated by creasing his lips.

"Harold, darling, tell them all about your big, little row-boats," said Nedda, irritated, annoyed with his prattle. "*Mister* Boudreaux drove up just a few moments ago. Darling, may I freshen your drink? An inch of Pinch, Honey? Right?" She spoke cloyingly, submissively, in a little girl voice followed by a practiced sorority smile. She pecked his cheek. There was no true affection between them.

Her voice quavering, "I'm so glad you two get to meet. Yes, yes, Chaim, I told Mr. Boudreaux what a *lovvvely* boy you are and what a *gooood* swimming instructor you are. I was so *excited* at my lessons." She cleared her throat. She kept calling him *Mister* Boudreaux, as if she'd forgotten his given name.

Chaim caught the Freudian slip, which betrayed their naked truths. Chaim's throat constricted. Did *he* get it? He was like a kudu in *The Green Hills of Africa.* Mr. Boudreaux seemed impervious to nuance and the trio ignored this potentially dangerous rogue elephant in the room.

Stella picked up the glare from Nedda's plump, pear-shaped, diamond wedding set. She jostled Chaim's arm and whispered into his ear, "Introduce me." He realized that he'd neglected common courtesies.

"Good of you to stop over, Mister Gold-*berg*," Hemingway enunciated.

"Mmmister Hemingway, thanks."

"Boudreaux," he corrected, looking strangely at the boy.

Bollix! "Uh... Mmmmister Boudreaux." Then, "Mmmmisssuus Boudreaux, tttthis is my friend Stella O'Shannahan. We were in a riot," he said, matter-of-factly. He was unable to stop stuttering.

"Yes, she said that..." Mr. Boudreaux said, sneering and clearing his throat. He had to sense that there was something wrong.

"*Enchanté.* I am *Missus* Boudreaux," she said, cool as a mint julep but she leaned hard on the *Missus*. There was her French accent again.

"I'm Stella O'Shannahan. Your home is...is," searching for just the right word, "*exquisité, charmant!*" They shook hands daintily, she, too, strutting her French. He saw Stella as so elegant, so poised, but she hadn't a clue of the subtext. For Stella, everything was just hunky-dory, but Chaim was amazed that Nedda was so cool.

"She's a piccolo player, Mrs. Boudreaux," said Chaim, nodding his head, to impress, to fill the awkward moment with something.

"She plays your piccolo well?" Mr. B asked, enjoying his crudeness with these children. Chaim saw his wife blanch, her face looking the color of the white in an hard-boiled egg.

"Harold!" Mrs. Boudreaux remonstrated, whacking her husband's wrist with the long stirring spoon, and splashed his drink.

"Goddamn you," he responded. These were hardly the romantic words from a man gone so long, yearning for his wife. This introductory palaver took but a few moments.

"What have we here? Wounded love-birds of paradise? Not from piccolo playing," Mr. Boudreaux said, in his most pompous way, inspecting the two pummeled patients, taking another gulp of his revived Pinch.

"We just met," Stella corrected. "Today... we *just* met." Stella picked up a *cloisonné* box, shaped like a bee. "This is cute," she remarked. "This must be very expensive."

"Here, let me have that," said Mrs. Boudreaux, snatching the box. White dust dotted the wings but she cunningly blew it away followed by a swoosh with her embroidered handkerchief. "I have to get after that Ping."

"These Wogs cost a fortune," Mr. Boudreaux lamented, tilting back his head, nose skyward, supervising Nedda as she cleansed the wounds. Officiously, he narrated, "Nurse when we married," then in orchestrated fondness, "No need to work, now."

Pronouns? Where'd they go? He was drunk, Chaim realized.

"A little gauze here, some mercurochrome there," sang Nedda, practically sounding like Julie Andrews in *The Sound of Music*... *the hills are alive*.... He admired her neck as she doted on Stella. The arch of her throat was poetry. Chaim remembered kissing her neck in the candlelight as she faced her dressing table mirror, his hands on her buttocks, when they sniffed her perfumes. Could Stella sense this?

"Regular John Glenn," scoffed Mr. B, and he drained his goblet. Chaim saw that Nedda felt mutilated by his behavior. She looked as if she'd been connected to static electricity discharges from a Van de Graaff generator Chaim had seen at the Franklin Institute. Ernest's, her husband's, specialty was whittling and chopping away at people until there was nothing left.

Hemingway brought out yet another sweating bottle of champagne. "Pernod-Ricard Perrier-Jouet, 1955," he announced in his monotonic voice. "Come hither and learn, my dear," he said to Stella. "Caviar's coming next week. Let me fill your flute," he offered, his eyebrows bowing like willow fronds, placing his right hand behind his back, pouring.

"To *new* friends," Nedda added. Her mascara had begun to run as she teared.

He fascinated Stella, though, apparently mesmerizing her with his soppy grandiloquence. He handed her the bottle, and she rubbed its neck up and down. "This must be so expensive!" remarked Stella. "This is my first champagne. May I please have the label? I never want to forget this night," she gushed.

"A champagne virgin," he leered. "Your French... *tres charmant.*"

"I'm in fourth year French. I recognize Pernod and Perrier."

Mr. Boudreaux almost drooled. *"Vous êtes prise d'une très bonne classe française, Mademoiselle!"*

"You are taking a very good French course," she translated. *"Vous parlez si formellement, Monsieur Boudreaux."*

He anointed her hand with a dramatic kiss. "You must come to Cannes for the season," he flirted.

"Harold will be at our apartment... alone," said Nedda.

A jealous ember ignited in Chaim as the cur peeled the label, handing it to her on a monogrammed, embossed, MB napkin.

"It... it's all so breathtaking," Stella gushed, and then she stepped over to a floridly genital lily painting. "Georgia O'Keeffe?" she asked.

"Know your art welllll!" he complimented.

Chaim fumed. Boudreaux's pronouns and articles convulsed in mocking laughter on the slate floor and lightning bugs twinkled and flitted between the lawn furniture in the velvet Lower Bucks County summer's eve. Cicadas thrummed. No one could have known what was about to happen, but Stella's foray into O'Keefe was like lobbing a hand grenade.

"Georgia O'Keeffe painted that one, too, there," said Nedda, diverting attention away from the clitoral lily to one without overt reproductive organ overtones. "This one, she called *Skye Above the Clouds*." Chaim saw Mr. B scowl. "It levitates one, doesn't it?" she hypothesized. Mrs. Boudreaux had her fill of her spouse's smarmy pedophilia.

"You knew Georgia O'Keeffe?" Stella questioned, incredulous.

"Art friends," Mr. Boudreaux boasted. "They're our kind of people," he said with that smug confidence Chaim knew so well from the YCC hoity-toitys.

This mention must have ignited combustibles deep within their relationship. "Stop! Stop, Harold! Jeez. They don't need to hear *that* story!" she bled, crying out. "Have another drink, fer Chris' sake!" Booze was their universal antidote to cruelty.

Unfortunately, fueled by far too much Pinch, Harold was like his eighty-thousand ton freighter: unstoppable. Harold's mastodon broke its corral.

"Harold, you know exactly what went on!" Mrs. Boudreaux exclaimed. None of this made sense. "Don't, Harold!" Frantic, she continued. She pleaded, evidently fearing the worst. "*Oh, my God*! You don't have to get into that. Oh, Harold! Harold, please! Please! Not with these children. Let it be our problem," she pled, her face glowing in humiliation and searing shame.

"Bitch! Whore! That young lover of hers!" He ranted and riveted on Chaim. Nedda dissolved into tears. Hemingway smashed an empty champagne bottle on the stone floor. He knew, he had to know about them, about Chaim and Nedda. What else could explain this?

"Harold! Oh, Harold!" Nedda screamed.

"Harlot!" Mr. Boudreaux raged and words spun in tornadic fury. "Daughter of Ethbaal, King of Tyre, Jezebel!"

Cymbals crashed, tympani rolled, trumpets and horns blared. It was Mahler's Fifth gone psychotic. Like a car crash, the evening spun out of control. Terrified, he grabbed Stella's hand . "We gotta get outta here!" he exclaimed, pulling her up as they rushed towards the Frog.

Mr. Boudreaux uncorked. "You fucked him! You bitch! Adulterer! Stieglitz? Huh? He's a fucking Jew, you know!"

He didn't stop at that. He looked directly at Chaim. "You God-damned Jews! Stay-the-fuck out of Christian womens cunts, 'swhat I say. You're not wanted!" He smashed another champagne bottle, a full one, on the stone slabs. Glass exploded everywhere. It was like a scene from a John Wayne movie.

Her Bass Weejuns squeaked as Nedda followed her fleeing guests into the driveway. "Oh, don't go! Please don't. We were having such a *nice*, nice, nice time. He doesn't mean it. He's had a long day... coming in from the Orient... don't go!" Then shouting at Mr. Boudreaux, exasperated, in her highest soprano, "Look what you've done! You sonofabitch!"

The bull in the china shop slammed his hummingbird to the ground with a blow from his right hand, bellowing, "You filthy cunt! Divorce me? You'll divorce me? I'll kill you. I'll break that fucking peacock's neck and shoot those god-damned dogs and kill you!"

She hit the ground hard in front of the Hispano-Suiza, a sobbing, disheveled form, like a squashed insect. Boudreaux knew, thought Chaim, he had to know. What a humiliation! That's what this meltdown was about. It had to be, and he was responsible.

To Chaim, one thing was certain: even if Mr. Boudreaux knew what had gone on between Nedda and him, Stella did not. "Ggggoood bbbbyyyyye," Chaim babbled, trying to be polite, and they left.

***

Out Dolington Road they sped, then down a series of narrowing country lanes until they arrived at 17 Woodfin Road, unpaved, on hard mud. "Here," she directed. They parked. It was dark but with a clear sky, star-filled. Both vibrated.

"Heckova first date," Stella said. "What about Mrs. Boudreaux? Should we call the police?"

"If we get the cops involved, he'll kill her. He owns the police... we'll be involved."

"Oh my God, you're right. My mother would not like this. She's not going to like any of this, anyway. Look at me. I'm a wreck."

Then she leaned over and kissed him on the cheek. "That's the first time I ever kissed a boy." She was thrilled with herself and, emboldened by champagne, she planted a Kathryn Hepburn kiss, full on his mouth. That brought a glow to her skin. "Oh!" she exclaimed, surprised.

He kissed her back, adding his tongue the way the books said, and he felt her braces. He was dizzy with hot adolescent fervor. Hesitating, unlocking the door, Stella said, "They're so rich. I've never seen anything like it. Her husband's a maniac. Is he always like that?"

"I never met him before," he said, then, pausing, "I'm gonna be that rich someday," he said. "But I'll be nicer." And with that he kissed her again pressing against her sharp braces. He tried to caress her right breast with his hand, as in *Peyton Place*.

She resisted, removing his hand. "You are a dirty little boy," she giggled. She'd been reading a purloined copy of *The Lovers' Garden*, that popular True Romance series book, and knew this was what she had to do, to resist, although it was not what she wanted.

They both smelled of Bactine and were plastered with bandages. "We're a pair, aren't we?" Stella laughed again. "I like the fireflies," she said and laughed a bit more.

"We call them lightning bugs, Photinus pyralsis," he said, knowing that he was showing off. "It's our state insect."

"Only you would know that! You're so smart," she said nervously, then dropping the window. A bunch quickly flew into the car. He liked her laugh.

"They're beetles, not flies." Lights snapped on in the entry to the doublewide.

"I gotta go." Kitchen lights snapped on and off again, clearly sending a message. "I want to stay but I have to go. That's her Morse Code," she said, but then she lingered. "You're so popular at school. I never thought I could talk to you."

"Wow! I thought the same about you."

"My mother would kill me if she knew I was with you. You're Jewish. We're Roman Catholic."

"My mother would kill me if she knew I was with you," he joked, and they laughed.

Lights clicked on and off, emphatically. "That's Mother O'Shannahan's signal for 'get in here right now!'" She laughed and kissed him again. "Could she be more annoying?" They laughed so hard that tears flowed.

"Let's go out Friday night?" she asked. "I won't tell my mother."

"I have to go to services but maybe I can get away. I won't tell my mother." They laughed more, kissed again, hugging. Her laundry soap smelled so pure. Neither one wanted the evening to end. Once more they kissed but, as the freckled Stella pulled away, she pressed his hand to her chest. Through her flimsy bra he felt her nipple and heartbeat, and that thrilled him.

The kitchen lights flickered again. "I have to go," she said and scooted away.

Exalting in his first thrill of infatuation, he piloted the Frog along the country roads, roads with twists and turns, with blind corners and lots of gravel, metaphors for his next decades. Exhilarated, he drove fast, too fast.

Lyrics from *West Side Story* flooded his mind:

One of your own kind,

Stick to your own kind!

But... as he swerved into the next curve... if he wanted Stella, he would have to confront his mother.

Blue... it was a blue grille... a massive chrome grille... 1959, blue Plymouth Belvedere Coupe... then, at the last moment, double headlights beaming.

The impact forces propelled him into a nether world.

Glass, like Mr. B's champagne bottle, like his tumbler glass when he smashed it on the floor... and crashes like Zildjian cymbals in Mahler's Fifth... with cow bells at a distance... and the lanterns from Nedda's home... and a Shofar far, far off... *teruah*. Then, the radiator hissed, accompanied by that sour smell of boiled over anti-freeze on a hot engine block as Officer LaGuardia pulled him free ... Officer LaGuardia.

He'd killed the Frog.

***

"Artie, he's waking. Did you hear that? *Kinehora*, Artie. But he's talking nonsense about Alfred E. Neuman. Jewish!" The voice was his mother's.

Arthur looked at his son and blamed him for this inconvenience. "What did you do to *get* here! God-demmit! Alright, I won't take a vacation this summer. We'll pay the hospital bill." He pounded his right fist into his left palm. "For today, Alfred E. Neuman *is* Jewish, goddemmit! Whatever he wants. *Oy vey*, I won't get new shoes."

Eva sucked in a breath. "Oh, my God, Artie!"

"What?"

"At least he's got on clean underpants," she said, gripping her husband's arm. "*Oy vey*."

The doctor entered, wearing a starched white coat, saying, "That's quite a boy you have. He'll be okay." Then the young doctor offered them cigarettes and all lighted up. "He's very bright."

"He's not so bright that this shouldn't have happened," Artie said.

He was groggy as the ER doors sprang open and Stella, her mother and two brothers swooshed to his bedside. Stella's mom was an appealing, tall swan with ginger hair.

His mother saw the family and gazed directly at Stella's neck. "So, who are *you*?" she interrogated, blowing smoke above Stella's head, like Alice's Cheshire Cat. It was her tiny gold cross which drew the attention. Chaim chilled.

Mrs. O'Shannahan stepped up and spoke to his mother. "Stella and Chaim go to school together. Stella had a *strange* feeling," she said, then, self-consciously, she added, "Oh, I'm Mrs. O'Shannahan," and extended her right hand. Her left ring finger was bare.

"My stomach's having a strange feeling," Eva said, sarcastically. "*Oy vey*," she uttered under her breath as the mothers politely shook.

Mrs. O'Shannahan was respectful, kind, and sympathetic. She had an appealing softness about her, a genial manner and placidness, which Chaim immediately liked, and which, evidently, she passed on to

Stella. When Mary saw Stella pick up Chaim's fingers, petting them, she wrinkled her brow.

Stella quickly released. There were those social boundaries everyone knew as two cultures collided in the ER. Evalyn, Arthur, plump Ruth, his sister, guarded his left. "The side next to his heart," Eva told people when she eventually recounted the evening at Rosenberg's.

"Estelle, did you practice your flute today?" Chaim asked, hoping to interject some levity and covered her hand with his.

"You sound like my mother!" she said, and everyone laughed. Chaim released his hold.

"He'll be all right," said Mrs. O'Shannahan and kissed his forehead. Evalyn glowered.

On their exit, Mary took Evalyn's hand and said, "He's a good boy. You're very lucky. I lost a child once... burned to death. You're very lucky."

As they drove home from the hospital, Arthur said, "Ya know that guy you like so much, Kookie Burns?" then he handed his son *The Levittown Times* newspaper.

Chaim nodded. "Yeah."

"He's gonna be over at Temple B'nai Shalom on Sunday. He's making a personal appearance for Hadassah."

"He's Italian, Dad. He's Catholic."

Shaking the newspaper for emphasis, vexed at Chaim's impudence, Arthur retorted, "no, no, says here that his name is Edward Byrne Breitenberger, from a good Jewish, New York family." Ever correcting his son, there was perpetual tension between the two.

"Mrs. O'Shannahan lost a child, burned to death. What a horror. Imagine the concentration camps, what *that* must have been like," Eva wandered. "I did like her," she said, but Chaim suspected that he knew her true feelings. She hated *goyim*, and he felt that she said that to placate him.

Arthur said, "The doctor thought he was bright. I don't know where he got that from. This accident was stupid." And they drove home in silence.

***

"Honey, some day you'll find your *besherte*, your one-and-only, like I did with your father," she soothed, pretending that he hadn't noticed her insults in the ER the previous night. She hugged him and tried to kiss his lips.

"Get off me," he protested, pushing her.

She smacked at him, he bobbed, but she landed the blow on his cheek. "Don't push me away! I'm your mother."

"Yes, but..."

Her palm struck him again. "No, 'yes, but.' I am your mother, and I can kiss you. Who *were* those people?" she persisted. His cheek stung from her battery.

The doorbell rang.

Behind black-framed glasses, Arthur's rounded head poked up from behind his *New York Times*, looking like an *Amanita phalloides*, a death cap mushroom, a human *glans penis*, a big dick, pushing through loam. "It's your hospital friend," he droned, resenting the intrusion.

Stella did not kiss the mezuzah. His mother winced at this religious felony as she passed into the kitchen area. Eva's black scowl took her towards the bathroom, lighting yet another cigarette on the way, vibrating with anxiety as this *shiksa* sullied her home, like *chumitz* at Passover.

When Stella petted him on his shoulder her hug was so welcome, so endearing. Then, she kissed him on his slapped cheek. He craved her softness. She smelled like fresh summer daisies.

"Your cheek? What happened?" Stella asked.

The Levittown floor plans were ranch style, an open kitchen, dining area and living room, without privacy. He covered his cheek with his palm but didn't answer. They talked in the living room, which looked like a reading room in the New York Public Library with periodicals everywhere. "How did you know to come to the hospital?" he asked Stella.

"Something happened, something inside of me happened, after you left."

"You think if people are close, they know these things?" he asked. "I've heard about that."

"Yes, they know these things," she answered softly and took his hand. "You were so lucky. I saw the Frog. It's totaled."

"That grille... of that Plymouth, jeez, I saw it coming at me, and I just lay down, and that awful crash!"

She hugged him again. "You went through a huge telephone pole. The cops at the scene said you were lucky to have lived." She held his hand and kissed his fingers.

"I think that engine block saved me; that V-8." He hugged her. "I remember the hissing from the engine and a sweet odor. It was my blood mixed with anti-freeze." As he told the story, he recalled glass, lots of glass from the windshield and headlights... a nightmare kaleidoscopic image.

"The other guy's fine. He swerved off the road a little bit, you didn't hit him," she said.

Chaim was relieved, but then a smoking figure loomed. Evalyn stood there, hair in tight pink curlers, a newly kindled Raleigh vibrating in her lips, smoke billowing from her nostrils. She targeted the smoke over Stella's right shoulder.

Stella rose into the haze and politely held out her hand. "We haven't properly really met. I'm Stella O'Shannahan."

"You're Irish *Catholic*, Stella O-Shann-o-han," Mrs. Goldberg replied, sarcastically mispronouncing the syllables.

"Yyyes, Ma'm," she answered, mannerly.

"We *are* Jewish," she said in the same snooty tone the elite Catholics used at the Club. "My son could never love a Catholic," she stated, tearing up, lips curling, as she retreated to her bedroom with, "Ours is a Jewish home."

"I had no idea I was intruding," said Stella, mortified with the humiliating affront. "My mother graduated from Vassar!" she screamed in tears, pushing past the aluminum storm door with the Old English font G in the center, leaving Chaim staring aghast as the flimsy aluminum monogram clattered when the door shut.

"Stella! Stay, Stella!" He sobbed. "Stella," he called after her as she ran to her car.

"You bitch!" he yelled at his mother who then caught him in a roundhouse slap, knocking him to the ground.

With *The Levittown Times* rolled in his hand, the Groundhog surfaced, enraged, but he was concerned about something besides his wife's left hook. "Look at this front page!" he yelled, more concerned with the newspaper headline than his son's abuse. "Those Goddemned kids," he spat.

She came at him again. "No goddamned *shiksas* in my home!" She beat him with her fists.

Artie intervened. "Eva! Eva! No! No! He's just a boy!"

"I'll be god *damned* if he's going with *goyim*! Not my son! It'll kill me!" Her *cloisonné* world crumbled as her son broke loose and ran out the front door, but the Frog was dead. Sliding into the front seat of their blue and white 1960 Chevy Impala, he twisted the key as his enraged mother banged her fists on the closed window, screaming, threatening. "Get back here!" she railed. The engine turned over, and he went.

4

Mélange à Trois

Stick to your own kind! rang in his ears but then, out in a corn field, through his tears, a sun sparkle attracted him, reflecting from a chrome bumper. It was Stella's dove gray Bug. The tiny car quaked with her sobs. "Why does she hate *me?*" she wailed. "She doesn't even *know* me."

Her raw emotion ripped his soul worse than his mother's assaults. "Stella, we still live the War. I hear about it every night at dinner. Roll down the window."

"The War?" she questioned as she opened to him.

"Yes. It's the War. Did you see *Exodus?*"

"The movie?" she asked. "We were in San Diego, then. That's when my father left us."

"Hitler killed six million of our people in the concentration camps."

"But that's before we were even born," she said, trying to make sense of this, of what to her seemed incongruous.

"It's not long ago in Jewish time. For my family it's yesterday. Our family lost cousins, aunts, uncles...everyone. We have no ancestral family."

"But how can your mother hate *me*? All this *goyim* this and *goyim* that. She doesn't know us! How can she hate my mother? It's so unfair." Stella pounded the horn and gripped the steering wheel. Her tears dotted the shaft, and the claxon sounded harshly against the silence in the field. She startled.

"That's *my* mother's spirit interrupting us," he joked. "She doesn't *hate* your mother," he replied, trying to mollify the effect of his mother's reprehensible behavior. "Jews have been persecuted for six-thousand years. My mother tells me that we can only trust Jews."

As he said that, he felt how illogical it sounded, but this was the effect of Eva's neurotic inculcation. "Stella, I'm so sorry about this. Please understand," he pleaded.

"She's pretty awful, isn't she?" she asked.

"Awful," he said and, through the open window, he kissed her tears on her cinnamon-speckled cheeks. Her natural smell was intoxicating. "Stella, we are alone in this world."

"Jews?"

"Yes. My mother tells me that we can trust no one."

"Chaim, you can trust me," she said and stroked his cheek. She was his bliss, and he felt warm and safe with her. She opened her door and came to him.

Pulling a sky blue, hand-made patchwork quilt from the trunk of the Impala, they nestled together, tucked into the rows of sweet, white corn, tassels glowing. Then, entwined, holding on for dear life, crying, snuggling, and concealed, he smelled the fertile soil and felt as if their lives and history had been momentarily protected from his mother's salvos. His mother's anguish arose from that European inferno, and his generation suffered.

His warm hands skied over her torso, and she pulled him closer than the moments when they danced at Zubarsky's home. Her breaths came hot in his ear, and he gently caressed her tiny breasts. She didn't push him off. She touched him fervently.

As he cruised over Stella's delicate, conservative mounds, he thought of Nedda whose breasts were more full, but he blocked those thoughts. Stella moved against his hands, but when he slid his palm towards home, between her thighs, she stiffened. "Noooo!" she moaned and withdrew. Reality intruded between them. "We can't do this. Oh, my God, I can't get pregnant!"

He ejaculated. A virgin, feeling his sturdy pulses, she remarked, "Oh. I've never felt that before." She barely knew what *that* was but her skin flushed. "We have to stop!" she gasped, withdrawing her hand, wiping the mess on his tee shirt, giggling, nervously joshing, "Boy juices." She continued, "My mother says, 'One sperm, and you can forget college.'"

Breathing hard, both surprised at what had happened, they lay there in quiet. Then she commented, "You look different than the Apostles. They have little hats." She giggled. How he adored her giggling.

"I'm circumcised."

"My brothers're always flappin' their things around, like lariats. I thought, well, maybe you'd have something more, more spectacular, the Chosen People 'n' all! Like Charlton Heston," Stella twinkled as they laughed. "Maybe one that did tricks."

"But he's Catholic, GI, I guess, government issue, straight from the manufacturer, right outta the box," he said. "I've got a slight modification." Their embarrassment abated as they laughed and had fun with each other.

"You have a custom ding-dong. Maybe it needs flames," she joked, becoming more bawdy. "Do I kiss nicely? I practiced on a peach," she said.

"Stella... yes... yes." They laughed.

"Then a tomato," she said and laughed.

"Oh, you're so naughty!" she said. "I like touching you," she said shyly, into his ear, gently emphasizing with an arm squeeze. Then she asked, "How did you find me?"

"I... just got out... and I found myself on Woodburn Road... and there you were in the cornfield," he said.

"I come here to think. This is my special field, my field of dreams. The Apostles make me crazy."

"Who are The Apostles?"

"Irish twins; John and Paul, my brothers." She laughed. "We call them The Apostles... there was another, Judas." He laughed as she continued. "There's no quiet place in my house. I don't have a bedroom. I sleep in the living room. It's sure not like Manor Boudreaux." Then she paused. "Hey, let's walk to the river. I like the trains when they come through here. Let's go!" She got up, kissed him, and ran ahead. "Catch me if you can."

Her thighs were beautiful and muscular as she ran like a doe. They raced to the Pennsy tracks alongside the Delaware River, parallel to the Delaware Canal. The tracks following the river's bend where the trains slowed in a rolling curl for an uphill grunt as they approached the Fairless Works, the economic *Ursprung* of Lower Bucks County.

Hand-in-hand, strolling, with sexual tensions subsided, a low rumble from the distance heralded a train's advance. A pair of brilliant locomotive lights grew in size, clearly visible even in the brilliant sunlight. As it slowly advanced up the gentle series of bucolic hills on tracks flanked by cornfields, it lumbered towards the plant. He whispered words that described its advance: "inevitable, unstoppable, pertinacious, incessant."

"What?" she asked, but by then the din was too loud to talk.

They smelled the diesel fumes and watched the leviathan with four engines approach. The sights, sounds, and smells coalesced in a turbulent undulation of machine upon the earth. "It's beatific!" yelled Stella and kissed him.

"What?" he yelled back, and they laughed and hugged in the warm, end-of-summer sun.

Ecstatically happy, swollen in that first blush of youthful love as the train approached, Chaim pulled out two pennies and set them on the track, saying. "Here's *two* pennies for your thoughts," but they couldn't hear a thing.

When the train shuffled past them, Stella saluted by flipping up her Vassar tee shirt, and her tiny breasts danced. The engineer blasted his klaxons louder than even his mother could screech. Chaim was amazed at her abandon. Her breasts were small, but she had rich, red nipples.

They hugged and waved at the tooting locomotive, arms around each other, kissing excitedly against the train's percussion. The cars rumbled by: husky, iron ore laden boxcars, ninety-ton chlorine tank cars, gondolas of potash and steel and coal, boxcars, open hoppers, and ballast hoppers heaping with the ingredients to fertilize America. The train resonated on the loamy earth like tympani, and it passed, car-after-car-after-car-after-car-after-car-after-car-after-car-after-car-after-car. Chaim Goldberg's lion was loose and strode the earth.

As if in slow motion, they thrilled at the centerbeam and bulkhead flatbeds with heavy industrial equipment as their massive wheels crushed the pennies, and the pennies bounced and danced into the rail bed: car-after-car-after-car-after-car-after-car-after-car.

The solid steel wheels rapped out slow sixteenth notes, one, two, three, four: The Penn-sy Line, The Penn-sy Line, The Penn-sy Line, The Penn-sy Line, The Penn-sy Line, The Penn-sy Line. The pennies symbolized their lives, their allegory of promise: The Penn-sy Line, The Penn-sy Line, The Penn-sy Line, The Penn-sy Line.

Car-after-car; triplets; car-after-car. Along the rail bed, the train split the quiet, and breezes ruffled and licked the wildflowers in a sixteenth note rhythm. Blessed were these flower children who waved their delicate anthers, filaments, sepals, peduncles, and stigmas, all, like Chaim and Stella, tormented and engorged by their concerto of reproductive frenzy.

God blessed these flower children: daisies, joe-pye-weed, spotted knapweed, evening primrose, white snakeroot, tickseed sunflower and pearly everlasting... car-after-car-after-car-after-car, cheered, the flowers. Then, as the train disappeared from the remote cornfield, their Night-on-Bald-Mountain frenzy left them in a dramatic quiet. For Stella O'Shannahan and Chaim Goldberg, it had been beatific.

When it got tranquil enough to talk again Stella asked, "Was I bawdy? I want to be bawdy!" Stella cheered, shaking her covered chest in the sun.

"Yes! Yes, you are bawdy!"

"Am I *avant-garde*?"

"Yes, *avant-garde*, too! I want to be *avant-garde*."

Stella bent into the rail bed and held the flattened pennies between her long flautist's fingers. "They're hot," she exclaimed.

"That's because of the sudden compression."

"How do you know that?" she asked.

"Physics, it's just physics."

"You are so smart! Look at Honest Abe's face! Squashed," she remarked, and in her concupiscent elation, she kissed Chaim's cheek. "I'm gonna keep 'em forever," Stella promised, and she did.

Chaim said, "Oh, Stella, we're wildflowers. Let's wave and dance in the sun. We must be copper pennies on life's rail."

When Chaim bundled up the blanket to place it into the trunk of the blue Impala, Stella laughed. She hugged it. "This is our loving blanket," and that was when his love for her began.

"That's a great name for it." Chaim then laughed and tucked it into the trunk, kissed her, and snapped down the trunk. "Holden Caufield was *avant-garde*! We can be *avant-garde* forever!" They couldn't keep their hands from each other, they were so pleased with their commotion, and they kissed more. "You gave that train engineer a treat." She'd surprised him, too.

"Oh, don't tease me. I just went a little overboard," she said, and they kissed again, happy with the commotion they caused. She pressed her chest into his, and he felt her warm buttons.

"A penny for your thoughts?" he asked

"Chaim, that Mr. Boudreaux was so scary," Stella said.

"He was like a big zit ready to burst. I've never seen rage like that before, someone so out of control."

"I have," she said softly, sadly, and he drove them away.

And God then sayeth: *Life will crush you on its tracks, taking everything; but you can make it. Though crushed by fate, you must make it.* Many years later he'd reflect and marvel at how wonderfully young they were then, so unscuffed by life— fresh and ebullient.

Following their morning that encompassed all emotions, they wanted to do what all teenagers do: eat. Chaim piloted to Chubby's Dairy Barn. Along the way, exhilarated, they sang, *I want to live in Amer-ica*, and he held her hand as they sang:

When love comes so strong,

There is no right or wrong,

Your love is your life.

Everyone knew Chubby's because of its landmark: a huge black-and-white spotted cow sculpture that topped the roof. Her name was Moo-lah, Mr. Calamari's favorite thing: money.

Chaim liked the Mafia ambiance, liked being a tough-guy. He liked the cryptic linguistic dodges, the euphemisms: *ice cream,* for heroin, *cabbage,* for money, *block uh ice,* for a dead guy.

There was another character whom he met, an angular man from South Jersey, Donny Fiasco, in stark contrast to Calamari's porkulence, who took care of everything "below ground." Johnny introduced him as "da' guy wit' da' cash."

Chaim showed off for Stella in their Mafia patois of euphemisms, leaning hard into his best Sout' Jersey accent. "Yeah, weez gonna have some ice cream, ya' know, with some corned beef 'n cabbage."

"What does that mean?" she asked.

"They'se gonna drop heroin with the Irish guys."

"Chaim, that's crazy," she laughed, at first. "Funny, but crazy."

"Yeah," he continued, "dems guys iz da' crazies." She chortled, returning his parody, and he thrilled.

Calamari and his comfortable club cronies attended, all wearing their after-golf white Sperry Topsiders. McGreedy and D'Maise were there, and there were two guys he didn't recognize, golf buddies, he assumed, wise guys probably from out of town, wearing Izod shirts stretched over their basketball tummies. The gaggle amply filled a corner booth, bellies over the table edge. Fiasco was there, he would remember when the FBI questioned him about that day. Calamari owned "da' place," and Chubby ran it. Calamari didn't hang out wit' folks he didn't know well. Big Tommy

Phillippo, Karen's dad, sat with them. None of them had a handicap less than 30.

"Hey, what's a few lies between friends," Uncle Johnny would say, while pulling bills from his socks to pay up at the end of a round. "It's no fun unless you're gonna lose somethin'."

To outsiders, the comrades would appear to be a cordial group of friends sharing a few laughs, some teasing, nothing more, but Chaim knew they were scheming. He knew the inside stuff, and he liked knowing their secrets. "Silenzio, omertà," Calamari said and cracked his knuckles. "Vershte?" he'd say when he bragged, about their turf and their operations. It was hard for Chaim to discern if Calamari was mocking him by using, what he considered to be, proprietary Yiddishisms. This language was not for goyim.

Mr. Calamari called to him, half-standing. "Hey, Jew boy!" Chaim's hackles raised, and he squeezed Stella's hand. "That's the Jew from the Club, Zubarsky's kid. He'll do it. I'll get him," he blustered.

Oy vey, thought Chaim, knowing this could be a problem.

"Dat's your goil?" Uncle Johnny asked, winking, lasciviously bouncing his bushy eyebrows. A haystack of lardy flesh, *The Squid* unrelentingly teased. It was like the day he crushed Chaim's fingers. "Hey, youse guys got a little beat up, we hoid. Youse nigger-lovers! Nice picture in da' paper!" He brandished the sheaf of newsprint, and the orangutans busted up, laughing, pushing the table from its position with their expanding bellies.

Calamari continued, "Hey, don't mean nuttin', kid. You kin be nigger-lovers. We's Kike lovers, too. Hey, you and da Miss Four-eyed Freckles, wan'u two take a ride to New Joisey for me? Lantic City? He'ahs a Grant... jus' a delivery; some stuff. Youse take da' ice-cream truck." The ice-cream truck was a plain, unmarked, white van.

"Dese guys," rolling his eyes to his entourage, "'zz my best friends," he said. In his gasconade, he went on, about American history, "especially 'bout dead presidents." He repeated his gem about Franklin on the $100 bill, saying, "Ee's da' only guy who waddn't President. Too busy 'ventin' 'lectrizity."

"Mmmmister Calamari," Chaim stammered, apologetically, "Wwwe, uh, got band. School's gonna start, and we got marching band practice."

One of the orangutans quipped, "She gonna play your flute?" Calamari smirked.

"Mister Calamari, you know I'd do it but..."

"*Mister* Calamari! I like that! Skippy's got some manners, everybody. We's all got our priorities. Next time." He waved two bills, wrinkling his brow as if to ask "sure?" but Chaim shook his head, no.

In the background, Andy Williams crooned "Moon River," and then came the station break, "WBCB, 1490 AM... Levittown, Fairless-Hills, Pennsylvania. Stu Wayne here with Stan Marks. Philadelphia Phillies baseball coming up soon. Stay tuned. Up next, 'Surfin' USA.'"

Zalingus, an adolescent Neanderthal, threw a handful of pennies onto the floor. "Fetch, Jew boy!" he yelled.

Stella startled. "Those were the guys in the riot."

Chaim reddened as Zalingus bent his left hand around a ketchup bottle, ran it up and down like a primitive hominid jerking off. The others, his friends, howled in black-hearted mirth. Seemingly an ocean away, on the other shore of the restaurant, Chaim saw an oasis with his band friends: Zubarsky, Goldberg, Zerovsky, Chernikov, and Neuberg.

"Hey, ass-wipe! Look at dis!" Zalingus called out. Oh, Christ, thought Chaim. It was the shower picture. He was sure the A&P photo processor would not print such a picture. Hysterical laughter drowned out radio baseball, and Zalingus pumped his curled hand again. "Queers!" he hectored.

Chaim flipped him off but Zalingus reacted, stood up, terrifying Chaim, who feared the hooligans, all of them, would attack. "Hey, bite my cock," the Cro-Magnon yelled, and protruding from his zipper was a footlong Chubby-dog with a mustard dot on the tip. Again, the café exploded with laughter. Chaim's face was hot with the humiliation and, seeking safety, he pulled Stella towards his comrades, the smart, weak nerds, eons more evolved than the Zalingus tribe.

"Suck it!" ridiculed Zalingus. He, like Calamari, wouldn't stop.

Chaim glanced at Bratstein, yearning for a reinforcement. Jules, the only Jewish Chubby's team ball player, cradled his *shiksa* girlfriend, Vicky Sackett. Chaim named her Vicky Suck-it. She had copper red hair down to her shoulders. Jules' entry to this inner *goyishe* circle came through Vicky's thighs. Surely, he could rely upon Jules for help, a landsman, a fellow Yid, but when Bratstein turned away, Chaim took a perverse pleasure. He'd seen the turncoat's mother, dead and naked, on a granite slab at Galzerano's Mortuary with embalming trocars protruding garishly from her neck, abdomen, and vagina.

A barrel-chested mill-worker, wearing a tattered and stained, gray, United States Steelworkers of America Local 4889 shirt, Jędrzej Tomaszewski, stood. Prominent in the community, the Polack rose, burger in hand, and wailed on the table with his free fist. "Stop it! I wanna eat my damn lunch!" he yelled while squeezing his sandwich. Two pickles and a tomato slice, slathered in mayonnaise, splushed onto the table.

Zubarsky stepped in. "Hey! Fuck you, assholes!" Zubarsky didn't swear much, but he was pissed. "Ignore them, Chaim. They'll wilt. They always do."

Until that moment, he'd been rolling out cinnamon roll dough, but Chubby, flanked by Mr. Calamari, joined with Tomaszewski, and the threatening trio stood in the center of the large dining room. They were a formidable half-ton of menacing, USDA prime beef, heavily marbled. Even within their depravity on other areas, they preserved a core of decency.

Chubby took center stage, white with flour, in an Asbury Park tee shirt featuring the Ferris wheel, and tattooed with the blue and red, eagle, globe, and anchor. The Marines graphics bulged on both exposed ham-hock biceps as he raised a large rolling pin. "Dat's enough," he said to the jocks. "Dis here's my place, and if'n youse guys can't behave," he shook the pin, and everyone knew what he meant. "Youse guys ain't no *lunch* mob." Waving the industrial-sized rolling pin, he threatened the unruly patrons. The crowd clapped approval.

"It's *lynch* mob, Chubby," Calamari corrected, and the goons sniggered, enjoying the malaprop.

"Hey, *fungul*," Chubby said, raising his rolling pin. "Up your ass, too. It's my place, and I don't need no fuckin' English teacher to tell me what's right. It's a lunch mob if I wan' a lunch mob." The crowd erupted in laughter, again, with the conflict. Tension eased, and peaceful country dining resumed.

"We saw the paper!" Chernikov said, looking like a young Groucho Marx with his big eyes, black hair, thick Ashkenazi lips, and bronze skin.

"We just saw it," said Stella, her brows twitching.

"You two are front-page news. It's all over TV, too!" Zubarsky replied. "You're famous. They called you 'civil rights activists!'" He shoved the paper across the table. There they were on *The Levittown Times*, front page, top of the fold.

The headline was spectacular in 26-point, Times New Roman, bold:

Levittown Racial Incident
Meyers Family in Hiding

They admired the dramatic picture in the newspaper with Chaim's arms wrapped around Stella, she burying her face in his chest. This was the caption:

43 Deepgreen Lane: Racist Rioters Smash Supporters; Scholar, trumpeter Chaim Goldberg, protects girlfriend, Estelle O'Shannahan, spelling champ, piccolo player, in clash. Credit Frank Cappa, Mangum.

Stella looked at the picture, encircled his shoulders, and kissed him on the cheek. "How did they know all that?" she tingled. "Look at you! My tough civil rights hero!" she exclaimed. "Those guys belong in a barn," she said, referring to the jocks. "Those pigs are insensitive to..." she struggled for just the right word. "Insensitive to... to nuance." Her verbal alacrity pleased Chaim. "I'm sorry about teasing you," she said to Chernikov.

"It's okay," he replied. Cherni was delicate.

Pizza arrived, and Chaim noticed the round wheel slicing through the sausage and pepperoni pie: slicing, slicing.

"*I* told the reporter," said Zubarsky, to Stella. "I... told him you played piccolo, that you won the spelling bee." Then, to Chaim, "I told him you were the smartest kid in the school. I know how much these human rights mean to you... to all of us."

Chernikov said, "Not so smart that we didn't get beat up!" The group laughed. Gobbling, the group of nerds and musicians traded war stories from the previous day, showing off assorted bruises and wounds. After they devoured lunch, Chaim said, "Let's go back."

As the group streamed out, the Seeburg Selectophone jukebox played Perry Como and Lena Horne's famous duet medley of the bird songs "Yellow Bird" and "Red, Red Robin," and then Deano Martin began, "Eeeeeverybody loves somebody."

"Stella, what happens to the Negroes happens to the Jews... and to women, children, prisoners. These are all human rights," he told Stella. "They're just like us."

***

About three hundred people filled Meyers' front yard. Chaim recognized Newell, a tattooed steamfitter from the mill who chewed tobacco and spat out great green, slimy hocks. His bald head shone as he incited the throng to boiling rage, raving, waving his hands, and screaming, "No niggers!" He held a green, Rolling Rock beer bottle.

"It's nuts to come back here," Zube said as the band kids looked out over the throng.

"No niggers!" the crowd responded. They stamped their feet, "No niggers!"

"Niggers will destroy our home values!" Newell yelled. The crowd returned the oath.

"No niggers!" Stamp, stamp! Vehemence! He went on and on.

An elderly frail man with a bad toupee peddled a two-wheeled Chubby's ice cream truck through the crowd. He chimed the bell and played the familiar jingle on the speaker. Frenzy and sour hate made brisk business.

A Bell heli, the kind weather crews used, with the big bubble, droned overhead as necks craned skyward. The pilot deftly descended, avoiding the overhead power lines, landing in the street at the intersection of Deepgreen and Dewberry lanes.

Chaim and Stella watched the copter descend slowly, swirling dust and debris everywhere. Then, the blades slowed and stopped, po-keta, po-keta, po-keta, and its bubble doors popped open. Heavily armed police guards greeted the two passengers, a man and a woman. The gold lettering on the sides of the dark blue fuselage said: Commonwealth of Pennsylvania: Governor.

The Honorable William Bingham, Governor of the Commonwealth of Pennsylvania stepped out. He could have gone head-to-head on stunning looks with Gregory Peck. He served as special assistant to U.S. Secretary of State, John Foster Dulles, under Eisenhower, and he knew what was right. He knew that what Bill Levitt set in motion with those restrictive covenants excluding blacks, was wrong.

But the woman, who was she?

"Oh, my God, it's my mom!" exclaimed Chaim.

Tucked into the crew of reporters with the Governor, Lower Bucks County Police Chief Verbecken escorted her. The Chief announced her as "President of the Human Relations Council." Crowd noise garbled much of the introduction. "My people, listen to what she has to say. Please listen." Everyone knew and respected Verbecken, a Delaware High graduate whose father had been a mill worker.

Eva Goldberg stepped up to the makeshift podium that efficiently appeared. A short, pudgy woman with a figure like a bowling pin, all *fa'pitzed*, wearing every bit of jewelry she owned, she looked over the crowd. Too much lipstick, he thought. She wore severe, basic black. Stella grabbed his hand. "Oh, my God!" she said, recognizing the woman who was so mean to her only a day before this evangelical experience.

"She's saddened that it's too hot to wear her mink," he whispered to Stella. "How did *she* get into this?"

Chaim had never seen his mother in such a role. In Chaim's view she lacked any true devotion to God. It was true, though, that she had been the *bona fide* president of the Jewish Community Council of Lower Bucks County, of B'nai B'rith, and of Hadassah, Chaim's feeling, though, was that she was insincere, a hypocrite. He felt that she craved attention and that this service was her way to attain adoration. The jewelry charms, necklaces, and bracelets she earned in recognitions along the way were her Girl Scout merit badge sash.

Chaim told Stella, "When she was president of B'nai B'rith, she got a candy-apple-red Studebaker Hawk convertible... brand new... for the year."

To Chaim's friends, Mrs. Goldberg was the lady who stuffed *kishka* in her kitchen, known as *The Kishka Lady*, the mother who smelled like boiled chicken, and the woman who made sugar cookies for home-room get-togethers. Chaim knew the true Eva: a self-consumed narcissist.

"Nigger-lover," someone yelled, but then the crown hushed. Her intensity, her gaze at the podium quieted them. She did have a magnetic presence, like Golda Meier. Mrs. Goldberg began, looking directly into the crowd. "You are right, my friends and neighbors. I *am* a nigger-lover!" The crowd inhaled and listened. "When you cry out, you are right! I am a nigger-lover. I am also a Jew lover, a Spic lover! I love Polacks and Degos, too. I love everyone in this state, my State, my Commonwealth, no matter what. I know all the words. Degos. Boons. Kikes. Micks. I know all these words and I abhor these words, all of them! And so should you."

A man yelled, "We don't have to live next to 'em!"

Another man bellowed, "Niggers 'n Kikes are takin' over!"

"This is all wrong. Listen to our leaders," she exhorted, and somehow what she said must have rung true because they listened. "This Commonwealth will maintain human decency, no matter what. This Commonwealth will assure law and order, no matter what. This Commonwealth will preserve religious freedom and defend against anyone who threatens the well-being of others for any reason, including the color of their skin... *no matter what!* It has to be that way or this... this *hate*," she emphasized, fists held at chest level, "crushes all of us."

They listened as she continued, "An upright man is a blessing, and the color of a vessel gives no clues as to its contents." Chaim heard her say, "Mark my words, Levittown. Levittown and this country will not tolerate bigotry and racism. This is a Levittown and an America blended from everywhere. The Meyers family is our courageous sister, like Rosa Parks, who would not sit at the back of any bus because of the color of her skin."

"You fuckin', bitch, Kike," came from a man in a black suit with black Foster Grant sunglasses. A would-be assassin jumped from the obscurity of a weeping willow, brandishing a pistol. Five policeman stormed him.

"Christ! He's got a gun!" someone screamed from the crowd but, implacable, she continued, as resolute as the Pennsy Line.

An acrid, sour vinegar odor permeated the crowd in the oppressive heat as the cops dragged off the gunman. Evalyn kept talking. Chaim's heart leaped. "Stella, I can't believe that this is my mother. She doesn't believe any of this. She hates *Schwartzes*."

The crowd surged, and eight burly National Guardsmen encircled her as her message rang with the clarity of the Liberty Bell. A gasket of husky state cops dressed in black, leveled shot-guns and maintained order.

"Let her speak! Let her speak!" The Governor commanded. His security detail stood straight. "She has the right to speak! No matter what!" The tension was like that preceding a southeast Pennsylvania electrical storm.

The crowd picked up the Governor's words, chanting "Nomatterwhat! Let—her— speak! Nomatterwhat!" Chaim heard an eighth note followed by triplets, and he squeezed Stella's hand. Ramrod straight, his mother didn't back down, and he was proud.

This woman was different from the mother he'd known to that point. Maybe there was some spiritual integrity there. Maybe he'd been wrong. He'd seen her as the mother who made bagels and lox on Sunday morning, who creamed scrambled eggs just right, who served kosher hotdogs and beans on a cold winter's day, and who sprinkled sugar on his bananas and sour cream, but not this. She was tough and courageous.

"Nomatterwhat!" they chanted and banged the rhythms on galvanized garbage cans.

"The Jewish Community, all the religious communities in this country are committed to ending these prejudices. Mark my words, Levittown! Someday a man or woman of color, be he black, red, brown, or yellow, *will* become President. Someday this country *will* stand with, united with, a man... a woman... of color. This is our America, my neighbors! This is why we fought this ugly War. The Meyers family wants nothing different from what you want: to watch TV in a quiet neighborhood in their own home. They are us!"

She was eloquent.

"Think about the Meyers family and their children. Do they love their children less than you love yours? Do they fret less when they see crabgrass growing in their lawn? Do they not *yearn* for a home in Levittown, peaceful Levittown? Don't make *hate* Levittown's middle name, Levittown's shame! This Levittown is our Levittown! This Levittown is our America!"

To Chaim, his mother was surreal. She spoke as if a ventriloquist had inhabited her body and mind. Chaim knew her truths, what she really thought, yet she said what needed to be said.

***

It was August the twenty-eighth, 1963, and at that exact moment, the Reverend Martin Luther King, from the steps of the Lincoln Memorial, looked out over a vast crowd assembled at the Washington, D.C. mall, speaking his dream: "This sweltering summer of the Negro's legitimate discontent will not pass until there is an invigorating autumn."

At 23 Deepgreen Lane, in Levittown that very day, the riots were over, and Evalyn Goldberg had done her job well.

The Trenton Evening Times ran Evalyn's phrase as its headline in its editorial: **LEVITTOWN'S SHAME**. Her picture stood obelisk-like before a rapt crowd. The caption read: "Evalyn Goldberg has a dream." That night she appeared on WCBS-TV, New York, and on WCAU-TV, Philadelphia. One reporter compared her to Israel's Golda Meier.

The next day the nation saw King in Washington juxtaposed to Goldberg in Levittown. At 22 Turnhill Lane, Evalyn Goldberg relished her fame as she treated reporters hungry for her story to apple strudel, rugalach, blintzes with cherries, latkes with sour cream, and Hungarian *beigli*. The famished journalists savored her philosophy and pastries and extolled her diplomacy in their print.

That Friday evening, the religious community, Quakers, Protestants, Lutherans, and Catholics, joined hands and hearts with the Jewish worshippers. The Rabbi spoke about human rights and human relations, these ideas of acceptance. Stella asked Chaim, "Why do the Jews align so closely with the Negros?"

"Stella, it's the same cause. We're against human oppression. We just lost six million of our people." She squeezed his hand.

Rabbi Fierverker honored Eva's work for her role in bringing together the factions. He noted that, "with *rugalach, hummantaschen,* and *strudel,* she restored peace to Levittown." She got a standing ovation.

Afterwards, he told Stella, "What a puzzle. You should hear her go on about *Schwartzes*." He didn't mention how she beat him. Confused when he went to bed that night, he wrestled with the question: Which mother was she?

She was both the mother who made him bananas with sour cream and the mother who slapped him so hard that he fell to the ground, the mother who made him laugh and the mother who made him cry. At the riot, she preached love, human rights, peace, dignity, and decorum, and then she slapped the crap out of him. To him, to whom she should have been the most dear, she was the most opaque. She was a hypocrite's hypocrite, yet she stood up to the mob. Which mother did he love? Could he love both of them? The answer came when she rested decades later.

Nightly, after the radio news on WOR, 710 AM, out of New York, Jean Shepherd spun stories of his imagined childhood antics. Chaim hung on every mesmerizing word as Shepherd's hypnotic voice allowed him to leave his mother's painful images. He wondered what it would be like to have friends who wouldn't taunt or beat him, to have a mother who didn't smoke and slap him, to have a father who would notice him.

He wandered far off from Jean Shepherd as he lay there in the still night, swathed in darkness. What a few days it had been: meeting Nedda, then Stella the very next day, the death of the Frog, Mr. Boudreaux, the riots. He oozed into a series of nocturnal thoughts about the day and rubbed himself, alternating fantasy scenarios between Stella and Nedda.

He looked at the right-angled, dark-stained mahogany veneer bookshelf, which the family toted from the Bronx when they moved to Philly and then, in 1953, when they lugged it to Levittown.

His father decorated the sides of a desk with dancing clowns, which he painted in black and white. The clowns, at his age of sixteen, then, reminded him of those troubling surreal images from Bergman's film, Det sjunde inseglet, The Seventh Seal. His father was as much of a quandary as his mother.

Chaim toiled endless hours at that desk and thought about painting over the clown images, about how surreal was his family life. The desk sat to the right of the angle-shelf, and to the right of that was the door, his portal to the world, his escape hatch to the world outside of his family.

The streetlight shone in his window, and in the penumbras he catalogued and arranged the volumes by subjects, authors, and how likely it would be that he would read them. From Chaim's childhood observations, it seemed as if his father derived his life's view, his experiences, from newspapers and from the books held in this perpendicular veneered case.

Chaim was most interested in the books that featured sex. He went to the cabinet and pulled out some volumes, many having authors' inscriptions: Hemingway, Faulkner, Fitzgerald, Sinclair, and Dos Passos. These had no sex.

A book of photographs of lesbians in action and another, a book of Picasso drawings, mostly nudes, had plenty of sex. The two Henry Miller Tropic novels lay, appropriately, atop each other, as bookends to Stieglitz's naked O'Keeffe book, complete with her hairy armpits... lustfully erotic.

His face glowed warm, and his crotch twitched as he recalled the Battle at Manor Boudreaux. He tried to caste that ugliness out of his mind, displacing it with thoughts of the shaved Nedda. He paged the Stieglitz book to see more of O'Keeffe's labia majora. If this was pornography, he liked it.

In Old Man and The Sea, Hemingway had written in blue ink, "il faut durer," one must endure, dated Christmas 1933: his dad was twenty-eight. In The Sun Also Rises, there was a black and white picture of his father with Hemingway, two soldiers defending the Sphinx, holding tennis rackets. Sandwiched between Dos Passos' Three Soldiers and Manhattan Transfer, Faulkner's works stood in a neat row, their spines aligned like intellectual soldiers on the edge of the shelf.

Back in bed and erect again, just as he entered climactic inevitability, Evalyn kissed him full on the mouth. Chaim felt wet saliva and cringed. "Get off!" he scolded. "Get off!"

Where had she come from? He hadn't heard her enter his bedroom. Her hand flew at his face. Those hairy fingers, the ones with the black hairs on top, the ones that smelled of tobacco, stung his cheek. "I am your mother!

Don't you push me away!" she scolded. Then, liltingly, "Honey, talk to me! What is going on with you... and that shiksa girl? You can't get abortions. You have to love your mother."

She had him pinned. "Kiss me... or I'll embarrass you. I'll tell everyone." Goo in his hand, he feared what she would do and whom she would tell. She opened her mouth, and he felt her tongue. This maternal humiliation transcended Karen's shower voyeurism.

"I can't breathe! Get up!" He struggled. He panicked. "Get off!" He wriggled, freed his hands from beneath the blankets, and pushed her from him as hard as he could, squarely on her chest. She flew away, across the room. Mighty, he was incensed and blurted, "She's a girl, Mom. That's all. A friend." He wanted to cry, but he couldn't show weakness and gratify her perverse satisfaction in knowing she'd wounded him so deeply.

She snatched a Macy's coat hanger from his closet and beat him. "You know what can happen, don't you? If she gets pregnant?" she screamed, beating him with each word and the hanger until it splintered. "That's it... for your life!"

"Stop! Mom!" he screamed. "She's not gonna get pregnant. She's Catholic! We're not doing anything, anyhow."

"I'll die if you marry her! You'll kill me." Evalyn sobbed, snapping the wooden hanger over her son's forearms. "She's not Jewish, your children will NOT be Jewish! She'll call you a Kike one day. Remember what happened to Mrs. Bratstein! Is that what you want?"

"Mom! Mom, we're sixteen! I'm not marrying anyone. I'm going to become a doctor. You know that. Don't hit me anymore!" He cowered onto the floor, sobbing, broken, looking at the red welts on his arms.

"You are obnoxious," she said, disappointed that the hanger had broken, and threw its remnants across the room. Then, as if a fairy sprinkled her with nice dust, she transformed from a rage-o-holic to silk. "Oh, Honey, you know I love you!" She grabbed him again and pulled him to her, kissing his cheeks, softly. "I'm your mother, and I understand your needs. I'll just get you a whore over in Trenton." Her attempt at soothing failed and annoyed him more.

My life is fractured, he thought to himself. I'm stuck in a mélange à trois, between three women. God, help me. Tasting his mother's spittle, he felt revulsion and shame, but what could he do? Zubarsky's mother didn't molest him. There was no way to get her to stop these intrusions. All of this spiraled in his mind like out of control kaleidoscopic glass fragments. Thank God, he thought, she doesn't know about Nedda.

"Tell me you love me," she demanded anew, grabbing his face.

"I love you," he uttered in order to cut her off, sobbing, hoping that if she got what she wanted, that she'd leave. He had to capitulate, and by that time he would have done almost anything to end the assault. Dutifully, he wrapped his arms around her as she'd instructed him from as far back as he could remember. The signal for the break in her storm, her adieu, came as a glowing button of her cigarette, which disappeared into the darkness.

He lay in bed wrapped in self-hate, wondering why this was his lot. Was this the mandatory Jewish experience? Was this what Zerovsky and Coleman experienced with their mothers? Was it Judaism he hated or his mother or both? How can he hate a dreidel? Hummantaschen? A menorah? A shofar?

What embarrassment. His alienation from religion came not from any fault of the ideology but from embarrassment. He was unworthy, not good enough "as is." He felt that a stock, "out of the box," Jew was not good enough. Even his dick was insufficient, requiring post-factory modification.

What confusion he'd created for himself between Stella and Nedda. Nedda was animal sex. Stella? She was pure and lovely and pristine. He had to have them both. But who will love me? he asked. Who will ever love me? His family was vapid and gave no security at all. His mother was sententious, fabricated from illusion.

Off in the distance, the rhythmic Pennsy Line wheels percussed as rapid kaleidoscopic images of his life fleeted by in a perplexing mess. What did his future hold? A deep, knife-like, inward sense of panic passed through him. How much battering and castigation can a mere boy withstand? Eva Goldberg's calumny and victimization knew no boundaries, and he felt as if he were smothering in one of the graves he'd dug with Chubby's backhoe. He was a shiny Lincoln penny on the tracks and, as the train sped onward, it crushed him.

Mélange à trois, he sighed. The house was finally quiet, but he heard the 2:47 AM out of Langhorne heading west, whistling far off. As the intense loneliness swaddled his ravaged mind, the train clattered on the tracks, whistling and sounding its horn into the night. How could the daisies and wildflowers sleep with all that noise?

Vacant, lonely, connected to nothing, he floated like Nedda in her lesson, a lily on the water's surface. Mélange à trois, mélange à trois, mélange à trois, mélange à trois, mélange à trois, and sleep arrived. The Pennsy Line, The Pennsy Line, The Pennsy Line, The Pennsy Line. He wanted to die... but he had so much to do. Achievement was his lodestar.

5

Vertigo

"Nedda?" he asked hesitantly.

"Yes?" she answered tentatively, circumspect, then glad. "Oh, it's yooou! Oh, Chaim, I'm so glad to hear from you. I didn't think I'd ever hear from you again. Yes, he's gone...Yes...Yes...I'd love to see you... Can you come over?" she sighed. "Now?"

He'd called her from the gas station, where in the men's room he found a large stainless steel rubber dispenser. *Use only for the prevention of disease, NOT for the prevention of pregnancy,* was the stern legal caveat. He bought one and slid it into his wallet.

He severed all Stella-thoughts and skedaddled to Nedda's. He needed real sex. He wanted a filthy slut, a whore, like Miller's books portrayed. He craved Nedda's vulgarity, her coarseness and her refinement, her sleekness. Yet at the same time, he wanted someone as dazzling and pure as Cinderella- Stella by starlight, his Madonna, with freckles, sprinkled with cayenne.

At about noon, he pushed open the already ajar castle door and entered. Sinatra crooned:

> **The song a robin sings,**
> **Through years of endless springs,**
> **The murmur of a brook at evening tides.**
> **That ripples through a nook where two lovers hide.**
> **"'Stella by Starlight.' Do you like my theme song?"**
> **she needled.**

He laughed. "Okay, Neddy, what a thrash that was!"

"I'm jealous. One thing's for sure, you won't take me to the prom," she joked.

Nedda wore her least: a red silk scarf; nothing more. She pulled the scarf up and down between her legs, pursing her lips, inviting him towards the library alcove. Surrounded by several small Titians, her setting resembled those of the great master, as she reclined on an antique Chinese day bed with intricate dragon carvings in the legs. The bed frame was permeated with a garlic scent augmented by exotic Asian spice smells— cumin and other aromatics— and the wood was dark Burmese rosewood, hand burnished.

Her eyelids drooped as she inhaled from a carved, green jade, hookah mouthpiece. "Opium from our Chinese friends," she said, exhaling. "Late 1700's, Qing Dynasty." She sighed. "Here," she said, opening her legs, allowing him to peak at her depilated lily. With her left hand, she parted her moist, pink lips, inviting him in coyly, tempting like Eve, and asked, "Love it?"

She placed the mouthpiece between his lips and whispered, "This is my dark, secluded place." Then, softly, dreamily, "Olé!"

Once he inhaled, she became a puma cuntress, half buried in oversized, silk-covered down pillows, a sensuous sexual pool. He dove in, headfirst.

Flamboyant painted flamingoes and peacocks decorated the support posts, all precisely painted in many red shades, tints, and tones: alizarin, crimson, brick, burgundy, cerise, cherry, chestnut, claret, copper, coral, magenta, maroon, pigeon blood, ruby, salmon, scarlet, titian, vermillion, and wine... passion reds. Fluffing her red scarf at him, she beckoned his approach, and down feathers floated.

Red, red, and more red, and blue, too, azure, beryl, blue-gray, blue-green, cerulean, cobalt, indigo, navy, royal, sapphire, teal, turquoise, and ultramarine, these Chinese designs were inlaid into erotic interlocking animal and human shapes, mother-of-pearl and gold-leafed bas reliefs in torrid sexual dramas.

Against this colorful palette, she was spectacularly gorgeous. "You like it? It's Harry's gift to me. He pays me well for his sins. Naughty, isn't it? But I don't mind being his whore."

He inhaled again and grinned. She was poetically lovely, beguiling in the soft candlelight that slowly bounced through the cut crystal goblets, each bearing the MB crest, with the matched set arranged on a table producing exquisitely choreographed mini-rainbows in the flickering candlelight. She squeezed her legs rhythmically together, clasping his leg then licking her fingers, and she teased, "Try it out?" She opened her legs, wide.

Swooning in rosewood oil scents mixed with her perfume, he sandwiched her face as his mother had done to him and boldly kissed her. She responded to his aggressiveness and rewarded him by pulling off his shorts and, as if he were a savory tart, she popped him into her mouth. He collapsed on the pillow and yielded to her as she enjoyed him.

Out of breath, he said, "I am so glad to see you," and all that had happened with Stella and the cornfield, the walk on the train tracks, the Meyers family, Chubby's, the car crash, his raucous parents, and band practice evaporated like water vapor from beneath his pith helmet, up in hookah smoke.

The opium...

and marijuana... and...

hashish...

...fairyland-like... lost in Nedda's labyrinth. She was everywhere, and everything slowed. She played him passionately as if he were her personal musical instrument. Saturated in drugs, they floated, suspended in an erotic ether.

Chaim breathed hard and pulsated, and she delighted in savoring every delicious custardy drop out of him, taking a fingertip and placing it into his mouth, and he tasted himself. "It's zabaglione," she laughed and cackled and took another sip of Courvoisier XO and gulped it all down in one divine, fabulous, forbidden... slow...desserty swallow. "Yum," she approved.

How long had it been since he'd arrived? Time vanished in this trance.

The usual divisions between clear ideas and remembered moments disappeared into a spongy snooze... and when they woke, he was voraciously hungry. Nedda provided him her specialty teenager-lunch: bologna and cheese with lettuce with just the right amount of mayonnaise on white, along with a Rolling Rock beer. "I've never seen anyone eat like you," she commented. "But that's okay, I've never had anyone fuck me the way you do!" she chortled.

Holding up the green beer bottle, its surface sweating, he looked through it, delighting in her naughtiness and the distorted images he saw through the bottle. "It's like your kaleidoscope," he said and slid the bottle into her pussy.

She gyrated on it, vigorously licked the tip, kissed him, and laughed. "Mr. Boudreaux's is a real hurricane, isn't he? I am done with him."

They inhaled again and floated away on her magic carpet.

Chaim marinated in his sexual juices but, since it felt so good, he worried that he'd been inhabited by Satan, Lucifer, and Beelzebub. Could anything be this delightful? He loved sex so much and he experienced a deep thrill when Nedda orgasmed, she always first. Then, he'd come, and they'd do it all over... time-after-time-after-time. The Pennsy Line!

Carnal umbras ravished him, consumed him, overwhelmed him, obsessed him, overtook him. He delighted when Nedda's clitoris and labia minora convulsed and her entire pelvis fasciculated in pleasure, and when she demanded her special back massage, she twitched...aaaahhhhh... until he went soft. Was this what happiness felt like? He craved this bliss and was fulfilled in giving this gift to her.

Driven, consumed by this wild monster residing inside of him, like a fatigued stallion with too many breedings, he was barely able to keep up with his school work. Three or four or five times a day he masturbated, but he could have done more. Once, he inserted his penis into a vacuum cleaner but, because of resultant chafing and swelling, it was only once. If this was the darkness of evil, he'd be a mushroom in Nedda's cellar and live there forever... then he thought of Stella.

***

Wobbly, he arrived late at Stella's home, feeling so devilish, so rebellious, with a rubber in his wallet. Maybe he could savor her charms, too. Self-deluded by Nedda's responsive performance, he was convinced that Stella would yield. Then the booze, opium, hashish, and marijuana ebbed, and his ebullience drained like cooling bathwater, leaving him in a dreary, depressed funk.

"Where have you been?" she confronted him, annoyed, brandishing their picnic basket.

When he said, "Iiii was at the Club," he realized that he was still stoned. He didn't like lying but what else could he do. He had to lie. She had yet to detect that his stammer intensified when he lied. His mother knew it immediately. "I don't feel so good. Maybe it's the heat," he said. "I need water," out of breath, like a distance runner at race's end.

"Ice?" she asked, servient but fuming.

As he drank it down, he hoped that she didn't smell the sex with Nedda but, a virgin, what could she know? Balancing his deceptions, silently they drove, she holding his hand, and he mulled. They proceeded down a farm lane where they came to a massive brick home, Federal style, with elliptical windows and white and black trim and an oxidized copper roof with ornate gutters and downspouts. He felt better after the water.

A dramatic horse track circled by a white fence spread before the home. Chestnut and bay Thoroughbreds grazed belly deep on rich, well-irrigated, emerald green orchard grass. "My Uncle Aku lives here," he said, and he drove up to the main barn. "I exercise his Thoroughbreds. But he's not really my uncle. My mother makes us call him that."

"She does control you," Stella said, with an acidic residue of resentment.

"Come on," he said.

"You were almost an hour late. Where were you?"

"Cutting grass at the Club... I told you," he said, well-schooled by his mother, trying to sound neither guilty or hostile.

They entered the white-washed barn, climbed as far as they could into the upper reaches of the hay stack, and soon they were cooing along with the pigeons. Their rough spots were gone, and Stella set out roast beef sandwiches slathered with a mayo and hot horseradish sauce.

"This is my favorite," he said, famished again. It didn't matter that this was his second lunch of the day.

He rubbed her chest. She was self-conscious about her tiny breast size, but she liked him touching her, and she said, "They both work," and kissed him. Her ire was gone.

Stella was like a gazelle, beautifully built, with long thighs, lithe, and accurate in tennis. He liked watching her serve, and he hit air balls that forced her to reach to the sky. He sang, "My heart and I agree, She's everything on this earth to me," and he kissed her deeply, emulating the lick on a margarita glass rim he'd seen in The Treasure of the Sierra Madre.

He tongued her salty neck and kissed her earlobes. "That's Stella by Starlight, Rapture so rare. You're all of this and more, You're everything I adore," he paraphrased while petting her red hair and enjoying her natural perfumes.

She sighed and laughed, "That tickles!" and they set aside their eyeglasses, but then a car engine interrupted. They froze.

"Oh, my God," he whispered and, leaning towards her, he inadvertently brushed his glasses over the hay bales, onto the barn floor twenty feet below. Then, the barn door slid on its noisy tracks. "I can't drive without them," he said. Pulling on their shirts, she replacing her glasses, they lay there, trapped, skulking, barely breathing.

Rusty rollers squeaked on steel tracks as the barn panel door opened. A pigeon pooped on Chaim's head, he farted, and Stella laughed, but the door noise concealed their commotion. He'd promised Uncle Aku that he'd oil that massive door. Acrid cigar and cigarette smoke was a harbinger for the visitors.

Once the door was opened, Aku eased his pride and joy, the newly imported 1962 BMW 5), metallic gray, into the barn. As he exited the car he bragged, "There were only four hundred and thirteen of these cabriolets built." Aku was a robber baron who loved being rich. "This is the greatest 'kown-try' in the world!" he exclaimed, triumphantly, flipping his ashes.

Clinging together they gasped, hoping that the interlopers would not notice his glasses below. Vertiginous, experiencing the waning effects of Nedda's medications, he gandered over the edge of the stacked hay at something he should not have seen, a sight ordinarily forbidden by common decency.

"That Chaim, he promised to grease this for me," Aku lamented, extending his hand to her as she rotated out of the seat from the low slung two-seater. Swiveling, Chaim saw familiar knees. She reached up to Aku and rose, festooned in a black, feathered, pill-box hat. They kissed. Chaim's heart sank.

"I have the same problems with him," Eva said. Chaim's guts twisted.

"Maybe they just came from some business luncheon?" Stella whispered.

Aku and Eva embraced in a long, lingering kiss. He held his cigar off to the side while, she, absent-mindedly, dropped her butt into a clump of desiccated alfalfa.

She sighed, "Oh, Aku," and surrounded his shoulders with her arms. They exited the side milking door, leaving the interlopers in the upper loft.

Chaim, humiliated and betrayed, had rivulets of tears streaming down his face. Stella cried with him. "It's terrible," she consoled, lacing her arm over his shoulders.

In a blind rage, Chaim jumped onto the barn floor, picked up his glasses, and hoisted a ten pound sledge hammer. He bashed the windshield of the precious BMW, then pounded the car's side panels.

"No! No!" yelled Stella, pulling his arm away. "Chaim! You can't!" but then smoke billowed from the floor. In an instant, yellow and red flame shards leapt up the stack surrounding them in a murderous fire curtain from the floor to the roof. Flames engulfed the car and blocked their exit. Chaim looked for a hose, but the nearest one was hooked to a hydrant at the other side of the barn, over seventy-feet away, through the fire.

"We gotta get outta here!" he yelled above the crackling fire and breaking glass noises. He pulled her through the bonfire.

"My brother burned to death in a garage fire," Stella said. "It was a long time ago. It was ghastly."

Chaim clenched her hand as they sped away. "I just hope no one saw us."

"No one saw us, Chaim. No one," assured Stella, returning his speculative squeeze. His dream of his final high-school year, how good it would be, was not turning out the way in which he'd hoped. Chaim sustained everlasting emotional fractures and never trusted his mother again.

Fire engines passed them. His scabs had just healed from the car crash and then, this. These scars were indelible.

***

Tisk, tisk, tisking away, pointing to the headline, LANGHORNE BARN BURNER! in the Levittown Times, Arthur sat down for dinner. Evalyn nonchalantly announced the success of the B'nai B'rith fundraiser and mused, "That fire must have happened during the luncheon. Aku was... at the luncheon."

Chaim left the table and vomited, reliving his view of the couple's BMW kiss.

In bed that night, he listened to Jean Shepherd but began to cry. What a betrayal! Evalyn heard him and entered his room. "What's wrong, Honey?" she asked, as if nothing catawampus had transpired.

He dreaded addressing her but managed, "I won't be able to ride Uncle Aku's horses." How could he possibly say what he wanted to say? You lying cunt!

"I'll talk to him. They'll rebuild the barn. The horses are okay, I'm sure." Then she kissed his forehead and left. He muffled his sobs in his pillow. Pernicious, kaleidoscopic discharges bombarded his weary psyche. Barn flames, fire trucks with sirens blaring, emergency lights discharging, lights, people, places and things all jumbled.

Nothing was dependable; nothing remained constant; nothing was predictable. His life was not orderly, like Mrs. Bliss' physics world.

6

The Day of No

October, 1963

Anna Zubarsky pushed open the front door to 353 Thornridge Drive and set down shopping bags. She opened the Coldspot, poured a generous glass of Chianti, lighted a Camel, and slammed the fridge. Then, she bellowed, "What a day at the mill. Youse guys, stay the hell out of my kitchen. I got dinner to fix." The boys loved Anna Zubarsky.

Years later when he thought back to those times, he realized that, had he known maternal love, it would have been in loving Anna. Following the barn inferno, mortified and morose, he flocculated like a catfish in muddy depths of despair. Bereft. He was bereft. He told Anna what he'd seen, and she chopped celery harder, almost whacking her finger. "Shit," she exclaimed at the near miss.

"I'm gonna hang myself," he told her.

She replied, "Shuddafuckup. Don't fuckin' do dat!" and smacked the back of his head with a cooking spoon. "I'll kill you if you do dat."

He cracked up laughing, and they both howled and hugged. She was the only one who understood his undercover life, and that was the reason the boys loved her so much; she understood.

"I'll take you into a bit of confidence," she said. "Me 'n Johnny, well... uh..." She shook her head back and forth. "We got together before the sheets wuz cold. Hey, shit, it happens."

Anna sprang like a rutabaga from sturdy Serbo-Croatian stock in Coatesville, Pennsylvania along the Brandywine River. Anna stood six feet, a Serbo-Croatian peasant woman. For glasses, she wore thick lenses in black frames which made her fiery black eyes look large and scary.

Her teeth looked like peasant corn kernels with wide interdental spaces, and she often spoke of her father, a "mean sonofabitch who worked hisself to death" at Lukens Steel. Camels were her brand; a heavy smoker. A foundation of sadness supported her vulgar bravado. She'd lost Mr. Zubarsky when Steve was in sixth grade, and it was about that time, just before Joe's funeral, when Chaim and Stevie became close friends.

"How do you shorten Chaim?" he asked his new friend when they first started playing together. "To Chhh?" They both laughed. Chaim wanted a nickname. All the popular boys seemed to have one.

The shunned Polack, Jew-genius, allied with Zube, the snubbed, agnostic Bohunk. In their make-believe ballroom, after school, they imitated Gene Kelly and Fred Astaire, tap dancing and jumping from furniture. They adored the Paul Whiteman Orchestra, and Zube loved Hal McLean, who played flute, clarinet and all the saxophones. Chaim worshipped cornetist, Bix Beiderbecke. They were different.

Anna was different, too, and direct: "Fuck 'em all, and tell 'em to go to hell," she said when the boys told her how they were mercilessly teased. They told her of the whispering campaign about her and Johnny that made Zube, a sensitive boy, a social exile. In reply, she raised her left middle finger, and they laughed.

Johnny "The Squid" Calamari was the president of Local 4889, a real union boss like Hoffa, and a frequent guest at Zubarsky's table and in Anna's bed, although he usually disappeared before the neighbors arose. He often said, "It's better to be feared than loved," and Chaim feared him, especially after what he'd done to his fingers. As late as October, he still had black and blue fingernails, what Dr. Katcher called subungual hematomas.

Chaim liked the medical lingo and admired Dr. Katcher.

The U.S. Steelworker's strike in the Fall of 1963 killed several union members. "The goddamned plant wants everything; and the workers? Bubkas! Nothing!" Anna said as she discussed the double-semi blown up in Feasterville. She chopped up tomatoes and garlic that October evening, sipping Dego red. Wine and cigarettes were her two main food groups... and "pork!" she joked, referring to Johnny Calamari.

Chaim sat across the table from Johnny when he described how a crane toppled Mr. Zubarsky into an enormous cauldron of molten steel. "Pfffffft! Vaporized." Chaim visualized a cloud made from human flesh vapor, like Auschwitz.

He thought about his parents' renditions of the glow at Buchenwald and Auchwitz. "The Nazis incinerated Jews like garbage," his father said, and he imagined the glow above the Fairless plant to be what Buchenwald must have looked like. How could someone fall into a vat of molten steel? Chaim could recite the names of the twenty concentration camps.

This was Yom Kippur eve, and Chaim forgot that he was supposed to be home for dinner. Spent from exhausting work hours, Anna entered the living room where Steve and Chaim played their instruments. "Shut the fuck up!" she screamed over the din. "I need some goddamned quiet!"

She, like Evalyn, was a screamer. "If you don't quiet down, I'm gonna put on Vera Lynn," she threatened as the boys listened to a Jimmie Smith organ album followed by the new Stan Kenton album, My Fair Lady -

My Way, then into Mo-Lasses, on Woody Herman's album Swingin'est Big Band Ever.

"Hey! Chaim! You're staying for dinner!" Anna commanded after they quieted down. He knew he should go, but he loved her and felt a part of this family. He was mad at his mother after the barn fire and wanted to injure her.

Then she burped, and everyone laughed. "Christ, when I come home," she slammed down a water glass, filled it with ice, and then poured in Chianti and lighted a cigarette, continuing, "I gotta have some goddamned quiet."

"One of a kind, huh," said Steve, taking pride in his mother's idiosyncrasies. Back in the living room, the boys displayed their album covers on the couch. On the Stan Kenton album musicians wore white tuxes, and they looked so, so cool. One day, Chaim wanted to wear a white tux and play on stage like Freddie Hubbard.

"Uncle Johnny's comin' over. Call your girlfriend, Chaimy. Get her over here. I want to see what everyone's talkin' about!" yelled Anna. He hated that endearing form, but from her, well, it was okay.

As the records spun, the friends paged through Playboy and Mad Magazine. Chaim pulled out volume K from the Encyclopedia Britannica. "I got a kaleidoscope from a lady at the Club," he announced. "Here, listen to this. 'Galileo invented the telescope in about 1609. He did not invent the kaleidoscope.'" The article went on in considerable detail. "Kaleidoscope means a beautiful form watcher."

Chaim's mind wandered, remembering how jealous he felt when the books arrived. One vulnerable afternoon they bought the collection from a Willie Loman character. "Looks great, don't it?" Anna said with pride when it arrived, admiring the oak bookshelf and the smart-looking volumes. "We are an educated family," she announced, emulating what the salesman told her. "Anyone can see that now." She'd purchased the American dream. "That Syntopicon, yeah, that makes it," she said. "All them great ideas," she sighed with pride at having attained such lofty intellectual rank for her family as she wiped Pledge on the cabinet.

In Chaim's culture, being educated was a status quo, as government issue as a circumcision. It was a mathematical "given." His family was educated, at least his father was, but they had no encyclopedia. One evening, at dinner, he asked, "Why don't we have Encyclopædia Britannica?"

"They'll never read any of it," was his father's disparaging assessment, taking another mouthful of stewed chicken. "That's goyische kopf. It's a catholicon."

Chaim asked, "What's a catholicon?"

"Don't be a dolt. Go to the library and look it up," slapped his father, sarcastically.

The phone rang, bringing him back to the present. "Answer the goddamned phone," yelled Anna, "Oh, Christ," she said and gulped more Maalox, chasing that with another water-glass of Chianti.

He lifted the black receiver. "Yeah. Hi, Stella! Oh, good. Mrs. Z, she's on the way. Her mom's bringing her."

"Hey, tell 'er it's Philly cheese steak sandwiches, so it's a good night." Then, to Steve, "Hey, asswipe, get your feet off that couch!" Everyone howled at her profanities. Then, to Chaim, "That's the couch where Joe and I made Steve!" The kids convulsed, laughing, and Steve blushed.

"Christ, I'm tired," she said, and rubbed her chest while whacking up onion, peppers, and lots more garlic. "Stevie, gemme some Maalox." Her metronomic chopping soothed Chaim. She sucked on her cigarette, gulping more wine while rubbing her chest, and toiled and burped loudly, and the teenagers chortled gleefully at her theatrics. Sometimes she even farted for them. Anna was an entertainer.

He rambled through the encyclopedia, enjoying the fresh vellum smell, that aroma of a new, unopened book, and remembered how he and Steve walked home together, hand-in-hand, from Manor Elementary School when they were in sixth grade, and kids teased them about being queers. "Fuck 'em," Anna's universal advice, made them feel better. She was on their side.

Awaiting dinner, he thought about Mr. Zubarsky's funeral. Frank teased his brother. "If you cry, you're a fag!" Steve didn't cry.

"Don't youse cry," Anna warned then. "No fuckin' crying." Then, he watched the Galzerano hearse deposit Mr. Zubarsky at graveside. Chaim remembered reading "Where death becomes art" on the rear panel. "Looey da G drove da hearse hisself," Mrs. Z said with pride. "People pay attention when dey know who you are."

Whack, whack, whack. Anna announced, "Chaimy, it's zabaglione for dessert!" Then, she burped loudly again and the boys laughed. She inverted the wine bottle and gulped down a water glass of Dego Red, inhaled, and, as a chaser, chugged the residual from the Maalox bottle.

The doorbell rang. "Stella!' Chaim called out. "You look fabulous!" Chaim smelled her perfume. His heart pitter-pattered when Stella entered. She wore an ivory colored, heavy, cable-knit Irish sweater her mother knitted. She had her hair up in some sort of thing with bobby pins, showing off her neck.

"Hey, dinner's ready," Anna yelled out, and she burped again. "That goddamned mill kills ya."

The boys, in unison, cut her off, chorusing, "but the money's good." Everyone laughed.

Fat Frank, Steve's middle brother, played both tuba and string bass. He'd been huffing and puffing into his tuba and materialized from the back bedroom, and everyone sat around the over-sized dinner table. "Oh, it's so good to have all of you here," said Anna, and squeezed Chaim's and Steve's hands. "Too bad Pauli's workin'. Save some for him, youse guys."

Then, "My sweetie's comin' over after dinner. He's takin' me dancin'... very elegant." She was so happy at that moment as she spun around, her apron and dress whirled from the forces. She piled steaming Philly cheese steak sandwiches onto an oval porcelain platter, then ladled pungent, garlicky marinara sauce with onions and peppers over crisp Italian rolls from Gambino's.

Chaim watched her knobby arthritic knuckles as she sprinkled red peppers over it all. Finally, she blanketed the feast with soft, grated provolone cheese. Oregano and pepper aromas wafted over the table and the meal began. Serving her family was Anna Zubarsky's zenith.

"No goddamned vegetables!" Anna announced. "Fuck it, you guys don't eat 'em. There's enough in the sauce."

Chaim whispered to Stella, "She's like this all the time. Just wait!"

Anna then suspended a huge, stainless steel, commercial-sized bowl onto the table that held a stack of French fries. She blessed it with a ton of salt. "Here, youse guys. This, you like! And you, too, honey. Stella, nice of you to come over. You're skinny. Eat up!"

Stella smiled and blushed.

Anna turned to Steve. "Stevie, these are your friends. You do the grace."

Chaim loved this part of the Zubarsky's family life. Everyone held hands around the table and he offered the blessing. "Bless us, Father, for this day and for what we are about to enjoy, and bless our friends, Chaim, the Jew boy," everyone laughed, "and his Mick shiksa, Stella," more laughter, "who sits at our table for the first time, and we hope that she will come back soon."

Chaim smiled at his teases, and Steve finished the blessing with, "and bless our daddy who is with you. Daddy, we miss you, but we send this aroma all the way to Heaven. In the name of our Savior, Jesus Christ, Our Lord, Amen." Everyone made the sign of the cross... including Chaim Goldberg.

"Stevie, that's nice," Anna complimented. "But maybe a little too much Jesus." Her thick, Coke-bottle, heavy, black rimmed glasses, much heavier than Mrs. Bliss' rims, magnified her eyes. She looked right at Chaim. "Chaim... sweeties, here, everyone, take Parmesan." This must be what family love feels like, he thought.

Anna's pupils flared wide as she elevated the crystal bowl but she let it free-fall into the plate of sandwiches. Her head fell. Those were Anna Zubarsky's last words. Anna Zubarsky had dropped dead.

There came a sick, smoonching sound as her head splatted into the softened sandwiches. The Philly cheese steaks then caromed into the French fries which flew into the delicate, cut-crystal bowl with the Parmesan cheese, which shattered on impact, and the whole mess spread onto the black tile floor.

Frank, terrified, wailed, "Mom!"

Immediately lifeless, limp Anna followed the food as she thumped onto the floor, tossing brilliant red, chunky marinara sauce all over the place. Marinara sauce with slippery peppers covered her face as she gazed up from the floor, her black-framed glasses dangled from her right ear, her nacreous, pearlescent eyes, wide open, stared at the ceiling, and bits of Parmesan cheese dotted her black coarse hair and her cheeks. She was hideous, and she reminded Chaim of one of those paintings at Nedda's... with all the reds.

Frank, the tough, no-crying brother, screamed, "Mom! Mom!" He was crying.

One second she passed the Parmesan cheese, the next second she passed. Lifeless. Death happens that fast, Chaim would reflect many years later, after he'd learned more about these transitions.

"Hey, asshole! Stevie, Jesus H. Fuckin' Christ! Call the rescue squad!" Frank ordered.

As Steve hurriedly dialed, there came a rap, rap, rapping at the front door, and Uncle Johnny walked in. A swarthy man, he had no idea what had just happened. "What the fuck!" he exclaimed, always a man of few words. "Who-done-dis'?" he blurted while extracting his Colt .38 revolver.

"No, Uncle Johnny! It's goddamned marinara," Frank pointed out.

Johnny looked at dead Anna, teared, registering what had happened, tucked in his tie and tenderly wiped off her face with a kitchen towel, but he was careful not to soil his expensive suit.

When the Lower Bucks County Rescue Squad arrived, the attendant took one look at her and stated the obvious: "She's dead. We can't do nuttin'." He wrinkled his face in futility and pulled his package of Camels from his shirt pocket. "Shiiit," he said, finding it empty, and flipped it into the sink, then exclaimed, "Jeez. Whadda goddamned mess."

Frank insisted, "It's marinara."

As they loaded her body, Chaim studied her open eyes that, by then, looked like hard, lifeless chestnuts. The attendant saw the open eyes, pressed them shut, and then, noticing her pack of Pall Malls on the table, lighted one up with the silver USW 4889 lighter she'd gotten for ten years of service to the union.

Galzerano's hearse rolled up the drive and, making death into art, neatly packed Anna into the back. They wrapped her in a white sheet, but the marinara sauce seeped through. Neighbors gasped at the gruesome scene, and red emergency lights created a surreal kaleidoscopic confusion.

Frank, frantic, yelled at the crowd of neighbors, shooing people away by waving his arms and protesting, "Get off the goddamn lawn. It's only goddamned marinara sauce!" Then, he jammed his double bass into his black 1960 Ford Falcon Sprint with its big V-8 and roared away.

The Victrola played Perry Como's album as Chaim, Stella, and Steve sat on the couch, mute, locked in disbelief, gazing at the mantel where Anna peered out at them from her wedding picture, complete with veil. The spiritual rent she left in their lives was like the gash in Nedda's oak tree, thought Chaim.

The dark living room was lighted only by a small lamp in the corner. Steve sat on the hassock in front of the couch, head in his hands. Chaim and Stella held Steve's hands and rubbed his back as they wept.

"Hey, buddie, come home with me," Chaim offered, extending his hand to his friend. Again they'd been welded together in death. In emotional fog Steve quietly pulled shut the door at 353 Thornridge Drive.

A record dropped, and Anna's LP, the Vera Lynn, began:

> **We'll meet again. We'll meet again,**
> **Don't know where, don't know when,**
> **But I know we'll meet again, some sunny day.**
> **Keep smiling through, just like you always do,**
> **'Til the blue skies drive the dark clouds far away.**

"Let it play," Steve said woefully, "She would have liked it." He snapped the lock.

***

"Where the hell have you been?" Evalyn greeted them, neglecting to notice that both boys were covered in marinara sauce.

"Mrs. Zubarsky dropped dead," he explained.

"What?" she asked, perplexed.

"Can Steve stay with us?"

"Oh, *oy vey*," came her sigh as the news sunk in. "Oh, my God! Anna? Your Mom? Dropped dead?" in disbelief, she cradled Steve's face in her hands and kissed his forehead. *"Oy vey.* Of course. What else could we do?" To Steve, "Come. Come with us."

Evalyn covered her head with a kerchief, blessed the candles for the holiday and then, taking pieces of black cloth from her cupboard, cloth kept for mourning, she covered the mirrors. Lights and reflections for the mourning period come from within a Jewish home.

By his age, at sixteen, he saw his family observances as pharisaic, wholly lacking in any deeply committed spirituality. What they did in the name of religion was a farce, a self-righteous show for the community, from which his mother achieved acclaim for her cooking, her social manipulations, and her political finaglings.

In Chaim's mind she was hypocritical, and their observances were procedural, absent any true belief; all lace, no fabric. His father toadied along like a lamb. Even his Bar Mitzvah had been a vacant experience, with nothing originating from his heart. Chaim despised this ecclesiastic charade.

Chaim and Steve realized how hungry they were at Erev Yom Kippur dinner. The family waded through boiled chicken and potatoes, with onions, garlic, and carrots. After the silent dinner, the boys heard Chaim's parents talking in hushed whispers. Evalyn said, "There's no one, Honey. Anna's family is in Croatia. They have no family." She worried over what would happen with Steve. "He'll be alone in that house."

Chaim was glad that his friend could be there and that they would comfort each other with this loss. In the bedroom darkness, Steve spoke, asked, "Want a cigarette? I have some."

Even though he hated cigarettes, he said, "Sure."

"To my mom," Steve said, lighting up.

Chaim commenced a coughing fit.

Hearing the commotion, Arthur entered. "What's going on?" he asked, meekly. He did not turn on the light.

Chaim answered, "Nuttin', Dad."

"Do I smell smoke in here?"

"Mom was just in here," Chaim answered, miraculously fluent in deception.

Arthur pivoted, closing the door, ignoring the obvious fact that he, too, held a cigarette in his hand. The boys laughed off this close call once the door closed.

After a few minutes, Steve asked, "Can you hold me?"

Chaim hesitated. Wasn't this what fags do? He slipped into bed with Steve, encircling his arms around his shoulder, embracing his friend. Two friends, lost puppies chilled by life's winds, comforted each other in a hollow, desperate time in their lives. They keened long into the night, entering sleep upon pillows wet with tears. Bobo, Steve's tri-color Jack Russell, jumped into bed with the boys, taking his position between them. Steve reached out, scooping the dog next to his chest, and Bobo licked his nose, then Chaim's hand.

The delicious Philly cheese steak sandwiches? The cops and firemen ate them, down to the last French fry. Anna would have wanted it that way. They did not go to waste.

***

Yom Kippur arrived on the twenty-eighth day of September, the tenth day of Tishri, 5724. It is the holiday of *no*, of self-denial. Not even Sandy Koufax pitched that day.

Among the observant, on the Day of Atonement, there is no eating or drinking, no wearing of leather shoes, no sex, no bathing, no washing for pleasure, no swimming, and no use of cosmetics or makeup of any kind. One sought God's forgiveness.

For breakfast that day, Eva prepared no scrambled eggs or bagels with cream cheese, dolloped no capers, sliced no onions or tomatoes, portioned no lox, served no savory jams or jellies, fried no garlic and onions, salted crispy, nor offered smoked fish or potatoes blistered in *schmaltz*. There was no family breakfast, no eating so much, as they usually did, that you could *plotz*. Chaim heard the *Shofar* blowing from his lost childhood. This is the Day of Nooooooo.

They fasted. There was no teeth brushing and breaths were rancid. Chaim eked out a perverse satisfaction from this bitter day of atonement. On this day the air was clear. There was no smoking in the Goldberg home. His mother locked her cigarettes in the liquor cabinet.

"Give me the key so I know you won't cheat," he needled her, gloating at her deprivation. She was already snarly, a mere few hours without her pacifier smokes. She scowled. Like a picador, he stabbed at her, pricking her for blood. "Every year you quit smoking, but only on Yom Kippur. I caught you last year. Remember?" he smiled, but his intent was vicious. "Give *me* the key."

She turned, lusting for her early morning cup of coffee with rich cream and sugar and her first inhalation, but it was not to be. Her hands visibly tremored. God watched.

"You're like one Pavlov's dogs," he bedeviled her, making her blood ooze the way Calamari stomped his blood from his fingers. She glared at him.

"*Genug!*" his father yelled. "Enough, we have to go or we'll be late!"

"You don't love me," she cried, a basilisk, able to kill with one glance and her breath. Tears streamed down her face. Chaim averted her gaze.

Then, seeing what he'd done, remorse overtook him. "Mom, I was just playing around. I'm sorry." He tried to embrace her, but she pulled away.

"I have to go to the bathroom," she announced.

As Arthur turned up the car heat on the way to synagogue, Chaim smelled smoke on her clothes. He looked at her and shook his head in disappointment. He looked at his mother, hating her, offended at yet another lie about her smoking. He wanted to kill her. She turned and wiped tears away. He'd broken her spirit.

Aku reeked of Tabac, a mens' fragrance he imported from Europe. Sitting next to him in the pew, Chaim, hungry, sickened and felt as if he would puke. Ilona wore a white mink and ermine jacket, although it was far too warm. She had primped at Rosenberg's Salon of Beauty, and she smelled of Killian, the new French perfume, billed as the most expensive in the world. By then, he knew his women's perfumes.

Stella entered late and sat next to Chaim. From beneath the hairdryers among the *yentas* at Rosenberg's, the news spread like flu. "That's his girl from the newspaper," a codger whispered.

"She's a *shiksa*," one woman muttered to her husband, nudging him with her elbow. Chaim felt exposed. His mother glared.

Tall, attractive, hair up, like a samba, Stella was a poetic swan of a woman. She had a smooth, graceful, curved neck, and he thought about how he adored kissing her, wandering through her lanugo with his lips. Though prohibited, he would not squelch such pleasurable thoughts on this day of *no*.

"My mother gave these to me to wear today," she whispered, pressing up her mother's diamond stud earrings. He kissed her left earlobe.

From behind them, came, "Irish Catholic! *Oy vey*."

"Stunning! A real looker," the husband replied. "A young Kathryn Hepburn."

"You're not supposed to be looking at *goyishe* women! Or any women," his wife chided.

"Don't pay any attention to them," Chaim told Stella.

In her mother's green, wool plaid suit with pink angora sweater, she looked so sophisticated. "My mother's pearls," she said and flopped the strand over her thin chain necklace, which held her gold cross. He chilled in guilt every time he saw that cross, knowing how deep his transgression hurt his mother. Yet, in this cauldron, he thought of what Anna would have told him: "Fuck 'em."

The Rabbi's Yom Kippur sermon concerned the consequences of hatred and of wrongdoing. Chaim and Stella looked at each other as he intertwined the Meyers riots with the theme of how God is an active force in correcting bad deeds.

"I learned, with great pain, that a woman in our community passed away yesterday, Anna Zubarsky, a mother, a community leader, a saint," said the rabbi. He extolled Anna, her family, her charitable ministrations. The Rebbi had worked with her closely in the betterment of the community. "We welcome her son, Steve. He is with us today. We include Anna Zubarsky in our *yiskor* service."

When the cantor sang Kol Nidre, Chaim and Steve sobbed. They mopped their tears with embroidered handkerchiefs Stella's mother made. Chaim, Steve, and Stella interlocked hands, daubing away their tears.

Did God punish him by killing the only person who loved him because of his impure thoughts? And he and Steve? He had no sexual thoughts, only friendship thoughts. They only slept together that one night. Nothing happened. Does God kill people just for thinking?

In the quiet of the synagogue, Chaim recalled the penetrating train rhythms from that warm summer day with Stella... car-after-car-after-car-after-car-after-car-after-car, The Pennsy Line, The Pennsy Line, The Pennsy Line, The Pennsy Line, The Pennsy Line, The Pennsy Line.

Remorse and guilt, remorse and guilt, remorse and guilt, then shame, shame, shame; bap, bap, bap, bap; one, two, three, four. These became his life rhythms. Then it was over with the sound of the *Shofar*; one long, cleansing Yom Kippur blast, *teki'ah gedolah*.

When the congregation finally spilled out onto the patio, many paid respects to Steve. The air revived Chaim as he and Stella stood with their friend. Aku approached and handed Steve an envelope. "You'll need this, son. It's from us," he said. "She was good to us."

Steve said to Chaim, "My mom made sure Rintala got his steel, sheet-rock, lumber, and workers." Chaim didn't tell Steve what Aku had done with his mother.

The barn fire blazed afresh when he saw Aku. It was hard to look at him, and they averted gazes. This was the first time he'd seen him since the fire. What pained him so was his mother's betrayal: she was a whore. She was a liar and a whore. He thought about the black silk douche bag kit in her purse and the pair fucking. Death had to be her penalty for such betrayal. God would approve.

When the sun finally set on Yom Kippur, the Goldberg family, along with Steve, sat at their modest Sears and Roebuck table to break the fast. The Rintalas, like vampire bats, thrummed in just after sundown. His mother excluded Stella, and Chaim fumed like a fumarole.

Grandma Cohen's crystal bowl was the centerpiece. "The fruit and nuts symbolize the sweetness of life," Evalyn said, smiling, enjoying the adulation with all eyes upon her, as she passed the bowl. Would God take her like Anna?

His inner anger seethed. "Sweetness of life," he mumbled cynically, skewering his tortured mind with images of the adulterous pair intertwined. You fucking, lying bitch, he thought. What sweetness had she brought to him in *his* life? She'd cheated him with her insincerity, her concept of perverted love.

Arthur commented to Steve, "I know it's hard for you to see sweetness in life at this time, but for Jews, even during the dark of the concentration camps, like a tree's roots searching for water, we find some joy. That is the lesson of Yom Kippur."

Chaim was enraged. He'd never heard his father make such a metaphysical comment, and he was angered, jealous that his father preferentially spoke to Steve and ignored him, his son. Did his dad know about Aku and his mother? He heard a din of massive steel train wheels, pounding, pounding him like that penny on the tracks, making him feel as if he were about to explode. Aku was a motherfucker sonofabitch who made him feel worthless, and he'd become his crushed penny. This betrayal felt like Calamari crushing his hand.

They ate *cholent*, beef brisket simmered with beans for about a day, prepared before Yom Kippur, so that, at sundown, it was ready. Evalyn cooked it on the sweet side with some raisins, garlic, paprika and pomegranate juice.

"*Halushkas!*" Aku exclaimed.

He should kill them, thought Chaim.

Then she said to Arthur, "Sweet, like my love for you. Kiss me," the infidel demanded with a dramatic flourish and kissed him, tarnishing his cheek with a garish lipstick smear. Then she kissed Chaim and sister Ruth and proceeded to Steve. "It's so good to have you at this time," she said, appearing gracious, but Chaim knew her perfidy.

Steve stayed again with Chaim. How could he go home? 353 Thornridge Drive lay vacant. No one was there. Steve tried to sleep and, in the bedroom darkness, asked Chaim, "Did my impure thoughts kill my own mother?"

"I was wondering the same thing. Don't talk about it," Chaim answered and rolled over, mulling the impure thoughts... impure thoughts. He sweated and his mouth was dry.

"Is God making an example of me?" Steve asked in the blackness.

"Shut up," Chaim answered.

***

Darkness descended over joyous Levittown like an eleventh plague: death of a parent. "We started coming here after we moved from Coatesville," Steve whispered as they slid into the pews at St. Joseph the Worker Church, on Penn Valley Road, not far from the Friends Meeting House.

Incense burned, and pungent smoke curled into the narthex. Chaim watched an ebony raven, perhaps Poe, the bird he named at the Club, flutter into the cupola above the altar. *And so faintly you came tapping, tapping at my chamber door.* Then, *darkness there, and...* and death of a mother and... *nothing more.*

Anna lay reposed amidst a field of lilies and white roses. They'd gotten the marinara off and her hair looked good. Her lips appeared as if she wanted to say something. Anna always wanted to say something. Chaim remembered her stony, chestnut eyes.

Nedda entered the sanctuary wearing a black mink coat, open in front, revealing a figure-hugging black dress, with a single strand of six millimeter pearls. Her stiletto heels clicked metronomic eighth notes on the marble floor. She joined Mr. Calamari and cronies, each of whom had a gun bulge beneath their black jackets.

Chaim recognized the singer, Giacobbe LaGuardia, the cop at his car crash, when he sang *Ave Maria*. His facial features made him look like that raven, dark, mysterious, deep sunken eyes and a *big-ah* beak.

"I'm an orphan," Steve sobbed. "A Bohunk orphan." And I'm a Polack... might as well be orphaned, thought Chaim.

In his bed that evening, Chaim missed Anna. He missed her flamboyant ways, her strength, the way she could make things happen. Most of all, he'd trusted her with his heart in ways that he was unable to do with his mother. How he missed those Philly cheese steak sandwiches and her *zabaglione*. Who would he talk to now? Then he dared to think his dankest, darkest thought. How would he feel when his mother died? Would he rejoice?

The only way to get through this wall of shit was to stop feeling. These days of *no* wracked him in mental anguish as he summoned his obliterator, slicing all that he despised into mental bits, then stowing the hurts in an out-of-the-way nook in his brain. He scampered back into his safe mathematical lair, like the bunny on the fourth green chased by the predatory raven. He slipped the laminated ivory over mahogany slide on his Küffel & Esser slide rule, hoping that Poe would not catch him out in the open, then slid the rule into its leather scabbard, and went to sleep. *Genug*. Jesus H., Fucking Christ.

7

Force Majeure

The modern plastic black button in the door handle looked like one of Anna's dead eyes. He pressed it and opened the entryway aluminum storm door, the one he'd remember forever, the one with the fancy, Old English font G monogram in cast aluminum, not reputable bronze. On the entry floor lay the daily mail, some with college return addresses, and then there was an inauspicious manila envelope addressed to him from *Scientific American*, New York, New York. He scooped it up.

Compared to Neddy's mansion, as he looked around, his home was a dump. He was distraught and wanted slick digs, like Aku's home or Nedda's. On his way to the Levitt, standard issue Coldspot, he tore open the *Scientific American* envelope and flipped through the heavy velum pages. The November issue felt like Zubarsky's Encyclopedia Britannica. He plunked down in his dad's living room reading chair and postponed his daily after school masturbatory ritual.

"Chaim Goldberg, Happy Birthday from *Scientific American*," he read, feeling as if he'd won an award. "From Uncle Elijah," it said. *Mirable dictu*!

He liked the hand calligraphy, like the Duchess of Yardley's note, signed in an heavy blue ink by the editor-in-chief, himself, Wassily Leontief. A Russian? Did Uncle Elijah *know* this guy?

The cover photo showed a silhouetted scuba diver in all sorts of complicated gear wearing headlamps, in front of backlighted bubbles, with this title:

Spelunking at 250 Feet
by Jacques Cousteau

Among the flotsam and jetsam was a flimsy, translucent letter: *Luftpost, Par Avion*, Air Mail. The stamp had a picture of Yuri Gagarin, some Russian writing, and a postmark, Gdansk, with no return address but addressed to Master Chaim Goldberg, penned in European letters, such as what he'd seen from Uncle Aku's European letters.

He slid a butter-knife through the top crease, slithering out the onionskin, written in soft, smeary pencil in Hebraic letters. The writing was faint. His father could translate. The missive was signed in cursive English: Uncle Elijah.

Returning to the magazine, he liked this new word: spelunking. The story was about people descending into the Cenote caverns on the Yucatan Peninsula, in Mexico, to phenomenal depth: 250 feet. What an idea, creeping into underwater caves. What if the light failed? The danger at such depth drew him, and he decided he wanted to become a spelunker, a deep diver... right then... in his parent's room.

Emulating the diver on the cover page, he held a flashlight atop his head. His heart beat quickly as he dropped beneath the surface of propriety, descending into his parents' pool of bottomless secrets.

He'd found her Ponds Cold Cream in that opaque jar which she kept on her dresser. Doing wrong was more exciting than masturbating. His mother was catering a lunch at the Kiwanis in Tullytown. He was safe for a while. There had to be more in her room, more exciting sexual items, revealing items.

Silently, carefully, he tiptoed and rummaged Dolores Del Rio's dresser. That was one of his derisive names for her. It smelled so luxurious, with her scented talc powder and perfume. Could he find evidence of fucking?

Alone in his Levittown shoe box, his hands swam past the Ponds, then through her silky underwear, sniffing and rubbing their softness on his face. He dizzied with the perfume odors. Inside a black silk pouch was that red rubber bag and beneath it was a plastic, flying saucer, a clam shell, which he opened. This was her douche bag and diaphragm, a teenaged boy's Holy Grail in parental investigations. Shall he borrow it? Maybe he could convince Stella to use it. His face flushed as he thought about sex with her.

In the drawer, there were some straight, tailor pins, and beneath her diaphragm paraphernalia he found an heavily tarnished brass key, stamped with Schlage. The key was tethered by a red string to a manila tag, aluminum rimmed, with the number 1610 in pencil.

He held her diaphragm and poked holes in its dome with one of the straight pins. Wicked! Emboldened by sexual rushes, he extended his search and, in behind an old Bell & Howell movie projector in a tweedy case on his father's side of the closet, there sat a large portmanteau.

The chest was unlocked, with a brown shipping label addressed to Mssr. Arthur Goldberg, Esquire at 410 East Albanus Street, Philadelphia, Pennsylvania, written in fountain pen by a European hand, with flourishes. He knew that his father trained in law, thus the Esquire. In the depths of the Depression work was scarce, and he later became a clerk with the Veterans Administration. His father's spinster sister, Miriam Goldberg, was the returnee. Perilously dangling by the last filamentous remnant of his superego, he hesitated. Dare he open this Pandora's Box?

The naphthalene smell of mothballs rose up along with a musty sealed up odor. On top of a stack was a green, heavy wool, Eisenhower jacket without epaulets or insignia. This valise appeared to be a time capsule.

The brown brim of an Army officer's dress hat stuck up as if whisked into view by the snap of a wrist brush in an archeology dig. In the center of the front hat panel was a brass escutcheon; its once gleaming pride, embarrassed by time, proclaimed: United States of America. An eagle clutched lightning bolts in its mighty talons.

Lifting the jacket, Chaim found a set of brass knuckles, a black, telescoping, heavy steel blackjack, and a soiled, blood-stained bayonet. His mind whirred in speculations. There were black-and-white photos and some watercolors titled "Morocco, Tangier Souk, 1938." Another, done in red pen and ink was of a black African woman, dancing with a spear. Finally, at the trunk's bottom, he found a Luger. On its left side, behind the hammer, in German was: *Deutsche Waffen und Munitionsfabriken, Spandau* with an engraved swastika, serial number: 2209.

Remembering John Wayne, he snapped the breech and was exhilarated by its crisp sound. The gun's density impressed him. It was much heavier than the play six-shooters he'd toyed with while playing cowboys 'n' Indians in grade school. This was real.

Naked and erect, he wrapped his fingers around the pistol grip and the power of mayhem surged through him. Thrilled, Latin expressions flooding his mind, and he shuddered at the thought that he could kill his mother with this. *Alea iacta est*, he whispered inwardly, as he approached his Rubicon: the die is cast.

His heart quickened as he fumbled through his father's phrase books in Chinese, Arabic, and German. He donned the jaunty Eisenhower hat and green jacket. He strapped on the snappy leather Luger shoulder chest harness, two inches in width, and secured the cold gun into its shiny leather holster. Then, he fastened the smart, three-inch, polished leather campaign belt around his waist. The leather smelled of Neat's foot oil. Christ, he felt tough!

He'd become John Wayne as Sergeant John Stryker in...the name came to him... *Sands of Iwo Jima*. *"Exitus acta probat,"* he proclaimed aloud, but he was disappointed at how squeaky his voice sounded compared to John Wayne's. He brandished the Luger and, swaggering, practiced returning it to the holster in his most rogue manner. He swashed and buckled until he could efficiently whip out the pistol. Ready for battle! The end justified the means.

Down he dove, plumbing the big chest's depth. There was... a... a... hhhhand grenade with the wire pin still in the lever. The grenade surface was cut into little squares, like a pineapple. It felt cold, Army green color, and had U.S. in black letters on the sides with a white star. He gulped and his heart galloped. There were other items including epaulets and a picture of his dad before the Pyramids with... with Ernest Hemingway?

There were other memorabilia: a brass bowl with Chinese writing and a Chinese dagger with an ivory handle, bound with gold brocade, with an inlay of a serpent with ruby eyes. Another book of sketches done in bright watercolors portrayed "Tripoli, marketplace, 1941." The writing seemed to be in his father's hand. There was a brass insignia bar with letters: OSS. One big one was for the hat, presumably, and there were two lapel pins.

He pulled apart a green civilian passport which revealed a street address: 882 Lennox Avenue, New York. This was his dad's distinctive script, and the document was issued December of 1942, probably just before he left for the War. There were passport stamps from all over: China, Poland, Germany, Egypt, Burma, Tunisia, Italy, India, Morocco. He hadn't exactly travelled *from* the Halls of Montezuma *to* the shores of Tripoli, but he'd been close. The dates fell between 1942 and 1946.

An enlistment paper showed that he entered the Army on 15 December, 1942 two days before his birthday... of 17 December ... 1905.

He paused.

Calculating quickly, he compared the civilian passport to the War Department document and noticed that his dad enlisted in the Army just two days prior to his thirty-seventh birthday. His fingers stuttered as he flipped the pages and came to the back. There it was: Date of Birth: December 17, 1905. He'd been born when his father was forty-two.

And paused again. His mother fabricated this tale that they shared the same birth date, December the first. He first heard this fable when he was very young but as he got older he became suspicious. It was statistically unlikely.

He vibrated in anger. More lies. His father, too, was a co-conspirator. Tormented, angry, something snapped inside and he lifted the hand grenade. *Exitus acta probat*!

Red heat surged through him like the barn flames. Engulfed in such a crimson rage, he went wild. His crazy mother hated his girlfriend and betrayed him with her lover, Aku. His birthday was *not* the same day as his father's.   None of his life was secure or was true and correct. He pulled the pin.

"What are you doing?" Evalyn shrilled. Startled, he opened his hands and the grenade bounced, then rolled in slow motion...on...the...linoleum tile...floor...roll-ing-be-neath-the-bed.

"Get the hell out!" Evalyn brayed. He held the pin in his hand.

But nothing happened.

***

He stood in the front yard of 22 Turnhill Lane in the persona of the jaunty Sergeant, wearing only the Eisenhower jacket, pistol belt and the jaunty parade hat.

The Pomerantz family paraded down the street in their fresh-from-the-lot-at-McCafferty-Ford-brand-spanking-new 1964 Ford Galaxie 500, 4-Door Hardtop, 57B with the 289 V8 and 3-speed manual, in fashionable midnight blue. Mr. Pomerantz honked.

Evalyn and Chaim, once oblivious to the world around them, gawked at the proud Pomerantz family, *en parade*, with their dirtiest laundry on display. She, like a bug discovered under a rock, and he, like a surprised mouse in a barn, scurried back into the house.

Smoke spewed from her nostrils as she exhaled her cigarette. Oedipus and Jocasta came at each other's throats.

"You're a racist! You hate Negroes! You hate Christians!"

"No, No!"

"You lied about Dad's birthday. It's here. In these passports."

"That's a mistake. The passports are mistaken."

Then it slipped out. "And you and Aku!"

"There's nothing between Aku and me! Why would you say such a thing?"

"You lie about everything." There was no more powerful a detonator for her madness than a confrontation over her own lies.

Then, "Honey, what are you doing?" Her eyes widened.

"God damn you! You witch!" he yelled, feeling so polluted, so soiled and raised the pistol.

"Oh, Honey," she sighed as she looked at the brandished passports.

"The passports are wrong," she protested. "He was with the OSS, he could have whatever dates he wanted... it's... it's *nicht gefährlich*, trivial. Oh, Honey, we're just friends, you know that. Oh, Honey, you know how you make things up. You're such a storyteller."

Trembling, blinded in indignation, gripping the pistol at arm's length, he eyed through the sights.

"No! No!" she screamed and his mind went white.

Glass splattered. Evalyn shrieked. Gunpowder smell filled the living room.

Clutching her chest, she cried out, "Oh, oh my God, what have you done?"

Chalky gypsum board particles, sheets that Aku's workers installed, flew everywhere in white clouds. Glass crystals lodged in the plasterboard wall where the bullet blast hollowed out a six-inch hole. When the dust settled, he'd blown away Bubbie's prized crystal bowl, the one Rumanian heirloom. Glass smithereens and gypsum dust sparkled onto the black, speckled, linoleum tiled floor and worn Persian carpet brought from Poland.

Shaking, weak-kneed, Chaim set the gun on the coffee table. Drenched in sweat, he panted. He went to her, hugged her, and sobbed. "Oh, Mom, oh, Mom." Folding into each others' arms, they retreated from this mortal precipice.

Thrusting his army regalia onto her bed, he donned underpants, white Levi's and a Madras shirt, ran to the car buttoning his shirt as he flew, then roared down the driveway. His Connies remained untied.

It had been a real sockdolager. In the rear view mirror, she stood upright, cigarette smoking between her middle and index fingers of her right hand. He'd transformed his bumptious mother into a pillar of salt.

***

Stella slid a red M&M into his lips. "That'll make you feel better," she kissed his cheeks as he told her what had happened. "I got my braces off!" she said.

Within moments they were in her bed. The fight with his mother had sexually energized him. He found Stella's warm, braceless lips to be juicy and luscious. Hormonally driven, their adolescent hearts beat their lovers' duet.

Stella was, in all ways, an irresistible aphrodisiac; the natural scents of her skin, her hair, her belly. The more he knew of her, the more he wanted. His feelings were intense, sensuous, insatiable, succulent, ripe. Clothes and good judgment flew as he cupped her tiny breasts. She moaned. "Oh, oh... oh." It was time.

She didn't stop him, and she undulated with increasing tempo. She could manage only vowels. Her oh's became ahhh's, then uh's. Nedda was like this, and on he rushed. Tantalized and excited by her reactions, they progressed in libidinous frenzy.

"Ohhh!" she moaned as he slid into her all the way. Then she stiffened, arms on his chest. "Stop," she protested, reason taking hold, pushing him off her. "Oh, my God, stop. We can't." But he couldn't wait, and he ejaculated as she rumbaed against him.

She sighed deeply. "Oh, my God," she cried. The two clutched each other for a long time. Then, catching her breath, she spoke. "That was better than M&M's, the red ones."

Seeing a blood smear on her thigh, he asked, "Did I hurt you?"

"No. I didn't feel anything. Nothing bad, that's for sure." She giggled.

"I brought this," said Chaim, and he showed her his condom.

She laughed. "That would have been useful a moment ago," she said, trying to be buoyant about what had transpired. "I don't know *what* to do," she said. "My mother will kill me. She's been worried about this."

She went on. "It's okay. I really liked it. That was better than M&M's, the red ones," she assured, repeating, and popped a favored one in his mouth. "I liked it. A lot. Oh, I do love you," she said, kissing him softly, this time brushing her lips across his. "Oh, darling, I'm just scared to death about getting pregnant."

Her "darling" was Lana Turner's intonation from a Carey Grant film. Even with her love, this sweet, gentle and purest distillate, he thought about Nedda's raw, uninhibited sex. He would never forget Stella's kiss.

"Your mother is a terror," she remarked when they cooled down, like a pie on a rack. He told her only part of what had happened, but not the shooting part. Parodying W.C. Fields, he mocked Eva. "She's a huckster, revealed; a prestidigitator, naked; a Svengali, uncloaked; an Houdini caught with a key; an illusionist with no smoke; a trickster with no mirrors; a swindler, with an extra ace; a deceptress with falsies; a delusionist who spikes drinks; a bamboozler with her hand in a man's wallet."

Rolling her eyes, she laughed. He loved to perform for her. "Yeeeeeesss," he said, mimicking Fields' drifting pronunciation. They had great fun entertaining each other.

Though they had rolled around before, this was Chaim's first time to observe her fully nude body. "What's this?" he asked, feeling a rough patch of skin on her left flank.

"A burn. I had an accident when I was quite young," she said. He wanted to know more.

Two roads diverged, and he wanted both. To have both he had to turn off his emotions, like a light switch, changing images when rotating his kaleidoscope cylinder. To have them both, he had to transform that which was morally true and correct into that which was untrue, and he had to ignore that. Could he be such an alchemist?

Decades later, he recalled the crystal bowl exploding, feeling trapped inside his kaleidoscope, as they ate individual colored M&M's on Stella's couch. That night, on WCAU, channel 5, they watched John Zacherle, as Roland, awaken from his crypt on *Shock Theater*, and all was well. And why was that night different from all others? Stella O'Shannahan lost both her braces and her virginity.

Laura Satanoff's husband, Al, the pizza guy, dry-walled up the hole in the wall, then Eva expertly spackled and painted it. No one could be so stupid and gullible, marveled Chaim, but his father gulped down the mendacity hungrily as if it were a generous helping of warm cherry strudel. The war between son and mother ended.

She piloted a red and blue-tipped EZ-Strik down the emery board, snapping it into flame. Every day began this way. He would smell the acrid phosphorous scent. Then came her rasping with her inhalation of her first cigarette, and the new day began. She had a perpetual hacking and coughing with wet phlegmy slime which she dismissed as "just a smoker's cough."

Her fire and smoke stink preceded the much more agreeable smell of Maxwell House coffee, potatoes frying in Crisco, of eggs and onions and garlic. How he hated those matches and cigarettes.

***

November 22, 1963, Friday, his mother's birthday, arrived as a slate-gray day, with the threat of snow. "President Kennedy will speak in Dallas this afternoon," said Stan Marks on WBCB. Off he went to school.

As predictable as was his mother's morning ritual of kindling the EZ Strike, physics maven Mrs. Bliss furiously filled four chalkboards every period. She was a calcium carbonate dynamo who wore powder-puff makeup, looking as if a box of Aunt Jemima pancake flour had exploded on her face. Her lipstick was always red, her hair severely slicked back, and she favored figure fitting, cashmere sweaters, with bland, gray or other neutral skirts.

Joining her necklace of petite white pearls, she wore stern, womens' military pumps, black, with solid cylindrical heels, which produced a distinctive klunk, klunk, klunk on the linoleum, making her way through the rows as she lectured. How different a heel tone and fashion style from Nedda, he thought, when she entered Anna's funeral.

Mrs. Bliss accentuated her academic look with glasses: thick, round lenses held together by a pewter wire frame. If Chaim looked at her in just the right way as she walked around the room, he could see her eyeballs magnified.

Earlier that week, he'd wondered about a brass insignia on her desk. "Captain's bars?" he asked, one day.

"You recognize those? Those belonged to my captain, oh, my captain: *Captain* Bliss," she answered sentimentally, with pride, eyes misting, lids reddened, and she grabbed a hankie from her sleeve. Regaining her composure, she told him, "Back to your slide-rule, Mr. Weisenheimer." It must have been recent, he concluded.

Wearing the same uniform, day-after-mundane-unimaginative-day, wholly lacking in ordinary emotional connections, she was a physicist who had hydraulic fluid for blood and universal joints and rods as her skeleton. She was reptilian, poikilothermic, but his question called forth her vulnerable human insides.

Earlier that academic year, on the first day of class, Chaim discovered a unity with her when she blundered, mis-pronouncing his name. "Chame?" she asked, pronouncing the "ch," as in chug. "Is that right?" she asked, killing the consonant blend.

"It's *Ch*aim," he answered, illustrating the guttural, dramatically flapping his uvula.... xha ... xha.... This articulation was second nature to him, having heard Yiddish and Hebrew spoken so often.

Well intentioned, she tried it several times. The kids howled at the entertainment and clapped when she finally succeeded.

"I hate it," he finally blurted at the end of it all and cried in frustration, tears streaming. The class became silent. Seeing how upset he'd been, following class, she told him, "Me, too. I hate my first name. It's hard having a first name like mine: Kitten. Well, you know," she said, pursing her lips, managing a smile. "It's not even short for Kathryn." He liked her then, and they became friends.

That was as close as she ever came to revealing her personal details until the captain's bars. Then the Bond movie came out, and one of the class clowns put a bumper sticker on the blackboard: Pussy Galore. She tore it off, threw it into the trash can and glared at the class. He told her he thought that was mean. He offered his hand in comfort, and she accepted.

She petted her captain's bars that day, November the twenty-second. He was drawn to her loneliness and liked her subjects, physics and chemistry. He marveled at her memory and energy as she filled the blackboards, brushing them with her breasts as she shifted the boards up and down. When she turned around to face the class, she'd created chalk pasties on her sweater, much to the perverted joy of the evil-spirited hooligans in the riot. Chaim hated them. For him, they were anti-intellectual sewage.

Chaim daydreamed that Friday, a little tired after lunch, and watched Stella, just two rows in front of him. He looked at her neck as she flopped her hair sideways as she took notes. Moonstruck, starstruck, hit in the heart by a meteor... he was in teenaged love and thought about what they planned for that afternoon after marching band; a tryst at her home.

Buzzzzzzz, buzzzzzzz, buzzzzzzz. Intercom tones jarred Chaim from thinking about biting Stella's neck. Mrs. Bliss looked up at the clock. The interruption was uncommon.

"Yes," she barked into the intercom microphone and, stretching up, her breasts brushed the wall as she reached up. The troglodytes giggled. She listened, straining to hear every nuance. Chaim feared he'd done something and was in big trouble. With his sooty soul he always felt as if he should be in the crosshairs of justice.

When she turned to the class, her facial pallor matched her gray cashmere sweater and equally gray skirt. She was unable to speak; her complexion, ashen. Tears welled in her baggy lower eyelids, then pooled, then gushed over, streaming down her face. She lifted the captain's bars from her desk and held them to her breast, then pulled another tissue from her sweater sleeve and snuffled.

She rotated the volume knob so they could hear the radio broadcast. Eyes riveted on the speaker box, altar-like, which was fixed on the wall with the blackboard, high above the class, next to the clock, in the center of the wall. Walter Cronkite presided. "The President has been shot in Dealey Plaza in Dallas."

She seemed faint and dropped the captain's bars, which make a dull thunk on the linoleum tile floor. The troglodytes no longer giggled.

Mrs. Bliss once told the class that, with a large enough lever and fulcrum, a person could move the world. The Kennedy assassination was that pry bar, a *force majeure*, and Chaim's world moved off its axis.

8

The Gift of the Tzaddik

Oswald's Dallas bullets fizzled the three Goldbergs' birthdays as the known world ceased rotating. What should have been his mother's birthday celebration on that precise day, followed by his birthday and his father's birthday, got lost in a moody assassination haze as the family wrapped into chairs before the beige wooden cabinet housing the fourteen-inch black-and-white Philco. He and Stella retreated to their homes, with love's labors postponed.

The Shabbat came in like a lion on 6 Kislev 5724, the evening of the shooting. Rabbi Fierverker praised Kennedy and concluded with "we have lost one of our own."

"But," he continued, jiggling his thin, right index finger heavenward, "as the Talmud teaches, disaster may be a sign that the *Tzaddik* is on the way."

"Amen," chorused the congregation.

It wasn't until late Sunday evening that they sang Happy Birthday for Eva. Chaim shivered as history reduced her birthday to an asterisk. He saw her, forty-five, disappointed in both love and money. She wiped off their meager Sears dining table as she mused. She openly admired the Rintala's imported, gilded Louis XIV table. "A real dining table," she sighed in her toil. She'd wanted a rich man, but she married Tevye, the fiddler, a *putz*.

Evalyn left school in the tenth grade, helping her family in Cincinnati by working on her father's horse-drawn vegetable and fish trucks. "You won't have to do that, *kussilah*. You will go to medical school," she promised him, when she told him that story when he fretted about paying for college. "You *will* become a doctor."

"There're no more horse-drawn fish trucks, Mom," he joked, and she hugged him.

After their hand grenade and pistol fireworks, homebound by snow and in the pallid sadness, they played ping-pong. Both were dedicated competitors. She called shots "in" when they were "out" and the opposite, when convenient. She raged as he picked at her bad behavior, like pulling on a scab, taunting her with "you can't beat me unless you cheat!"

She huffed and puffed, and they dueled, a butt hanging from her lips at each serve, smoking her way through a pack of Pall Malls until ashes floated like snowflakes onto the table. "If I win, you have to quit smoking," he said, exacting his price.

Then, she missed his left-handed, cross-table smash to her weak side. Weary, as one of her smokes burned the edge of the table, she smoldered in disgust. She knew he'd bested her and threw her paddle at him. He ducked just as it whizzed over his head and it bounced off a lamp, smashing the bulb. In the darkness, he'd won.

"Not as bad as my bullet!" he baited and laughed.

"I *will* beat you," she vowed, searing him with her eyes, and on they grappled. But his zeal exceeded hers, and he had to win. He'd studied Lombardi and knew that losing wasn't his option.

It felt so life-and-death, this mother-son competition, as they entered the fourth set, score *even-steven*, as Eva called it: two each. At dawn, though, depleted, they were just whacking the ball back and forth, doing silly trick shots, and they became distracted in *remember when* conversations from his childhood. They'd softened. Even Coach Lombardi had room in his heart for love, and they wound up like kitties rolling in strands of yarn, the pair splayed out on the living room sofa, both in tears. "Mom, I'm going to be gone soon."

"Oh, Honey," she sighed, kissing him. "Don't talk about it. I know you have to go, but it's so hard." She squeezed him like her beloved mop, tears gushing.

"That's a tenth-carat diamond, Mom," he said when he gave her his gift. He was proud that it was so costly. "You can show it off at Rosenberg's."

He'd selected an eighteen-karat gold trumpet charm for her bracelet, engraved to memorialize this birthday: 11-22-63. "Mom, I love you so, so much," he said when he handed her the tiny box, and he believed what he said.

"Oh, Honey!" She laughed and cried again and they mended together the edges of their ripped feelings.

"I'm sorry I... I nearly killed you," he said woefully, but then they erupted in fits of hysterical laughter. They always ended these explosions with laughter.

"Oh, Honey, don't make me pee my pants!" she exclaimed and they hugged. In the absurdity of it all, the conflict really ended. Even after the news struck about Jack Ruby that Sunday evening when he gave her the gift, the two found enough space to laugh in the hollow of worldly despair. The gladiators had reconciled, and he was relieved.

"If you don't let me go, I'll never come back," he said. She clung to him, and he felt so guilty about nearly shooting her. They never completed the final game of the final set, but each understood the score.

"Why won't he talk to me?" asked Chaim, frustrated by his father.

"He'd like to, Honey, but he can't." Then, "I never told him about what... what went on. It would just make him crazy."

"So you put a ping-pong table into the living room?" he asked.

"Egg shells," she replied, and the exchange ended, leaving him empty, feeling so inadequate, so meager. None of it made sense, but they'd sanded the rough edges.

His father's rages terrified Chaim. "I don't know what I may do," Arthur often would say. "I won't be responsible for what I'll do if you make me *uber dem kopf*," and Chaim worried about setting loose an incubus.

Many years later he reflected upon that year and remembered that, even then, he saw his family as cockeyed and distorted, like images reflected from bent carnival mirrors. Artie wanted peace and quiet, to remain unmolested, preferring to lose himself in the intellectual mazes of cross-word puzzles. His version of reality popped like a mushroom out of the humus of the *New York Times Book Review*. He interacted little with his son, treating him impersonally, more like a gladiola than his own flesh and blood; an inconvenience rather than a pleasure.

Chaim was, inescapably, much like his father. He, at that naive age, fashioned his life from a collage of movie images, mental clippings from newspapers, and weekly immersions in *Time, Newsweek, US News & World Report*, subscriptions his father bought eagerly from the Willie Loman character, the same one who had elevated the Zubarskys.

Before a mirror, Chaim emulated his father's speech mannerisms, his intonations, his walk, his hand gesticulations and, on paper, even his handwriting forms. Splenetic, his father sulked endlessly, a hermit, a rabbit, concealing himself in his warren of books and newspapers. He did not admire his father's choleric ways, yet he emulated them. Chaim Goldberg was a serious lad.

Arthur worshipped what he described as *important literature*. His heroes' booty were Nobels and Pulitzers, and these prizes formed fundamental entry credentials for this literary omnivore's vicarious life.

Of Bellow, he predicted as if he knew him, "He'll win a Nobel Prize, you'll see." He set down *Henderson the Rain King* and added, dropping another cold turd in his son's lap, "Saul Bellow doesn't have time to waste."

But what did his father know of life? He seemed so much like an eggplant. Chaim resented these aspersions. Chaim was not a wastrel. How much harder could he work, he thought, when he turned in at two AM? He twisted internally, wanting to achieve, to be the best. He felt wrung out, strangled the way his mother wrung out her halogen impregnated mop with her reddened hands.

He yearned to know his father, but all that he had available was that dark wood veneer bookshelf in his room housing a collection of the ends of conversations. If Chaim asked him about a book, he'd reply with a cryptic "I'll let you know" or "I'll write you a letter." The books were like photographic negatives out of his father's mind.

"He's a true intellectual," his mother justified, as if his reclusive and ascetic ways were the preferred parental norm. "Honey, he loves you, but he's not able to show it," she'd say, excusing his detachment. "He's just not able to talk." These incongruous excuses sounded like Campbell's fatalistic *jus' is*.

Chaim peered into his kaleidoscope, entreating, asking, *mirror, mirror on the wall, who am I*? What he got back was gobbledegook.

Sunday night, before returning to school, he pondered, weak and weary, and sensed someone near. He looked up. Over his shoulder was his dad. "Here," he said and handed him that week's *Time Magazine.* "Look on page sixty-four. There's a story about Culley College in L.A.. They call it *The Princeton of the West.*"

Slide-rule in one hand, he accepted the magazine. "Thanks, Dad," he said. His father often pulled stories for him from the *New York Times* and other sources. That was their way of communicating. His father seemed pleased and exited, like the Raven, saying nothing more.

He was working on physics problems about centrifugal forces, and it was almost midnight. Should he have invited him to talk? He seemed as if he wanted to talk. He slipped the slide in and out on it tracks and divided the size of the continent by the speed of his train heading west, calculating his travel time to get to L.A.. At an average speed of fifty miles an hour, he could be there in sixty hours; divided by twenty-four, slip, slip, two and one half days... or by jet, at five hundred miles an hour; six hours.

Freedom was six hours away... but, at that moment, unknowingly he sped towards a deadly detour.

Leaving would be hard, not only for him, but also rough on his parents. He was sorry to hurt them but it was time to go. *Holy Mary, pray for us sinners now and at the hour of our death. Amen.* Then he crossed himself. And after he'd said it, he wondered why he'd done that, but it brought a sense of calm. Such a miracle, he exclaimed inwardly in his best Yiddish accent.

In one of their make-up sessions, her lungs cigarette damaged, she wheezed how hard her life with Arthur had been. "It's like walking on egg shells around your father." He hated that expression... egg shells. "You have to be careful what you say to him," she told Chaim, dropping her head. "He's too sensitive."

It took a lifetime, and untold hours of on-the-couch psychoanalysis, to escape the effects of these mendacious parental gravitational fields.

Eva, on Monday, silently left his birthday gift on his bed. He took it as an apology. Finally it was the correct Delaware High letter sweater. The previous year she'd disappointed him with one in black, with orange stripes on the left arm.

When she asked him why he did not wear the sweater, he told her. "The kids in Yardley wear white sweaters with the orange and black bands, the *in* kind." He'd been so disappointed. The "out kind" were black with orange arm bands and, at Glick's shoe store, were three dollars cheaper.

"Oh, what difference does it make?" she asked, missing the social cachet point, so vital to teenagers. "Honey, your father's *spurovdik*, cheap. What can I say? He doesn't like to spend money. I bought it with my money, from catering," she told him. "I love you," she said.

"But does he love me?"

"Honey… Honey, don't be so sensitive. Of course he loves you." He hated her calling him Honey. She left him alone in his room while he opened the box. It was the right sweater, and she'd sewn on his high school letter, a small black "D" with orange trim, with Band written in black script over the orange. She did love him, and he felt her warmth when he wore the sweater at the school bus stop.

She could be so loving, he reflected, like the silks in her dresser drawer. He didn't know then, that in her era, in her sparse Cincinnati childhood, there was no social cachet, nothing extra. They needed food.

He waited until August, as he packed his suitcase to leave, to open his father's gift.

***

"It was addressed to me," he protested, then angry.

"But you can't read it," she bickered.

"*Schrei nicht*, you two," Arthur yelled from his reading chair. "Let me see it." He squinted at the translucent onionskin paper, raising his eyebrows, and asked Chaim, "Did you know about this?"

"I don't read Yiddish, Dad," the impudent whined.

"Imbecile, did you *look* at it?" Angry, his father joined his wife in the bullying ridicule.

"Just enough to see that it was in Yiddish. I don't read Yiddish." Chaim was mad that they challenged him. What they discovered was Uncle Elijah's note, the one that came with the *Scientific American* spelunking issue.

"It's half Polish, half Yiddish," Arthur said.

"I don't read Polish," Chaim said, defending himself in his view, insolent by his father's European standards.

"I don't like your tone. *Oy*, that Elijah," said the father as he scrutinized the faded onionskin below his reading lamp. "There's some news about organizing labor unions in *Gdansk*." Then, lips moving as he read, Arthur exclaimed, "Eeeeva, Elijah's coming! To us." Then wondering aloud, "But when? He doesn't say." Arthur figured aloud, "Hanukah? Maybe then. That's when he would come."

Uncle Elijah was Arthur's cousin, but Chaim knew little more about him than that. "He's my second cousin; much older than me." Then he went on, "The Lubels lived in Brze⊠nica, four miles to the east. His family were the tax collectors. The proles at Ellis Island shortened it from Lubelskie… and they gave us my mother's maiden name. Our name was Zachariascj. You didn't know that," he said, speaking to his son… but the revelations were reluctant.

"You didn't tell me," said Chaim. By this time in their relationship, Chaim resented his father's cryptic ways. He softened. "Tell me more.

What was it like where you grew up?" This familial nourishment sent zesty thrills through him.

Artie became animated. "My mother mixed sawdust into the pumpernickel dough to make it go farther," he said. "He's a Communist."

"What does he look like?" asked Chaim.

"He's a *tzaddik*," said his father. "He *looks* like a *tzaddik*." Then he shut down, drumming his fingers on the chair cushions, holding the letter, and tears streamed down his cheeks. "I haven't seen him in... Eva? What's it been?"

She wriggled her face to mean, I have no idea. Chaim recalled Rabbi Fierverker saying that the Kennedy assassination may herald the *tzaddik*, The Prophet, that the *Moshiach* would come. *Oy vey*! Was Uncle Elijah *that tzaddik, Eliyahu Ha Navi*, the one for whom they always left a vacant chair at Passover?

***

They tiptoed into her virgin territory and Stella, curious at first, quickly transformed into as sex-crazed a hedonist as Chaim. "My clit's on fire," she joked, mastering their increasingly bawdy sex language.

She'd been hesitant to talk about her sexuality, but soon it became hard to ignore; after he fingered and licked her into pubescent frenzy, *it* was all they could think of. Driven by hormones and overwhelmed by burgeoning love, these two joked about opening Stella's Box, like Pandora's Box.

"Can hornitis be lethal?" he asked her, and she giggled, twiddling her fingers on her mouth as if to contain her sexual urges. She reveled in triumph when he spurted, and he swooned in her orgasms. They had such bawdy adolescent fun!

With Aku's barn in ashes, his car became their loving venue. They kissed, sweated, curled up, and slid against each other until they were raw, never once watching an entire drive-in movie. The first time she sucked him and he came in her mouth, he was embarrassed and apologized. She gagged. "I wasn't expecting that," she said. "But I'll do better next time," she promised, and she did. "You taste salty, but sweet," she giggled, and he adored her accepting naughtiness.

Sometimes Stella's bedroom afforded them relaxed privacy and he lingered, tonguing her. He sucked her clit amorously, giving her full benefit as a graduate from Neddy's tutelage. Then, she told him, "I want you to come in my mouth. I love your taste," and she pleased him with her desire.

He had two women, but Chaim Goldberg had some serious flaws: he always wanted more.

***

"He's gone. Come over... *now*," she had ordered and clinked the phone receiver.

When she dropped her dressing gown, Chaim drew in his breath, aghast, and turned away from the sight. "Oh my God, Nedda. Oh my God! What a sonofabitch."

She looked so forlorn and crumpled.

"He's a sadist. He could only come after beating me."

His swan had sustained caning blows everywhere, and the bruises were purple, black and blue, hues he'd seen only in the darkest of paintings, her paintings. Was this one of the reasons for their art collection? She selected the paintings.

Her skin tones around the wounds ran from cobalt, manganese, and cerulean to pthalo and ultramarine, with a generous intermingling of all values of cerise and darker reds into a complete palette of ugly violet hues.

"*This* was *my* Christmas gift," she cried. Cruelly humiliated and emotionally crushed like a mosquito, contorted, she sobbed, "I wanted to please him. I loved him."

Chaim held her and soon they lay in bed and cried together. "After a while, his shipping company practically collapsed. Calamari's competitors from New York, and those out of Hoboken, took their shipping contracts. They wanted to ruin him... us."

Nedda knotted an embroidered handkerchief, crying. "He was here for a week. He raped me again and again. It thrilled him. Oh, I would have done anything for him. I loved him so. Then he threw me down those stairs." She wailed. The bruises told the tale.

"He fucked me relentlessly. He whipped me with canes. He tied my hands and feet. I sucked him, as he instructed; I tried to do what he wanted. When I pleaded for his mercy, he made me finance him. He beat me until I agreed. Then he fucked me. *My* money fronted all of this." She held her head in her hands. "Chaim, I'm tapped out. I'm broke. I'm beaten. He really fucked me, Chaim."

Chaim gulped. He was a kid. This was right out of De Sade's *Justine*, *Juliette*, *120 Days of Sodom*, and *Philosophy in the Bedroom*, all found in his father's reading shelf.

"Boudreaux Lines is the only shipper of medical opium to the U.S. for processing into morphine. We *own* those BNDD agents up and down the East Coast. You can't imagine how much money is in this."

"Who knows about this, what he's been doing?"

"No one... until you. Chaim, they make heroin."

"Nedda, you are up to your neck in trouble."

"There's only one way out for me."

"How?"

"We have to get rid of Harry." Nedda looked at him with a grave gaze. "I'm free only when he's dead."

"Dead? Bbbbut how?"

"All you have to do is *talk* to Uncle Johnny," she said. "Just a few words. He likes you. Jjjjust… talk to him." Nedda slid her tortured body into her vermillion, silk pajamas, and cloaked herself in a yellow and red Pendleton wool bathrobe in the Santa Fe pattern. She then wrapped her arms around his neck, kissing him, running her hands over his crotch, gripping him again. "I have big plans for you," she murmured.

"I don't want to hurt you," he said.

"I need to be fucked," she said, and then energized, frenzied lovemaking followed. Afterwards, she said. "I'll feel so much better, doctor. Here, let me show you something." He liked her calling him *doctor*.

She towed him through a network of poorly lighted serpentine stairways in the back of the mansion to a dark hallway in a false attic on the fourth floor. A heavily patinaed door panel with a lintel so low that he bowed his head to enter led them further.

In the dull winter light, the only illumination came through a stained-glass panel. Dust had collected on its sill, and there were desiccated flies and a few hornet bodies, their wings delicate and dry in the filtered rays. "The light makes it looks like your kaleidoscope, doesn't it?"

"You know how much I treasure that… the kaleidoscope… not the dead flies."

She laughed. "You're an idiot." They played well together, this older woman capturing his youth. Then, they came to what appeared to be the end, but it was a six-panel bas-relief of oxen, horses, and foxes. She tapped it on one side with her flashlight, and it opened into a closet.

At the back of the closet, she pushed open yet another door. "Cold, huh? This space isn't heated," she said, noticing him warm a foot with his hand. "How's that?" she asked, grasping his foot and warming its sole with her breath.

A steep stairway descended into darkness.

He placed his hand on the volute and wiggled the newel post, which nearly gave way. The handrail and many of the balusters were loose. "Watch out. If you fall down those steps, you'll wind up in front of the old coal furnace, in the basement, four-stories below us," she said.

"Chaim, these passageways were for the maids, which allowed them to clear chamber pots from the bedrooms. People were modest in those days, and no one wanted anyone else to see their poops!" She took pleasure in her vivid narrative. "So, unseen, the maids hauled them out every morning. The estate potters took great pains to create attractive vessels, and they threw everything into the gardens."

"Remind me not to eat the broccoli," he quipped, amazed that an estate would have its own potters. Then, they entered a small, low-ceilinged room at the top of the stairs, and she switched on a dangling light bulb.

"Just a minute, now." She tapped on another panel inside this small room where they bent over, allowing them to squeeze in. Chaim saw whips and chains, manacles, leather thongs and a black leather mask. "For slaves?"

"No," she said, sorrowfully, "for me."

"Oh, my God," said Chaim.

"This was his sex dungeon, and he did what he wanted with me. I was his by contract. I was his sex slave." She showed him the contract.

"You agreed to all of this stuff? The beatings, the humiliations. It says here 'The slave agrees to accept any punishment the master decides to inflict, whether earned or not.'"

"Here," she said, interrupting him, ashamed. At the back of the small room, she inserted her fingers into a crack, and another panel gave way to a black cloth. "See?" she asked, pulling it aside. Banded bundles of

Hamiltons, Jacksons, Grants, and Franklins. Gold bricks lined one wall, and there were black leather wallets.

"Diamonds," she said.

"My God, we are a greedy pair, aren't we?"

She punched him in the chest. "Don't be an asshole."

He read "1.02 c-t, VVS1, E." The stones showered them in sparkles.

"It's portable money. There are packets of rubies and sapphires. That's what was going on in Thailand and Cambodia."

An array of handguns sat on a small table along with neatly packaged bricks covered with butcher paper like those in Chubby's ice-cream freezer. "Heroin," she said. "He skimmed all of this from Johnny. Millions in heroin."

She handed him a fistful of bank books from all over the world: Bank of Shanghai, Bank of Tokyo. "He's visited every major city in Asia: Bangkok, Singapore, Kuala Lumpur, Dehli."

"He's stolen millions... many millions, Neddy."

"He delivered unto Johnny what was Johnny's... and siphoned off commissions, what he could get away with. Twenty million by my count."

"This... is not compatible with life," whispered Chaim.

"See? I knew you were a smart boy... and he must pay for what he's done to me. I am not his sex slave." She kissed his cheek and slipped her cold fingers into his crotch. He got hard and she squeezed. "If you loved me, really loved me, you'd do me this favor."

"What?"

"You know that Moses killed his Egyptian slave master."

She spoke emphatically, but Chaim looked at her cockeyed, responding, in disbelief. "But you are not Moses, and I am not Rigoletto."

"Chaim, it's *exitus acta probat*," she said.

"The end justifies the means," he muttered, recalling the Boudreaux ethic, the bronze plaque, and nearly killing his mother. "What are you saying? You can't be serious."

"I have been your whore. It's time to pay up." Emphatic, she looked up at him, her deep blues afire. Kneeling before him she looked up and slid her chilly hand into his orange and black Delaware High sweat pants. Holding him, she warmed him with her breath. "I picked you for this, and I fucked you silly all summer long, and now you belong to me... I own *you*." She licked him. "You want me, don't you?" Lustfully coy she teased, "It's my way or the highway."

"Oh, yes. Ohhh yes. I want you in the worst way... bbbbut... what you ask is not a favor." She grasped his testicles and squeezed, pulling down. "Hey, that's too much," he objected.

"You're right. It's not a favor. It's *do's*. You *do's* what I tell you. Just imagine what it would be like if Harry did this. He'd tear them right off."

Chaim groaned. She squeezed his nuts hard. "I'm going to barf." She released.

"See how easy this is?"

"Hhhhow? Wwwwith a gggggun?"

"Too complicated. Tooooo bloody. We'll kill him with your favorite weapon: words. You simply tell Johnny where his stuff is."

He could almost hear her sprockets spinning like a newsreel.

"Why can't *you* just tell him?"

"For a smart boy, you're dumb. Why do you think?" She played him like a trout. "If I tell him, he'll know you're fucking me, and you do not want him to know that."

"When I tell him, why won't he kill me?"

"You don't deserve killing. He'll see you as a loyal friend, a trusted ally. He likes you... really."

"There's mmmmmillions." He looked down at Nedda, her mouth toying with him, licking him. "So, all I have to do is ttttell Mr. Calamari... ttttell him... I fffffound these?"

"That's all you gotta do, pretty boy... and I let you go," illustrating her point by removing her hands from his genitals. He was powerless against her as she stretched his scrotum and stroked his balls. He exploded and she drank down his goodness.

"I watched you all summer, and I knew you would help me," she said as they nestled into her bed. She could be so sleek and soft like all that ermine and perfume. "You are such a pretty boy. I love your red hair. Enough business, sweetie. Don't leave me wanting you again. Come, before you go," she said. "Fuck me one more time."

A dazzling woman, after they dallied, she reached beneath her bed and pulled out a Christmas-wrapped, red box with a great, fancy, intricate green bow featuring gold thread intertwined all through it. "Here, this is for you. It's *your* Christmas gift." She kissed the box and handed it to him.

"Oh, Nedda! But I don't have anything for you," he sighed, embarrassed and deflated.

"Oh, yes, you do. You just gave me your Christmas gift... talking to Johnny." Her eyes glimmered. "Now, open it."

"It's so beautiful I don't want to disturb it," he said as he carefully pulled off the tapes. "It's from Saks Fifth Avenue. I've never had anything from SFA." It was a set of gold cuff links with diamonds in the center.

"My commission," she said, then crying.

He reacted. "What's wrong? Did I do something wrong?"

"Oh, no, you did everything right. You are so... so pure, so clean."

"Then why are you crying?"

"I bought your gift before Harry came back, and I hid it... and when he was raping and beating me, I thought about you and how lovely you are and what a nice lover you are... otherwise, I would have died, I'm sure. Your spirit came to my aid, and you saved me. It makes me cry to think about what Harry did... but... but I kept thinking of my gift to you and your gift to me. I knew you would help me."

Gently, he tucked her into bed. "You are so bruised."

"It's what I need now. Fuck me, fuck me hard, once more. I know you can." She pulled him to her. "You'll do it, then?"

"Yes, oh, yes, Nedda."

As he drove away, he recalled how Stella showed up after his car crash, how their spirits joined. He shivered, realizing that he could drown in this torrent of danger but, like Superman weakened by her kryptonite, she'd rendered him powerless and exhausted.

***

"It's for *goyim*." That was how his family celebrated Christmas, ridiculing the Christians. For Chaim, it was hard to miss that the rest of his known world came to a screeching halt. He enjoyed Christmas. He was sickened by his family's hypocrisy. They were as prejudiced as those they criticized.

Since Anna's passing, Steve moved in with the Goldbergs. Arthur swallowed hard and added, "We'll do...both...Hanukah and Christmas."

On Christmas Eve, the family hung the Zubarsky's family ornaments on the tree and Steve explained each one. Evalyn lighted the menorah for the first night of Hanukah, which, coincidentally, that year, began on Christmas Eve.

"God will forgive us," Chaim heard his father say to his mother, and what an irony it was that a *goy* delivered good cheer to his generally sour home life.

Christmas Day arrived on a Wednesday, decorated with delicate snowflakes fluttering down in the still, icy, Lower Bucks County air. A cheery fire crackled in the red-brick fireplace that divided the kitchen area from the living room. There was no style at Turnhill Lane, as with the Manor Boudreaux hearth, which featured polished river rock and was large enough to cook in to feed a regiment during the Revolution.

Offsetting Yom Kippur's denials, they indulged in a late breakfast. Steve had never eaten lox or creamed herring, and he was a good sport. "Don't ask for bacon," Chaim warned with a smile.

"I know *that*," he said as they gobbled it down along with smoked whitefish on bagels. Steve liked the Jewish foods, and that pleased his hosts.

"I love the scrambled eggs with garlic and onions fried up in *schmaltz*," said Chaim.

"*Halushkas, Steve-ala!*" Eva exclaimed, licking sour cream and herring from her fingers, reaching for the smoked whitefish, smacking her lips, pleased that her special guest enjoyed her menu selections. She adored Steve. "You're becoming Jewish, Steve-ala."

Christmas tree, gifts, fire crackling, they nestled into a Norman Rockwell cornucopia. So that's what it felt like to have Christmas, Chaim thought, to be one of them.

Arthur, dressed as Santa, appeared with a *yiddisha* Ho, ho, ho!, chuckling, "If only Rebbe Fierverker could see me now!" he mugged as the flashbulbs burst. Chaim was surprised, seeing his father show off. How jovial. How rotund.

Arthur Goldberg was forty-two when his son was born. To Chaim, he remained a polemic, life-long. It would take another thirty years for him to understand his father's life arc as an introverted, intellectual, naturally taciturn Polish Jew. By the time Chaim came along, Arthur had survived the pre-WWI ghetto deprivations, emigration to a new country, learning a new language, and then endured unemployment in the Depression while trying to support his family of seven. Ghastly WWII experiences in the worst theaters— Burma, China, North Africa— deleted his life dreams and took his hope away.

Whenever Chaim asked his father about his childhood and Poland, he replied, "I forget it."

Steve and Stella, Aku and Ilona, and the Goldbergs crowded around the table when Eva brought out a ham, Rumanian style. "This isn't *kosher*," she sighed, seeking absolution.

Arthur kidded, "Eva, God will forgive us. This is a mitzvah." It was hard for her to violate the dietary prohibitions, although Chaim's family was not rigidly observant.

Baba ghanouj, hummus, garlic, paprika, onion, and clove, the pungent and complicated aromas from Europe, wafted through the tight Levitt-rambler kitchen-dining area. Eva had spread Bubbie's best embroidered linen tablecloth and set out carefully ironed napkins and gleaming sterling silver napkin rings, each monogrammed with a C, for Cohen. "These are my mother's, from Budapest," she announced, as she added the final polish.

Stella remarked, "It looks so elegant," and her approval pleased Chaim. She picked up a monogrammed napkin ring with a C. "These are lovely." Hearing this, Eva managed a smile, and Chaim was proud of his mother's indulgence.

The monogramming made him feel as if he'd succeeded in borrowing elegance, as if he partook of the social cachet. This microscopic detail, these engraved napkin rings, buttressed his sense of family worth.

Evalyn asked, "Please, Stevie, do your grace?"

Steve followed with his prayer:

Father in Heaven,
We praise You for giving us Your Son
To be our Savior and Lord.
Bless us all as we gather here today,
And let us live happily in Your love.
Hear our prayer, loving Father,
For we ask this in Jesus' Name. Amen

At the mention of Jesus' name in her home, Eva visibly gasped and, uncharacteristically for her, gulped a whole cup of wine. Stella and Steve, according to their custom, crossed themselves but then Chaim did the unthinkable: he made the sign of the cross.

Evalyn wailed, "Christ, what was that?" Everyone laughed as she juxtaposed the Christian epithet with her Jewish values.

"Mom! I do it all the time at Zubarskys. So what?"

"I'll give you so what," she replied but eight pairs of Jewish eyes glared at him, still laughing. Then, fate intervened.

"Goddemmit! Offen Sie die Tur!" a man yelled from outside the entry door. He had a heavy European accent. "Goddemmit!" He banged so hard on the flimsy storm door that his father's rose trellis quivered.

Eva called out, "Oh my God, Artie. Look who's coming to dinner." A small, hunched-over troglodyte stood at the portal. He had a long, flowing white beard and wore a black mink kolpik and was clothed in the black Hasidic caftan.

Arthur chuckled, grinning in disbelief, and called out, "Elijah! You came! You came, my old friend. What a wonder. Come in. Come in." Ordinarily, his father had no remnant of a Polish accent, but when he saw this man, his accent returned. The visitor toted a large leather valise, a violin case, and an assortment of smaller bags. He smelled of garlic and sour perspiration.

"Get his cases," Arthur ordered Chaim.

With more animation than Chaim had ever seen, his dad turned to all of them, gleeful and excited. "Cousin Elijah's a Communist," he announced to all. He laughed, then informed, "I can say that now that McCarthy's gone," mopping his forehead with a table napkin.

A commie at our table! thought Chaim. Aku and Ilona rolled their eyes in unison, and Stella placed her hands on her cheeks, amazed.

"I've only heard of Uncle Elijah," he said to Stella. "He sent me a *Scientific American* subscription," he continued, omitting his spelunking episode. His mother blanched.

Stella whispered to Chaim, "I've never seen a Communist."

Elijah and his father embraced in the Polish way, arms and lips everywhere, and Chaim saw rare tears in his father's eyes. "You came, Elijah. You came!" His father was overwhelmed with emotion. Artie said to the guests, "We haven't seen each other in, how long? Thirty years?"

"Your family sure is different from mine," Stella whispered. "We're so... so reserved."

"Arthur! Look at you!" Elijah exclaimed in a thick guttural Yiddish accent. He shook Artie by the shoulders and the two embraced again. Elijah smacked the back of Chaim's head as a greeting. "*Boychick*!" He was "old-country," and at seventeen, Chaim knew of the European custom not to talk to children. Uncle Elijah pinched Chaim's cheek, saying "Shaving, *Tzatzkela? Nu?*" Many of Elijah's statements came as questions.

Chaim sensed a satisfying vinculum between him and Uncle Elijah, pulling the two together across the generations. A thrilling man, dramatic in his person and dress, he looked so otherworldly, so transcendent. He had a huge, white-and-black peppered beard, *ein Grossbart mit payas*, long curled side-burns, *tzitzes*, the prayer braids at the end of the *tallis*, and the distinctive Hassidic black hat, which he removed and under which he wore a black yarmulke. Physically, he was elfin, diminutive, smaller than Arthur. But, spiritually, he was a mythic, larger-than-life figure.

Eyes widened as they welcomed this exotic creature. Elijah hugged and kissed his way through the guests, and he shook Steve's hand. "*Solch ein Mensch!*" he complimented. "Zo handsome, *zehr grosszügig.*"

"Noble," Chaim translated to his astonished friends, raising his eyebrows, underscoring his Uncle's compliment. "He likes you, Steve."

With his stubby, yellow, nicotine-stained fingers, Uncle Elijah combed through his massive beard that ended at mid-chest. The cousins spoke both Polish and Russian... languages that his father had told Chaim he'd forgotten.

Elijah was Arthur's first cousin from his father's side, not truly Chaim's uncle. Following the family convention, they called him Uncle. Unlike Uncle Aku, who was not blood-family, Elijah *was* blood-family. Both Aku and Elijah were uncles who were not really uncles. Elijah was a union boss, organizing workers all over Poland, based in Gdansk, where "the weather is better," he joked. He related news alluding to, in whispers, *connections* in San Francisco, at *The Chronicle*, and getting workers "vat dey de'zerve."

When he finally engaged Chaim, offhandedly, he said, "Use your brain, *Boychick*. You never know when you'll need it." It seemed as if Elijah heard English phrases, cobbling them together, but not quite correct in American English usage or context. Elijah was anti-establishment, ready to overthrow the government: a true Anarchist, a Nihilist, an authentic Communist hippie.

Following dinner, Elijah pulled out a flat box, a fine, rich, red leather bound box imprinted in gold on the front cover. "Mahjong," he explained in his Russian accent and handed it to Evalyn. "Ve'll play zoon." Tobacco smell permeated the room as cigarette smoke tentacles turned and undulated around noses and beneath chins, encircling ears.

Elijah seemed to know everything. "I teach you," he promised. Chaim felt as if he were the *Vilna Gaon*. He spoke with such admirable confidence and energy. He was the *tzaddik*. Reb Fierverker was right.

Then he said, "*Tzatzkela*, for you!" The endearment comforted Chaim as he pinched his cheeks again, cuffing him gently in the face. His hands were soft and smooth. From behind Chaim's ear, his cigarette-stained fingers produced a double eagle, twenty-dollar gold piece, minted in 1854 with the SF mintmark. "From San Francisco, the best place in the world." Everyone laughed at the illusion.

After dinner, Uncle Elijah went on like Willie Loman, producing items from his corpulent, travel-scuffed leather suitcase, adorned with stickers from world destinations. The full valise popped open the moment he released the clasp, like a pair of pants girdling a bulging tummy when the button breaks. Being "full," for Europeans, was the ultimate luxury after so much deprivation.

Then he unsnapped his violin case, showing gifts wrapped in the Polish newspaper, *Arsenievskie Vesti*. "It's the *Gdansk Times*... better than *Pravda*." He looked at Aku, winking mischievously, and showed off an offering of cod, smoked whitefish and herring, and mackerel.

Chaim unwrapped the crinkled, fish-oil permeated front page, dated 2 September 1939. It felt like torah scroll, written in Polish, and there were no pictures. Uncle Elijah saw him glance at it.

"You don't read (trilling the r at the back of his throat) Polish so vell? Dat vas the day after the Nazis invaded."

Arthur broke in. "Elie, *genug*. He doesn't need to know about that. It's over. Forget it."

Those around the table winced with the strong aromas as Uncle Elijah handed Eva more greasy packages, one of smoked, black cod, heavily oil-stained, and several packages with herring. With considerable pride in his stumbling English, he showed off a massive package of red lox. "You don't show up *mit bubkas, Boychick,*" he said, whacking Chaim's shoulder with the package to make the point. Chaim loved the inclusion and attention.

Elijah was animated as he pulled out his treats, making side comments to his cousin, in Polish and German. *Halvah!* He said, thumping a brick of the delicacy onto the table. Then, from another stinky, tattered and scuffed leather suitcase, he produced cartons of Eastern cigarettes, passed the packs across his nostrils, whiffing the fine delicacies, then rubbed them through his beard. He handed a carton to his father, who *kvelled* in boyish pleasure.

Uncle Elijah turned to Chaim. "*Besser als Sosnowica,* Arthur." Then to Chaim, "*Zo, Wildechiya, vat denks du?*" intermixing English and Yiddish and German pronunciations. "You don't know about *Gliwice,* do you?"

"Elie! *Genug!*" commanded Artie, trying vainly to distract his relative. "Not tonight, *Bitte.*"

"But we have something to say? Hmmmm?" puzzled Elijah, not letting it drop, riveting his searing eyes at Chaim, like a jeweler inspecting a diamond. "Mmmmmm?" It was what Chaim recalled many years later, that piercing Gdansk inquisitional gaze, fearing the pandemonium to follow.

Chaim's question was simple. "*Gliwice?*"

Uncle Elijah pulled at his beard, and the adults looked at him for a clue as to what might happen. They looked at Arthur. Chaim expected an explosion, as when he saw the hand grenade roll across the floor in his mother's bedroom.

But no answer came. He must have considered the consequences and all breathed a sigh of relief. They laughed with the captivating raconteur as he returned to his show-and-tell of Eastern-bloc cigarettes. There was

Sobranie, written in English and Cyrillic, then Djarum, Tor, Ziganov, Karelia, Borkum Riff.

Uncle Elijah's gifts came in different packages and, through this curious man, soon emerged a peeping-Tom glimpse into his father's life in pre-war Poland. Out came three huge bottles of Russian vodka, or "wod-ka" as they pronounced it.

He set thimbles on the table, and the adults began drinking. After consuming a half bottle of the *Stolichnaya*, Uncle Elijah started to hum a Russian song. Russian cigarette smoke, heavily perfumed and exotic, curled upwards.

Chaim hated smoking and cigarettes. He objected once when he was very young, seven, perhaps. His mother forced him to go to the store and buy her cigarettes, and she slapped him across the face so hard that he spat blood. "You'll do what I goddamned tell you to do." She wailed and jammed a quarter into his tiny hand, shoving him out the door into the snow. He screamed hysterically in defiance. But this scene was different.

Uncle Elijah took up the neck of his violin and tuned the strings by twisting the pegs. "Gdansk Symphony, *jah*, before *Krieg*," he said with considerable pride. "Played with *Willie Hess*," he said. It was as if he unwrapped a badly burned part of his soul, bringing to life, again, the war's garish wounds.

From his seemingly bottomless case he pulled out a two-liter bottle of *Luksusowa* vodka. "Polish!" he said. "Best," needling Aku, holding the bottle at arm's length. "Better than Russian!" They laughed so hard at the good natured teasing and, in that instant Chaim peeped into the structure and comfort of a pleasing family.

Arthur disappeared out to the storage shed, and when he returned, he held a cello in one hand and a bow in the other. Chaim's spelunking had been deficient; he knew nothing about his father as a musician. "Elie, remember *Kujawiak*?"

"Of course!"

Ein bissel shiker and crying, they hugged each other. Through Uncle Elijah's window, he visualized the boys in their Polish *stetl*. Elijah's violin had a dark patina and smelled of sweat, Turkish tobacco, garlic, vodka, and rosin. "We play now *Kujawiak, Gorenka, Kamarinskaya,"* Elijah told the group. "Polish and Russian *titties* from childhood."

He looked at the guests, wondering why they looked so puzzled. "Whaat? You say that? *Titties*?" He laughed.

"*Ditties*, Uncle Elijah," Artie corrected and everyone chortled. To illustrate, Arthur said *titties*, and copped a feel of Ilona's left breast, much to everyone's hilarity. Aku glared. Eva turned away.

Stella said, "I can't believe this!"

Killing off a few notes, they made it through the Hungarian Rhapsody, and Elijah hoisted another engraved silver thimble and exclaimed, "A toast!" Then standing, "This is to the fall of tyranny. That sonofabitch! Fuck Mr. Eugene McCarthy!" And, gulping and refilling, "*Fuck* the Czar!"

"Fuck McCarthy! Fuck the Czar!" the two gleefully cheered like naughty boys.

Elijah insisted that the teens indulge in the vodka. As they drank it down, he refilled their thimbles, Arthur disappeared, then returned with a *balalaika*. How could he have missed that, too? Chaim wondered.

The two plucked like madmen, then sang, then danced, kicking legs, waving arms with blue smoke blowing all over the living room. For Chaim and his friends, ghetto Poland bloomed in their living room.

"*Hier, Mann*, trrrrrink!" commanded Uncle Elijah, pushing another thimble to Chaim. He gulped. "Arthur, watch the Bar Mitzvah boy *trink*!" commanded Uncle Elijah, his white beard bouncing down to mid-chest.

"I just turned seventeen, Uncle Elijah! I'm not a boy!"

"L'chayim!" he toasted, smiling at Chaim. *"Ein Mensch!"*

Everyone partook. Stella gulped, grimacing as the hot liquid coated her throat. Zube's eyes glazed with the powerful drink.

"Has he had a woman, Arthur?"

"Elijah!" Eva protested, eyes darting towards Stella. The Rintalas guffawed. Most good Catholic girls would have been out the door, but Stella embraced Chaim and pulled him near.

Ogling her, Elijah twinkled innocuously, *"Oy vey!* Jah, *nun. Nu, d*at's *eine Fraulein."* He pulled on his beard and stuck out his furrowed tongue.

Stella blushed. His vulgarity was clear.

Evalyn, remained stiff-lipped, enduring this *traif* girl in her home. It was as if she'd found *chumitz*, forbidden, leavened bread, in her cupboard at Passover. Stella, emboldened by vodka, took her hand, and Eva eased, returning the friendly ovation.

Elijah was a lion. In him, Chaim saw a real *mensch.* He reminded him of the life passion of his trumpet teacher, Herr Knauss, and of the Hemingway bull fighters.

Elijah poured yet another round, insisting that they all drink. Chaim gulped, and they danced more. The world twirled in kaleidoscopic prisms, whirling, hands on shoulders, bouncing up and down on bended knees, flying, turning, candles blazing, music, loud. He wanted to be just like Uncle Elijah. His * face hurt from so much laughing...

And the next thing he recalled, he was puking his guts out in the toilet.

Morning, and his brain was sore. Elijah was gone. Chaim felt as if his head were a lemon and someone squeezed it through a sieve for juice. As he hung his face into the toilet, the last thing he remembered was Uncle Elijah whispering. *"Shema Yisrael Adonai eloheinu Adonai ehad,"* *davening,* swaying back and forth, standing close to God.

Christmas, 1963, was the Goldbergs' first, last, and only Christmas. Chaim saw his father transcend his corporal being, culling his youth-spirit from Poland the way one digs potatoes. Through that kaleidoscopic picture, decades later, he nostalgically reminisced over that night as a rare and treasured family apogee.

Chaim saddened when he returned from that mythical village place in Eastern Europe to Estate Goldberg, his mundane 900 square foot home in Levittown. The magical kaleidoscope stopped, and the house was quiet, sullen again. He knew of the gifts the magi bestowed, but this had been the gift of the Tzaddik.

Thinking back decades later, after that evening, Chaim saw his parents in a different way, in a heroic way, that had been wonderful. He'd felt the war and its aftermath as a personal event.

The day after Christmas, Stella and Chaim exchanged high school rings, class of 1964. Hers was tiny, delicate. She wore his ring on her gold necklace with her cross, and he wore hers with his mezuzah chain. They were going steady, and his heart quickened when she came into a room. Was she his *besherte*, his "meant to be"?

Thoughts of Nedda's luscious, round cantaloupe buttocks insinuated between dreams of Stella's breasts. He missed Nedda's smooth and delicious honey-pot, yet he hungered for Stella's warm mouth and soft hands. He had to have both.

There remained one final point in this equation. He hadn't told Uncle Johnny about the bankbooks, and there was another mistake. He wanted to call Nedda, should have called Nedda, but he hadn't. He worried that there would be hell to pay.

A few days after Elijah disappeared, Chaim ambushed his father in his reading chair, smoking. "I never knew you played cello or the balalaika." He held his report card and wanted to give it to his father but dreaded the drill.

"I don't."

"Yeah, you do! I never knew you could do that."

"Do what?"

"You played really well. I never knew you could play! How did you learn?"

"I'll write you a letter," he replied, never looking up, his face buried in *Un di Velt Hot Geshvign*, Elie Wiesel's book. "I'm busy."

He looked at the cover and his father asked, disappointed. "You don't even know what this is, do you? The English title is *Night*, about Germany."

"Dad, here's my report card."

The elder looked at the card, blasé, annoyed at being disturbed.

"Did you see my grades?" He sought an accolade.

"What's this B?" he asked, picking the one fault.

Chaim wanted more. "Dad, I got into the Honor Society and... and I got an A in physics. I just about got all A's."

Arthur adjusted his glasses, knocked the ash from his cigarette. "Except for this B in Latin."

"It's a B plus."

"What's so hard about declensions? This guy," pointing to *Night*, "was on the best-seller list! Elie Wiesel didn't get a B plus in Latin."

"And Steinbeck won the Nobel Prize... who never graduated Stanford. I'll do better. You'll see." He was crestfallen. His father wanted him to be "like" other people. He was never good enough but, in frustration, there was something he wanted to know. "Tell me more about growing up in Poland, more about you and Uncle Elijah... about *Gliwice*."

"There's nothing to tell. We grew up. I forgot it all. Not now. I'm busy," he said, waving him away with his novel. "Now here's a real intellectual. This's what you should be. Yes, Wiesel. Be like Wiesel."

Chaim teared at the snub and walked to his bedroom. "I like Steinbeck," he retorted. He did not know at the time that this asymptotic nearness was as close as he'd ever get to knowing his father. At the time he knew nothing of Eli Wiesel.

***

The New Year's Eve party for 1964, at WFIL-TV, on Dick Clark's American Bandstand came next, on national TV. Cousin Brucie would be there. George Michael was coming along with Fabian, Philly's own.

The Dovels! Fabian! They would sing *Bristol Stomp* and *Why Do Fools Fall in Love* and *I Want You to Be My Girl*. Yes, yes, yes! They would sing "No, No, No!" In hormonal frenzy, everyone would attend.

He and Stella would slow dance together to *Moon River, Volare*, and *I'm Mr. Blue*. What a magical night it would be. Chaim almost drooled in anticipation. This was his first New Year's with a date and their first New Year's together. Strains of Leonard Bernstein's *Tonight, Tonight* echoed in Chaim's mind. And, if he were lucky, he'd get Stella to go all the way.

"I don't give a good goddamn about you and your friends," Evalyn snarled emphatically when he unwrapped this plan. "You're not going!"

These kinds of negotiations, he'd learned over the years, were always high-pitched, heated, and painful, but he could win if he persisted long enough. Then she would relent in frustration, when he'd worn her down.

"Mom, we'll take the train. It goes right to the TV station. Fabian's going to be there," he exhorted. "Please," he exhorted, then digging into his bag of manipulations, waving the red cape, "Mom, Dick Clark 'll have Negroes."

Like a picador, he'd weakened her. Evalyn, adamant, scowled, "You're *not* going! Jewish boys don't go to *goyische* parties. It's *goyische kopf*." She was spitting, she was so mad.

Then, Arthur got into it, whining. "Eva, he's going to college next year. Let'em go, already." They negotiated in Yiddish. "How much trouble can he get into?" he heard his father say, surprised that his father had such temerity and took up his cause, opposing his mother.

Arthur interceded. "He's gonna go one way or another. We can't really stop it. In a few months he's gonna be gone. He'll be out of our hair."

"O..." snapping an EZ Strike, "K..." inhaling, acquiescing, with a dishrag, wiping nonexistent *schmutz* from her already spotless, stainless steel sink. "We'll drive you." She dumped a cup of bleach into a mop bucket and filled it with steaming water, and the acrid halogen fumes permeated the kitchen.

"Eva, the whole point is that the kids get to do this. It's *their* party," said his dad.

Evalyn started to cry. "I can't believe you're graduating."

He looked at her, sullen. "Mom, I want to go to California. I want to go to school in L.A.," saying what he needed to manipulate her, "to be near the family."

This was music to her ears, her son going to college. "We'll find a way, Honey," she said.

"Oh, Christ," came the grumble from the living room. "Why the hell can't he go to Penn State like everyone else?" Arthur screeched like a bulbous blue Hyacinth parrot, from his perch.

"I'm not *like* everyone else, that's why. Maybe I'll get a scholarship. I read that story in *Time*. It's a great school." With that, tears flowed.

"You don't come from a family like those at that fancy country club. I'm not paying for you to go to any goddamn beach. You're not going to L.A.," Arthur threatened.

"Artie, *schrei nicht*. Honey, we'll find a way. You'll get a scholarship."

"Mom, don't cry," he said and took her in his arms affectionately, knowing how effective this ploy could be.

"I am dying thinking of you with that girl, the Catholic. My grandchildren will not be Jewish." She thought a moment, "Three-thousand miles... you'll be far away from her in L.A.."

"All we're doing is dating, Mom," he whined. "We want to go to a dance." He soothed, omitting the couple's plans to wind up at Culley together.

Chaim heard Arthur angrily smack the folded *Wall Street Journal* against his reading chair. "The boy's grown up, Eva," he mumbled. "Goddemmit, we can't afford L.A.! You know that!" Then, "He'll have to go to Penn State... for medical school, too," with more muttering.

"Kids grow up, Artie," she said, resolutely, then lobbying. "*Oy vey*. What can I do?" She plunged the spaghetti mop head into the steamy, strong bleach solution and wrung it with her bare, sore fingers. "Just don't dance with *Schwartzes*," she screamed, dissolving into tears. He'd won.

9

Off Kilter

"Your hands are sweaty," he said to her.

"I guess it's hot in my gloves," she replied. He slithered his arm around her shoulders, which she ordinarily liked, but she pushed him off. In the lightless tube, the train squealed along the tracks to 60th and Market and, in the chill, after a zesty cold walk with blustering wind in their faces, they turned down to 46th and Market, where they marched up to the TV station and entered entertainment's razzle-dazzle world.

"It's so glamorous," Stella remarked and squeezed Chaim's arm, and whatever fever she'd caught seemed to have vanished as they waded through picture-flashing paparazzi.

Inside, as they funneled into the tight corridor leading to Studio B, lights blazed, and they met scores of students. Tony Gaddella, producer, and Eddy Battista, floor manager, awaited. Tony began, "Kids, this is a national feed. Twenty million people will see you dance."

Gaddella went on. "So, no nose picking; don't cough. Guys, this ain't no baseball game." He grabbed his crotch, and the girls howled. "If you're not dancing, get off the stage."

Battista cheered them on. "Kids, dance like everyone's watching, 'cause they are. Our ratings will go through the roof. Smile, smile, smile, kids. You're on camera all the time."

Then came Dick Clark who looked spray-painted with thick make-up, like Mrs. Bliss's paint-job, and his forehead beaded in sweat beneath the lights, creating wet, caked blotches. He had armpit blotches.

"I thought he was much younger," Stella commented.

"Kids, American Bandstand has some surprises for you this evening!" he said as the make-up people fluttered around him, wiping his face, daubing at him with poofy sponges, reapplying make-up, and pulling out the white crepe papers from around his shirt collar.

Studio B was small, with three bulky color WFIL-NBC-TV cameras. The studio had football jerseys and bikinis strung on the walls behind the bleachers. Full New Year's Eve decorations festooned the studio.

"It's hard to believe we're here!" Stella screamed over the music and, back home, Levittown cozied in for the show. For Levittown, this was as big as when pitcher Joey Mormello won the Little League World Series in 1960.

Dick Clark took the stage, peering into the camera with the red light, and the floor director counted down on his fingers. "Three, two, one!" and pointed to Dick.

"Number one in 1962, number one in 1963, and number one in our hearts in 1964, Chubby Checker's here!" A three-foot high, red and yellow neon sign blinked: SCREAM!

"Raised right here, celebratin' Sout' Philly, he's our own, and he's gonna debut a new song for 1964 on American Bandstand's New Year's Eve celebration! It's 'The Mashed Potato'!"

SCREAM! blinked the sign, and they let loose!

And so it went: bumpity, bumpity, bump. Chaim was an awkward dancer, always feeling uncoordinated... but Stella, now, that Irish girl had rhythm. She showed him how to move and danced to song after song.

Minutes before midnight, the network linked to Los Angeles, where Elvis Presley greeted everyone, dressed in his Army private's uniform. Then, drum roll, lights flashing: SCREAM!

Dick Clark announced, "American Bandstand is moving to L.A.!" Flashbulbs ignited. "It's the first trans-continental, simultaneous, live, split-screen broadcast!" You would have thought a man walked on the moon!

Dick Clark announced, "Now, the countdown into 1964!

"Five!

"Four!

"Three!

"Two!

"One!"

Dick yelled so loud that even without microphones, they probably heard him in L.A..

In their own world, Stella and Chaim kissed, flashes burst, the nation watched the confetti cloud fall, and balloons bounced. It was 1964... but there was something off kilter. It wasn't like the Kennedy assassination weekend, not like that at all, and maybe it was nothing, he told himself. He sensed something wrong... with Stella.

Sweaty and fatigued after all the falderal, chilling in the cold night air, the two adorable lovers sauntered arm in arm to Market Street towards the train station. "Jeez, it's cold," Stella said, grabbing on to him.

Maybe there was nothing wrong, he hoped, but instinct told him there was. At the intersection, five Negro guys harmonized the doo-wop song *In the Still of the Night* around a steel burn barrel, watching a small TV set. They had created an antenna from a pulled-apart wire coat hanger which they had then wrapped in tin foil. The antenna looked like a popcorn popper.

When Stella and Chaim passed the quintet, they sang out, "Happy New Year," in five part harmony. G... E... C... like the NBC chimes. The tenor called out, "Hey, ain't youse two the guys we's jus' seen on Dick Clark? Youse famous!"

The bass congratulated them. "That was one fine kiss!"

Then, snapping fingers, they continued. *"In the still of the night I dream of you. My life is empty, girl, I don't know what to do. I hear your footsteps."*

Chaim shepherded Stella down the stairs into the subway. "This 's where I get out for my trumpet lessons at Curtis," he said.

"Was that the Five Satins?" she wondered.

"I'd like to thank the guy who wrote the song that made my baby fall in love with me," echoed off the stairwell's yellow-tiled walls.

In asphalt darkness, the Pennsy Line pounded its way back to Bucks County. They curled up until they reached the Langhorne station, then got into his car and switched on WBCB, where Brenda Lee sang *I'm Sorry*. They dallied.

"I have a surprise," he said, feeling heroic, and pulled out his wallet.

"That rubber again?" she teased.

"Nooo." He pulled out a shiny key, the one he'd found spelunking in his mother's drawer. "I think I know where this goes."

She grabbed his crotch. "I know where this goes," she toyed.

***

Chaim assured Stella. "If this works, we're in. I figured it all out. The barn scene, her douche bag, and the key in her pouch; she visits him when Ilona's away."

"I hope you're right. I'm cold."

"See the keystone? See the number on the key? Sixteen-ten? They match."

She kissed his cheek. "You're so smart! But the last time we came here, it didn't work out so well... that barn fire."

"Just don't light up. I think we're okay," he joked, giddy with anticipation. "The manor sets on the original Anchor Run estate that quartered General Washington and his officers."

"I'm impressed."

"When I saw the number in European handwriting, it added up. They're away, in Europe. It's okay," he assured. He twisted the key in the lock. It stuck. "Shit, it doesn't work."

"It's a sign... maybe we shouldn't do this." She took the key, blew on it, wiped it, warmed it, and tried again. It opened.

"Great, Stella," he complimented her.

"I give good blow jobs, don't I? We're a fine team." Rolling her tongue over her lips, she laughed. They laughed.

When he switched on the lights, Stella gasped. "Gad, it's... gaudy." The interior design contained a confusion of *nouveau riche* Erté design elements, far too many mirrors, and Louis XIV furniture pieces thrown into a *forme fruste* misunderstanding of old Europe. "There's no theme... other than too much money," she said. "I'm shivering. Get me to a warm bedroom," she said, clinging to him.

He snatched up a bottle of forty year-old Courvoisier VSOP, and the brazen burglars made their way up the narrow back stairway. "Aku's so fat he can't get up these stairs," he said.

"That Christmas was something else. I think I'm still hung over," she said. "And your Uncle Elijah! What a stitch!"

Once in the bedroom, candlelight glowing, in delicious, clandestine, irreverent delight, Stella guided his hand. What he felt was smooooth.

"Do you like it? I want to be avant-garde for you!" She exaggerated her French accent. "Lady Chatterley shaved."

"How European!" he replied, stroking her sleek mons as she rubbed on his thigh. He loved her velvet, but this sleekness was so erotic, so naked. It was a sign that she really loved sex, too, his sex; that she wanted him.

"I want to shave you," Stella said, but she started laughing. "Why do they have a drinking fountain next to the toilet?"

"It's a bidet, Stella. I thought it was a drinking fountain, too."

"What's it do?"

"Here, watch." He turned it on.

"Oh, I get it! Ol' Faithful," she joked as it gushed upward and she splashed him.

Back in bed, both shaved, they undulated against each other, passions engorged. He pulled out a joint. "Here! You'll like it."

"Chaim, you are such a bad boy... a good bad boy, but I just know I'm going to get into a lot of trouble with you." Soon, they were very stoned.

Chaim handed her his one-and-only condom but she said, "No... you don't need it."

"Why? You're safe?"

"Why?" she questioned rhetorically, and her mood changed. "I'm pregnant."

She forced a smile, then sobbed. Their joyous buzz left. "You're joking? Just 'cause we're stoned?"

In the soft candlelight, Stella looked at Chaim, tears streaming down her cheeks. "How could I have let this happen?"

But then he held her and cried. "Oh, Stella, we created life!" he said. "Oh, my God." These two bonded at the hips and in their minds. "But how can we look upon a baby as a tragedy?"

She placed her right hand over his mouth, drawing him closer. Cold and, by that time, very loaded, they shivered and pulled the covers over them. Then giving into the warmth between them, speechless, they made love and, when they were exhausted, she spoke. "I have to do *something*, but what?" Her copper red hair glowed in the candlelight. She was glorious.

"We're seniors. If... if... we married," he mumbled, running the permutations. They could barely speak.

"You have to go to medical school. I want to be a teacher. We can't. We just can't. These are our dreams. We're too young to let this happen. It's my fault," Stella sputtered.

"It's not *your* fault. It's my fault, too, my sperm." His mind raced. His guilt boiled. "We're not in a novel, like those imaginary people in *Peyton Place*. This is real. We made love."

"If I have this baby, I have to give it up for adoption, they... they... won't let me continue school, and I'll never graduate. I'd have the baby in July. If I have a baby, I'll never go to school." Her voice was frantic. "My Mom was lucky. She made it through Vassar. Our dreams are not in the past tense."

Chaim's instinct was to run, to avoid this. Run? Whaddaschmuck, he thought. Run? Where? He was a *mensch*, like Herr Knauss. Herr Knauss wouldn't run; he couldn't run. This was his baby.

It was the new year, and there he was in bed with her, naked, very intoxicated, not thinking clearly. "God is watching, Stella," he said. He thought about Elijah, speaking to God then of Zero Mostel as Tevye. "If I were a rich man," he sang, wishing none of this had happened.

"You are so silly," she teased, whacking at him.

Chaim spoke in a Yiddish accent, simultaneously mixing Tevye, Groucho Marx, and Henny Youngman, trying to be upbeat. "Vy should ve be sad about a baby? A baby, our baby, is not something vhich is sad. A baby is *nachas*, joy!"

"But you are not the *vone* who is pregnant. This won't wreck *your* life. You can't *bili-bili-bom* this away, Tevye, while you sit on the roof, fiddling."

"You're Catholic. What do you think about an abortion? We're taking a life?" he asked, squirming, remembering the horror of Cathy's self-induced yet failed abortion in *East of Eden* where she nearly bled to death.

She replied, "And you're Jewish. Jews deeply feel the value of life, too. We've heard your mother go on and on about the concentration camps and her reverence for life and that whole thing with the Meyers family... the sacredness of life." She hugged him and felt part of him in her, inside her, his soul was in her, in the form of their baby. "Chaim, I want your baby, our baby."

He was terrified. His life would be ruined. "Not just because we're stoned? That is what you want?" he asked, trying to support her, saying what he knew she had to hear but not saying what he meant or wanted.

"Oh, yes... yes," she affirmed.

This unborn child intertwined in their inchoate futures. He tried humor. "Stella, you sounded just like that girl in Peyton Place... with Rodney... and the football game."

"Stop! I'm trying to be serious," she said, annoyed.

He couldn't face it. "I'm trying too. I'm just so stoned." He went on. "Can I tell you something? I've never told anyone about this," he said. They lay together covered by a luscious Swiss eiderdown comforter that the Rintalas brought back from their European travels, tenderly speaking, soul to soul.

"Yes, you can tell me anything... but (giggling) I want hearing *you*, not Tevye," she said.

"When I was in my Bar Mitzvah class, we met with the rabbi on Sunday mornings. He went on and on about God and the Torah and teachings." Stella nestled into his chest. She loved hearing his stories. His calm voice soothed her. "He'd found a robin's nest, and there was one blue egg. I daydreamed. I couldn't help myself. It was such a beautiful blue egg, and I touched it, and the shell broke. I broke the shell. I pulled away my finger... but it was too late. He saw the goo on my finger right away and got very mad. 'Goldberg! You destroyed life!' he bellowed and the class winced.

"He thundered like God himself, Stella. It was an earthquake. I expected a lightning bolt. He went on forever about me killing that unborn chick and how we must have reverence for life. He knew the egg would never hatch, but his point was that we never know what will happen with life, that we must honor and protect life even if we are unsure about its existence or viability."

"And that's how you feel about our baby?"

"Yes. Yes. It's sacred and we must protect it."

"It?" Stella laughed. "It will be a boy or a girl, not an *it*!" She played with him.

"Oh, my poor little pronoun!"

"Stop it!" She whacked at him again.

"Our baby," he said, and the thought returned to him like an echo. His mother? He was terrified, unable to confront such a serious matter. Chaim played with her, singing, "*Do you think, do you think he'll be a boy? My Boy... Bill? He'll be tall as a tree? ...he'll be a spittin' image of his dad?*"

Stella laughed. "*Or she may be a girl; you gotta be a father to a girl,*" she sang from *Carousel*, which they'd seen on Broadway only a few weeks before.

Chaim thought carefully about what he was about to say. He listened to her rhythmic breaths as she lay on his chest.

"Can I tell you something else?" he whispered in her ear, hugging her from behind as they lay together.

"Yes, tell me anything."

"I love you, Stella, I do. I really *love* you."

She turned over and kissed him. "I love you too, I really do," she said.

"And we'll be together always, Stella. My Mother be damned. It's us, forever. We'll work our way out of this." They kissed again and he felt welded to her soul for all time. The marijuana wore off, and she wrapped her arms around Chaim's chest. This was the best place he'd ever been, and he was so glad that he was hers... *bili-bili-bom*.

The new year 1964 was full of hope and, when daybreak came, they feasted on optimism.

***

Home. He was in perilous inner turmoil. There was no cigarette smoke. The house was still. No one was awake. On his bed, he spotted a message his mother had written: Mrs. Buddo — driveway.

Mrs. Buddo? Who else? He wrinkled his lips and headed out. Six new inches of snow concealed the manor driveway curve as he followed partially concealed tire tracks and nosed slowly towards the main house. Deer munched alfalfa remains which the horses had tossed out of their corrals. How different the estate looked from the summer, when the copse in the grotto near the barns grew lush and verdant and the gorse swelled with flowers.

The white J-12 was nowhere in sight. The tracks must have been Nedda's, he surmised. The manse was dark and a white owl settled onto the garage roof, tearing at something. Not a creature was stirring, not even a mouse, except the owl.

Snow crunched in the dry air as he approached the main double doors. It was too quiet as he tiptoed up the unshoveled stairs, and he slipped, stumbling, on the icy treads. Ping Pong? Where was he?

Once inside, he heard flowing water from upstairs. She must be taking a bath. He eased. All was well. He looked forward to having sex with her when she was fresh, so warm from her bath. "Nedda?" No answer.

"Nedda?" His voice resonated off the marble floors, echoing through the high-ceilinged rooms. There was a scratching sound, and then he heard the opening trumpet solo from Mahler's Fifth Symphony. The turntable must be spinning. Diapason triplets: bah, bah, bah, baaaah. She must be up there. She loved Mahler. Bah, bah, bah, baaaah. Imbalance, dizzy, off kilter... *teki'ah, shva'rim, teruah.*

The house was a farrago with food dishes here and there, all licked clean by the dogs. Ping must be off for the holiday. Was Hemingway skulking somewhere, but his land yacht wasn't there? Maybe it was in the garage? Where was he?

She must be in the bath and couldn't hear, he reasoned as he ascended the curving, cherry wood staircase, patinaed by age. There was a bloody handprint on the newel post. His heart beat faster and then he heard bah, bah, bah, baaaah, and the final melancholic triplet, culminating on that high note. Da, da, da, deeee. Dread infused his heart.

Advancing to the first landing, blood tinged water trickled down the marble floor, dripping onto the white oak stairs, then onto the ornate cerulean blue Persian rug, and it was just starting down the staircase.

In the icy mansion air his breath frosted, as in Chubby's subterranean freezer where they held their precious ice cream. By the time he traversed the black and white marble-floored foyer, his optimism precipitated out like ice crystals.

Nedda's Chinese red kimono, the one with the vermillion and cobalt blue dragons, the one upon which they'd made roiling love on the antique Chinese day-bed, splayed out on the floor before the bathroom, water-soaked, its color darkened, its wetness not a remnant of their passion. Thoughts of polishing her toned body with almond and rose oils intervened.

Bah, bah, bah, baaaah. The foreboding funereal notes haunted him and bounced around. Bah, bah, bah, baaaah. The notes seemed louder and even more onerous... and then the tympani rumbled, and cymbals crashed.

"Nedda! Nedda!" Frantic, insistent, he bleated but no answer came.

Peering into the bathroom, he faced the massif of the claw-footed porcelain tub, the one in which he'd received his orientation to her tonsorial requirements, making her body smooth and oiled.

The tub glared at him, like a taunting animal yet surgically stark and white, inanimate, emotionless. Her hand draped over its edge. Nedda, unlovely, lay there, submerged. He screwed down the faucets, pulled her expressionless face to his chest, eyes unfocused, blankly gazing up, pupils dark... lusterless eyes, no sign of life; like Anna's chestnut eyes.

Don't let it end this way, he pleaded, but whom, or what entity, did he exhort? Nedda? Or did he speak to God? He wanted his mother's comfort. Mom! He summoned her. Then he felt shame over his weakness and placed his nose at her mouth from which no breath came. He pressed her chest, pounded on her, shook her, rattled her vigorously, and rolled her back and forth. Water sloshed out of the tub and from her mouth.

"Nedda!" No answer, no life. "Heeelp," he called. "For the love of Christ," he yelled. Hail Mary came to mind. No help came, no life... she was gone. Scooping his arms into the freezing water, he shivered as the water soaked him and overflowed the tub. How different this was from the summer when she'd floated like a lily pad on his hands and from their baths together when he'd shaved her legs and succulent petals.

Her face was as purple as an eggplant, arms mottled, eyes, nacreous white, limp arms and legs. Lifeless, he lifted her. She had a deep abrasion on her right knee, but it was bloodless. The white subcutaneous tissue was pale.

He stumbled on a hard object on the mosaic-tiled floor, almost dropping her. It was her Beretta. "Jesus Christ!" he exclaimed as the pistol slid along, caroming off the wood molding, stopping its spin behind the toilet in a pool of blood.

He smacked away two empty bottles of Dom Perignon, 1954 and one of Henri IV, Dudognon Heritage cognac. She drew in a breath. He breathed. She breathed. He finally exhaled, in relief, realizing that he'd held his breath for a long time.

She sucked in and then let it go, emitting a stertorous, feeble, slow gasp. Soaked to the skin, he was freezing. He shook away the chill and repositioned her again, splashing more water over the gunnels. Finally, carefully, he delivered her into her bed. He shivered. Time expanded.

He shucked his sodden clothes, paced to the fireplace, and scratched a blue, red-tipped E-Z Strike into flame. The fire was ready to go. Good ol' Ping. He touched the match to the paper and kindling, and the fireplace burst into life. "I'm gonna call an ambulance," he said aloud.

"Nooo... nooo." Slurring, in a whisper, she said, "I'm okay... just some pills. Don't... don't call anyone." Dare he ignore her and follow his judgment and call an ambulance? She sat up and let loose with an explosive torrent of vomit, dark red, purplish magenta with crimson flakes.

Chaim recoiled. Dried puke crusted her blonde hair and, in the new effluent he saw pills, white pills, silhouetted in the dark red, acid fluid, tinged by the cognac. Such a beautiful woman could not produce something so repulsive, Chaim thought.

Her bedroom was overdone in Nicolas Pineau style, complete with Antoine Watteau and François Boucher paintings and on the Louis XIV Rococo ornate bed stand, defiant like a rook in checkmate, sat an amber prescription bottle: Miltown. Empty.

He'd learned about dangerous Miltown, a soporific, in his lifeguard courses and inspected the pill bottle: Nicholas Palumbo, MD, 717 Bayonet Street, Trenton, New Jersey. There had been thirty dispensed, and in the vomit, he counted twenty-two pills; at least eight were missing.

As her lids dropped, tenderly, he encircled her torso with his arms and drew her close to him to transfer his body heat. She remained flaccid. He entwined his legs around hers and, with his hands, massaged her icy torso. He held her wrist and she responded with a more vigorous pulse. "Nedda! Nedda! My darling, my dear!" he'd never spoken endearing words like that to her but out they came. "How many did you take?"

She mouthed a word but her tongue was thick.

"I counted the pills, Nedda."

"How?"

"In your puke."

"In my puke?"

"I love you, Nedda. I'd do anything to save you."

Groaning, but stronger, she said, "Oh my God. No ambulance. This'll get into the paper. Johnny," she mumbled and drifted off.

"Johnny? Uncle Johnny? He's part of this?"

She snored. He was furious with her yet frustrated that he could do nothing more, except to wait. And what did Johnny have to do with this? He got up to pee, but she clutched his hand. "Don't leave me," she entreated, grabbing his penis.

"I'm just gonna pee." He kissed her hand. "Lemme go."

When he returned, she sat up in bed looking like a ragged raccoon, mascara smeared all over her face, lipstick smudged, appearing to have aged ten years. He whispered, shocked, incredulous. "So what happened?"

"Newyearseve," she slurred. "Johnny's coming to visit... but he didn't show up. Didn't call."

"So it's you and Johnny?"

"Oh, Lover Boy... you know I like you athletic types." She nipped his right nipple and continued. "Jus'adrink." She was woozy, and it came out as one long boozy word.

"The pills?"

"I got mad." Her strength increased. "I opened Harry's goddamned prized fucking bottle of Dom Perignon, and that three-thousand dollar bottle of panther-piss cognac. I just took one pill to go to sleep, and... I guess I ate the rest." Not making much sense, she looked at him, sad, forlorn. "With ice cream." He saw the empty carton of Breyer's vanilla fudge on the bed stand where her pistol usually sat with a spoon sticking up.

"So you took a bunch," he said.

Histrionic, she went on. "Harrythemutherfucker didn't even call me."

"Mmmmister Boudreaux?" he had to clarify who she meant, with pronouns flitting like fireflies, but she passed out. He tried not to laugh. He'd never seen her carry on like that and she was unintentionally humorous.

When she roused several hours later, he did what any good Jewish boy would do in such circumstances. He heated up a can of Campbell's Chicken Noodle Soup and it was Mmm Mmm Good. She drank it down, wiped her hand though her hair, and anguished, "I do not belieeeeve what I did." With a long, hopeless, sigh, she said, "That was terrible. I am so sorry! Forgive me."

She was disconsolate. "No one loves me! On New Year's Eve! Where-the-fuck were you? You were with that redhead, that high school flute-player?" Her voice ascended an octave.

"Estelle? Stella?"

"I know what her name is. Why didn't you call me, at least? I would've sucked your cock... and hers too."

He couldn't laugh. "I didn't know if your husband was here and I don't want any more of him."

"He's gone. He's left me for Sister-Little-Fucking-Cunt, Clitoris, I call her. They went to our Paris apartment for New Year's." She screamed out. "That asshole's hauling drugs all over the world, fucking anything he can... and I'm here in this goddamned prison."

"What do you mean?" he asked and looked around the room. All of this was wrong.

"Jeez, you don't know? He's Calamari's shipper. Boudreaux Lines are the freighters on the River Styx."

"Boudreaux Lines?"

"Lines of coke and bundles of heroin! That's Boudreaux Lines. They'd be bankrupt if it weren't for me. Who do you think supports Rintala Construction and all those companies and Chubby's? He can't afford his Mercedes by selling dime ice cream cones at race riots."

"So Rintala's in on this?" He'd seen the pieces to this felonious jigsaw puzzle, but finally he learned how the parts fit together.

"All of 'em. They're all criminals and I'm sick of it. Even the 4889 Steelworkers. Then she asked, "Did you mean that? You said you love me? Do you? Do you love me?"

"Yes, Nedda. I do love you. Yes, I do," he said and he meant it.

"Oh, Honey, you're so young and so adorable." He liked it when she called him Honey. Then she continued as they lay in her bed. "You're a kid, and I shouldn't be doing this. It's statutory rape, fer Chris' sake. I'm twice your age. You're not even eighteen yet. Oh, but I do like you, a lot," she said, grabbing his penis and kissing the end, "and you taste scrumptious."

In her bedclothes his lion detected her perfumes, but he wondered if the faint vinegary smell was Johnny Calamari's or even Harry's scent. They made wonderful, passionate love, and afterwards, she lapped their pool of sweat from the pond between his chest and abdomen.

Her face rested on his chest and she said, "Chaim, you can't love me. What you love, my child, are your orgasms," she said. Wistfully, she mused, "Oh, pretty boy, it's too bad that you are so young and I am sooo married and this is sooo off kilter."

He teared with her confounding complexity, and she kissed his lips. "I do love you Neddy, I do."

Chaim looked at her. "What?" He could tell she was thinking of something weighty, something important.

"My darling, my young, sweet darling boy. I'm so sorry I hurt you." Atop of him again, she gyrated her hips, riding him, and he breathed in deeply, his hands smoothing her breasts. He was at his peak. "We were together, when? About six weeks or so ago? Well, I missed my period. I'm pregnant."

Instantaneously flaccid, his dreams turned to smithereens, and his world tilted off kilter.

"Lover boy, if you love me...." She trailed off.

10

Drinking with the Devil

Two women pregnant! *Oy vey*, unthinkable, absurd, Tevye mocked. Chaim vibrated with anxiety, aghast. He couldn't tell Nedda about Stella, and he couldn't tell Stella about Nedda, and he could never tell his mother. How right was Mrs. Bliss who always said, "One thing about statistics, everything does happen."

Stunned with her news, Chaim wandered towards their marital bedroom. He was like Inspector Clousseau, seeking clues about the antecedent events. She halted him. "What are you looking for?" she queried. "I'm here." Wrapped in her purple silk peignoir, she stood behind him. "It's time to shower, loverboy." She dropped her gown.

"He's gonna kill you," Chaim concluded, matter-of-factly. "Okay, Neddy, I'll do it. Oh, jeez, Neddy, I do love you."

"Chaim, you're such a good boy." She rewarded him with passionate lovemaking and they rested. "I'm feeling better. Thanks," she said.

"I can't believe you're pregnant."

"Me, either."

"What are we going to do?" he puzzled.

"I don't know," she said. "Call me? Tomorrow?" she asked. He said he would and exited.

As he plowed her driveway, snow flew and he ruminated over his decision. Those bank books had it all: millions, and the jewels and drugs. He had to save her, didn't he? He swaggered with Harry's death warrant, like the gun-slinger, John Wayne, avenging his woman's suffering. Harry the Bee was Evil. He would be Good and he couldn't change his mind.

Lights on high beam in the pelting snowstorm, he faced a wall of kaleidoscopic white. Squinting through his thick, fogged glasses, navigating like a blind man with his cane, he made out curbs and tried to stay between them, guided only by his feel for the invisible centerline. Nedda's near death consumed him, and he felt fortunate to have intercepted what was certain to have been her final breaths. He flicked the brights on and off to better interpret the road, then he used his fingers to scrape the rime from the inside of the windshield. The headlamps were useless.

"Whose woods these are, I think I know," he repeated aloud, feigning confidence, shooing away his inner demons. "His house is in the village, though," he continued... but what was that line about the queer horses?

The logistics of getting two abortions boggled his mind... and becoming an instrument of death for her husband. It was too much to think about. Everyone knows that you can get an abortion over in Trenton, but under what door would he slip the cash? Maybe he should just kill himself. This murk descended like a curtain, like creek silt.

Death evolved into reality. As when he cracked the robin's egg, taking a human life no longer hid in the shadows as an abstract concept. He shivered at what he needed to do and tuned to WBCB, Levittown, Fairless Hills, AM 1490 where Bobbie Gentry crooned:

I got some news this mornin' from Choctaw Ridge.
Today Billy Joe MacAllister jumped off the
Tallahatchie Bridge.

Was he going to be like Billy Joe? Trenton makes and the world takes, he brooded. And what if Stella, his dear and wonderful sweetheart, decided to do something like Nedda? "You're not the one who's pregnant," Stella had said. He put that thought out of his mind.

Well, Billy Joe never had a lick of sense, pass the
biscuits, please.
There's five more acres in the lower forty I've
got to plow.

What Trenton uses, the world refuses. He mumbled that phrase over and over, listening to Billie Joe's lyrics that lacerated him like glass shards in his kaleidoscope.

The windshield was frozen. He pounded the dash in frustration and stopped. It was dark, and tears came, making it all the more hard to see through the pie-tin sized snowflakes. He felt as if he were being sucked into the flakes. It was hypnotic.

I'll have another piece of apple pie, you know it don't
seem right.
I saw him at the sawmill yesterday on
Choctaw Ridge,
And now you tell me Billie Joe's jumped off the
Tallahatchie Bridge.

The lyrics taunted him. Do it! Jump!

He was flying, flying, flying. Then, whomph, a distinct halt. Horns. He'd slid off the road, down an embankment in this snowstorm. He pushed the driver's door away but snow poured in and then he couldn't close it. Snow avalanched in when he rolled down the window and terror filled him as the wet snow set up quickly.

He struggled like his sister's black cat in the pickle jar. He was in a pickle with angles and gravity against him. Stuck. Shit! Frantic, he pounded the horn and steering wheel. Off in the distance he heard his mother's comforting words. *Schrei nicht. You'll be okay, Kussilah. Teruah*... bah, bah, bah, baaaaaah.

He recalled a pleasant time with his father, when they lived in New York, in Manhattan, when he towed him along in a snowstorm. His hands were so cold, and his daddy warmed his fingers and hands as they walked, and then blew warm air on his red fingers and put one hand into the pocket in his daddy-coat. They trudged along in the driving snow to the Horn & Hardart Automat. He remembered his dad's after-shave, Old Spice, how wonderful it smelled when his daddy kissed him. His dad pulled him into Horn & Hardart and he made a big deal that he didn't pee in his pants and bought him baked beans and a hot dog. He loved his father then and he was sure his father loved him. He was three and he'd discovered bliss.

Then he returned to the reality in the snow bank. God, he was fucked! In his old, new car, which Zubarsky named the Clot because its faded paint was so purple, Chaim felt pressed, closed in, pinned. He clotted in the Clot. *Honey, I'll send help*, she said to him. Mom! He felt his mother's spirit. Mom! He cried out. "I'm screwed!" Claustrophobic, he hyperventilated as the sensation of being buried alive in snow squeezed him. He squirmed. Was he going to die down there?

He thought about discovering poor Nedda in her watery tomb. Panic took hold as he looked into Anna's dead face. Out! He had to get out. He began to breathe quickly, and then he heard a loud tap on the window. In a deep baritone, came salvation. "Hey! Snow White! You okay down there?"

Salvation? But it was Beelzebub, himself, in the form of Johnny Calamari. What was *he* doing here? Mom! How could you? Honey, you gotta take what you can get. It's a holiday, Honey, he heard her say. It's *besherte*, he heard her say. Meant to be.

At a time when everyone else in Lower Bucks County was snugasabuginarug, Mr. Calamari was out on the road. "Hey, you! Down in the ditch!" Then he snarled, "Yeah, it's me, you faggot, nigger-loving, Jew."

"You hit me!" he yelled.

"Yeah, an' I'm gonna hit you again. Putz, you're in a pile of shit. I been watching you!"

Chaim was terrified. What did he know?

"Go get one uh your fuckin' Jew-lawyers an' sue me. I'll fuckin' leave you, Snow White. The big bad wolf'll eat your guts by the time your lawyer arrives!" he hissed. Wearing a red and black checkerboard, heavy wool, hunter's jacket with matching cap and a bow on top, Mr. Calamari looked like the Elmer Fudd balloon at the Macy's Thanksgiving Day Parade. He would have been funny had he not been such a malevolent figure.

"I'm stuck!" yelled Chaim.

"No shit," came the sarcastic gnarr.

"Get me out! Gemme out!" he pleaded, even more hysterical.

"Got any green, Princess? Youse Jews always got money," goaded Calamari. "Twenty bucks, kid, ta pull your sorry ass out... today's a holiday, too." He raged on with heavy bourbon fumes in his every breath. "I *know* what you been doin'. Youse rich Kikes, youse think you own the whole fuckin' world, 'n'you don't! Youse guys got too much money, wit your fine clothes and, heck, all's I got's dis' tow truck, six kids, 'n' I pull smart-ass faggots like you out of ditches on New Year's 'n' I *know* what you been doin'."

Chaim was getting colder. "Twenty bucks," he answered. Was it preferable to freeze to death rather than to put up with this orangutan? His inebriated savior dug away the snow and pulled open the door, letting more frigid air rush in. Just having the door opened lessened his claustrophobia, but he was cold, Nedda cold. Once free, he sucked in a massive breath and clumsily burrowed partway up the slope, exhausted.

"Cold as a witch's tit, huh? You almost made it to the fifth hole! At the Makefield Country Club's golf course... fifth tee, Snow White. No Jews at that club, neither, Putz," needled The Squid, guffawing.

Chaim stood next to the tow truck, its diesel engine rumbling. He ignored the fumes and was soothed by the exhaust warmth. He saw the red-and-gold lettered sign: Calamari's Tow Truck & Recovery. Its yellow lights swirled. There was a cartoon squid character in pink with eight tentacles attached to little cars. The tagline read: "You goes or we toes!"

Calamari's face was cobbled, and Chaim noticed that he'd carved his nails down to the quick. He had bits of red flesh at some of the nail beds, and the cuticles were raw. Chaim had to turn away, his facial skin was so bad. His complexion was hot, aglow with the bourbon flush. In the bitter cold, the nodules looked as if they were, each, at the bursting stage.

Mom, how could you send *this* to me? Beelzebub winched the Plymouth out of the ditch, and finally Chaim nestled into the truck cabin. "There's no heater in this goddamned thing, Skippy. Sorry." Sadistic Calamari seemed almost empathetic.

"It's okay, Mr. Calamari. I'm grateful you got me out." He shivered and, as he warmed, he inwardly offered a thanks, Mom.

"Okay, Putz, da' cabbage." Calamari ridiculing him with *Putz*. It annoyed him and he made an error, incautious when he opened his wallet. "Putz, Putz, Putz... whaz's dat? You got *more* money you didn't tell me 'bout? Sonofabitch." He smiled a threatening, wicked smile. "Ohhhh, dat's not so good."

"Johnny," Chaim protested.

"It's *Mister* Calamari, you little fuckin' Kike liar!" Angry, chomping on a stale, unlighted, stinky, cheap cigar butt, he pulled the other twenty from his wallet. "I oughta push your ass back down there, you nigger-lover, Jew. You won't be needin' dat bill in dis snowstorm when you freeeeze to death!"

Calamari's drunken meanness was too much for Chaim and he started to cry.

"Hey, you *are* a little crybaby, faggot!"

"I'm *not* a faggot," he sobbed. "Iiii got two women pregnant!" It slipped out. Did he really say that? Yes! Yes, he did, and the story came out, bursting forth like pus from one of Mr. Calamari's facial cysts.

"What? Putz! Whad a stallion! You? Who?" He was amazed! "Who's da' mares?" he asked and sniggered. He hesitated. "Fuck! Spit it out!"

"Stella O'Shannahan."

"Dat goil you wuz wit at Chubby's... an' da' other?"

"Missus Boudreaux."

"You got Nedda fuckin' *Boudreaux* pregnant? 'N' dat chick I saw you at Chubby's wit? Really? Dat's innerestin' news." He dropped his jaw. "I like you bedda now." Then, brooding, "Man, you got no idea wadda hornet's nest youse into, Putz!" he exclaimed. "Jeez. Dat pussy's da' Mercedes-Benz piece uh ass! Her husband's gonna fuck you up! You know who *he* is?"

"Some sort of shipping guy?"

"Shipping guy?" Almost boasting, "Harry da' Bee's a *Capo di Tutti*, you idiot! He's a kingpin in Asian drugs. He's da *Capo di Capi*! He's like duh Babe Ruth uh ice cream. Man! Dinga-fuckin'-linga! You fuckin' idiot! Harry da Bee is da *Capo di Tutti Capi*. He brings all dat good vanilla ice cream to Philly. Harry the Bee's da man! Stings like a Bee," he said and boxed his hands like Cassius Clay, wham, wham.

"You'll be chum. You'll be like a rabbit wit' da' eyes ate out if he gets ahold uh ya." Chaim imaged Poe pecking the eyes out of that rabbit. Calamari crunched his knuckles to emphasize his plight. He resented this uneducated, white-trash moron making him feel like an idiot.

"You gotta tell your parents, kid. What da fuck you gonna do 'bout dese babies? You can open a goddamned fuckin' nursery school!" He giggled sadistically.

Chaim felt sick. Whatdafuck *was* he gonna do? The weight of his predicament hit him hard. Calamari was right, and this was all wrong: the end to college, to his life, to Stella's life, to Nedda's life.

The song lyrics returned:

> **And Mama said to me "Child, what's happened to your appetite?**
> **I've been cookin' all morning and you haven't touched a single bite.**
> **...And she and Billy Joe was throwing somethin' off the Tallahatchie Bridge**

"What should I do? Jump off a bridge?" he questioned.

Calamari rocked, laughing so hard at the incongruity of the concurrence of moral remorse and culpability creating inner turmoil and shame to the degree that it would force a suicide. He gasped, laughing. "No, you stupid fuck! I thought you wuz smart. You get 'er fixed."

QED! *Quod erat demonstrandum*, as Mrs. Bliss wrote on her chalk board.

"Do I have to 'splain everythin' to you? Youse s'pposed to be a fuckin' genius."

"How? How'd you do that, ggget it fixed?"

"Every bitch in heat in five counties dat gets knocked up winds up in Trenton. You get an abortion. You're rich. Jus' rent a bus, round up your ho's and get 'em abortions. Just buy it. Quick as dat. Badda-boom, badda-bing. You don't even have ta' go. Jus' getta bus. You can fuck 'em again in two days."

Calamari would not have anguished one second over crushing that robin's egg. In his culture, there were garage sales on lives. He was closer to dogs than humans, but that gave dogs a bad name. Chaim marveled at how hard he was, how he lacked any sense of humanity.

"Abortions over in Trenton?"

"Trenton makes, the world takes, Putz."

Perhaps he shouldn't have, but he asked the obvious. "Mr. Calamari, what are *you* doing out on New Year's, on a night like this?"

This question must have been like a dental pick in one of his few nerves because he responded like the cowardly lion in Wizard of Oz. "You know kid, this ain't the end of the world. There are solutions to problems like this." The loving father replaced the boisterous tow truck operator-assassin. "Me? Hey, Chaimy, okay... we's friends. Call me...yeah," he struggled, "call me Uncle Johnny."

"Yeah, okay, uh, Uncle Johnny, how come *you're* out here?"

"You don' know when to quit, do you? I work all da' time," he said, ever evasive. He could never answer a question just straight-on. Surprisingly, he 'fessed up. "Da' ol' lady threw me out!"

"On New Year's Day?"

"I was a baaaad boy, Chaimy" he said, pulling off his Elmer Fudd hat, then shaking his head side to side.

"What'd you do?"

Sheepishly, "My snake got loose. Oh, Jeeez. You know dat physics teacher with the nice tits, Miss Kitty with da' titties?"

"Mrs. Bliss?"

"Mrs. Bliss. She was married to Pippo, my brother, 'til he died."

"You fucked your dead brother's wife?" Her *O Captain! my Captain!* flashed in his mind, and the Captain's bars clunked in his mind the way they did when she dropped them on the floor.

"Yeah. We kep' it in da' family, you know." Johnny tried humor. "Hey, Putz, the angle of dangle equals the heat of the meat, times the mass of the ass. She's a physics teacher, fer Chris' sake."

This was incongruous for Chaim. Here was that fatalistic *jus' is*. He couldn't help himself and laughed. Then Johnny joined him.

"Your dead brother's wife?"

"Yeah... well, it ain't pretty. She's got dem nice tits."

Chaim took in a breath, warming a bit, and pushed to what was his worry. "What do I tell my parents?"

"*Oy vey*, oh, jeez, kid, you jus' tell 'em."

"It'll kill 'em."

"It'll kill 'em if you don't. You can put your money on dat horse. There's no such thing as a secret like this. You want control," he said, crunching his knuckles producing that distinctive walnut-shell crunching sound. "Dey's gonna die anyway. We's all gonna die."

"You're not going to tell anyone, are you?"

"Me? I'm no whiny bitch, like dat Karen Phillippo, dat coochie. What she did was dirty... at Chubby's. Ohhhh... Me? No, I don't say nuttin'. Uncle Johnny's lips are," and he pulled his thumb and index fingers across his mouth, "zzzzipped."

"Okay, kid, so you're not a fag. You probably do suck cocks, but I like you." The Squid extended a tentacle and they shook. Had he gone Looney-Tunes? Could he actually like this harmful Neanderthal?

Calamari's hand was the size of a Chubby's porterhouse. "You're gonna do some favors for me now, yeah? I know about you, but we's friends, sooos." He pulled out a bottle. "Here, kid, you gotta drink on dat. Dis here's sixteen year old Hirsch... made by dem Jews but it's da good stuff. Fagetaboutit."

"Uncle Johnny," he tried to protest, feeling like his mother's floor mop, dirty, twisted and wrenched in ugly swill. There was this perpetual *quid pro quo* with Johnny. It would be very wrong to trust him... very wrong.

"Drink it, or I'll know youse a pussy. I'll make you suck my cock." He laughed. "*L'chayim.*"

Chaim wanted to puke thinking that his lips would have to touch Johnny's pucker spot, but he had do it. The medicinal liquor burned, and his host laughed. "Yeah, dat's good. So's when I call you, you just do what I tell you to do. Simple? Here's your money back. You're gonna need it," he said.

"But if we'uns gonna work together, don't ever, never, ever fuckin' lie to me... an' here's my brother-in-law's phone. He ain't 'xactly a doctor no more, but he knows his business. Da girls from At-lantic City go there. Name's Nick the Razor," he said, slashing his index finger across his neck. "Nick Palumbo, good Guinea. Tell 'm Johnny, Uncle Johnny, sent you. He's a little expensive but maybe he'll give you a two-fer." Johnny was so impressed with himself as he nudged, laughing himself sick again, that he honked like one of Nedda's fat geese.

From behind the open door, a satchel tumbled into the snow and a severed hand fell onto the trampled snow. "Oh, shit!" Calamari exclaimed. "You wasn't su'posed ta see dat, kid! We been busy. Guy lost his hand." His eyes must have flared in surprise because Calamari exclaimed, "Putz! What are you lookin' at?" He threatened. "You didn't see nuttin'! Nuttin'!"

What Chaim saw was the satchel and a left human hand wearing a blood-stained wedding ring. As Johnny replaced the money he snatched the hand by its stiff middle finger. Johnny smelled like the inside of a bike tire, a metallic zinc, rancid, rubbery smell. The bourbon odor mixed with the scents of citrus Vitalis, and cedar English Leather.

"Don't stare at da' pigskin, kid. You gotta learn to stop dat. Gives you away," he chided. "It's like poker, *versteh*?" Johnny, after his lesson in concealing criminality, twisted Chaim's arm hard, hammer-locking him, and slammed him brutally, flat-faced into the snow. Loving Uncle Johnny reverted to Mean Johnny the Squid. His face in the snow, Chaim recalled that August day in the YCC locker room when he'd crushed his fingers into the floor like Italian wine grapes.

"Hey, asshole," he said, and jerked him up, onto his feet and jammed him into the cash cab. "You could wind up like dat guy who lost his hand. I could kill you, kid," he said, "but I won't. We's business partners, now, so I won't."

"Mmmmister Calamari?" he asked, hesitantly. "We'uns friends? Iiii'm sorry."

"Yeah, okay, Putz. Whad? Call me Uncle. I like dat."

Terrified, he realized that then was the time. "Here's somethin' dat'll in'erest you," and with that, Chaim handed him the sheaf of bank books.

Mr. Calamari scrutinized them. "Ohhh, yeah," he admired. "Yeah, I forgot deese. I musta' left 'em somewhere." He pulled out another bill, a Franklin. "Good work. Dat money's very clean, kid, very, very *cleeeean*." And then in his ominous, shadowed manner, "Dis'll help dat very bad memory you got, won't it? Don't forget who's your friends, Putz," he snarled and crinkled the bill, then stuffing it into Chaim's jacket. "Have another drink, kid. You done good."

Calamari continued. "And do forget what you jus' saw. Dis didn't happen. None uh dis'." He pointed his finger like a gun, cocking the trigger and shooting. "You do not remember. Omertà. *Verstehst du*? Nuttin'! Two things: one, do not ferget; da other, ferget. Got it? One, two! Badda-boom, badda-bing!" He cracked his knuckles again. The sound was sickening, but the image was as crisp and clear as the Franklin. He was supposed to not forget, to forget.

Chaim ignored his illogical rant and asked, "Uh, Mr. Calamari, Uncle Johnny, why do you call me Skippy all the time?"

"You like Putz beddeh? It's cause when I fuck you up the ass you'll be like peanut buddah!" He laughed heartily. Chaim gulped. His humor would only make sense to Yogi Berra and to Knuckles "The Squid" Calamari. Terrified that his vigorish would be exorbitant, he knew that he had no choice. Mrs. Bliss' centrifugal forces, $a=v2/r$, pulled apart his universe, and his kaleidoscope whirled out of control.

Besides, Hirsch bourbon was made by the Pennsylvania Dutch, not Jews... and those bank books... Harry created them. They were all in Harry's name. Despite his bourbon-dulled senses, Chaim saw a way out as he emerged from his séance in the snow.

His parents... he couldn't dodge this. He had to tell them. Yes, he'd do the right thing and tell his parents. They would accept his flaws and love him. He was confident that they would help him. They would understand. He would follow his mother's advice and turn over a new leaf.

He'd straighten up and fly right. Relief came from his decision to confess. Drinking with the Devil brought him to this epiphany. He'd confess and that would make it all right. The weight of his oppressive wrongdoing lifted.

11

Mea Culpa

Death, his death, weighed on his shoulders, like Calamari's counter-weight in the locker room when he tried to stand. Was this how impending death felt, how Christ felt when he struggled on his cross? What was he going to do?

He knelt, making the sign of the cross before he entered his Jewish home. *Confiteor Deo omnipotenti, beatæ Mariæ semper Virgini, beato Michæli Archangelo*, he whispered. He'd become such a bad Jewish boy.

A blue smoky haze floated above the Sears table, poufing around the Levitt-fashion, stainless-steel light fixture which hung above the kitchen table, the tobacco scene punctuated by clicking and clacking of ivory mahjong tiles. Uncle Elijah held court along with his mother, father, and that painfully skinny woman he abhorred, Laura Satanoff, the *yenta* from across the street. He loathed her eerie plastic dentures, and he could see her pink, flesh-colored plate on the roof of her mouth when she laughed. Her dental falsies clacked like mahjong tiles when she spoke.

"Nice that you could attennnnnnnd, *Tzatzkela*," Elijah sighed, drawing out the words sarcastically. Rising only half-way, he tapped his right index finger on his pocket-watch face and set his eighteen-karat gold Patek Philippe before him.

Bleach fumes told him that his mother was mad as hell. "*Setz, Dich!*" she commanded, in her adenoidal Yiddish. He should have been home much earlier, but how could he possibly explain what had been going on? Only lies would help him but he promised to reform, to lie no more.

The four sat like an appellate tribunal around the dining table, tiles banging, smoke fuming, with Elijah's pocket watch adjacent to the red mahjong box with Chinese writing. They'd drained the vodka bottles as they gossiped.

"God bless our friend, Mr. Calamari," Laura said as she placed a tile. "Al's finally working," she said, wrinkling her brow. "Otherwise he'd be here. Mr. Calamari, what a *mensch*, got him work out at the mill. Thank God for Uncle Johnny." Her adulation of his torturer was like drinking vinegar for Chaim. They had no idea what sort of person Uncle Johnny really was. The smell of Johnny's BO, that rubbery stench of a bicycle inner tube, hung in his nostrils.

Evalyn brought out a cherry kugel, steaming, rich in cinnamon and raisins, butter dripping over the sides. "*Halushkas,*" complimented Uncle Elijah, "delicious." After they gobbled, Elijah announced, "*Jah...* time to sleep! *Schlaffziet.*" The creases around Elijah's eyes deepened, accentuating the age difference between his father and uncle-not-his-uncle. With finality of the evening, he snapped the watch cover shut.

If Chaim confessed to his parents, it would precipitate a nuclear holocaust, but he could trust Elijah, the Prophet. In the bedroom, his uncle entered a different world as he recited the *Shema*. This was his moment. Dare he? In God we trust, maybe, but dare he trust Elijah, the *tzaddik*? Hesitating, like testing thin ice with a boot toe, he asked, "Uncle Elijah?"

"Shaaa. I am getting close to God," he whispered drawing the tallis over his head as he began his prayers.

When he was done, he spoke. *"Jah, Tzatzkela. Vat villst du?"* Elijah sat on the bed with his *tzitzis* still over his head.

"Can I ask you about something?"

"Tzatzkela, jah, vat, zwar? Yezzz, tell Uncle Elijah."

"But you can't tell anyone."

"Checka, the KGB?"

"No. No. It's nothing like that." Uncle Elijah smiled, waiting.

He told.

Once it was out, Elijah sat mulling on the bed and ran his bluish fingers with paper-thin skin through his hair and then ran them pensively through his long, bushy beard. He tugged his beard once more with both hands, the way one strokes a horse's tail, hand over hand– thinking, thinking, thinking. Then he wriggled, *"Oy vey, Tzatzkela,"* and sighed.

Chaim watched his eyebrows buckle, wondering if he should speak. By then the *tzaddik* rubbed his hair, removed his yarmulke, replaced it several times, and pulled anew on his beard. He didn't light a cigarette. A bad sign.

But then, like a summer sunrise, came the *Tzaddik*'s impish smile. With his hands, he clamped Chaim's face, drawing him nose-to-nose. His garlic breath, augmented by heavy smoking and too much alcohol, was putrid. *"Sechs million. Sechs million, Tzatzkela,"* he said, smacking the top of his right hand against Chaim's head. Chaim gulped, imagining vivid kaleidoscopic images of what must have spun in Uncle Elijah's head.

Then, looking up in discordant glee, Uncle Elijah snapped an EZ strike and lighted up. A good sign. *"Jah! Wunderbar*! Wunderful! *Wunderliche Nachricht*! Wonderful news!" He snuffed the match-head between his fingers. As Tevye would have done, the *tzaddik* bolted to Arthur and Evalyn's bedroom, where the unsuspecting parents, hearing the commotion in this cramped home, stood in the lintel; she in curlers; he in his robe. Chaim stood behind Uncle Elijah.

"Artie, Sie wird ein Zadie sein!" Elijah sang out. "You're going to be a *Zadie! Wunderbar!*" he exclaimed, joyfully smacking his hands together, dancing around. *"Zwei!* Two! *Zwillingen!"* Elijah howled.

Reb Tevye flashed across Chaim's mind when Elijah asked, *"Wann sollen wir eine Hochziet machen?* When do we make the wedding?" Not even Shalom Aleichem could help him. Unthinkable, absurd.

***

"Stella! Stella!" he yelled like Kowalski in *Streetcar*, his world in smithereens, banging her window, freezing, clad only in pajamas and sneakers. She lifted the window and Chaim blew in with the spindrift snow, the prodigal flopping onto her bedroom floor like a carp. "What are *you* doing here?" In her flannel jammies, the ones with Curious George all over them, she said, "It's past midnight." She wiped her eyes and grabbed her thick glasses.

She smelled delightful. "Stella, Stella, I have to talk with you." She caressed his face, kissed him, pulled him into bed with her and, as they wrapped their arms around each other, he search for succor.

Stella gushed, "I have something wonderful to tell you."

He interrupted her. "Stella, you're my best and only friend, I love you so much."

"I know. I love you too," she said. "But what is it at this hour? We have to be quiet. No more *you know,*" Stella cautioned. "But we can do this," she said, sliding her hand into his pants. She'd taken over her brother's small bedroom. All that had gone wrong for Chaim evaporated as they released their sexual energies. Afterwards, entwined, he whispered into her ear. "I have to tell you something."

"It's okay," she calmed and hugged him. He felt so secure, so loved.

"I don't know where to start," he said and tears welled in his eyes.

"Your mother again?"

"I feel... feel... so ashamed."

"What happened?"

Selectively, he recapped how he wound up like rime on her windowsill, but he remained cautious about the truth, the whole Nedda truth.

"So, after fucking her all summer, she wants you to kill her husband? Chaim, this has to stop. You can't think only of yourself, at least not with me."

"Okay, I won't see her again... like that," he promised.

"Wait until I tell my mother about this," Stella said.

"You're gonna talk to your mother about this?" He was incredulous. "I can't believe you'd talk about this with your mother?"

"Chaim, mothers and daughters talk. I tell her everything!"

"Everything? Not in my family. We don't talk about anything," he said.

He encircled her torso and held her close in a blanketed cocoon that held their chrysalis of their future together and, finally, he slept.

At daylight, Mary, tall, statuesque, thin, stood in the doorway wearing a Navajo-patterned, Pendleton bathrobe. "Good morning, you two." Mother Mary, backlighted by the sun, had a halo behind her and radiated goodness, her wedding-set diamond, a memory of things past, glinted on her right ring finger. Her sprinkled cinnamon freckles on her cheeks and nose she shared with Stella.

Chaim's back stiffened, embarrassed. He pulled the quilt to his neck, averting her face. "It's okay, Chaim. It's a small house. I'm jealous, though. I wish I had someone," she kidded. "I'll fix breakfast. The boys'll be up soon. You like pancakes and bacon? You eat bacon?"

Chaim nodded. "I love bacon."

Then Mrs. O'Shannahan added, "I went to Vassar, yes, but that was just good fortune. I came up the hard way, Chaim. I understand all of this and

211

none of it surprises me. You're just a boy becoming a man and that's how boys *become* men. Fortunately, this will all work out just fine... now."

Stella said, "It'll be okay, Chaim." In the background he heard strains from a Chopin sonata... a Horowitz recording.

"What do you mean?" he asked, amazed that she didn't see his conduct as morally putrid.

"Stella didn't tell you?" Surprised, she glanced at her daughter and smiled. Chaim looked at Stella.

"That bit of news I had to tell you? Yesterday, my period came. I'm not pregnant... and," she pulled out a gray packet of Enovid, "my mother got me these."

"Too much holiday fun, too much twistin' 'n turnin'. winked Mother Madonna, "and maybe Elvis and all that Bandstand commotion. He'd make me late, just lookin' at him."

Chaim felt his burdens vanish with their kindness and was astonished with Mary's open expression of her own sexual desires.

"I was looking forward to being a grandmother, but not now. Stella's *my* love child."

"What a nice mommie!" Stella said, blowing a kiss to her mother. After waffles, sausages and bacon, the boys clamored all over like monkeys. Chaim really liked them. It felt so good to be with a family.

Chaim's spirits and penis perked up as she slipped off her flannel nighty with the Curious George pictures. He and Stella took a shower. This family seemed to function well without secrets and deceptions. He lathered Stella's red hair and she caressed him in the steam. They shared nearsightedness, both wearing teaseable, thick prescriptions, but in their ardor they'd retained their glasses, so he removed both pairs while kissing her torso all the while and rubbed her face.

In the spongy air she blinked a few times and, his vision unaided, he noticed that her green eyes seemed so much smaller, unmagnified by lenses. "I can't believe you told your mother about all this... and she got you birth control pills."

"That's how it is when we love a person, Chaim," she said, matter-of-factly. She was so sure, so certain. Her care for him felt like summer sunshine, the way he felt in the cornfield that previous summer.

He wondered what it would be like to feel such parental love, to be enveloped like that. He felt so hollow, as if that part of him, which he knew should be there, was absent. Something changed. "Why are you crying?"

Her back muscles stiffened. "I want to understand all that you told me. First, you've been seeing Nedda through the summer and never mentioned a word to me about what the two of you have been doing?" Tears streamed down her cheeks.

"Nnnnot all summer. I mmet her first, before I even knew you."

"One day?"

"I saw her at the Club but we didn't really, well, you know, until August, when she gave me the kaleidoscope."

"One day, Chaim. It was one day."

Chaim did not like this interrogation and slid his leg between hers as the water sprayed over them. Her thighs snapped closed with the vigor of the steel jaws of a muskrat body trap.

"She gave you a lot more than that kaleidoscope. Then, you and I met and we, uh, you know."

"Yeah."

"Then came the Meyers family, and we went over to Nedda's, and Mr. B went nuts...and you never mentioned that the two of you had been playing ping-pong, as you call it." She was as steamed as the shower mist. "And now she wants *you* to kill her husband? She picked *you* for this assignment?"

"I don't have to *do* any killing, jjjjust show him the books... to Mr. Calamari." He neglected the fact that this was already a done deal, that he was deceiving her.

"He's that big pig at Chubby's," she said.

"A big, nasty, dangerous pig," he said.

"But you will set in motion forces that will kill this man? How can you ignore that, at some point, someone will kill you? Or us? These people didn't go to Miss Vanilla's School of Charm, Chaim."

He hung his head. Her calm worried him. Then, whispering, "Meanwhile, your mother hates me because I'm Catholic? What an irony. You Jews are God's People and you behave like this?" He was getting ill wondering where this might be going. He depended upon her, needed her.

She continued to piece together the factual history. "Then, after our New Year's together, you went over to see *her*? To fuck her? After *our* evening in Philly? Chaim, that evening meant something to me! And she was nearly dead? You pulled her from the bathtub?"

"Are we breaking up?" The shower water turned cold.

"No. We're having a shower and a chat, but I want to know what I face." She squirmed. "I'm pretty pissed. I feel...so betrayed, so used. Am I just a convenient sperm receptacle, like one of your... rubbers?" Icy water shocked them as she fumed. "Let's get out of here. We've used up all the warm water and Mother Mary Magdalene's next."

Could he salvage anything here? He wrapped her in a Turkish bath towel hoping this filigreed explanation would satisfy her. "She showed you this, this treasure trove, and she asked you to *kill* her husband?"

"Not *kill*, exactly. I didn't have any choice."

Stella laughed. "Oh, now I understand. She... she extorted you... told you if you wanted to continue fucking her that you had to kill her husband? How do I ever trust you? This is insane. We can't tell my mother this. She'd go to the cops."

"So what do I do? I'm in this, and I can't get out!"

"I? Hey, buddy boy, it's not 'I.' It's *we're* in this together— or not me. They know who I am, too." She thought a moment. "Whose hand was it?"

Chaim shook his head. "I haven't seen anyone walking around with one hand. I guess the rest of him is in a worse predicament."

"Don't try to get out of this by being funny. Then he pulls you out of the ditch and gives you a hundred bucks and tells you that you're gonna do work for him?"

"I've been working for Chubby, you know, on the bbbbackhoe, ddddigging a few holes, and I made some deliveries for Uncle Johnny... just a few. No big deal. I needed new tires."

"So for the price of a few tires, you're willing to whack a guy? Johnny is Johnny The Squid, Uncle Johnny Calamari, the way you say it? That Johnny? Being on the same continent with those guys is wrong. Don't you *see* this?"

She blazed. "You need new glasses! Drugs? Money? Murder! What? What else? There's more to this. I know that. You're gonna get killed. Chaim, we're gonna get killed. I'm gonna get killed." Then she cried.

He wondered. Should I tell her about what I didn't tell her about? Nedda's baby?

"Chaim! Do you think you're James Bond? You're in this up to your ass! And he knows... about *me*! This isn't Ian Fleming, Chaim. This is real!"

"It'll be all right." And he hadn't told her that he'd already done the deal, that Calamari had the bank books.

"Chaim, if Harry dies, you're a murderer. How can we talk about life together when you're killing a guy?"

"I'm not killing him. I just..."

"How can you be a doctor? I... can't be with a murderer. Oh, my god, Chaim!"

His anguish over possibly losing her was too much. "No more Nedda," he said with affirmation, but how could he keep this promise?

"*No more Nedda*," she confirmed.

"Give back the bank books. Let her kill her own husband. Why did you agree to do this? Do you... love her?"

"He was so bad to her," he justified. "He almost killed her, Stella."

Mary tapped on the door, interrupting them. "You two okay?"

"Yeah, Mom. Just fiiiine." Stella said, sarcastically. Then, she sobbed on her bed, wiping her tears and muffling her sobs, pulling her Curious George doll around her head.

***

Queen Clorox hung in the air. It was Friday, January the third, 1964. With any luck, his parents would be somewhere else. Arthur had carpooled to Philly for work at the Veteran's Administration, and Evalyn's car was absent. He hoped that she was gone for the day. He wanted to go to his bed, pull the covers over his head and... die. Inside, he felt like badly scraped knees.

As the World Turns raged on the Philco in the living room. She must be around, he surmised. An empty pack of Raleigh's lay crumpled on the kitchen table. She must have gone out for cigarettes. He slipped into his bedroom. Elijah's bags were gone, but on Chaim's desk he found a small rosewood box with ornate gold inlay, presumably one which Uncle Elijah left.

Pulling it apart he discovered that he'd nestled the precious pocket watch and gold chain. There was a penciled note in Yiddish. Chaim wound the watch, slipped it beneath his pillow, and listened to its heart beat.

Without warning, she swung open his bedroom door. Like a banshee, she'd nailed him. Worse than Karen Phillippo, she'd caught him, cock in hand, stroking. He shot his wad a foot into the air and it came down, splat. Boingo!

She pounced on him, beating him with both fists. "What's wrong with you? You're a sex pervert! How could you do this to me? I'll get you a whore over in Trenton, goddammit. What's wrong with you?"

Across his chest she lay, pinning him, as his poor penis shriveled to the size of a miniature snack hot-dog, the kind of *hors d'oeuvre* they serve wrapped in dough at *bar mitzvahs*. He couldn't move, but he was very strong and freed himself. He shoved her away, pulled on his Delaware High sweatpants, the ones with the falcon on the left thigh, and stood there as she raved. Again, she offered to get him a whore over in Trenton. Her other major threat was "I'll take you to a psychiatrist!" He stifled his laugh.

"The ovens at Auschwitz haven't even cooled and you do this?" she raged, but what was she upset about? As she yelled, he retreated to music and lyrics:

When love comes so strong,

There is no right or wrong,

Your love is your life.

"I have to show my face at Rosenberg's. How could you do this? This is the last straw." Then it came, her blockbuster, her ultimate threat. "You're going to a... a... psychiatrist!"

"Mom, nnnnno one knows! Nnnno one knnnnows!" he repeated.

"What are you going to do?"

"Stella's nnnot pregnant, she had her period!"

"Oh, great! So, no problem? No twins?"

"No twins. There's no twins, Mom!"

"Elijah said that there were twins? He said, *'Zwillingen'*, twins!"

"No twins, Mom. There are *two women*; *each*, pregnant! Two *different* women! *Nicht Zwillingen*! Iiiii tttttthhhhhought I ggggot two women pregnant," he stuttered. It was out.

"*Oy vey*! Can it get worse! Two? Two women! How did you do this? Who's the other lucky woman? I'll beat the living shit out of you right now if you don't tell me. I have to know. I'm your mother. You have to tell me."

"Mmm... missus Boudreaux."

"Oh, my God! Nedda Boudreaux? I thought so. She was the one who wanted her driveway done, wasn't she? I guess you plowed more than her driveway. Chaimala, don't you *know* who she is? What the hell's wrong with you? She's Calamari's woman, Johnny the Squid's mistress. He's been *stupping* her... since God knows when."

Evalyn cried uncontrollably in between her vile threats and exhortations. "He'll kill you! He'll kill your father. He'll kill all of us. Don't you know about him? That's why they call him Johnny the Squid. He lurks in all that blackness, all that ink. Oh my God, what have you done? Oh, honey, he'll kill your sister."

As far as he knew, he'd been merely having Meaningless Sex 101 with a beautiful woman. He had no inkling about her and Johnny. Calamari, with his many tentacles could cut off his fingers, his genitalia, tear out his tongue, cut off his lips. He'd never play trumpet again, especially if he cut off his hands... the way they'd done with whoever owned that hand.

"Calamari's gonna find out and when he does— and when he does— he's gonna kill you... and us. He'll rape your sister." She repeated, tearfully, "He'll *rape* your sister." She clutched her chest. "*Oy vey!*" She burped loudly. "Is that what you want?" She clutched her chest.

"Mom! Mom!" he screamed, scared, remembering Anna when she dropped dead.

"I'm okay, Honey." She buckled, theatrical, but with real gripping pain. "It's nothing serious, honey... just my ulcer... it's bleeding," she asserted. "Oh, honey!" Weak, she made her way to the bathroom, hung her head into the toilet and spewed bright, red blood and gastric contents.

Chaim relived Anna's and Nedda's cataclysms. "Mom! I'll call an ambulance. Mom! Oh, my God, Mom! Don't die." He felt so culpable for all of this. He held her shoulders as she let loose again.

What had he done? *Oy vey! Zvvvvvvvvilllingen!* echoed in his head. He was the master of disaster, destroying everyone and everything in his path. Oh, Uncle Elijah, what have you done? *Zvvvvvvvvilllingen!* His mother was right. He should never say a word about nothing. Never tell anyone what you are thinking. Trust no one. Mahler's bah, bah, bah, baaaahhh reverberated in his head. Then, the *Shofar... teki'ah gedolah.*

12

Chump Change

He reverberated with worry like a tympani head as he wiped her cheeks, lifting her face from the toilet bowl. Fourteen years later, when his own life fell into ashes, he'd reflect that she'd been his first patient. How he did love her. At that moment, then, pulling her away from drowning in the white toilet bowl, he keened for his devastated childhood, and asked for her life to be spared. Again, she erupted.

He ministered her and thought of that mustard plaster she had cemented to his back when he was so young. How angry he'd been with the pain, but she had meant well. Then she had soothed his blistered skin with Crisco and wiped away his tears. That was how her love always came: pain and soothing. And when he told her about Jeffrey raping him, she slapped his face in disbelief. His lips bled, and that was her love, too. He should drown her as he'd done with his sister's black kitty.

He tugged fretfully at his pillow that night, repositioning his arms and legs as night terrors pricked him like the wicked glass shards from his car windshield. Fat fingers with bloody fingernails grabbed him, massive arms with tattoos of threatening demons and devils and dragons darted past... and he saw a ghastly port-wine splotch on Calamari's face... looking like a distorted garden vegetable.

Enmeshed in glistening Brylcreamed hairdos, he heard dissonant Mahlerian church bells in f-sharp minor, the din of Scotch glasses tinkling, waves cresting from martinis' sloshing olives with red pimentos, all of it peeking at him like malformed, engorged clitori, Manhattans and Rob Roys all set in neat rows, and all of this chummed his sleep into smithereens and splintereens with harsh sounds of bones crushing and gnashing knuckles crunching and someone hidden in the penumbra of it all with a meat cleaver, hacking off his right hand... wild libidinous women. He jolted awake.

What if Harry the Bee got nuts and did come after him? Had he gotten so far into this, taking Stella with him, that he, *they*, couldn't get out? What would happen when generous Uncle Johnny turned back into the rapacious Mr. Calamari and would no longer accept a clever juke for an answer?

How much sadness could he endure? He felt as if he had swum into the deepest, darkest cave; a spelunker without a headlamp. I'm just a kid, he protested.

Dreaming again, his mother snoring by his side, he rebuked his errant penis, which he felt had nearly killed Neddy. You mischievous wise guy, he railed. He took a scissors to continue where the *moile* left off. Capped mushrooms danced... He would kill this miscreant troll that controlled him. You got me into this, you incorrigible rapscallion. You must die, he said in his dream. Then, dreaming, the tension passed and he nuzzled between her legs sucking her, his tongue where it shouldn't be, adoring her... but who? His mother? Nedda... Stella?

She stirred. "*Oy vey*, Honey, I still feel sick. You got *two* women pregnant?"

"Mom, Stella was never pregnant. She just missed her period."

"But, but," she sputtered in disbelief. "The other? Mrs. Boudreaux? But, how? You know there are things to prevent this!"

"That's what I was doing in your bedroom that day. I was looking," he responded timorously, recalling his sadistic moments poking holes in her diaphragm. Should he tell her?

"For what?" she asked.

Overcoming the deepest shame, he told her. When he finished, she revived with a cigarette, smoke then curled through her nostrils and she said, "*Oy vey iz mir*. So what are we going to do? She's Johnny Calamari's girlfriend, *Kussi*. Everyone knows that. What's *she* gonna do? Is she mad at you? Does Uncle Johnny know?" She muttered. "No. If he knew... *we'd all be dead*," answering her own question. "I'll have to get him some money. Where can I get that sort of money?"

"Mom, we're all friends," he protested. "I can trust her. I have no idea if Mr. Calamari knows or what he knows. He doesn't know that we've been seeing each other."

"You only hope." Angry, then. "You know, for a smart Jew boy, you're an idiot! Three can keep a secret if two are dead. You can trust no one! Have you learned nothing?" Evalyn sniffed and tears returned. Chaim braced. "That man... do you know *what* that man is, Calamari? He's *Mengele*. We need the *Moshiach*."

As if that hadn't been enough guilt, she tore his heart apart with her sobbing. "I don't want to lose you!" she wailed. "I can't lose you. You're my only son. You carry on our name, our Jewish name. You can't marry *goyim*. My grandchildren will not be Jewish. You can't. It'll kill me. You're my only son. You came from me, you are me. You have my blood in you. Promise me, Chaim."

She grabbed his right hand and placed it directly on her breasts, covered by an apron. "Feel my heartbeat. You will stop my heart if you do this. My heart is yours." She was so impassioned. "You will stop my heart, and we will both die. You must give them up. If you continue, I'll say *Kadish*, and for me, you will be dead."

Shrill anger boiled. "Is that what you want?" Shaking, then, "Do I have to kill you?" she asked, and delivered an installment on that threat with a vicious backhand across his face.

"Okay. Okay. You won't lose me," he whined holding his cheek. She'd knocked his glasses to the floor. As he picked them up, he knew that what she asked was not possible. She'd mortally shamed him.

"You are not going to take that whore to the prom! Assimilation is destroying our people and you are not going to the prom... not with... her!"

She went on and on. "I'll tell you something, too, Buster! One day, she'll look at you and call you a dirty Jew! Mark my words." The words flayed his soul. "You can't take that whatshername, Estelle, to the prom! That's it. *Fertig*! *Genug*. No more of that girl... and stay away from that Mrs. Boudreaux. Do you hear me? I'll find you a date!"

With her left hand, as she'd done in the past, she imprisoned again his right hand on her left breast, over her heart. He was humiliated with his handful of maternal tit. She noticed the morning sun glint off something in his bed. "What's that?" she asked, picking up Uncle Elijah's watch and chain. "Where did you get this?" she accused, suspicious, as with his gift kaleidoscope, always mistrusting. He felt raped, as when Jeffrey violated him.

"Uncle Elijah left it for me." Here, read this note."

"It's in Yiddish," she observed, inspecting the penciling in ancient scroll and translated:

Tzatzkela, this is for you. My father gave it to me for my Bar Mitzvah, and I pass it on to you… plus a little something else.
Love, your uncle, Elijah.

"What do we tell Dad?" he wondered aloud.

Without missing a beat, she confabulated, "I'll just tell your father that Uncle Elijah made…a mistake. Yes, that'll work. I'll tell him that you told Elijah you were *dating* two girls, not *mating*. Yes, an honest language confusion. He doesn't have to know. He'll believe it. Uncle Elijah, after all, he's such a story teller. We must not upset your father and this will make him happy. Ahaaa, dating, not mating. Easy to confuse." She swaggered in her triumphant arrogance, brewing her clever deception, delusional that someone might accept such a ruse.

The boy watched this mother at work, dazzled at her expertise, creating an *honest language confusion* in her sea of mendacity. "I have to keep the peace," she said. What difference did fact or truth make if the lies maintained the peace? The lies were like control rods in a nuclear reactor, keeping the reaction from destruction. *Exitus acta probat.*

After reading *1984*, and under his mother's baton, he'd polished his Orwellian double-speak, seeing truth-telling as inconsequential and expediency and calm as the most utilitarian goals. As long as the lies maintained an illusion of serenity, of harmony and quiet, the home was happy. His conclusions? Truth created disaster; lies insured tranquility. Lies were good; truth was evil. Lies were better than truth.

But Chaim, child on his quest to manhood, knew right from wrong. He had that right. Truth is like a mathematical proof, Q.E.D. Truth had to eventually supersede lies, or the world order would fall apart. But why? Truth was the fallen soldier in his family's neurotic battles. He could ignore that only so long.

The pair entered the kitchen. Their nimbus clouds cleared like a lifting weather front, and she chopped up a banana, added sour cream, and sprinkled on a healthy dose of sugar. "For sweetness in life," she said, then, setting it before him, told him, "I always feed you first."

She was bone tired. "I'm going to take a nap, *Kussilah,*" she sighed but, first, with a knitting needle, she popped a hole in the pole of an egg. "Do you think these other kids have a mother who works the way I do for you? You have clean sheets, washed and ironed clothes, and a good breakfast every day. No one has a kitchen this clean. You can eat from this floor. This, I created for you. This is what makes you successful."

She descended into her familiar soliloquy. "Here, look at my hands," she offered, opening her raw, bleach-damaged palms. "I would sell my body in Trenton if I had to, to get you food or clothes...to make you a doctor. I'd be a whore for you." Putting her lips on the shell, she glutched down the egg yolk, emptying the contents in one revolting slurp. Chaim thought about crushing that robin's egg as she drained life out of that white, chicken's egg, draining his life along with that yolk.

"It's good for my stomach. But this is what you do to me. My ulcer. Never forget that you are my son. On my knees, I scrub these floors for you. I get down on my hands and knees and wash these floors for you. I scrub your shit out of the toilet with my bare hands... for who? You! For you! I haven't bought underwear in years. I borrow jewelry. I work so that you will go to college, so *you* can become a doctor."

She whispered, "This is what it means to me to be a mother; *your* mother! For you. I beg you, do not abandon me. All I ask is that you do one thing for me... only one thing. You break up with that girl. I don't care what you do with that slut Nedda, but you cannot marry a *Shiksa*. You will kill me!" She punctuated this by lighting another cigarette, taking deep, portentous, drags.

She cradled his face into her two hands, the way Uncle Elijah did, and looked him dead on in her eyes. She looked into a soft face, one with the lightest beard, one that barely needed shaving, "Marry a *shiksa*, and you will kill me."

She kissed him full and wet on the lips, running her tongue between his lips, rubbing his torso, drawing him near. Chaim stiffened and pushed her away. She grabbed his face again. "Say it!" she threatened. "Say it, or I'll smack you again."

"Mom, I love you," he said reluctantly.

"… and…"

"… more than…anybody else."

"Kiss me," she demanded and he did. "On the lips." She held his face. And he did. Her kisses were punishment by submission.

He was powerless against her, like Superman buckling against kryptonite. Surfacing like an out of air diver, he had to make it to August with his escape to L.A. with Stella, and he'd never return.

***

When sunrise finally came, the clouds luminesced, all dressed in pale yellows and reds, creating a scene from Nedda's bedroom like her René Genis watercolor. He hadn't slept much and felt dreadful, hung over, as he crunched his L.L. Bean's through the brittle ice and hard snow on the Delaware's banks, stumbling along, dejected, alienated.

He came upon a rusted steel body trap with a muskrat frozen solid, its front legs snapped, with a ghastly *risus sardonicus* showing its incisors. *Ondatra zibethicus*, he recited, like a prayer; its Latin name. In the middle of the river, a beaver family swam upstream. *Castor canadensis*, he noted.

How much like that muskrat he felt; trapped, like his sister's kitty in that pickle jar. As a child, his mother tortured him by pulling down his pants and she'd smack his turtle and dumplings, as she called his genitalia. The memory was too excruciating. Following his latest skirmish in his Pubic Wars, he felt purple, as purple as Nedda's arm, battered and mushy like an overripe purple plum.

He wanted to kill her, to exact retribution for all that he'd suffered. She'd get hers with that perforated diaphragm. She was a rodent, and she deserved to suffer, to die, in a steel muskrat trap. When she got pregnant with that faulty diaphragm she'd have to bite off her legs to get free of that surprise. She could find her own way to a Trenton abortionist.

In his mental funhouse mirrors the reflection he saw was a distorted image, that of his eggplant father, a Jewish *nebbish*, a *putz*, a useless failure, a rabbit. He did not want such a life. He had to be more... like Catholics, like those who seemed perpetually unruffled, diamond glazed, who wore plaids, whose smiles showed off their toothy, joyous grins, exposing rich, healthy gums, like the Kennedys.

Economic survival was never a concern for them. They never felt a wolf at their door. They had old money, they had new money, they had money. No one killed six million of their *mishpochah*. No one wanted to exterminate them. They were God's chosen people, not the Jews.

It was bitter, ten degrees, near sundown, wind blustering, and all the ducks and geese had gone south. How had he gotten sucked into this mob vortex? And this craziness with his mother. Now, clutched in winter's fist like Mr. B's grip, he made his way through the crusted ice and snow, reliving summer and his first night with Nedda, Harry the Bee's wife.

Then, he thought of Stella. This was their place, where he and Stella intertwined all summer long, where the Pennsy lumbered, serving the Fairless Works. He looked at the trestle where they'd watched the train fly by, lying on their backs, watching the train overhead, where Stella flipped up her tee shirt and he saw her symmetrical cone-shaped, porcelain breasts, each capped with a sweet raspberry.

What a glorious insouciant summer it had been, resplendent with the flowers. Wistfully, wishing for summer's return, his skin chilled as he walked along on the ice, downriver from where Washington crossed the Delaware, Christmas Eve of 1776.

Skipping flat stones across the ice and out into the water, he repeated *mea culpa*, *mea maxima culpa*, and breathed to himself, inhaling the frosty, desolate, lonely air at the river's edge, the dead souls from Washington's army looking on knowingly. They knew revolution, upheaval for justice, those men of wisdom; cousins, as they were, to the paintings, the captured history in Nedda's paintings. He wished he had a cap as he warmed his ears and nose with his gloved hands. What a fiasco his truth had become.

He wanted to go to college and become a physician. He had simple choices. He could tote a stethoscope in medical school or an M-16 in Vietnam's rice paddies. He'd get drafted for sure when he turned eighteen if he didn't go to college on his pathway to medicine. His mother inserted her pry bar into his life's concerns like someone opening a can of paint. He felt as if things would start popping off, like snapping violin strings.

Without warning, the ice gave way and in he went, like the diver in the caves, hitting the deep river bottom. He shoved off the silt, then bouncing up, beneath the ice, swimming towards a light spot... as when he crashed his car. On the surface, he'd lost his glasses, sputtered, and was terribly cold, bones aching.

Once he made his way to the river bank, miraculously, he found his glasses in a fold in his jacket, then he spotted a Galzerano hearse driving along the frontage road. In the tiring light, he waved to them but the hearse flashed its lights, honked, and kept going. At least I'm not *in* the hearse, he rationalized when he returned to the Clot, shivering.

He recited Frost's verse:

Whose woods these are I think I know.

His house is in the village, though;

He will not see me stopping here

To watch his woods fill up with snow.

Shivering, he ran the heat up all the way, but the windows fogged, and he remained very cold but grateful that he'd survived this spelunking.

***

"I fell in the river," he told her. He wanted her. He needed sex. Sex would make him feel better. He needed food, too.

"Come over here— right— now. I have to talk to you." Nedda was emphatic and not listening to a word he'd uttered. "No. Don't say anything." Her speech was unclear. Did he detect a slur? "Juss come over here. I neeeeed you."

When he arrived, she looked at him, disheveled. "You really *did* fall in the river." Then, setting that aside she demanded, "You have to drive me."

"I'm soaked," he protested.

She bobbled in the foyer. "It's okay. Just drive me. Wear Harry's clothes," she insisted. He'd promised Stella that Nedda was out of the picture, but he couldn't help himself... he needed her in the worst way.

"Where to?" he asked as she led him to her husband's dresser, from which he selected a full change. The clothes were far too big. "The shoes won't fit," he said. "Too big."

"No one can fill those shoes," she smirked. "Ping's clothes'll work."

Ping's clothes were in Harry's closet. "That's Pierre Cardin," she said, pointing to a black tuxedo, then she installed studs with bold diamond cufflinks in the heavily starched shirt, saying, "These are Harry's... keep 'em. He doesn't need them."

"Where're we going?" he asked. Nothing with Nedda was unadorned or simple.

"Here," she said, handing him a pair of gleaming black crocodile formal shoes. "Wear these. Ping wears these for dinner parties. The Governor came to the last one, and Kurt Vonnegut attended." As they walked through the kitchen, she embraced him. "You look like James Bond."

Chaim turned over the engine in her bulky, black, Mercedes 600 with ruby red leather interior. He felt so royal behind that wheel. She held a large crystal, MB snifter, full of Courvoisier VSOP. It was a dark, moonless night.

Finger-pointing directions between sips, she directed him to where death became art: 3500 Bristol-Oxford Valley Road, Galzerano's Mortuary. "Drive to the back," she ordered. This was Bucks County's largest mortuary, family owned by Calamari's sister-in-law's family. Lou Galzerano and Johnny Calamari were tight and, unlike Dr. Palumbo, dealing with living situations, Galzerano handled the other side of the coin. In one way or another, it was all in the family: life and death.

Chaim piloted her land-yacht Mercedes to the back parking lot. A bank of lights glared. He panicked, surprised, and exclaimed, "Whatthefuck!" He knew that this could be the sort of situation from which some people do not leave, except processed *through* the mortuary.

"Don't worry. Dis ain't about you. It's a social gathering. They like you, kid," she said, lapsing comfortably into her Sout' Jersey accent, kissing his cheek. She handed him the last of her Courvoisier. "Finish it," she ordered. "You'll need it." Wow, she was edgy.

It looked like a Lon Chaney "gangsta" movie with fifty gorillas, each in black, each, thug-like, milling around. Many puffed hefty cigars, with gun outlines like misplaced sporrans bulging beneath their black jackets.

The party moved into a capacious room with a slab concrete floor and a drain hole in the center, and on two sides of the room, against the wall, there were six stainless steel, gleaming cremation ovens. Stark. Nedda squeezed his forearm. "It's okay. Just wait." Potted dead lilies, asters, mums, roses and carnations, all white, looking like dead soldiers, lined the floor along the walls.

Chubby asked his cronies, "Is he here?"

"Where is he?" came back the crowd murmur.

Nedda wore a luxurious black mink coat, neck to ankles, a white ermine hat, very chic, with six inch "fuck me" heels, black, patent leather. And between top and bottom were her glorious legs and torso, as if a morsel from a Dior advertisement in *Life Magazine*. She delighted when the men gaped at her, much like her show at Anna's funeral.

A dozen gym-fresh bodyguards, each with a Kalashnikov, banana clip in place, stood at the ready. Chaim worried where this was headed as a black 1963 Mercedes, an *S-Klasse Grosse Heckflosse*, windows black-tinted, slowly entered the drive, scraping the undercarriage as it bounced over the concrete lip and berthed like a yacht.

The driver and four more guards took their positions behind the car as Don Calamari stepped out. He looked like Black Mike Sylva in Cheney's 1920 role in *Outside the Law*.

Stella slipped out. "Chaim! Chaim!" she called out terrified, then clinging to him.

Mr. Calamari said, "Putz, sometimes I gotta have insurance."

He and Stella hugged. "I'm okay," she assured him.

"I'm so sorry, Stella, for dragging you into all this." She gripped his hand.

"It's okay. I'm okay. I'm here with you, with us," Stella said.

Donny Fiasco, from Chubby's below-the-ground operations, shouldered a huge AK. He was big, a robot, and an easy six-foot, seven, three hundred and fifty pounds with a flattop.

The Calamari massif, looking like Sicily's Mount Etna, stood in sartorial splendor, with a blood red lining to his jacket, stark in contrast against the shiny, brushed, stainless steel ovens. He wore a pearl white shirt, black tie with a gold stickpin, housing at least a five-carat diamond, and his right pinky sported a smaller diamond ring set in gold. Mr. LaGuardia lighted the boss' cigar and, appearing so relaxed in this element, he puffed the *Hoyo de Monterrey* into flame.

Chaim thought about that day he squashed his fingers. That was the same cigar smell. Pictures of ovens at *Auschwitz* and *Bergen Belsen* passed like movie film over the sprockets in his mind as he chilled, drawing Stella near.

"*Amicos*, thank youse for comin'." Mr. Calamari welcomed many of the men individually, paying some compliments. "Mr. Puzo, nice job for us over in New Brunswick wit dem guys from Bayonne, and Mr. Evangilisti... your daughter liked my wedding gift?"

Nedda narrated, "Uncle Johnny took out her old boyfriend."

The master was dapper, suave, and worked the crowd in Jimmy Hoffa's cordial and affable style. "Dere's a message here. Everyone's gotta know da rules. Have a drink." Don Johnny presided.

"Everyone from the East Coast is here," Nedda told Chaim and Stella.

"A little business. I am pleased to announce that Mr. Rintala's takin' over Asian shipping. He don't know no Chinese, but he knows his way around Customs." He encircled Aku's shoulders with his brawny arm. "There has been a vacancy, as many of you know, and Mr. Rintala will fill it." The crowd clapped approval, many laughing. Chaim surmised that there was some *in* joke. What did he not know? "Now, everyone fill up!"

Clearing his throat with another sip of Scotch, Uncle Johnny continued. "Dis is a sad evening. Ahhh, maybe not," he smirked. Someone, *sotto voce*, translated English into Italian to a few fellas. "Make sure they unnerstan' my jokes," he said to the translator.

A hearse dieseled into the lot, bouncing a bit, too, as it rolled over the driveway lip, then backing towards the ovens. Six pallbearers hoisted the body bag onto a stainless-steel gurney. They really strained. "Who's in the body bag?" wondered Chaim aloud, and Nedda responded with her index finger over her lips.

"We're sayin' good-bye to a brother, a man who made a few mistakes, and such mistakes are regrettable, but unfortunately not forgettable, not forgivable," Uncle Johnny continued.

"Looey da G." Mr. Galzerano, zipped open the bag. Chaim nearly barfed and Stella squeezed his arm. The body had been hacked and slabs of meat hung from the corpse.

"Harold Boudreaux was my friend until I found out he liked vanilla ice cream, he really liked it, and he tried to set his-self up over in Trenton with his own ice cream parlor wit' our money." Mr. Calamari raised the bank books. "There's no secrets, my friends... and stashing money in foreign bank accounts, it jus' ain't safe."

Stella blanched. What Chaim had done, ratting out Harry to Johnny, got this man killed. Chaim sickened, knowing that Stella would make that conclusion.

Calamari continued. "I do not have competitors. My money's, my money; my ice cream's, my ice cream. Youse guys do pretty well wit me, pretty, pretty, pretty well. This is not goooood. A very unfortunate accident." He punctuated his point like a percussionist by cracking his knuckles, crunching, like holiday walnuts.

Nedda leaned into Chaim saying, "'*This* is whatthefuck'sgoin'on,'" and with droll self-satisfaction, she smiled.

"Road kill," someone called out.

"Sonofabitch," another called.

Harry's left hand was gone.

"Animal," someone commented, and many cupped hands over their mouth to stifle laughter ... or vomiting, or both.

"He took his own life when he saw how wrong he was about some of his decisions," said Uncle Johnny. There was a distinct violaceous bullet entry wound at the back of the head and the left eye was blown away. How he must have suffered, Chaim empathized.

Calamari's facial tensions showed his wrath. "He took his own life," he repeated. "He was glad to die. Guilt does that. Very sad. So now we will say good-bye to our misguided brother *who took his own life*. Mr. LaGuardia, you singa his last song."

LaGuardia's tears at the end were theatrical perfection. "That's *Vesti La Giuba* from *Il Pagliacci*," Chaim explained to Stella, recognizing the aria, "about the clown tormented by the suicide of his unfaithful wife."

Nedda whispered to Stella and Chaim. "My dad named me after the clown's wife, the soprano. I selected the aria. It's fitting, don't you think?" Nedda was as much a backstage manipulator as was Calamari, the varlet. It was as if Chaim roomed in a pit of cobras. Stella looped her arm tighter into Chaim's arm. She dressed L.L. Bean; Nedda wore Pierre Cardin. He took comfort in wearing Ping's tuxedo. Anything less would have appeared disrespectful and parsimonious.

He compared smells. Stella's fragrance was milky, natural, fresh, chocolate, like M&M's. Nedda was expensive cognac with *L'Heure Bleue*. Mr. Calamari jolted him back by rapping on his glass with a shining dirk he pulled from beneath his coat. "Mrs. Boudreaux, it's your time."

Center-stage, in dramatic Nedda fashion, she began. "This man raped me." Tough guys quailed. Part of her was able to cut dangerously close to their bones. Chaim squeezed Nedda's arm and, on his other side, Stella gripped his hand. He flashed on Nedda's torpid image in the bathtub, submerged, near death, her mottled skin, her aphotic eyes. He couldn't get that image out of his memory.

Calamari withdrew a black, Louisville Slugger and extended it to her, handle first. "Our men do not assault our women," he said. Nedda removed her mink, handed it to Chaim, and gave her white ermine hat to Stella. Nedda's figure-hugging, red lamé YSL dress was breathtaking. Fifty men creamed. On her right leg, an angry blue-yellow bruise showed through the side slit in the dress.

A string of lustrous, natural, Mikimoto pearls with an eighteen-karat gold clasp encircled her refined neck. In each earlobe set a dazzling, two-carat diamond earring. She had lovely, sculpted hands with tapering fingers which, in candlelight, he recalled, had encircled him.

Nedda proclaimed, "Out, out, damned spot," and brought the bat down across Harry's mutilated face, bashing his brains out the back end, like cauliflower. The cranial vault gave way, tissues weakened by putrefaction, splurting, sounding like a collapsing, dropped watermelon. Blood, brains, and pus, splattered poor Mr. LaGuardia, who had not repositioned after Pagliacci's final notes.

"We are *famiglia*! Share wit' your family. Don't none of youse guys ever forget dis. Do not steal money from *La Famiglia*," spoke the *Capo di tutti capi*. "Don't none of youse rape our women."

Calamari gave Nedda the severed left hand which she then flopped onto Harry's chest, the hand still bearing his wedding band and added her gold band in the palm. A loud cork pop came from a bottle of Remy Martin, Louis XIII cognac and Nedda anointed the corpse with a gush of this holy water. The cost, Chaim knew well, since he'd signed the delivery invoices: $10,000 a bottle.

Stella stood there, pupils dilated, freckles aglow. "How were you involved in all this?" she asked, deeply perturbed, grimacing. Chaim preferred to concentrate on the dead flowers, but she pinched him.

When Lou fired up the glinting Shivang Cremator Number I, manufactured in Gujarat, India, it was as if Beelzebub arrived, laughing. Mr. Calamari lifted his hand to flip a shiny, newly-minted penny onto the corpse. Johnny quipped, "He's worth at least that much now." Fire and ice, he thought, recalling Frost's words. Harry perished twice.

Splashed by the cognac, Calamari wiped off his black framed glasses with his red silk handkerchief, but steam from the sizzling tissues clouded his lenses, anew. As the Flames of Hell consumed Harry Boudreaux, the crematorium room smelled like Texas roadside bar-b-cue.

Lou Galzerano slammed shut the stainless steel door, and the party began. "Our trucker friends donated all this filet mignon and lobster. Eat up, brothers," Mr. Calamari said. "Dat's *zabaglione*. Dem berries wuz swimmin' in Panama, yesterday." Uncle Johnny levitated at his social pinnacle, but his grammar deteriorated the drunker he got. More Courvoisier, more Glenfiddich, and Midleton Very Rare Irish Whiskey flowed.

At the end, Mr. Calamari poured the ashes into the crematorium sewer hole. "His final resting place," said Uncle Johnny as he flushed the drain with an industrial black hose. Then, he picked a puddle of gold from the drain cover and handed it to Nedda.

Harry the Bee was a bad man, and he'd gone out of his way to deserve this end, but Aku Rintala, sonofabitch, should be in there with him, thought Chaim, for what he'd done with his mother. He, too, deserved the baseball bat and the Fires of Hell.

The regicide was complete and, at the very end of the ceremony, Mr. Calamari tapped his dirk on the lip of his crystal Scotch glass. "One more announcement. Everyone, listen up. One more important announcement. We have a new member of our family, a real *mensch*."

Everyone looked around, wondering. "It gives me great pleasure to tell you that Chaim Goldberg has joined us. He's our brother." Mr. Calamari grasped Chaim and kissed him full on the mouth and handed him a snifter of Courvoisier. "A toast to our new brother," he said. Chaim almost fainted. This was what Mr. Calamari meant, then, on that night he hauled him out of the snow bank. Stella's jaw dropped open.

At dawn, after a night on weird mountain, it was over. As they departed, Mr. Calamari draped his arm over Chaim's shoulder. "Hey, kid, Omertà. You unnerstan'?" He sounded like Barry Campbell with his "you unnerstan'." "If you ever... evvvvv-uh breath a word about any of this, you will follow Mr. Boudreaux. And, kid, youse one of us, now, so you protect dis family, dese interests now."

Then, he turned to Stella. "Got that, Tootsie? Same for you."

"I heard Pippo died in an accident," Chaim said as they entered Nedda's Mercedes. "Was that true?"

"It was like an accident, alright. His car blew up," Nedda explained. "Pippo took out Joe Zubarsky, Anna's husband, over union leadership. There was a problem in Bayonne. That's when all the trouble happened with Nick."

"Nedda," he said as they nestled in, "you got some scary friends."

"Better friends than enemies," she replied. "Blood's thicker than water, but money's money."

***

"What was all that mumbo-jumbo about?" seethed Stella. She'd said very little during the cremation ceremony.

Chaim tried to soft peddle his involvement. "No big deal. I've done some deliveries for Mr. Calamari, but I have no idea what I delivered. For one, maybe the biggest, all I had to do was to drive."

"Chaim, you are so full of shit. Calamari killed his own brother! You are in this all the way. You are one of them, and you and Nedda sucked me into this insanity. When my mother finds out she'll kill me. You saw what they just did to... to poor Mr. Boudreaux!" Crying, she was hysterical and furious, squeaking, "What did you do? You helped to kill a man. I have to know! Leave out nothing."

"Stella, all I did was drive a white panel truck with Michigan plates to Baltimore."

"No, there was more to it."

He had to tell. "Yeah, okay, so, in Baltimore, I changed the plates to North Carolina, delivered the load to a warehouse on the harbor. Some guys unloaded it. They signed a manifest, and I took that back to Johnny. Back in New Jersey, I changed the plates to Maine plates. That was the deal... just don't have plates from the state I was in. What's wrong with that? I needed the money."

He patted his pay envelope. "When I returned the truck to Mr. Calamari, he was very happy and gave me this. Stella, I can get new tires. It's college money."

"How much's in the envelope?"

"Not a lot... chump change."

"How much?"

"Five hundred... in Grants."

"Fifties!" she remonstrated. "You're starting to talk like them." She was hurt, very hurt. She didn't take it well. "That's twice what my mother makes... in a week. Chaim, you're the chump here. They whacked off Harry's hand. What do you think they'll whack off us?" She dissolved in tears.

"Oh, Stella," he said, trying to dismiss her unassailable logic.

"Chaim, so you fuck her all summer and tell me you love me?" What a mistake it was to let her into his world. How much like his mother he'd become. "And your future, our future, with these monsters? Chaim, let me tell you what's wrong 'wit dat'," she said, parodying his affected South Jersey accent. "This is criminal. You got a guy killed, Chaim. That's what's wrong. Mr. Harry Boudreaux, like him or not, he's dead. Are you going to build your life, my life, our lives with... with... filthy lucre?"

"Oh, Stella!"

"Don't 'oh Stella' me, Chaim Goldberg. Mr. Boudreaux was scum and, yes, he deserves to die, but Chaiiiim, killing someone is wrong. If you do not see how wrong these people are, we are through. I mean it. Look what you've gotten me into! And they wanted you to be part of that. You just got a promotion for killing Harry."

He tried to ignore the stark truths. As she ranted, he thought, I've become a professional liar, like my mother.

"And a criminal, too. You're no better than Calamari. You can't pretty up this pig, Chaim. We have to get out of here... get out of Bucks County, Pennsylvania; away."

The fact was that he liked being a swaggering gangster. He liked having a roll, the heft of cash. He liked Nedda's sex, but losing Stella was too much. When they parted, trying to make light of this confusion, he teased, "It'll be okay, Tootsie."

Her look was severe. She recruited every facial muscle in her contempt. "May God damn you," and landed a sound slap on his cheek.

***

In his bedroom, while one problem had been incinerated, another problem remained. What were the answers to these questions? What was the question? How would Robert Frost have solved this equation?

Vince Lombardi, help me! He agonized. Nedda? How to tell her what he must tell her, that he could no longer see her? He had to tell Stella about the prom. How?

He'd become like one of those crazy Rumanian carnival jugglers he'd seen on Ed Sullivan, tossing plates, balls, and Indian clubs, entangled in a net of mixed metaphors of moral gravity. It was impossible to keep all of these deceptions, illusions, tricks, and feints simultaneously up in the air.

He caved in and began to cry. Would his life be without lenity, a solitary figure, always alone? He heard a baleful *shofar* blow... *teki'ah, shva'rim, teruah, teki'ah gedolah*. Please, he pled, scare away my demons.

13

Small Talk

The angry lovers sat on her bed reading aloud passages from Lady Chatterley, intertwining fingers and toes, listening to cuts from *Joan Baez/5*, her new album, pretending as if things were hunky-dory.

Was he really unable to take his precious Stella to the prom? He'd parsed it, avoided it, talked around it to himself, pretended that it didn't exist, convinced himself that it was no big deal, but this obelisk he was unable to ignore: his mother had the power.

He'd drifted off and heard Stella say, "I like it when you shave me. Your touch is deft and lingering." She chuckled. "That's what DH would have said." He marveled at how well she'd developed her natural sense of eroticism.

"What?"

"Oh, I was just thinking it might have been nice if we *did* have a baby," she said, coyly.

"What!" This surprised him because he was thinking a much divergent line. He had to tell her about not taking her to the prom. He backfilled, diplomatically. "Babies are different than puppies, Stella. Someday we'll have a baby when I'm a doctor. Why can't we just practice?"

Frustrated in not having sex with her, he was angry that she required him to give up Nedda, and since the cremation they walked around Nedda, never mentioning her. Chaim saw his concubine daily, engaging in elaborate ploys to deceive Stella. Following his trysts with Nedda, somewhat sexually relieved, he'd visit Stella.

"Stella, we could, we could get married and have our baby, our lives together. We could, we could do it." He couldn't bear to lose her. He saw Stella ponder, and both kids stewed in the worst cauldron of immature indecision. What he wanted was sex, and he'd say anything to get it. Stella adored him, worshipped him, and he was confident that she would weaken.

He could tell that she liked what he said when she sighed, teetering, drawing him into her, arms around his shoulders, kissing him gently, in her special way. Then she said, "Chaim, it's not our time. This is not something we should do now, and anyway, what about your mother? She hates me. She hates me for something over which I have no control, being Catholic... and being me."

But this palaver amounted to eiderdown, and was not what was really on the day's agenda. "Stella, I have to tell you something," he began. This was like the time he blurted out his secrets with the Squid on New Year's Day.

"I don't like it when you say that. The last time was not good."

"My mother, you know what a bitch she is."

"Oh, just say it!" she snapped, patience fleeting.

"She won't let me take you to the prom. She's going to get me a date." There it was. It was out.

Stella steamed. Tears welled. Furious. "Get you a date! Yeah? I'll get my own date. Someone else will love my shaved pussy... which I did for you. Chaim, what is wrong with you? I'll find a guy pretty quick who'll love me, really love me, who can get away from his mommie. He can fuck my ass whenever he likes."

Where did she learn about that? "Stella, no, no. Don't say that!" The thought of her having sex with another boy was cruel. Their bond tore. He entered a primordial jealous rage and was angry about his enforced splitting with Nedda. He had to keep Stella.

Loneliness terrified him and being without a girlfriend would be awful. He didn't know what to do and slid his hands between her legs and spread her legs. She was moist. Her thighs parted. He'd solve it with sex.

"That's all you want: sex. If I have sex with you, everything is just fine, but you can't go up against your own mother? Go fuck your Nedda bitch." She pushed his head away from her, crying. "You can have me or your mother, but not both. And no more Nedda!" Snapping her legs shut, she closed that chapter with finality.

They'd never had such conflict before. "This Nedda thing, it's wrong. It's perverted. She's twice your age. My mother says it's dangerous. I know you're seeing her. Do you think I am that stupid?"

"I'll stop seeing her. Promise. I told you that already. I haven't been with her since we talked." He lied.

"How did we get roped into that cremation mess? If you hadn't called her, we would've been somewhere else."

"Stella, you're right. I shouldn't have called her." He tried to sound remorseful but, even as he spoke, he was confabulating his excuse for his next visit to Neddaland.

"Why *did* you call her? You wanted to go over there and fuck her, didn't you? You're an animal!"

"It's not like that, Stella. We're... we're friends, you know. I love you. I'll do anything for you. You knnnnnow that!"

Stella glowered at him. "Have you told her that you love her, too?"

"No, Stella," he lied.

"I have to be sure about what is going on here. I have to know the truth. You and your mother make up your lies *du jour*, whatever fits, but I have to know what's real." She was wrung out, eyes red, and removed her glasses. "Look, buddy boy, we're going over there for a talk or you and I are through!" His heartbeat tripped.

***

Eunuchoid Ping glided into Nedda's lavish parlor supporting a large sterling tray holding a complete Ming porcelain service. "Tea," he announced, smiling, his tightly braided queue bouncing as he giggled. He'd anchored his top knot with a carved green jade barrette, and he adorned the pigtail's end with a yellow orchid. He smelled of sandalwood incense.

A few days after their meltdown, Stella calmed down and they visited Manor Boudreaux. Jolly flower arrangements brightened the home. The feel was much different than during Harry's reign. She'd tied back the window coverings, and the rooms were light. Clove and sandalwood incense lent an introspective tone to the scene. Harry the Bee's pall and all of his heavy furniture was gone.

"What brings you two here for such an emergency visit?" Nedda asked, taking a lady-like sip of Earl Gray and biting into a chocolate pirouette, careful not to munch too hard and muss up her red glossy lipstick. Part of Nedda was a street brawler; part of her was royalty. She and Chaim's mother were chameleons who could easily blend into social propriety. "Trouble in Paradise?"

Chaim cringed. She could be so sarcastic.

The chunk of gold was hard to miss. It was a man's, gold, Rolex, President, named for President Eisenhower, the kind Johnny Calamari wore, which sat on the glass coffee table, between the *cloisonné* box and a silver and crystal *Lalique* lion figure, on his haunches, in roaring position. Stella eyed it, and so did Chaim. Nedda snatched it up, placing it into her sporran.

"Nedda," Stella began, her voice descending a nervous half-arpeggio. "Chaim *told* me all about you two. I know what's been going on." Chaim exhaled as he looked at Stella, dreading the Armageddon sure to follow with the exposure of his dual lives.

Poker-faced, Nedda listened.

"But you tell me. I want to hear it from you... especially you," she demanded.

Nedda was as divisive as his mother, and he knew that she was conjuring what she needed to say, what she could say, what she had to say but, but, mulling most upon what she must not say. The best deceptions, he knew that she knew, resided in information incompletely provided.

She looked perfectly respectable, one-hundred percent country club, sporting a heavy fisherman's sweater, cable knit, handmade in Scotland, no doubt, ivory in hue. Her left ring finger was nude. Nedda burped. "Excuse me," she managed, quickly covering her mouth and ran to the bathroom.

She returned looking ashen when she reappeared. "I'm pregnant. I'm really pregnant." Then, recovering, "This is morning sickness." She urped again, ran off, and returned.

"Congratulations, then," Stella offered.

"Oh, it's not a *congratulations baby*. I'm having an *abortion*."

Stella and Chaim blenched. He hadn't told Stella about this.

Nedda sniffled. "Would you two come with me? I can't do this alone. I need help."

"To where?" asked Stella.

Stella and Chaim looked at each other. He fidgeted. Then Stella asked the indelicate but obvious question. "Chaim's?"

"No," she answered.

Chaim registered Stella's relief, but she was relentless. "Mr. Calamari?" She'd noticed the gold Rolex, too.

"No."

"Mr. Boudreaux, then?" Stella was competitive with Nedda's level of sarcasm.

"You don't quit, do you?" Nedda laughed at her own peccadilloes. "I am just a gutter whore, what can I say? That fucker raped me and… and here I am, pregnant with a dead man's baby. I can't do this alone," pleaded Nedda.

"Does Mr. Calamari know?" Stella asked.

Nedda dropped her face. "No. we don't talk too much lately." She sipped her tea and laughed, "I guess you see me as a pathetic slut."

Stella softened and reached over to Nedda, grasping her hand in friendship. "I don't," Stella answered. "You had no choice."

"Chaim told you what happened?" asked Nedda.

"What happened, when?" asked Stella.

"On New Year's," said Nedda.

"I thought he was with *me*," said Stella. "I suppose I heard some of what went on. What *else* happened?" she asked, perplexed.

Nedda said, "I nearly… took my own life. Everything came in on me. He told you, you said?"

"I'm getting used to hearing parts of stories. Go on," invited Stella, dagger-eyes at Chaim, but genuinely concerned about Nedda.

"I was here all alone, and it was New Year's Eve, and I knew, or at least I thought I knew, that Harry was in Paris with this woman he-doesn't-know-that-I-know-about-but-I-do... and here I was all alone." She pulled up one of her embroidered MB monogrammed linen handkerchiefs, daubed her eyes, and wrung it into a rope. "Look, I am teetering on a mental breakdown with this." She was convincing.

"Well, tell us anyway," said Stella. She'd eventually become a criminal prosecutor.

"Oh, Chaim already knows about this, maybe some of it anyway."

"But this is new to me," Stella said, eyes askance again, bobbing her head, listening intently. "I'd like to hear this whole story, your version."

"I have to tell someone what happened," said Nedda.

Chaim felt the poke of truth, like a needle entering his skin as Stella answered, "We're listening."

"Someone was in the house. Ping was gone. I went into my bathroom and there he was."

"Who?" asked Chaim. "I didn't hear this part."

"I thought I told you," said Nedda.

"No. This is all new to me, too," said Chaim. She pitched the curve balls, like his mom, he thought... always something hidden, always one more unrevealed fact.

"Harry had crept up the back stairs from the kitchen. I thought I was through with him for a while. I thought he was in Paris with that princess bitch, that Danish cheese sleaze with bleu cheese in her twat." Nedda laughed through her sniffles, knowing that her audience appreciated her hyperbole.

Stella and Chaim laughed along with Nedda and, in unison, they asked, "Then what?"

"He was drunk," she said, breathing heavily. "I tried to get away. He followed me into the maids' hallway behind the bedrooms. I yelled at him. He wasn't going to rape me again. I ran down the back stairs. I had to get out of the house, but he chased me. He laughed at me. He'd come to kill me." By this time, Nedda had crumbled in a pool of tears. All levity left. "He had that meat cleaver."

Stella took up her hand. "Annnnnd?"

"He laughed this wicked, doomful laugh. You heard it when you were here. I ran up the stairs, and he cornered me in the bedroom, pinned me down on the bed, and took great joy in forcing his way into me. I kicked and screamed. It was awful, but I couldn't keep him out of me. Then I don't know what really happened. I bit his arm as hard as I could and I yelled at him. 'Enough,' I yelled.

"He forced his cock into my mouth and slapped me, and I bit him as hard as I could. There was blood all over the place, and he vomited and fell back. He came towards me.

"So I grabbed my gun. It was over in an instant. I shot him right in the chest. There was blood all over."

Chaim and Stella listened, mouths agape.

"This happened at New Year's Eve. Johnny was coming over for a drink, and it's lucky he came because, when I shot Harry, his body weight, he's huge, he pinned me in the bed, and I could barely breathe. He was as heavy as a horse. Johnny got him off me, and we cleaned up the mess. Johnny took Harry away. It was all too much for me. I fed his cock to the dogs. It was self-defense."

Stella was dumbfounded but asked, "Did Chaim kill him?"

"No. Chaim played no role in it. It was like what Johnny said." The pair listened intently.

"So, Chaim's role, anyway, fell apart?" Stella probed.

"When Chaim came over, I'd been so out of it. I wanted to end it all. I'm not sure I knew what I was saying." She went on. "Harry was dead by the time Chaim gave Johnny the bank books."

Then she broke down. "Look, I need help. If you refuse me, who else can I call? A next door neighbor... to help me get an illegal abortion?"

"It's sure a lot different than a cup of sugar for a cake recipe," said Stella. They reached a caesura.

"Ping!" She tingled her engraved sterling silver bell and he appeared.

"Martinis, please?" she asked him. Then to the duo, "I need a fucking martini."

Moments later, ambiguous Ping, wearing an iridescent azure silk kimono, brought a large silver tray while balancing a sweating crystal pitcher. He smiled. A delicately built man, he announced, "Martinis! Dry, just a hint of Noilly Pratt, Madame," then bending at the waist, setting down the silver tray. "Gilbey's, Hemingway's favorite."

Nedda looked up at Ping, who tilted his head to one side. He smiled and recited in his thick accent: "One martini, about right, Madame. Two, too many. Three, not nearly enough!" He giggled. "James Thurber!" Ping giggled more, delighted with his recitation. "Le-ah-ning Engrish," he said as he floated away towards the kitchen.

Nedda poured into delicate, frosted, carved crystal, monogrammed, conical martini glasses. She raised hers and toasted, "To friendship." She contemplated, then seeming jubilant, she raised her glass again, "To the Three Musketeers." They clinked glasses.

"Did Chaim tell you about *our* scare?" Stella tried to drink the martini, wrinkling her face. "What is this? This isn't like that nice champagne we had here in the summer."

"Ahh, the panacea," laughed Nedda. Chaim was much relieved when the conversation detoured away from his philanderings.

"Ukkk," Stella exclaimed. "I've never tasted something so awful. It's like airplane glue." Then she continued, "My period was late; scared the daylights out of us. My mother nearly had a stroke." She gulped it down.

"Well, I *am* pregnant," Nedda said, patting her tummy. "This is no scare." She twisted her hands in anguish, then she swilled her martini, leaving a distinct lipstick impression on the glass lip just above the MB monogram. She threw the martini glass into the fireplace where it shattered. "God, that feels good. He's gone. That's the last of him."

Chaim downed his second martini, grateful and relieved that this baby was not his.

"The thought of destroying this baby makes me sick but I can't have a baby from a man I hate," said Nedda.

"... and killed." Stella added. "Oh, I didn't mean it that way. That sounded... mean."

Nedda teared and her mascara smeared her cheeks. "That prick deserved what I gave him. I'd do it again."

Nedda continued, "How can I say this about my baby? I'm awful to say such a thing. It would kill my poor mother. How can I do this? But I have no choice."

"Do you have to *tell* your mother?" he asked Nedda.

Stella interjected. "Chaim, you know how we girls are. We tell our mothers everything." Chaim found it hard to imagine such intimacy with his mother, father, or anyone. He trusted no one.

"Nedda, you're not a slut. You just like sex... Just no more with my boy. Okay?" Stella said pointedly, nodding at Chaim.

"When's your appointment?" he asked.

"Now. God, I hope I've had enough to drink." She downed one more martini. "Three's the charm. For steady nerves," she said and away they went.

***

Chaim felt so rich piloting Nedda's Mercedes. The trio sat in the front seat with Stella in the middle and, as they crossed the river, he noticed the *Trenton Makes* sign. How many times had he made this trip? This ride was unique, and he knew then, that he would never forget this passage. "The House passed the Civil Rights Act," Nedda commented, crunching the Sunday New York Times, trying to mollify the uncomfortable silence.

Chaim nodded *uh huh*, and Stella tried to make small talk. How to behave when we are going to get an abortion while pretending that nothing is wrong? he wondered.

"You went to Vassar? My mother went there," Stella said, but the small talk was ineffective, and Nedda wiped her tears, and by that time she'd become silent, scanning the stock market charts, burying herself in the financial news. "The Dow hit 800," she said, then gave up on the pleasantries and rested her head against the window. The crossword puzzle on her lap blotted her tears.

He returned to a time when he was small, when he and his mommie traveled so many times over the bridge to see Dr. Katcher in Trenton. Plagues visited him. He was a sickly child, suffering from measles, mumps, chicken pox, colds, life-threatening bee stings, giant urticaria, and at one point he had a touch of polio and his legs weakened.

When they lived in Philly, briefly before moving to Levittown, he had pneumonia. He shook with rigors, breathed eucalyptus steam from a boiling kettle, and she'd placed a mustard plaster on his back that badly blistered his pearl white skin. Avrum Labe Katcher, MD then harpooned him and, miraculously, within a few hours, though tortured by the mustard plaster, *touchas* hurting from the injection, he was cured. Penicillin was the magic bullet, and he wanted that magic. He exalted in that magical feel of being a healer.

A heavy brass nameplate, Nicholas Palumbo, MD, marked the red sandstone home, located in Trenton's historic district just blocks from the Delaware River shore. From what Chaim had heard about Nick the Razor, he was Dr. Kildare's moral antithesis, a medical rapscallion. Someone had scratched out MD. The Dominici Foundry made this brass plate, too, as at Nedda's manor. It was all in the family.

This was Trenton's backside, a once affluent neighborhood, that by 1964, had degenerated to slum. The faces of many vacant homes, gaunt, like spirits, watched them. There was a corner store that had broken windows with "niggers" spray- painted on its chartreuse door that hung from one hinge like a beaten dog's limp ear.

He was curious to meet Doctor Nick as Nedda, making small talk again, prattled, "Nick the Razor got in a bar fight and slashed a man's throat." Small talk.

At 717 Bayonet Street, the address from the prescription bottle, the trio ascended the gray, granite stairs, twirled a bell, where, in the foyer, a stylish man greeted them. He wore a greasy, Kookie Byrnes pompadour. A thin, furry caterpillar moustache slept upon the vermillion border of his upper lip, which Chaim vividly remembered from Harry's wake.

A gold pinky ring featured Jesus' head with small, pinhead-sized rubies for eyes, then finished with a small pigeon-blood ruby in the mouth, making The Savior look like a beady-eyed, Satanic ambassador. "Doctor Palumbo," said the man to Chaim and Stella as he embraced Nedda.

Nick was an effusive host, adorned with a gold brocade, burgundy smoking jacket and a heavy, gold, garish crucifix with diamonds pavé set on the cross arms. He was draped in plush camel hair pants, finished by a white shirt and a snappy paisley tie. "Did you see the Beatles on Ed Sullivan?" he asked. "Those guys're gonna go somewhere!" Small talk.

His aroma was Tabac, that cologne Aku imported, and he smoked a Sobrane Turkish cigarette, Uncle Elijah's favorite, which he swept around flamboyantly in a garish gold cigarette holder as he escorted them down a set of steep, poorly lighted stairs, then taking them into musty, dank-smelling catacombs. He looked nothing like a Dr. Kildare.

Chaim picked up the iodine scent of surgical scrub soap, so familiar from Dr. Katcher's office.

"I do what I can to heal love's labors lost. Pennsylvania makes it a felony to even provide birth control information to a person less than eighteen. Imagine! How archaic!" He giggled in falsetto. "So Victorian."

As they walked, he warned, "Mind the coal." It was very warm as they wound past the raging furnace with its mountain of anthracite. "We burn garbage in there," he said, as Chaim skirted a pail of kitchen debris. His mother's prejudices made him chill at the specter of patronizing a Wop doctor, a Guinea. He felt as if he were trading with the enemy, betraying his own kind... but he wasn't the patient.

Then Dr. Nick pushed open a plain door where he'd created an opertory, and the Betadine smell became more apparent. The white painted suite featured an operating light, an examining table with stirrups, gleaming stainless steel surgical instruments, and a B&D autoclave. "I don't have much in the way of anesthesia but it's okay. This don't take too long."

The smarmy abortion mill was faultless, smelling properly medical with plenty of iodine, isopropyl alcohol, and mercurochrome. It was as spic 'n span as Dr. Katcher's office or his mother's kitchen. You could eat from the floor, as his mother often remarked. His diplomas impressed. For this Guinea kid from Trenton's Hell's Kitchen, it was all orthodox.

Chaim inspected a poster about the evils of syphilis, which hung on the inside of the door. "Yeah, those treponema'll get ya' every time," the doctor said. "Watch where you put your dick, kid."

Turning to his patient he inquired, "Nedda, my love, how *are* you? That was a real homer at the wake." He tried to be light, then, to Chaim, "Good choice, joining us."

Nedda, visibly anxious and shivering, not laughing at the macabre reference, clutched Chaim's hand for support and produced a fist full of Grants. "Here, Nicky."

He waved her off. "*Bambina,*" he said in a friendly way, "your money's no good here. Youse faaaamily." He brushed her cheek with his womanly hand.

Nedda replaced her wad. "Uncle Johnny doesn't know about this?"

"Unless you told him. Just us. Hippocratic Oath. Nice and private."

As Nedda readied, Chaim told Dr. Palumbo, "I'm gonna be a doctor."

"Don't be a doctor like me, kid. You *look* like a doctor, studious, a good Jewish doctor. Don't give your mother *agida*, the way I did. Give your mother *mazel*. Give her *naches*!"

"How do you know so much Yiddish?" Chaim was amazed.

"Are you kiddin'? I went to Jewish schools. N-Y-Jew, Einstein. I could *bench* with the Hasids! I read Torah."

Chaim and Stella held Nedda's hands while the doctor placed the ether mask. Handing Chaim a small can, the doc instructed Chaim. "Just drip some on da' mask. Not a lot."

Then, to his patient, "Nedda, honey, deep breath," but she was already asleep.

He positioned her in the stirrups and placed the weighted speculum. How awkward it was to see her vagina in this clinical way. Stella held Nedda's hand as the doctor worked. "Seven percent solution," Dr. Nick commented to Chaim, as he pressed a saturated sponge into her vagina. "Just like Sherlock Holmes." Then, to asleep Nedda, "Baby-doll, dis is gonna hurt a bit, some cramps." He was a caring man, Chaim thought. Guineas could be good doctors.

Working deftly, he narrated. "I'm dilating the cervix."

Stella, looking at what resembled a bar tender's spoon, asked, "What's that?"

"A curette. I scrape…" he began and Stella wobbled and slumped to the floor.

"Don't pay no attention to her," Dr. Palumbo commanded. "You gotta be a doctor now. Your girlfriend 'll be okay."

A light knock at the opertory door interrupted, and in walked Mr. Calamari. Chaim gasped. Wearing his familiar black, ankle-length mink, cigar smoking, he filled the door. "Nickyyyy, howzitgoin'? She okay?"

"She's fine, Uncle Johnny. Jus' fine. We got ether goin' here. Be careful." The Squid stubbed out his cigar.

Dr. Palumbo did not look up from his work, wiping away some blood while inserting a generous wad of gauze sponges. "We're done."

Mr. Calamari saw Stella woozy on the floor and lifted her into a chair. "Okay, sister?" He offered his paws. "Dis ain't as much fun as dat party, huh?"

Dr. Palumbo handed Stella a stainless-steel kidney basin, which she promptly filled with gin-scented vomit.

"Too many martinis, huh?" Nick quipped.

Mr. Calamari set a manila envelope on a side table. "Little somethin' for you and your good mother, Nicky," he said, in his husky voice. Then, Mr. Calamari, on his way out, asked the doc, "You're commin' fer da' christening?"

"Uncle Johnny, wouldn't miss it. This is what, your fifth? Fifth grandchild?"

Calamari lifted the corners of his mouth, pleased at the results, and vaporized, like Beelzebub, walking towards the raging furnace.

"I'm so embarrassed," Stella said, sipping water.

"It's okay. Some people don't take to this much," he said. To Chaim, Dr. Palumbo pointed out the tissue anatomy. "Here's the brain and the heart. The baby is actually distinctly recognizable at this stage. We got it just in time, though. A few more days and it woulda' been too big, too dangerous."

Stella sat on a chair and gulped more water. "Those martinis," she said.

Chaim examined the white gauze pad: a baby boy. The fetus had transparent skin and was half the size of a newborn cat. Chaim was deeply moved, chastened, as he felt the power of sperm and egg and he teared up, thinking of that blue robin's egg and his mother sucking the very life forces from that egg, and this fertilized embryo; its potential gone.

Dr. Palumbo, silent, pinched a hemostat onto the delicate tissue and plopped the fetus into a bath of formaldehyde in a glass specimen jar, then screwed down the cap, where it would swim in its sepulcher for eternity. The doctor placed the jar among his museum of several hundred squelched, anonymous lives.

Nedda's eyes glazed as she pulled a blanket around her shoulders.

"I wanted to become a heart surgeon, like DeBakey or Barnard. But dings didn't work out. I just made more den what DeBakey gets for his surgeries," Dr. Nick said, waiving the manila envelope. "Uncle Johnny's very good to me, takes good care of me... not a lot of competition. It's all about money."

He continued, "You know, Chaim, dat's youse name, right? Bad name, but youse a good kid. I can see dat. As a doctor, we do dings dat people do not know about or unnerstan'. This is a good deed, a *mitzvah*, not 'xactly da *naches* ding, but a good deed, nonetheless. Good deeds are important too. More important dan money."

"Can we take it? Him?" asked Chaim, feeling that Nedda would want the fetus, home, with her.

"Sure, I don't care." Dr. Palumbo handed him the specimen. "Don't mean nuttin' ta me." Chaim knew it would mean everything to Nedda.

In a low, sincere, voice, Chaim said to Doctor Palumbo, addressing the doc, "You're a *gutta nishumah*. I want to become a doctor just like you."

It was over.

***

Nedda, groggy from the anesthetic, leaned against the Mercedes window again. "So Johnny showed up," she questioned. "I don't know how, but he knows everything. Let me see it," she said as she cradled the specimen bottle and they drove west over the Trenton Makes bridge into the incendiary orange, red, yellow, and purple sunset.

He thought about that scene in *Lady Chatterley* between Connie and Clifford where he proposed that she have a baby with another man and he thought about Nedda's life, how this would resound through her life for years. Chaim recalled Connie's line to Clifford, *And wouldn't you mind what man's child I got?* Nedda'd done the right thing, gotten rid of a wrong man's child.

As they approached Manor Boudreaux, Nedda broke down, weeping uncontrollably. "What have I done?" Tears soaked her blouse. Stella hugged her. "Oh, my God, what have I done?" Her recriminations and remorse had ambushed her. In her kitchen, the three sat as Nedda poured a tumbler of Gilbey's gin, no ice, gulped it and swallowed hard. Her nostrils and cheeks flared. Nedda was unable to look into the jar. "I really wanted my baby."

Stella fortified her by holding her hand.

"But not that baby, not with that man, not now." Her tears flowed. "I'm done with him," she said and, teary-eyed and profoundly sentient over the day, the three embraced.

They left her with a generous bowl of Campbell's chicken and rice soup. As he drove Stella home, he said, "I missed Friday night services. My mother's going to be upset."

"You missed something else, too."

"What?"

They parked in a furrowed cornfield about a mile from her home. "Today. Today's Valentine's Day."

"Oh, Stella! I'm so sorry. With all of this..."

"You showed more love today than anyone could. You were very brave. I am not mad at you any longer."

"But Stella, I forgot us, our day."

She put her fingers on his lips. "Shhh. It's okay. I have something for you."

"You do? Oh, Stella. I forgot. I'm so sorry."

"I think it's gonna be okay," she said as she gently pushed on his chest so that he reclined. Moving her hands to his belt, she unbuckled it and unzipped his pants, smiling, and said, "You deserve this. Happy Valentine's Day... but one more thing, Chump: you better change."

Cassius Clay defeated Sonny Liston, and Chaim's guilt stung him like a bee, but Stella made it all better.

***

A week passed and a faculty academic committee selected him for an astronomy class as a *Promising Young Scientist*. He never felt like a promising young scientist, but this was another plume in his mother's cap.

This tasty pre-college *hors d' oeuvre* of freedom would allow him Thursdays away from home.

Whistling when he got home from school, happy over this new award, his mother ruined it. "You're taking Martha Hymen to the prom. Her mother says that she thinks you're very nice."

"She's Jewish, Mom. That's your only criteria." Chaim growled, "So, Hymie Chaimy's taking Hymen to the Prom?" He laughed at her, slamming his books on the dinner table. A salt shaker tumbled to the floor.

"Don't be insolent to me. Look, goddamnit, you go with a goddammed Jew or no one! Your *goyisha* girlfriend drives a Nazi car!"

"So do the Rintalas!"

"That's different."

With all the goddamns, Chaim started to laugh. He'd named Martha, Zitty-Tittie because she had bad zits and smelled like the astringent, benzoyl peroxide. She had ungainly, heavy breasts and fat calves, and he was sure her chest was a garden of pustules and comedones. She was so unappetizing that guys joked, "I wouldn't fuck her with your dick."

"What's so funny?" wailed his mother as he smirked. He went to his room and slammed the door.

Martha played third clarinet badly, often honking like a goose. More than taking her to the prom making him ill, withering to his mother's powers enraged him. What would James Bond do? What would Nick the Razor do? He envisioned slashing his mother's neck. He rubbed Uncle Elijah's pocket watch, his talisman, and fell asleep.

14

Love's Labor Lost

He dreamed. Smothered, as when the snow came in his window in the car in the ditch, in the storm, as when his mother pinned him and forced her kisses upon him, as when cousin Jeffrey pushed his mouth onto his cock. Wriggling away from the baby spinning in the specimen bottle... chasing him... the baby, hideous, grimacing at him, the hands swirling in images of red...and dead Anna, nacreous Nedda...chased by Zitty-Titty, whose face looked like a vivid collection of scarlet, conical Mount Fuji's with oozing, purulent sores...as ugly as Johnny Calamari when he was in the ditch.

Thoughts whizzed. Think like Uncle Elijah, he told himself. *My brain is my best tool*, he thought. Uncle Elijah, the *tzaddik*, a wise man, a righteous man, a man who could think, the *Vilna Gaon. Think like Uncle Elijah...* and the answer to the prom dilemma became clear. He woke with a start, hair wet, sweating.

***

It was Prom night, and what a ploy his mother perpetrated.

260

The requisite three stars appeared in the evening sky. Prayers, wine, spices, and lighting the *havdalah* candle, marked the close of the Shabbat. Everyone took a sip of wine, and then, with a drop of wine between her fingers, his mother extinguished the candle with an audible hiss.

Chaim was *uber dem kopf* angry as Martha and her parents convened at Eva's festive, narcissistic table, replete with Bubbie's hand-embroidered linen tablecloth. The observant Hymens made a concession to eat at Goldbergs, who did not maintain separate kitchens. On this night, Eva prepared chicken. The Hymens were *very* Jewish, kosher Jewish. Following the rules of *kasruth*, Eva prepared a "safe" meal: chicken. She served the family on paper plates and plastic forks.

Chaim sickened with Evalyn's pretextual *Havdalah* performance as she slathered on ultimate *yiddishkeit* like *schmaltz*. It was *Bubbelah* this, and *kinehora* that. Chaim wanted to disappear. Arthur, too, seemed to endure her performance, as she interwove *Yiddish* into English to make their family seem *more* Jewish. You were born in Cincinnati, *fer Chris' sake*, he wanted to yell across the table, although *Yiddish* was her *Muttersprache*.

"*Geh, fress*," she said, fake smile smeared like bad lipstick across her face as she served dinner. Chaim felt that his mother regarded him as Martha's husband-apparent and the stud for her many grandchildren. What she wanted was to curry the Hymens' favor, and all of this insincere manipulation envenomated his bloodstream like bacterial toxin. He felt he was dying from a form of cultural sepsis.

Chicken, boiled, and boiled potatoes and boiled carrots disappeared in a greasy, salty blur across the table, and Mr. Hymen told a stupid story about his notions store. Eva reacted as if he were Don Rickles at Grossinger's, letting loose with fusillades of "oy, *oy vey, oy gevalt!*" accompanied by dramatic hand and facial gesticulations. "*Zo komisch!*"

He wanted to barf.

At the meal's end, Mrs. Goldberg clunked dishes into the soapy water in the stainless steel sink. Kodaks burst like Martha's flaming pustules. *Trink, l'chayim, to life, to life, l'chayim,* he could hear the wedding *b'ruchah* clanging like bells in Mrs. Hymen's brain when she cooed, "They're so cute together."

"Aach! *Zo ziskeit!*" joined Eva, tweaking her soon-to-be-daughter-in-law's tarnished cheeks. By comparison, Stella's complexion was a flawless peaches and cream... and Nedda... Chinese porcelain... the finest.

Martha's mother said, "That son of yours, a real *Mensch,*" and Evalyn *kvelled,* pinching Martha's cheek once more as she faux-admired her.

"*Schoene punum,*" Eva said, about the pock-marked donkey. Martha Hymen was the anti-*schoene punum.* Obligatory *mazel tovs, meshugges* and *naches* flowed and by the time dinner ended, Chaim was ready to *plotz.* His parents were authentic Catcher-in-the-Rye phonies.

As far as Eva Goldberg was concerned, the ink on the marriage contract, the *ketubah,* was drying. He shuddered just then as he thought of Nedda's baby-boy-in-a-bottle, swimming in eternity, in quest of its unformed soul.

Chaim wore a baby blue tux. He wanted black and no frilly pirate shirt, but Evalyn wanted baby blue with the frilly pirate shirt. "I pay the freight," she reminded him, and so it was. "*Schoene punum,*" she said, pinching his cheeks, *kvelling* in her triumphant *nachas.* She made him feel like a two-year old with a stinky pile of poop in his pants. He was that humiliated and at her mercy.

Mrs. Hymen coaxed him to pin the corsage on her donkey, but he focused on her flock of pustules raging in her cleavage and a thumb-sized, chicken grease spot from dinner on her dress, just above her left nipple. He faltered, distracted by a vision of her nipples, sure that she probably had one black, wiry, curling hair growing from an areola, like his mother.

"Oh, let me do that," Mrs. Hymen said, annoyed, jamming the pin into her daughter's hefty bosom such that a blood mark oozed through to join the chicken grease. Martha brayed and baby's breath flecks lit on her fat spot, making it appear even more obvious.

Eva pinned his red boutonniere into his lapel and flashbulbs dazzled as they prepared to leave. Mrs. Hymen invited Mrs. Goldberg, "We're sitting *shiva* for my mother. Come over."

"I'm sorry. I didn't know. When?"

"Two days ago."

"I... we... didn't know," she repeated.

"She lived in Pennsauken... well into her seventies. A survivor."

"*A leben ahf dir,*" Eva exclaimed, continuing her *Yiddishkeit*. "You should live and be well," she said and kissed Mrs. Hymen on the cheek. Eva was ebullient, taking this intimate invitation as a sign of acceptance. "Thanks for not cancelling tonight. It was good of you to come. Your mother would have approved of him."

"We're so glad Chaim asked Martha. She... she's not much, *zo* shy, zo... *heymish,*" she whispered, *sotto voce*, to Eva, but Martha heard and grimaced. She held her hand over her soiled bodice.

It was a sad reality, but Chaim realized that she knew she was not attractive. She sheltered her glowing cheeks with her hands. She was beyond *heymish*: she was ugly. *Ein chazer bleibt a chazer,* he said to himself, a pig remains a pig. How was he going to get through his night?

The witches congratulated themselves on the spell they'd cast. "*Zayt mir gezunt.* To life, to life, *l'chayim, mazel tov... l'chayim! Imyirtseshem,* may God be willing. *Gott sei dank*!" the mothers went on, and on.

Everyone waved and joyous tears flowed as the couple backed down the driveway on their way to the prom with the two mothers clucking over what to prepare for the *shiva* visitors the next day. They cackled that in a few years, *a'livei*, may it be so, they would have a new life and a *bris* to make. And Chaim thought about Nedda's baby swimming in eternity.

In the car, Martha slithered her corpse-cool hand into his. "I have to drive," he said and withdrew. She scowled. He felt sorry for her and guilty at hurting her feelings. He was not an unkind boy.

Nedda had been in the ugly doldrums following her abortion, but the kids energized her. She had a Polaroid camera and snapped their pictures. "He's very handsome," Nedda said to Martha," about Steve. "Better looking than Gregory Peck."

The plan was simple: trade dates at Nedda's. Chicanery... just what Uncle Elijah would have done. He bamboozled the bamboozler-in-chief. Martha, however, didn't know about this switch. Steve laughed nervously. He knew. As the two couples readied, Chaim, with Stella present, unwrapped the plan. At first Martha teared. "I didn't want to go anyway," she said, but Chaim could tell that he'd hurt her, too. He felt so guilty. He'd known the pain of not being picked for sandlot baseball and football because he was "no good."

Martha teared up. "I didn't know." Her mascara dribbled down her cheeks. "My mother made me. I hate you," she yelled.

"Here, here, one of these 'll make it right," Nedda said, offering her a stiff martini.

"Oh, never mix, never worry," Martha said and gulped it down.

Chaim laughed. "Where'd you hear that?"

She looked at him, the alcohol taking effect, "Virginia Woolf... that play... remember? We all went. That was Martha's famous line... my namesake."

"I'd forgotten," Chaim said. "But it was Honey."

The alcohol emboldened her. "Martha," she retorted. "Martha, like me. *I* said that."

"Honey," said Chaim but Stella jerked his arm.

"We have to go," said Stella and gulped down her drink. "I've grown accustomed to these." By the time Stella and Chaim left, they'd swilled three martinis and the two piggies went to market, while Steve, Martha, and Nedda stayed home.

"Want to try something, Stella? I have some pot," he offered in the school parking lot. It was heavily laced with opium.

"I'm kinda drunk," she said.

They toked up.

Stella said, "Is it supposed to feel this way?"

"Yeah! You're stoned."

"I like it," she said and he was glad. He liked corrupting her.

Stella's mother had created a dazzling satin, scarlet hue, figure-hugging strapless gown, which was a tough order because of Stella's "tiny tits," as she joked. "There's not much to hold it up," she bantered. "Fried eggs. Wow. I'm really talking."

"Stella, just let it take you. Here, take my hand. I'll never let go."

Sixties rock 'n roll tunes spun, and it was even better than the New Year's Eve party. "I feel the drum beat, the bass guitar," said Stella, hugging him.

"Great," he said and kissed her.

After a bunch of fast songs, and what seemed like a long time, they swayed to *Blue Moon*. "Remember that song? It was our first dance over at Zubarskys," he said, "from *Malaya*, Spencer Tracey's film."

"Valentina Cortese sang it," she said.

"You know your movies," he said, encircling her waist. "But Andy Williams made it big." Small talk. "What's that perfume? It makes me weak," he sighed, nibbling her neck, feeling very high.

"Do you like it? Mmmm," she murmured in his ear, placing more of her weight into his arms. "It's my mother's love potion number five, Chanel Number 5."

He hummed the melody in her ear. There was more than small talk going on. She stiffened and asked, "Are we really going to be together?"

"Yes," he said. "It's us, forever...I love you," he said, a bit unsteady on his pins, as the duo twirled at the song's final phrase when he softly crooned in her ear, *"moon river and me."* Again, he hugged her and sang, *"Ca-li-fornia here we come."*

Chaim felt something inside of Stella dramatically slip, one of her tectonic plates. She jolted, stiffened in his arms... seething. "You tricked her... this was trickery. This whole thing was a swindle!" She was very angry. "That was so rude! Are you ever going to be able to conquer your mother?"

He felt weak, impotent, and she riddled him with her clarity. "You're afraid of your mother. You want me because I am easy. You love my sex, but not me for me. I can't endure what you did with Nedda... and Martha! You can't treat women that way."

"Stella, that's the pot talking. Nedda and I began before we met," he protested in high pitch. "And what I did with Martha, was for you. Stella. No, Stella!" Even as he said that, he felt as if his mother had formed his words. "That's not it at all. I do love you. I do, but Stella, she's my mother. I need my parents for school."

"Maybe when we get out to California she'll be far enough away so you can think about *me* and be a man," she blazed. "Chaim, you have to want *me*... for *me!*"

His best laid plans began to unravel quickly. Fervently, he wrapped Stella in her mother's white mink stole as they went to the car. "People are noticing, Stella!"

"I don't care. They *should* notice. They should notice *you* and what a bum you are!" She pulled away from him, sobbing, and smacked his face. What he feared most was the possibility of losing her, but he wanted to believe that it was the booze and dope talking.

Wrestling in his car, her lips fiery hot, she unzipped him and got him real hard. "Oh, Stella," he panted, ready for her pleasure, thinking that this would be like Valentine's Day when he'd been the hero.

"Nedda gave you the pot?" she accused. "You fucked her?" Then, just as he came close, she squeezed him violently. "Go shove it in that Jew-bitch. Go fuck that girl your mother fixed you up with, that pig you were supposed to haul to the prom. Go get rid of that thing with her! Or Nedda. Go fuck Nedda! Go fuck 'em both. Go fuck yourself."

"Oh, my God, I was so close."

"Close to what, you asshole. You weren't even close. You deal with your mother or we're through. Get her out of our lives. I told my mother you are my one and only. Get your mother out of our lives or we're through!" Stella pulled and twisted his penis. He bellowed. Stella cried.

Chaim was stunned, realizing that his mother's prophesy had vested. He felt their love fracture and the pain shot through him as if from a splitting tooth. Was Stella like all *goyim*, as his mother told him? Was his Stella one of *them*?

"Bbbbuuut, Stella. I am so sorry," he pleaded and he meant it.

***

Not a creature stirred at Manor Boudreaux. The manse seemed to hover in candlelight. Stella and Chaim cooled down from their car meltdown. The alcohol and pot effects were gone and, while her Irish nature was quick to explode, her natural habit was to forgive.

Steve's bituminous black Ford Falcon sat in the drive where the Hispano Suiza once sat, next to Martha's yellow Buick. On this night, dogs snored in the library, and the Dutch Masters' eyes were shut as they, too, slumbered. Guarding the entry to the library, a grandfather clock, handmade in Germany, its finials heavily gilded, chimed— one, two, three — a portentous, descending B minor, Mahler arpeggio.

In the guesthouse, the fire crackled and, soon cocooned in each other's arms, too tired even for teenagers to fondle more, they took refuge in deep, nurturing, healing sleep. They woke on March the first, the day after the prom; Sunday.

Brunch took place in the estate sunroom gazebo, overlooking the stables that reminded Chaim of the Paris Tuileries Palace he'd seen in Janson's book. The glass-encased fishbowl had white-painted steel-framed window panes. Tropical plants grew everywhere. Outside, spring glowed, and crocuses nosed into the sunlight after the punishing winter.

In post-prom haze, Chaim and Stella enjoyed the irises, gladiolas, orchids, and ferns. There were antheria, plumeria, and gardenias. Lotus blossoms floated in a koi pond. These fish were Ping's delight. The sunroom was lush with potent flower perfumes enriching the senses.

"Ping does all of this," Nedda announced as they took their places at the wrought-iron-framed table with a thick glass top. Steve, Martha, Chaim, Stella and Nedda, five of them, sipped fresh-squeezed, frosty, blood-orange juice as Ping entered with platters filled with pancakes, sausages, sheared eggs with chives in cream, fried tomatoes, and scalloped potatoes in cheese sauce.

"I picked a special *Pouilly Fuissé*," Nedda said, filling unadorned crystal glasses. "All the monogrammed everything... is gone. I couldn't stand it. I felt as if we lived on one of his ships." Chaim felt nauseated and didn't feel as if he could drink more alcohol.

"*Côte Mâconnais*," Stella read, but without thinking she said, "I remember when Harry gave me that champagne label..."

Nedda cut her off with a head shake, in effect saying, No more Harry talk.

Across the breakfast table, Chaim and Stella looked at Steve and Martha, who self-consciously giggled. Steve looked like the cat who ate the canary.

"You two?" Stella quizzed.

Steve and Martha grinned and kissed. "We're ready for college." Their blushes betrayed any attempt to withhold their naughty story.

After the filling meal, each paused, napkins and utensils supine, when Nedda asked, "Could you stay a moment longer?" She led her guests outside where they stood beneath the ancient oak with its rotted core, thick as three whiskey casks. The leaves were emerging. Nedda produced the Henry VIII *cloisonné* box, cradling it at her waist. "I do not want this life to go unnoticed, to end in a drain, or his precious spirit to remain in this bottle forever."

Weeping like morning dew coursing down a winter window, Nedda tucked her blonde hair beneath a hand-knit, cream-colored wool cap. She handed Chaim the specimen bottle. "Can you do this?" She appeared faint, her knees weakening as the fumes expanded into in the fresh spring air.

Formaldehyde dripped onto the ground as the almost colorless baby tissues flowed onto a piece of black towel. All eyes teared as the vapors enveloped them. Nedda spoke. "This was Henry VIII's. He used this box for his chocolates, the sweetest, and most precious delights in his life, and this baby was mine, my baby, my sweetest and most precious delight. My baby must have a name: John Fitzgerald. This box is his repose."

The dogs— Kafka and Freud— seemed to understand the holy nature of the assemblage and rested quietly, politely, at graveside. Reaching into her memory Nedda recited, paraphrasing, as she quoted Ecclesiastes:

> **To everything there is a season,**
> **to every purpose under heaven.**
> **A time to be born, and a time to die;**
> **A time to kill, and a time to heal;**
> **A time to love, and a time to hate; a time of peace.**

"Chaim, please say something," she asked. "With your gift of words, it would be a poem."

Here's what came to his mind: *"Shema Yisrael Adonai eloheinu Adonai ehad... a closeness to God."* Then each added loving words for John Fitzgerald.

When Ping's moment came, he spoke, as was his way, softly. "I must... want purify my soul. Truth, now. You call me Chinese; I not. The Mister bought me. He call me Chinese. Call me Ping. I Japanese. Very bad man." His voice strengthened as he became more confident.

"Name, not Ping. Name, Akio Wakabayashi. Am Japanese. I, *Akio*. I, Shinto. Baby's soul not to leave earth alone. Prayers with baby. This is *hinden-igyo no gi*. Name most important."

Nedda set the tiny casket into the grave. *"Gusen no gi,"* Akio said and whispered a prayer in Japanese and lighted incense sticks, which he placed around the grave.

It was done. John Fitzgerald, love's labor lost, was on his spiritual way. Years later, at his mother's graveside, Chaim would remember this moment. The sun shone through the trees, wispy clouds played above, and the baby's soul rested. Chaim, Akio, and Steve moved a heavy granite boulder onto the grave and an engraved plaque read:

John Fitzgerald
1964
...loved

There was no surname.

Nedda said, looking at Chaim, "He would have been compassionate, like you, what you will be, a leader of men." She really did love and admire him, as young and as ill-fit as he was for her, he felt, and he loved her.

As they walked away, Chaim looked at Akio's offering, a thimble of rice wine and a lotus blossom along with a small dish of rice on top of the grave.

Leaving Manor Boudreaux, he and Stella drove in a calm silence. How self-conscious he'd felt with his two women. Then he thought about Akio and his own name. "I guess I have to accept my name, don't I?"

"A name is who we are. I don't know who I'd be if my named changed," she said. "If I weren't Stella O'Shannahan, who would I be?"

***

His funk passed, it always did, and after a few days Chaim got up enough courage to show his father his acceptance letter from Culley College. His reticence was over what tumult that announcement would cause, but this silence he was unable to maintain. Besides, this was great news. He would leave for California, and he was ecstatic.

"No! Absolutely not," Arthur raged. "We can't afford it. Los Angeles is too far." Once again, his brooding father dashed his ebullience.

"I can help with the money, Dad," he squealed.

"What? With your ninety-cent an hour job? Why the hell can't you go to New York? It was good enough for Dr. Katcher."

"Artieeeee?" Eva scolded, sloshing a bucket of her caustic mop water onto her husband's ire. Chaim thought, Artie, farty, what an asshole.

Adamant. "You're not coming home at Christmas, then. There won't be enough money. It's just too expensive." He was mad. Mrs. Goldberg twisted her black eyebrows at him. They left the discussion with ragged edges, but he knew that she would make it work. By August he'd be gone to Culley, to L.A.. She was more than his equal force. His father didn't have a chance against her.

15

Mit und Drinnen

Passover, 1964

At the back of the Brunswick Theater, a matinee, the pair snuggled into the plush red velvet seats. They welcomed the healing dark therapy of electrons washing over them as *Judgment at Nuremberg* played.

"This war never leaves you, does it?" she whispered, intertwining her cold fingers into his. Her lips brushed his ear as she whispered, "I am so worn out. I couldn't have done that. We would have had to have our baby. I want ours, Chaim."

He inhaled as if to say something, but an elderly couple shushed them, turning and scowling. He anguished. Stella squeezed his hand and he returned the pressure, kissing her neck, but rustling the popcorn bag. The seniors turned their black-rimmed eyes at them again.

Following the three-and-a-quarter hour movie, a catharsis took place. In the theater parking lot, in the Clot, he spoke. "That baby was the most perfect being. He was the most *perfect* being. It's hard to imagine that such a little bit of goo creates a new person. When the doctor scraped it out, I saw it breathe. I did." Then he said, "When I poured the baby into the casket I saw its tiny hands." Stella sighed, then cried.

As they drove back to the Pennsy side, she held his hand and he talked. "Remember the robin's egg in the Rabbi's study? This was more real. I've seen too much death, Stella. Anna, Bratstein's mother, Harry the Bee... Nedda had been so close."

"And my brother Judas, Chaim. Remember Judas... him. He was a good boy... just seven... in that garage fire. The gasoline just exploded. It was horrible."

"And that was when you got burned?" She nodded. "Well, what happened?"

"Oh, Chaimy, please don't make me say it... it was just too horrible." She sighed. "We'll be out of all this soon... when we go to California."

He liked hearing her say that: when *we* go to California. "I have something I have wanted to tell someone for a long time."

"Tell me. Trust me, you must. You can tell me anything."

"This is really awful." He was so overcome he pulled off the road onto the Weathergreens Used Cars lot. Finally, he'd found someone whom he could trust. "You are the only one who I could ever tell this."

"Tell me. Go ahead."

"My sister had a tiny kitty. It was black. I stuffed it into a pickle jar and drowned it."

Stella gasped. "Oh my God! How old were you?"

"Seven. I remember it so well because that happened right after my cousin, Jeffrey, made me..." He stopped. "Oh, Stella, please don't think I am terrible."

"Tell me. It's okay." She petted his hair and kissed his cheek.

"And my cousin Jeffrey... made me suck his... dick."

"Oh."

"It was horrible. Then he teased me and called me 'blower,' and we got into a big fist fight. I smashed a pistachio ice cream cone in his face. I told my mother, and she smacked me for lying and making up stories... but that's what happened, Stella. I swear. That's when I drowned my sister's black kitty. I am sure God will punish me for that. Sometimes I feel as if I just can't go on. I was sick seeing the wet kitty, motionless. I wanted to kill my mother... and I harmed my sister, Ruthy."

He cried and quaked. "Oh, Stella, am I a killer? Am I going to become a murderer? Am I going to be a thug? Am I going to kill myself?"

"No, Chaim! No! You're not. You're a wonderful boy. You're loving!"

"What am I going to do? I feel responsible for all these deaths." The truths spilled out. "I see the images of the frog in the chlorine vat and the dead kitty. My mother told me that I would kill her... if you and I stayed together."

A tapping on the window with the end of a long black flashlight interrupted them. It was a bald, burly man. "Can I help youse? Youse wanna buy a car or sumptin'? Looks like ya' need one."

Chaim hit the gas pedal on the big V-8 and spun it out of the parking lot. "Chaim! Chaim! Watch your driving!" Stella screeched, correcting the steering wheel as he reefed the Clot back onto the road. "Chaim? My God! Pay attention! No more accidents!"

"It was awful when Beelzebub appeared... when Beelzebub came to Earth from Hell and consumed Harry the Bee," he blubbered.

"What are you talking about? Where's Beelzebub in this?"

"Will God consume me? What can I do to make the demons leave? Will I spend eternity in a cremation oven?"

"Chaim, Chaim! You're not making sense. Don't believe your mother. She's crazy." Stella jostled him. It was as if he were absent, as if his mind had gone somewhere. He was paralyzed, palms sweating, and he'd stopped in the middle of the road. "Get… get onto the shoulder!" she ordered, glissing into her high soprano.

They were at their special field of dreams, where they first lay together in the cornfield in the summer, where they first unrolled their loving blanket. "Stella, Stella," was all he could manage, and he gripped her. "How can I be so flawed? Everybody thinks there's something wrong with me," he sobbed, and together they shook, hugging each other. "There is something very wrong with me."

"Oh, no. Oh, no," she whispered, then "poor boy," and petted his sweaty hair, and held him for the longest time. "You're a genius, and they're jealous. You're such a good boy." She rocked him, both crying as he descended into a watery abyss, like the spelunkers, without an headlamp or direction, fleeing his mother's halogenic onus.

They could delay no longer. It was time to go to the *Seder*… without his Stella.

***

Chaim loved the *Seder* foods, especially the ceremonial, sweet, Concord grape wine, Manischewitz. "Man-O-Manischewitz, What a wine!" went the radio and TV commercials and, when Chaim parodied the jingle for his family, everyone laughed.

Steve and Miss Zitty-Titty, his mother's invitee, arrived right on time, an hour before sundown. Martha had been such a good sport about the prom, so he wasn't mad about her. She'd been kind to him. He was bitter at leaving Stella home with her family, and that indignity was like a maul splitting his inner being. This time, this time, he planned to even this score by surpassing that puny ping-pong game vindication.

And so it came to pass that on the fifteenth day in the month of Nissan in the year 5724, twenty-eighth day of March 1964, Passover began at sundown, on a Saturday. Easter began the very next day. He liked *Pesach*, a joyous holiday without contrition, where the only suffering comes from awaiting the meal, delayed by the telling of the story. This *Seder* night at Manse Goldberg would differ from all other nights and remain a memory for all of his time, albeit not an happy one.

The Rintalas berthed their new Mercedes 500, fresh from its trans-Atlantic delivery. The car added some class to his pathetic neighborhood, he thought, and he hoped that the neighbors would have an eye-filling gander. He'd been telling people that he was from Yardley, hoping that no one would trace his umbilical cord to Levittown.

And, yeeees! Was Ilona was all *fa'pitzed*! As she removed her black mink coat, she bemoaned her ostentatious afternoon at Rosenberg's Salon of Beauty where she endured the wops, Darlene, Rhea and Betty, preening and stroking her, transforming her into Aku's regal feline.

His mother nervously jangled her charm bracelet as she smeared her chicken-greased hands on her apron when Ilona unwrapped their plans for Europe in the fall. "We're picking up Aku's new Ferrari... a little shopping in Florence."

When she finished, Eva said, wistfully, "Honey, I'd like a pedicure."

Arthur said, "When I get a raise. I work for the President, you know."

His mother stood at the stove, a Jewish-mother icon, up to her elbows in chicken fat, carrots, celery, apples, cinnamon, and cigarette butts, grimacing. "Oy, what I do for this family." Chaim saw her notice Arthur's attraction to Ilona and she frowned. When he copped a lascivious feel of Ilona's luscious *tush*, Eva slammed a large steel spoon on the counter.

Evalyn's Raleigh burned away as she drew heavily on the butt, a frustrated drag, curling her lips into the end, huffing smoke through her nostrils and mouth above the pot of boiling chicken soup, just as she plopped in the matzoh balls. The steam caught the updraft, shrouding the stovetop in her smoky exhalation.

His father turned to his wife with a dumb Alfred E. Newman smile, in innocent quandary, as if to ask, "Is there something wrong?" She frowned.

Chaim felt betrayed. It felt like his mother's familiar slaps on his face all at once. She'd blindsided him. His father was less than a man.

Stella, her tiny breasts, her nipples, of kissing her, those thoughts made it better. He wanted to be with her, to bite into succulent ham and mince pie with people he liked, with people who would be nice to each other. Chaim thought of Nedda, too, of her thighs, of tonguing her most delicious parts. He was *mit und drinnen*, roiling, churning, his fuse smoldered, but not yet *uber dem kopf*. Like the Pennsy Line, his plan rolled along.

The Pomerantz family burst through the front door. Mother Rifka, wearing hideous red lipstick and a black bird-feather hat with stupid black netting, perpetually peeved, entered first, nattering endlessly about sales at the A&P and how "they never have what they advertise." Hairy tits, Chaim thought.

Chaim then focused upon her husband, Schmuel, the *schmu*. His mouth was filled with too many unattractive, stained buck teeth, and he wore a herringbone sports jacket with clashing plaid pants and white-buck shoes. Their costumes alone maddened him, and he was further incensed by Schmu's harsh, black glasses with thick rims that reduced his already beady eyes to marbles.

Oh, Christ, he was upset.

To his mind, the Rintalas were social climbing phonies, using cash as an unguent to mollify their snooty behavior. They sniffed at Schmuel Pomerantz, dismissing him as an undistinguished postal worker. In fact, the War pre-empted his engineering studies at MIT.

Rifka, despite her degree in philosophy from Barnard, drew no acclaim, and they called her *Schmata*, a dishrag. Chaim laughed at the hypocrisy, for neither of the Rintalas finished high school.

"Help me, Kussy," his mother interrupted his reverie. Together they slipped in the extension leaves to the gray, Sears Formica table, then pulled a card table next to it and covered the joint between the sections with Bubbie's long, hand-embroidered linen *Seder* tablecloth.

The Pomerantz kids, Shelly and Michael, about Ruth's age, took their places at the *Seder* table. All of them irritated Chaim. Levitt homes were small, and the guests scrunched close to one another. It was too hot. He sought *nouveaux riche*, and this was no *riche*. He preferred the spaciousness of estates Boudreaux or Rintala. He was ready to *plotz*.

The table was set. In addition to the Goldberg parents, the cast included Zube, Martha, Chaim, sister Ruthy, Aku, Ilona, Rifka, a big breasted, *zaftig* woman, and Schmuel, the *schmuck*, Shelly and Michael, their twins, of ten years, Ruth's age.

Who's afraid of Virginia Woolf, hummed Chaim.

Eva shooed Arthur to the head of the table, a position he gingerly accepted. She sat at the opposite end, nearest the stove. Why didn't his parents sit together? His father was a limp-dicked figurehead, a poseur.

Dark ties set on stiff, starched, white shirts, like exclamation points, each cuff with links, all the men cloaked in black suits. The women were all *fa'pitzed*, dressed to the nines— jewelry galore— with far too much perfume, as it was their cultural way. Boys sported flattops kept sharp with pink Butch Wax, that military hair goo that made them smell like babies.

And the girls? Ruth, flirting with puberty, wore a spaghetti-strap dress, but poor, dowdy Martha reminded him of a horse blanketed for winter, draped in a featureless a-line skirt with a fluffy white blouse and her mother's pearl necklace. Too much Spray-Net produced the look of a half dome of a bowling ball.

Fresh zits glowed in her cleavage garden accompanied by her industrial moniker scent: *eau d' benzoyl peroxide* skin cleanser. Her scent reminded him of Dr. Nick's operatory and the whole of Nedda's abortion experience. He was, however, grateful that she was a willing accomplice to the prom night switcheroo.

At table center sat the traditional porcelain *Seder* plate portraying pictures of matzoh, maror, parsley, lamb shank, egg, wine, and the *hagadah*. The smells? *Oy vey! Halushkas!* Ordinarily, these smells would have calmed him.

His mother boiled, preparing *csirke paprikás*, chicken paprikash, and the scents of onion, garlic, and paprika, aromas which would water any mouth. He peeked into the cauldron and saw the sauce, sumptuous, colored like Nedda's Willem Kalf painting that depicted a lobster with Cassius Clay-sized claws, ready to be eaten. He boiled along with the chicken in the pot.

Had he not blown away Bubbie's heavy crystal bowl, it would have been the centerpiece. Cigars were *en flambé*, and Manischewitz flowed as Uncle Aku began to sing the *Havdalah* prayer to end the Shabbat before they could begin the Seder. Chaim mulled the horrid barn scene again and remembered the Luger's location in the closet in his parents' bedroom.

As part of the *Seder* ritual, Arthur, chirped like a cricket, "We leave an empty seat for *Eliyahu Ha'navi*, for Elijah the Prophet."

There came a rap, rap, rapping, at the bungalow door.

"Who?" cooed Arthur, then sounding like an owl.

Mr. Pomerantz quipped, "It can only be Elijah!" Everyone laughed.

Splendiferously attired in an ermine jacket, a black mink hat, beard to his waist, smoking his hand-rolled Turkish, Borkum Riff cigarette, toting a large box, who else?

Schmuel chuckled, "It's *Doctor Zhivago*!"

Aku teased, "It's the *Vilna Gaon!*" Chaim knew the *Vilna Gaon* was Elijah of Vilna, the ultimate scholar, after whom Uncle Elijah had been named.

"*Ein Trinkspruch*! A toast!" he said and handed out a one-hundred-dollar bill to each guest.

"Benjamins!" Chaim exclaimed.

Everyone lifted a goblet and drank, each fondling a bill, each wondering what was going on.

"Are these real?" Schmuel teased, ever the postal provocateur.

"I robbed a bank!" he answered in jest.

The *Seder* went on, but Elijah's mood darkened during the four questions. Arthur grasped Elijah's left forearm to calm him, and the *tzaddik* cried. "Elijah, you're not in Auschwitz anymore. This is 1964! It's okay, now," said Arthur who knew Elijah's fears.

With Arthur's brush on his forearm, Elijah pulled back his shirt sleeve, revealing a violet forearm tattoo. "Jah. Auschwitz. *Eine kleine geshenk*, a Hanukah gift. He recited: "A-7-7-1-7. *Meine nahme fur vier jahren*," and he cried. "Every *Pesach*, I show this."

Steve, who, seeing the tattooed numbers, became ashen. "I've never seen anything like that. That's as close as I have ever come to the Holocaust."

Elijah sobbed and the Holocaust spilled onto their *seder* table. Arthur grasped his cousin's hand. "It's hard for him. It was November the tenth, 1938, in Berlin. He was there at the *Fasanenstraße* synagogue."

"*Gliwice*?" Chaim guessed. He'd heard much already about the *Kristallnacht* massacre.

Uncle Elijah said, "I was organizing workers at the radio station when the Nazis came in and killed everyone. Only two or three of us got out."

Silence.

"June the first, *mein Geburtstag*," said Elijah. "The day they executed Eichmann. Best present ever: nineteen sixty-two."

That's how it was in Chaim's home. *Der Kreig* was ever present. After that, the *Seder* moved on with the Ten Plagues. "Blood," Elijah said, dipping his pinky into the wine and making a crimson drop on the napkin. Each person recited one plague, with the last one falling on Chaim.

"*Death* of the First Born," said Chaim and he, too, dipped into the wine. Trenton makes and the world takes, he thought, remembering Dr. Palumbo scraping away John Fitzgerald's life. Chaim felt so confused and guilty, as if he'd killed a first-born son, like his sister's cat, like that frog, and visions of Nedda, Anna, and Harry. The smell of putrescine clogged his nostrils and hung in his mind. He was no better than Eichmann, the murderer. Ba, ba, ba, baaaahhhh.

Ilona cleared her throat, maybe wanting to insert some levity, innocently asked, "Where's that nice girlfriend of yours, the one with all the Sassssooned red hair... that Stella?"

Evalyn hacked and replied for him. "Easter's tomorrow, and she couldn't come. Her mother wouldn't let her come... the *goy*."

Zubarsky and Martha looked at each other, rolling their eyes like cat's eye marbles. Steve twitched uncomfortably.

She'd lighted the fuse that time. "You let her come for Christmas!" Chaim detonated.

"Easter is *her* holiday," replied Eva. "She needs to celebrate that with her Christian family." She spoke in her *simple tone*, as if explaining the obvious to a preschooler.

Chaim exploded. "There are two more plagues... my parents!" All sucked in an audible breath.

"Don't start, Chaim. You'll upset your father," Eva pled.

"I *want* to upset my father," he said to her, but then, he turned to Ilona, "My mother hates her because she's Catholic, and *she* wouldn't *let* her come!"

"I shouldn't have said anything. I didn't know," Ilona apologized and glowed in embarrassment, then draining her wine goblet.

Evalyn laughed nervously, then to Chaim, "Yyyyyou told me she couldn't come because of Easter or something like that. She has her dinner with her *Catholic* family."

"You hate her because she's Catholic. You are the biggest hypocrite in the world!"

"Chaim!" Arthur admonished.

"She hates Negroes!" Chaim sputtered.

"I love Jackie Robinson!" she protested. "Wwwwwilllie Mays! I love Willie Mays!" Everyone watched as she went on. "She's *chumetz* in our Pesach home! What the hell are you going to do? Marry a *Shiksa*? Why don't you just go out and... and... marry a *nigger*!" Then she fell apart sobbing.

Arthur, frazzled, tried to soothe her. "Honey, we were having such a nice dinner!" he sighed wistfully. Then, to Chaim, "Look at what you've done. You imbecile."

Seething, roiling, Chaim ran to his parents' bedroom. It was time. He slipped his hand into the space where the Luger should have been but it was gone. Foiled. Surprised, sheepishly, he returned to the dining room where everyone looked at him. They had no idea why he'd left.

Aku's mastiff face curled as he torched a Partaga then disappeared like the Cheshire Cat behind a dense smoke screen. "Keep your powder dry, buckaroo. Shut...up!" he barked. "Si'down!" he ordered.

His admonishment had the effect of an apt punch to Chaim's kisser. Then, Aku drained his wine goblet and he saw that his wine was dry. "Arrrrtie?" he asked, holding his glass to show that it was empty and motioning to Ilona's vacant chalice as well. He wiggled the stem. "See?

Less than a thimble of wine, Artie, Artie, Artie, *etwas mehr, bitte. Wir sind durstig.*"

He was *shicker.*

"We can't have run out, but where is it?" A dramatic, conjuring pause followed. "Oh, noooow I remember," he said, trying to right his capsized host's boat, and portioned the remainder of the bottle into several glasses. "It's in my wine cellar... the car."

"*Ein bissel schiker,*" Aku teased, tension easing, then waving his index finger. "You don't hold your liquor, Artie, the way you used to."

Eva, hands tremoring, inserted a cigarette into her lips, looked for a match, found none, bent over into the stove, and touched the cigarette tip into the glowing filament. "Ahhh!" she squawked like an angry hen, retreating as flames sprang from her hair. She smacked her forehead, but the incinerated hair filled the kitchen with disgusting sulfur smell.

Chaim wisecracked, "It's God's way to tell you to quit." She sneered, her eyebrows meeting in a furrow over her nose, and Aku chuckled.

Hefting a whole case of Manischewitz, Arthur reappeared. The pores on his nose vibrated. A varix bulged on his forehead. Lobster-faced, he riveted his gaze at Chaim.

"You! You!" He pointed his finger at his son. "You, you... sonofabitch." He *fanfaed,* he spat, he was so mad. "*Nudnick!*" he screamed, eyeballs red, and then he farted.

Chaim, and all assembled, erupted in hilarity. It *was* funny. Supporting the heavy wine case on one hand, teetering, face aglow, freckles jumping, he splatted a gooey rubber onto the table where it landed between the triangle of the *maror, charoset* and horseradish, the three points, neatly describing a plane, Chaim immediately noticed.

"What the hell's wrong with you!" he oathed.

Laughter stopped.

Like a hand-grenade detonation, his vituperation came, a bitter mixture of even parts of outrage and disgust– primal, biblical, like Harry the Bee. Arthur pounded the table so hard that every wine goblet tumbled over, creating a sanguineous wash onto the white tablecloth. He was *uber dem kopf*!

Evalyn, grimacing, pleaded, *"Gor nisht*, Artie!" But it was too late, as she turned from the stove, both hands filled with the tureen of *csirke paprikás*, ready to present her *magnum opus*.

Arthur, eyes flaring, entered his Rod Laver backswing and, inadvertently, he smacked Evalyn, knocking the steaming cauldron from her hands. The ceramic bowl hit the table and the chicken pieces set off on their last lugubrious flight. Fight and flight panicked in the brisance as a crimson tidal wave splashed onto the black, speckled linoleum tile floor. The dinner was ruined.

Chaim delivered a solid punch into his father's left jaw. Arthur recoiled as he went down, their lives and family splattering into smithereens, like Bubbie's bowl.

Ruth cried.

The Pomerantz family gasped.

The Rintalas froze.

Zubarsky's and Martha's mouths opened wide.

Shelly and Michael gasped.

And Elijah? He'd drunk too much and had been fondling Ruth's thighs under the table, and now he scampered out the door, like Alice's frightened white rabbit.

Arthur lay in a miserable puddle of Man-O-Manischewitz, Whaddawine. Every red hue, value, and chroma bathed the white tablecloth. Glasses smashed, his heart broken, tears dripped into the mess of wine and pungent, oniony csirke paprikás which would have been savory and delicious.

Chaim, once drooling with food appetite, was overcome, seeing what destruction he'd wrought, gloated in the satisfaction of schadenfreude. He'd created a fête bachique, a Bacchanal, a fête surprise, a surprise party. He plunged in his dirk to the hilt. "You fag!" Chaim screamed at Arthur. "I hope you die!"

A rude pounding on the front door interrupted this cuddly family debacle. A black Pennsylvania State Police car with lights ablaze, reminiscent of the riot scene at Deepgreen Lane, sat curbside.

Arthur, dazed, stood up from the mess. "I'll take care of this," he said ineptly. He was a comedic *Complètement en Charge du Projet*, like Peter Sellers' Inspector Clousseau.

Chaim's brain whirred in French-isms. The scene was macabre and sadistically perverse, *déjà vu* from the night Anna dropped dead. But why the cops? No one had called them.

Wearing the broad, navy blue, flat-brimmed trooper hat with a tight gold braid trim, the officer's head was angular, features hard. He was the kind of man who shaved twice a day, his head seeming as if it had been chiseled out of a block of Pennsylvania bluestone, as if he ate nails for breakfast. "Elijah Lubel?" he questioned. "Is he here?" The policeman who filled the door was as massive as one of Nedda's oaks.

Arthur looked up, lips quivering, answered, "Not here."

The officer poked into the kitchen dining area. "This looks like an Irish wake. Jeez, what happened here?" he asked.

"Our *Seder*," answered Arthur, disoriented and crestfallen at the outcome.

"I thought youse guys were... calm."

Schmuel the Schmuck called out, "Hey, aren't you O'Malley? For Penn State! Joe O'Malley! Nittany Lions?"

The officer was a dutiful beagle on scent and would not be distracted. "Is he here?"

"Why Uncle Elijah?" Arthur asked the policeman.

"Robbed a bank."

"Robbed a bank?" repeated Arthur, dumbfounded.

Pomerantz ignored the disaster. "Hey, Joe, tell me about Rip Engle."

Arthur quizzed, "How do you *know* it was Uncle Elijah?"

"Left this here Polish passport. Lists your address. But if he ain't here, I gotta go," he said and vanished into the violet night.

"Joe was a legend," Mr. Pomerantz said to no one in particular, pleased to show off his sports acumen.

Chaim rejoiced. The *Vilna Gaon* was an idiot, a fraud.

Zubarsky and Martha? They never intended this, but the strife at Goldbergs brought them together again. Martha asked Steve, "Wanna see *Les Quatre Cent Coups* and Truffaut's new one, *Jules et Jim*?"

"It'll be nothing compared to this evening, nothing," Steve remarked.

"You can understand them at least. They have subtitles," she said as off they went. Chaim hung his head.

In the night kitchen, all was dark, and Chaim pondered weak and weary as his mother sucked a Raleigh. "Why did this have to happen?" she asked rhetorically, exhaling heavily in despair as she snapped on the light and filled her mop bucket with steaming water, creating her phosgene wash. She strangled the spaghetti mop and water coursed into the bucket.

This was her angry *Reinigung mit Bleichmittel* tantrum, purification with bleach, which she did when she was *vermischt* and *mishugge*. The odor was like the chlorine vat when he executed the frog, like the WWII trenches, he postulated, when the Nazis gassed soldiers with phosgene. His mother had Clorox in her blood.

Teeth clenched, facial muscles strained, she looked up at him from her steaming mop bucket. "Bastard," she slapped his face. "Someday I'll be gone and you'll remember what you *did*."

He sat there silently, face stinging, unmoving. There was nothing further to be said then, and he retired, listening carefully to her familiar mopping swishes as she punished every nook and cranny.

Intermittently through the night he woke and heard her crying and sobbing. He suffered along with her, feeling such remorse. Her life and dreams had gone so terribly wrong, and his dishevelment destroyed her party.

He dreamed fitfully. Is everyone's *Seder* like this? *You are such a disappointment*, his father's words, reverberated in the wastrel's mind. Maybe he did need a psychiatrist. A whore over in Trenton just wouldn't do much for this problem. He wanted to *become* Holden Caufield, a figment of J.D. Salinger's imagination. Uncle Elijah was real. He laughed at the absurd theater of the day, a day as dramatic as when Anna dropped dead and equally red.

Spleenful in his thoughts, contrition came. How could he have hit his father? He woke. In the moonlight he noticed a stain on his sheets: blood. His father's blood stained his knuckles. He heard his father whimpering in his bedroom next door. Should he go to him, to comfort him?

Overwhelmed, exasperated, and exhausted, he mumbled to himself, trying to find cheer. "Man-O-Manischewitz, Whaddawine," but it wasn't funny. It was all a vivid mess of *csirke paprikás*. Elijah, a Holocaust survivor, had a concentration camp number. Until that moment the War seemed distant, but there it was, so personal at his *Seder* table.

When he woke the next morning, he had nasty finger mark bruises on his left cheek and the beginnings of a black eye. It took two weeks for the visible black and blues to vanish, but inwardly, in his deep down spot, he never forgot that slap and all that it represented. That Passover of 1964 had come in like a lamb but went out like a lion... a raging lion.

16

Centrifugal Forces

Secrets shadowed his successes like a watermark in fine linen stationery. Because of Evalyn's formidable meddling to dismantle his love affair with *traif* Stella, Chaim was seldom home, preferring to caress and dote on his girl at her home where mother Magdalena Mary plied them with an inexhaustible supply of colored M&M's.

His parents prickled over his perambulations. Where were you? Where are you? Where will you be? When will you be home? This was the inquisition gauntlet he ran.

At this time, he'd lose his sense of self. Who was he? His various alter egos competed for his attentions as he gulled and gaffed his wicked parents. He'd gone over an edge between truth and fiction and transformed into Pagliacci, the cuckolded clown, a fop. He was a betrayed Rigoletto, a jester participating in murder. He was Shecky Greene's Swiss cheese, with more holes than substance, a personality filigree, *Filigreto*. Or... and he laughed... *Chaimeleon,* his mother's equal at disguise and deception.

Nedda had led the naive dupes into perilous waters, t-boned, as they were, by crime in devilish fog, and they felt as if they were sinking... like the *Andrea Doria*. His dilemma was that he wanted both women, and to perpetrate his deed he had to lie to the girl he adored, Stella, the one who should have been able to trust him most. He betrayed her.

Often he felt that Nedda didn't care about anything more than the contents of his zipper.

How could he do such things? Had he no morals? Was he that vacant?

But why? Why was he so driven that one was not enough? Every bit of ethos held that his impulses were wrong. He cheered himself on and created Cunnilingus Man, a heroic, tireless, insatiable lover. This character was a porno-*übermensch*, whose abilities far exceeded anything Clark Cunt imagined. He needed his pizza cutter to separate these deeds, to allow him to continue. But what he was doing was wrong and he knew it.

He had a naughty mind which he could share with no one. Did Ward and June Cleaver actually get naked? Did she ever beg him, "Oh, Ward! Fuck my ass," Neddy's favorite treat? Did Harriet ever suck Ozzie's cock? Did he come in her mouth? He fantasized Harriet grabbing Ozzie's gigantic ostrich, demanding, "I'm gonna suck it dry."

Missus Bliss once said, "A mass undergoing curved motion constantly accelerates toward the axis of rotation. What *kind* of force is that... Goldberg?"

Hearing his name, he looked at her like a doe in headlights. "Huh?"

He saw the equation: $a = v2 / r$, almost falling from his chair wondering, fearful that she had somehow read his pornographic mind... especially after Calamari's confession.

"*Mister* Goldberg, are you listening?" she probed, like a dentist finding a cavity.

He pictured Miss Kitty's titties bouncing on Uncle Johnny's chest. "Centrifugal force?" he answered. It was the only thought that came to mind... other than, May I please fuck your ass? He would have asked her very politely.

"Brilliant," said Mrs. Bliss, and he felt the angel of academic death pass. He was angered as he realized then that not every child suffered maternal beatings and paternal shunning and no one, he was sure, had fantasies like his. These thoughts terrified him.

But, like the spelunkers, he could escape. Every Thursday at two in the afternoon, a joyful and promising young scientist ejaculated out the school double-doors as he swam like a good sperm to the intellectual eggs at the Franklin Institute and then on to his musical Mecca, Philadelphia's Curtis Institute of Music. It was on these trips that he loved his parents so much, as he awaited his August skedaddle to California, when he would leave them behind forever and love them more.

He cared little about astronomy, but what's a little math when compared to freedom? He dozed in his final afternoon, hearing something about Lord Kelvin and absolute zero, slept through several stultifying chalkboards of equations and proofs, then on the fly, he grabbed a salt pretzel with yellow mustard, and hustled to Curtis, at Broad and Locust Streets. That he relished. He ran up the granite steps and gently tapped on the solid maple door, C-103, for his lesson with Herr Samuel Knauss, principal trumpeter of the Philadelphia Orchestra. He both loved and dreaded Herr Knauss.

Knauss often called him *Goldstein*. An intense, often livid Hungarian refugee, had a thin, affected moustache. A demanding, sarcastic perfectionist, excruciatingly thin, he chain-smoked and yelled through the lessons and smacked Chaim's left hand with the baton whenever he failed to pull out the third-slide for D's and C sharps's. "Goldberg, *Du bist ein Schmendrik. Oey vey,*" he'd say in despair. He'd end many sessions with, "*Zo*, next week, *ein bissel mehr* practice?" Chaim was frustrated that he could never reach Knauss' degree of perfection.

Why didn't he just quit? He would never quit. He loved the trumpet. He loved Herr Knauss.

Strangely, his sardonic relationship with the *maestro* felt so *normal*, so comfortable, so much like a combination of his own father, Uncle Elijah, not-his-real-uncle, and Uncle Aku, also not-his-real-uncle. Herr Knauss was the only man who paid full attention to him, at least for the paid hour, which often went late. Chaim interpreted the lateness as a personal indulgence, as a sign of affection.

This was his last day. Knauss taught in a short-sleeved white shirt which uncovered a blue smudge on his left arm, like Elijah. The tattoo series began with letter A. "Vat? Vat do you look at zo?" he scolded when Chaim first saw it. "Pay attention to the notes, not my numbers."

Then, he asked him to play the Arutunian. "*Ausgezeichnet, jah*, perfect," he said. "I played that when I came to America, for the composer himself. He directed us at this very concert hall."

Chaim dipped like a hummingbird into a flower's corolla, sipping the sweetness he craved. "I'll miss you," he said, tears flowing and the maestro, too, cried and hugged him.

When he walked to the train that night, sad, sniffling, he thought about how his teacher had suffered in Auschwitz and thought about Uncle Elijah and *Kristallnacht*. Then, he heard someone on a lone tenor sax playing jazz at Ruggiero's, a music and repair shop off Rittenhouse Square. He listened at the door and hesitantly peeked in.

Gorgeous, rhythmic, undulating, seductive music pulled him in. The saxophonist looked familiar, a handsome Negro. "You're John Coltrane! I just got your album, *Love Supreme*." He looked at the worn Selmer.

"Ain't *you* the smart boy." He extended his hand. "Wit good taste in music, too." Chaim listened for a while, and Mr. Coltrane offered some parting advice, "Don't waste your life in music."

"I'm going to become a doctor," said Chaim.

"Yeah, now dat's da way to do it," said Mr. Coltrane. "We need more doctors. Don't need no more trumpet players..."

On the train, exhausted, he was elated. In one fabulous day, he'd been complimented by Samuel Knauss and noticed by Mister John Coltrane. Knauss's *mein Sohn* and Mr. Coltrane's endearment felt so different, so comforting, so opposite from Knuckles Calamari's derisive "Putz" and the bitterness which dripped from his father. With what kind of alchemy could he transform these men into his father?

What a sick fuck was Calamari! And Aku? Aku, his motherfucker? Uncle Elijah was a bank robber. Maybe his father wasn't so bad. In deep thought, plunging into the tunnel, he wondered where his own train headed as the Pennsy Line cars approached the Trenton Makes bridge.

A priest squeezed next to him. The priest smiled and extended his hand. "Remember me? I'm Father Barczak, from Mrs. Zubarsky's funeral. What were you doing in Philly?" They shook.

Chaim answered, "My father's funeral." The words fluttered out like surprised quail in a field. Why couldn't he have answered, "I had a class at the Franklin Institute and a trumpet lesson?"

The priest, concerned, compassionately offered, "Bless you, my son." Then he asked, "May I offer you a blessing?" He didn't wait for a reply, pressed his hand onto Chaim's head and recited:

> **May the peace and blessing of almighty God,**
> **the Father, and the Son, and the Holy Spirit,**
> **descend upon you. May His Grace remain always.**

He made the sign of the cross and shed tears. Chaim felt awful as he realized how he'd injured this innocent man. He was mortified at what he'd done.

He had to get away to survive. It was kill or be killed. Finally, a little after midnight, he turned the key at 22 Turnhill Lane, and entered the kitchen to do homework in six courses. Drained, he asked forgiveness. Bless me, Father, for I have sinned. Then, he purged Father Barzack and his parents out of his mind, plunged his head into a pillow of simultaneous equations, and fell asleep.

***

Pressing her finger on his lips, she interrupted him, saying, "That man needed killing. Some people need to be killed. I did him a favor."

Chaim writhed when he was with Nedda. How differently he saw her by then. She was like a night terror conceived by Lord Kelvin himself. If Mrs. Bliss had hydraulic fluid in her blood vessels, Nedda was at absolute zero, as cold as liquid helium. She chilled his insides. He felt so guilty about her conception despite her assurances that John Fitzgerald was not his… but he could have been, he speculated. They never spoke much more about the baby. He felt so culpable over the events leading to Harry the Bee's death and to the baby's demise. He ceased naming that tissue blob. To personify "it" was foolish. He rolled his pizza cutter and excised "it," the whole incident with Nedda and her baby and the abortion, all of it. He could only cope with *it* if *it* no longer existed. Even more than that, Nedda was ruthless.

He felt Nedda's heartbeat on his chest. Try as he would, he was unable to excise the image of those primitive, tiny hands swirling, swimming in the formaldehyde. *It* remained a person, with him forever: John Fitzgerald. Everything about Nedda and him had changed. What they continued were sexual calisthenics, not lovemaking. This was not love.

***

Senior Skip Day arrived at the end of May. As he drove along, hand in hand with Stella, he thought.

In the weeks following the *Seder* debacle, as always, his father forgot about Passover, or so it seemed. That was his family's form of forgiveness, to move on, to say no more, to forget... like what he was supposed to do with Calamari... to forget the maiming, the death, the destruction that he'd seen, heard, smelled, and experienced, to erase it as if it had never happened, like Mrs. Bliss' chalkboards.

When his father asked Chaim to write a letter to Uncle Elijah, he instructed, "Just tell him what you're doing. He'll be glad to hear from you. He's in Gdansk for a while. I'll address the envelope." He complied but knew that his uncle-not-his-uncle was in prison. His uncle-not-his-uncle was a bank robber, and everything that he'd experienced about his piety was a hoax. Elijah was a hoax, and all of Chaim's respect and adoration had been misplaced, all based upon fraud. That he knew.

"Take that turn," Stella said as he headed to Mantaloking and then to the west, to Barnegat Bay, the beds for great East Coast oysters. "Are you here?" she asked. "A penny for your thoughts," she invited. His reply came as a hand squeeze. What more could he say?

In the warmth at Island Beach State Park on the New Jersey Shore the two teens, wrapped in their loving blanket, like mating turtles, hidden away behind a tall dune, snuggled and petted to the complex rhythms of crashing waves. He remembered splushing Joanie Hoffman-Willberger's hair.

In the local tradition, a throng of hormonally crazed seniors from Delaware High School melded in the sun. Distant from them, detached, they watched the kids on the beach, content to look. "They look like they tumbled from this new Binney & Smith box of forty-eight Crayola crayons. Look at their bathing suits." He read the colors from the crayons. "Apricot, carnation pink, gold, mahogany, orange yellow, periwinkle, and turquoise blue."

"Oh, Chaim, you are such a dreamer," said Stella.

Stella sketched the scene with her new, yellow Dixon-Ticonderoga, number two, with no teeth marks. Together, wordlessly, they colored with her crayons. She drew them. He wore a king's crown, and she wore a queen's tiara. She wrote beneath the drawing:

This is me

This is you

I love you

A little beer, a little pot, they were all seniors, they threw caution and their seeds to the winds. "Our private dune," Stella exalted, rubbing his thighs, and he felt their future heading to California. Chaim clicked on Uncle Elijah's red GE transistor radio, on which he picked up WFIL, *I love you, yeah, yeah, yeah.* "What if someone sees us?" she asked.

"Nobody can see us here," he whined. "Who cares?" He thought about Joanie and her breasts in August at this same beach, in this same dune.

"I care. Shhhh," she said, pressing her finger on his lips, shushing him the way Nedda had done only a few days before. "We can't do it out here." She kissed him. "There's too many kids," so, slipping her hand inside his shorts, she satisfied him. "Later, when we get home, we'll do it," she promised. "Everyone will be gone to the fair. Promise."

Trusting chemistry (for she was on the pill by then), he calmed down and, with her promise, they joined the besotted bar-b-cue. Chernikov showed up with the band kids. They boarded his dad's 1932 Chris Craft, a gorgeous babe of a boat with gold-painted letters on the stern: The Avante Garde, Barnegat, Sout' Jersey.

With its sparkling brass and chrome, it was a seagoing version of Boudreaux's Hispano Suiza. Its horns blatted spectacularly as the kids skied. From frosty green bottles, they guzzled far too much Rolling Rock beer.

Later that evening, they made athletic, teenaged love, and with Stella screaming wildly, then like Nedda, Chaim felt like John Wayne, as if he'd gotten the job done. She smiled up at him, saying, "This was the happiest day of my life."

"Me, too," he said, kissing her.

"Let's remember today forever, just like this," she said.

Holding Nedda's kaleidoscope up to her eye he said, "Here. Look through this."

She pushed it away. "That's Nedda's. You told me you'd gotten rid of it."

"I'm sorry. I meant to," he lied. He would never part with that kaleidoscope and had to lie or risk Stella's tears. He remembered the priest's tears when he lied to him. Then, she softened. She always did after he behaved badly.

***

On his way out the door for school he asked his father, "Are you coming? It's at two." He had to know how important this was to him, in the way that Uncle Elijah's attendance meant so much to his father, even if Passover hadn't turned out so well.

Any good Jewish boy most of all wants to give his parents *naches* at any awards ceremony. He hadn't told them that he'd speak at graduation, leaving that as a surprise for the end of the week. What he wanted to avoid was his mother's extravagant cheek pinching and embarrassing *kvelling*. He dreaded her salivacious kisses and wiping away her wetness.

At the breakfast table, his father shook the New York Times. It annoyed Chaim the way he folded the paper lengthwise, then further folding it into such a rectangular, neat form. "Three civil rights workers are missing, and this is all you can think about? You're not going to win anything. They're so many others. What have you done?" Chaim hated him so deeply and wanted to punch out his lights again.

"You'll never know unless you come," he taunted back. He was hurt and wanted to goad his father.

"Do you want me to come?" asked Arthur.

"Yes, Dad. I really *want* you to come."

Wrinkling his brow, brooding, he asked, "What do you know about Aku and your mother at that fire?"

Surprised, he froze. Like dried, yellow, picric acid, so potentially explosive if jostled, the lies themselves were part of the family's layers of uncomfortable distortions that needed more lies to create stability, even if the peace were evanescent. "I was at school," he answered.

Artie muddled and the creases in his face deepened. "Well, I'll see what I can do. The President doesn't give us much time off, you know."

"So, you'll be there?"

"I'll write you a letter," he answered, annoyed, with his standard cryptic reply, gathering up his newspapers and briefcase, just as his car-pool ride showed up. His father never saw Chaim's tears that morning.

"Is he going to come?" Chaim, crestfallen, asked his mother that morning. Since the *Seder,* his relationship with his parents had been understandably strained but, as always, after a few days, everyone just *forgotaboutit*, and life returned to normal. Chaim felt shame when he thought about that gooey rubber retaliation. What a bang for his buck that created. Truffaut would have loved his father's *uber dem kopf* conniption.

"My Dad's meeting with the President and just couldn't make it," he'd told Steve, who wrinkled his face, eyeing him with his usual skepticism over his wild stories.

Proud and optimistic, he'd worn his white letter sweater with the orange and black stripes. He felt like such a loser, a jerk, and he was sad. He liked his white Levis, tight fitting, a madras, short sleeved shirt, burgundy, Bass Weejuns loafers, each with a shiny 1964 penny, and white socks. His hair was short, a flat-top, and he was rubbed, scrubbed and buffed. After all his self-castigation, he felt ready to win, and why shouldn't he win... something? In for a dime, in for a dollar, he thought, repeating his mother's *non sequitur*.

To have his father attend this ceremony would have been the best award ever, the only real award he ever wanted. How important a job could he have? President Johnson could get on without him for a little while, couldn't he? A wave of despair splashed over him. Without his father's acknowledgement, he was a turd; with it, a king, like Stella's crayon picture where they wore their crowns... like Herr Knauss' approval.

And Nedda? Would she attend? He'd invited her. He thought of her plump nipples and darker areolae illuminated in the previous afternoon sun as she looked down upon him.

And the band played on. When he saw his mother enter the gymnasium, Arthur was with her. Chaim *kvelled*. Arthur limped along with his short right leg, freckled face, black-rimmed glasses. He was there. He'd come, he'd come. Chaim wanted to yell, he was so happy. He waved to them. Evalyn was all *fa'pitzed*.

Chaim pointed and waved to Zube. "There's my dad!" Zubarsky, buried in the sax section, saw Arthur and waved back. His *mishpocheh* entered in the middle of *Under the Double Eagle*. With his parents and sister came the Rintalas and the Rabbi and his wife, Sadie, the Pomerantz family, and the Satanoff's. The Beth El contingent came. Tevlins, Karshes, Glicks. His spirits soared with pride. Chaim felt as if they'd come for him. He'd won his first prize.

A past moment flashed in his memory, a time when they lived in Philadelphia on East Albanus street and all was happy, and he walked up the street returning from a day at kindergarten, and he saw his father's gray Hillman Minx. How his heart leaped then. He returned to the icy childhood day when they walked to Horn and Hardart in the snow.

When the awards assembly ended, Chaim had cleaned up with academic awards and won best overall student. His parents teared in pride. They won the parental *naches* Superbowl and became celebrities in the stands. People reached over to offer congratulations and shook their hands. Had no one but his father come, it would have been enough. *Dayanu*!

Mrs. Bliss approached him and surrounded his shoulders with her arms, kissing him gently on the cheek. "Here, keep these always." She pressed the captain's bars into his hand. "He was a doctor, a young doctor, like you'll be, a surgeon, a young surgeon." She was tearful. "You are the best student I've ever had. God bless you," she said.

He was overcome with her emotion and then realized that his parents flanked him and heard every word. "Good bye," he said, and shook her hand and held the bars in his hand afterwards. He, too, teared up.

Eva asked, in the tone of mistrust, "Who was that?"

"My physics teacher," he answered, and they left it at that.

As Chaim exited the gymnasium with his parents, Mr. Beveridge, the principal, approached and congratulated them. "Your son did real well. Terrific speech, wasn't it?" Then to Chaim, "You've done a wonderful job here, young man."

Then, to Mr. Goldberg, Beveridge commented, again, "He's a fine young man." Arthur gasped as Mr. Beveridge shook his hand. "Boy's got real genius, one of the best boys we've ever graduated. He's got that mark of greatness. He'll do some great things."

Arthur wrinkled his forehead, freckles jumping with the puzzling accolades. "I never thought he'd amount to much," Arthur said, grumbling.

"Rumor has it that he's good on a backhoe!" complimented the principal.

In his form of joking, Arthur said, "What? He can't even drive a car right."

Chaim was mortified with this hieratic Willy Loman barb. He wished his father would have stayed at work. It was so painful. Then, from behind came the sound of walnuts cracking and a Tabac cologne scent wafted over him. Nedda stood there with Uncle Johnny, who handed him a manila envelope with Chubby's Dairy Barn as the return address. "Cream of the Cow," was the tagline, embossed with a smiling Moo-lah picture.

"Ya' can get some ice cream, too, for your family," he said. "I put some free tickets in there. Hey, Chaim, we gotta talk soon."

"Thanks!" Chaim acknowledged. That was the first time Mr. Calamari had called him by his name. Calamari's right eye twitched. Chaim knew what he meant and answered, "Yes, Mr. Calamari, we'll talk."

Nedda demurely complimented him, limply shaking his hand. She captured his eyes, and he was able to turn away. He felt as if he blushed and hoped no one noticed. She wore a Dior, salmon colored dress and a brilliant Vera scarf. He felt nude, as if everyone looking at him could tell their illicit history. He buried the envelope in his sports coat, in the inside pocket.

Chaim wanted to disappear when, as they exited the gymnasium, the Squid floated towards his dad. "I wanna shake da' stallion's hand dat made dat kid," he said. "He does great woik."

Arthur looked at him and wrinkled his face. "I guess he's pretty good. He struggled, at math."

"Math!" Calamari howled. "You don't know nuttin'. You should see dat kid wit a ten-thousand pound backhoe. The kid's a fff..." editing himself, "genius wit a backhoe."

Arthur repeated, "Backhoe?" shaking his head, hearing again that reference. Chaim curled his lips as he saw him mouth the words: *genius* and *backhoe*. These words seldom come in the same sentence. "I wish he'd pay more attention to his studies."

"What's with you and the backhoe?" asked his dad as they went to the car.

He couldn't completely deny the backhoe. "I just wash their backhoe for a couple uh bucks."

"But you don't actually operate the backhoe?"

"Of course not. Way too dangerous."

What more could he want? Chaim would never be able please his father... never. It was all a blur and, as quick as a flashbulb's burst, like the Meyers riot, it was over.

Later that evening, in bed, he puzzled over the day's events. What connected Arthur, Elijah, and Herr Knauss with the priest? What was it? These thoughts of unfinished business sent him into his father's bedroom where he saw him reclining in bed in his underwear. His hand was buried in his underpants. Arthur looked up and smiled, pretending he'd been scratching an odd itch. "Who was that guy who came up at graduation?"

"He's just a guy I know. I do some work for him." He was glad he didn't pursue it, but everyone knew Johnny Calamari. Everyone except his dad.

"And the backhoe? Everyone knows you work a backhoe? That's very dangerous work?"

"It's a joke. I just help."

"You can really run a backhoe?"

"Of course not. I'm just a kid." He paused. It had to come out. It was like pus in an abscess. "Dad, I am so sorry about... the... the Seder." Chaim slid next to his dad the way he did when he was much younger, worming his way beneath his arm, like a puppy.

His dad wrapped the boy in his arms and acknowledged the hurt with, "It's okay, my son. You're a good boy. I'll be all right."

He looked at his dad's bristled face. He wanted the endearment to feel loving like Herr Knauss' mein sohn, but it didn't. Beneath his tortoise-shell glasses, his dad's eyes were tired. He commuted to Philly every day, leaving well before dawn. "I'm going to miss you when I go to college."

"I'll miss you, too," Arthur said and kissed his son's forehead.

Excited, he showed him the letter from Culley College in Los Angeles. "Dad, I got in. It came yesterday."

Arthur looked at it, rubbed his finger over the embossed seal on the letterhead and adjusted his glasses. "Nice letterhead. Must be a very expensive school with letterhead that nice." Then, "It's an awfully long way away. You won't be able to come home for Christmas, you know. I don't know how we'll ever pay for all that."

"Dad, it's the Princeton of the West," he countered, trying to persuade.

"If you go that far, you can't come home," he stated.

Emboldened by his mother's assurances, he said, "I know, Dad, but it's time for me to go. Mom says I'm... I'm going."

"That mother of yours, she's like Rommel," he said and kissed his son's forehead again. For that brief moment, all that had happened that year evaporated, all the vehemence he'd felt and acted upon, all the awful things that happened with Uncle Johnny, Uncle Elijah's craziness, the sting of his mother's betrayals, lies, and beatings, all of that, all of it went away. With his father holding him, he felt whole, as if something made sense and he tried to imagine what it must feel like to be in a family where people didn't gore one another.

When he returned to his room, he clicked on his transistor.

Amazing Grace, how sweet the sound

That saved a wretch like me!
I once was lost but now am found,
Was blind, but now I see.

When the song ended, Chaim was in tears, thinking about the priest and his blessing with God's grace. The announcer intoned in sing-songy Negro patois, "Dat was'uh Diiii-nah Washing-ton and Quincy Jones singin', backed by the Allegros. Yeah. It's eleven fity-nine, in da' PM, an' dis is WTNJ, Trenton, New Jersey, man, seven nine-dee on da' AM. What Trenton makes, the world takes, evvverybody. G'night, evvvverybody." Then the tone... weeeeeeeee. "Yeah, Trenton. It's midnight."

Chaim pulled the covers up to his shoulders, smelled the new linens that his mother had washed and placed on his bed. It had been a good day. With the graduation praise and awards, he no longer felt like garbage, but what a wretch he'd been, he lamented. How lost he'd been, like Holden Caufield, but he knew then, at that moment, he'd found his own direction which would transport him away to America's great West.

After all this struggle, he'd found himself. He could see, like the *Amazing Grace* guy. He created a moment when he was gleeful and optimistic and felt much loved. His mother got what she wanted— bragging rights at the salon.

When he opened Uncle Johnny's envelope, he laughed. He'd adopted Uncle Johnny's affectation of calling Franklins, Benjamins. Ten of 'em, he counted, a thousand bucks. He'd tucked them into a Hallmark card with some stock gooey poetry crap. Beneath a picture of Bambi, Uncle Johnny had written, "Good work, Putz... tomorrow."

With this stash, he'd be able to come home for Christmas and have some cash left over to buy his car in L.A.. Then he thought about Uncle Johnny's price tag, how squeezed he felt, and what he'd have to do for him. Jezuz fuckin' shit, he said to himself, in dismay and disappointment, as the illusions faded, the way they all do after a magician completes his show and you realize you've been tricked.

Filigretto, the liar, that part of him, wanted to rampage's D-8 Cat through everything around and destroy it all. What should have been the best of days were the worst of days.

17

The Sound of Silence

"California, here I come." He sang the lyrics and then went into:

> **"Tall and tan and young and lovely,**
> **The girl from Ipanema goes walking**
> **And when she passes, each one she passes**
> **goes— ah."**

He looked at Astrud's photo on the album cover and imagined sunny California in a few short weeks. What it would be like to bask there... *like a samba.* After the graduation, Mom made a party for their friends. He smiled, kissed all whom pomp and circumstances required, and endured their gin-saturated air kisses. He wore Captain Pippo's bars.

"You're not going into the military?" asked Chernikov's father.

"No. Got these as a gift today."

"That's a good gift," Mr. Chernikov said. "I never got above corporal."

"He was a surgeon," said Chaim before his mother pulled him away to show him off to her women friends from Rosenberg's.

With his obliterator, he excised his parents' exhortations and warnings and sighed wistfully about sun and sand and crashing waves in the distant great Pacific, the warmth in winter, the lure of Hollywood, the freedom of being at college, of what it would be like to leave, forever, Bucks County and, best of all, of extricating himself from the giant Squid's tentacles. He was ready to saunter into President Johnson's Great Society.

Eenie, meenie, minie, mo. He dallied with Neddy two, three times a week, swimming in her pool, touring her deserted, lonely body, all the while teeter-tottering on elaborate deceptions to keep it all from Stella and his parents.

The Clot became Chaim and Stella's mobile bedroom and, when the weather warmed, their pelvi gyrated on their loving blanket in their cornfield to the train's metronomic steel rhythm. The Pennsy Line... The Pennsy Line... The Pennsy Line... car-after-car-after-car-after-car... ahhh... oooo... ahhhh.

Neddy, he fucked. Stella, he loved. He stayed with Neddy often at her pool, and they smoked an awful lot of marijuana and opium. He'd gotten to like the opium mix with Pinch. Then he lolled with Stella through the summer doldrums waiting for college.

Sometimes, he worried that his sexual drive controlled him, but his obliterator worked, and he detached segments of his life from all others, like dollops of batter in a cupcake tin. His parents didn't bother him much so long as he didn't bother them about money. He'd cached his cash in Aku's cigar boxes and, in his mind, he was already on the Malibu beach... tall and tan and like a samba... Eenie, meenie, minie, mo.

***

Materializing from within a cloud of Hoya de Monterey smoke, Calamari intercepted Chaim on the John Deere while he was moving boulders the size of Stella's Beetle at his country estate.

"Nice rockery," came the familiar voice as the Squid crept out from behind a lilac bush. "Looky, Chaim," he puffed, his gray cigar smoke disrupting the still atmosphere. Something was up, Chaim knew, whenever he uncharacteristically called him by his proper name. "There's a ship comin' in tonight, in Wilmington. I need some transportation." He fanned out a flush, five Franklins. "It's from Hong Kong. You know the dock 'n all."

Chaim amassed nearly three G's in his cigar boxes. He felt sick, though. It wasn't as if he'd renounced his love of money, but he knew he had to stop this or... or worse would happen. He knew what was going on. This was serious drug running... serious. There would be guys all over with big guns. The munitions would be like Harry's wake, but without the entertainment element.

Stella would go nuts if she found out, and he could get killed or worse... busted. Getting sucked into one of those predictable tornados would destroy his life. "But Uncle Johnny," he whined as he thought about dishonoring his parents. He had some basic ideals, fer Chris' sake.

Calamari was a predator. Chaim felt the lion sense his weakness as he pushed. "Listen Putz, I need you. Dis' is our deal. Take da' money an' we'll be even," Calamari growled as sweat beaded on his forehead and a drop plopped onto the bills.

"It's a double semi."

"What's it got?"

"You don't ask. It's just paper... yeah, printing paper."

"In a double-semi?" asked Chaim in a conversation like the one they had when he was stuck in the snow and Johnny told about Mrs. Bliss. Truth was that Johnny was a big bull-shitter and liked to brag.

"There's some scrap metal, too. Dat's why. Look, you just drive it outta Customs and take it to Pennsauken. Dat's all ya gotta do. Hand da' guy the papers and drive. How hard's dat?" With that he added another fan of Franklins, and he wiped his forehead with his forearm. "Take da' money, you little fag," he insisted, irritated at his fief's reticence.

"Uncle Johnny," he protested. He knew the score. This truck was probably filled with heroine, currency, and gold bullion... millions.

"Don't gimme dat shit. I took good care of you. I pulled your ass outta dat snow and youse made a lotta money wit' me. All ya' gotta do... Look, you get your diamond ring if you do dis' for me."

"Iiii ccccan't. It's too dangerous. I donwannagetcaught."

"Get caught? Look, Chaimy, we got the cops taken care of. Think about it. Hey, you get your ring." He got off the tractor and vomited into a lilac bush. He liked the ring idea and knew that they had the cops controlled. He'd seen LaGuardia in action on both sides of the fence. The boulders became ballast for the empty trucks when they would sink them along with anyone who got in their way.

"So you'll do it?" asked the Squid with a tone of optimistic skepticism. Wouldn't anyone agree to such a deal?

Chaim gave in, and Uncle Johnny delighted, then sealed the deal by kissing him on the lips. "Omertà. Just meet the ship, my son," he said, whispering the ship's name like a prayer. When he drove off, Chaim rubbed off Johnny's slime, but he liked it when Johnny called him *my son*.

There was another undeniable component for Chaim in this tight-rope act. He liked being an outlaw, and there was no net.

***

He bounced the Clot's shiny new Goodyears into a parking spot about a half block from Dr. Palumbo's. Curbside, he opened the velum, S-T volume from Zubarsky's Britannica which had a section on syphilis, where he read about *Treponema pallidum*, a "Gram-negative bacteria... a chronic human disease."

Chaim shuddered as he read. So this was what Dr. Palumbo's poster was all about. The article described how spirochetes screw into tissue, into brain, especially. To attend Culley, the college required what Dr. Nick called his "Syph Test." He checked the new tire against the curb for scuff marks and locked the door. There were no blemishes.

"Ya' gotta keep your dick in your pants, but if you've only fucked two women, you ain't got it. It's dem women on trains; whores," said Dr. Nick, elated. "Yeah. Got my license back!" He glowed with pride.

"Ya' got yer money?" asked the re-frocked physician, most concerned with getting his money.

"Yes," answered the graduate and crossed his palm with a Jackson, the way one would place a salami slice onto a piece of pumpernickel.

"Here," he said, to Dr. Nick. "Give Uncle Johnny his money back. It's all the money he paid me. *You* take it, Dr. Nick. Give it to him." There were two cigar boxes full of cash.

"You can give back the cash, kid, but it's more complicated than that," the doc explained, accepting the boxes, held closed by rubber bands. "This ain't no... club, Putz. You jus' don't quit us," Nick said, derisively. "Weez, well, you know, *family. Capiche*?" His distinctive pinky ring flashed in the light, it eyes glowing. "You can't undo the ties."

"Don't call me Putz. Uncle Johnny did that, and I hated it." Chaim had begun to feel more bold. "I'm no pussy anymore," he said. "Look, how *do* I get out? Help me," he exhorted. "There's gotta be a way."

The doc withdrew the needle from Chaim's vein for the blood sample and filled the test tube. "Here's your TB test," he said, pressing the dime-sized rubber stopper with four small needles into his forearm. Then, with a flourish, he picked up his burning smoke, precariously balanced on the counter's edge, took a ruminative drag, and dramatically blew smoke through his mouth and nostrils. Then, nonchalantly, he tapped the tortoise shell cigarette holder mouthpiece on this upper teeth.

"Give me your hand," he demanded and grasped his hand. Chaim shivered. Then, from the syringe and needle, which he'd removed from Chaim's vein, he squirted a sanguine pool into Chaim's hand.

Through a thin-lipped depraved smile, he said, "You die... like Harry, or you evaporate, like Joe Zubarsky, you remember?, and hope to Christ that they never find you. It costs blood, your blood... then you leave."

Chaim's knees buckled as he rose up to leave and the doc supported him. "You'll be okay, kid. Chaim. Jus' do it. We need you to do it. You know." Chaim knew the meaning of the euphemism, *leave*. Harry left. He knew what Nick the Razor meant.

Donny Fiasco and LaGuardia, the Shrimp, met him at his car. Chaim thought about bolting. "Get in," commanded Fiasco and, as Chaim opened the door to sit in the driver's seat, Fiasco, with his hips, shoved him to the center. The Shrimp, smelling of fresh garlic and Aqua Velva, slid into the passenger side, wedging him between them.

Simultaneously, the two skewered him with guns to either side of his chest like a rotisserie chicken. It was a rainy, late summer afternoon on the banks of the Delaware on the Jersey side as he looked across the river to the steel mill. Fiasco jammed the gun barrel into his ribs. "Look ahead." Fiasco moved to the back seat, behind Chaim.

Fiasco demanded, "Drive, dumbass."

"I cccccan't see," he complained. The windshield fogged completely.

Fiasco jammed the gun again into his left ribs. "Wrong answer. Drive." Chaim smeared the windshield with his sweaty palms as LaGuardia pushed the gun barrel into his opposite side. Thus pinioned, the barrels created terrific pain. Chaim wriggled.

"Dese guns have hair triggers, Putz," Fiasco said. The only witnesses would have been sea gulls. A raven tore at a dead rodent, reminiscent of last August at the Club. "Stop," commanded Fiasco at the most remote spot on a receding sand spit, which would soon disappear as the tide washed up the river, leaving no traces.

Aqua Velva Man grabbed his hand, doubled back his thumb in the joint and squeezed. "No... ddddon't, Mr. LaGuardia." Chaim protested. "Whaddayawant?"

Fiasco said, "Aaaall about Mister Calamari. Youse a fuckin' encyclopedia. See, we know Uncle Johnny's got somethin' planned an' didn't tell no one 'cept you. An dem bank books." questioned Fiasco. "You're his girl."

Feeling his thumb sliding from its joint like a chicken thigh joint, he forgot what Calamari told him he was supposed to forget, and told about the books, aaaaallll about the books. "An' da' boat?" came the question with another cruel squeeze. "The name of da' ship?"

"Iiiii ccccann't," he said.

"Sure you can. What do you like better? Your thumb or the name of dat ship? You got two thumbs, you know." He began to see blue, the pain was so intense.

"Sssssss," he began.

The two chuckled. "Yeah... we're listening."

"Oh, fuckin' shit," Chaim said, reacting to the pain. Omertà rang in his ears but then he saw blue.

"Dat's not the name." Fiasco ridiculed but let off the pressure.

"Ch... chh... *Chasing the Dragon*."

"Where, exactly?" demanded his tormentor.

"Pppport of Wilmington, Delaware Terminal Operating Company."

"Pier?"

"Sixty-nine." Oh, Christ, he ruptured like a stinky carbuncle.

Then he was alone. His heart raced as he remembered those gun barrels, point blank, and he rubbed his distressed thumb. He'd soaked his pants. Beelzebub appeared, mocking him and laughed. "Youse in biiig trouble, now," the spirit said, and Chaim vomited. Frantic, he was relieved to find a dime in his shorts pocket.

As he pressed the coin into the slot, he felt the phone booth accordion door against his right side. "Putz, Putz, Putz," said a man in an accusing tone. The voice was familiar and onerous and the odor of Jade East and VO5 was equally, sickeningly familiar. "Who's dem friends you got?" The bi-fold squeezed until Chaim was trapped against the phone-booth housing. His assailant pushed hard. Chaim could barely breath.

"Hello! Hello?" came a woman's voice from the phone receiver and then waaaaaaaa, dial tone.

"Mmmmister Calamari. Let me loose."

"Let me loose?" Calamari reached into the booth with his hand-tentacle and grabbed Chaim's neck, squeezing it hard. Then Calamari wriggled fully into the booth, pressed his massive belly against him so tightly that he couldn't move. "I told you I was gonna fuck your ass, Putz, you little prick."

"Pleasssse, Mr. Calamari," he whinnied. Any bravado he once had melted like chocolate against Calamari's body heat. He smelled *Architeuthis dux*'s sour sweat, feeling what he hoped was a gun up against his ass. Chaim hated himself for being such a geek, recalling the Latin name for *squid* at a time like this.

"Whad'ya' tell dem guys?"

"Nothin'. They jus' said 'hello.' Nice guys, you, know."

"Bedderbe nuttin'. I got a little somethin' for you right now. You gotta get over to dat bitch's place and drown her. You unnerstan'? Drown her. Dat's what you gotta do. She knows everything... everything. If you don't, I'm gonna drown *you*. You work for me or you die, Putz."

As quickly as he appeared, the Squid vanished, leaving nothing more than his black ink trail of coercion which melded into the fog. Calamari looked as if he'd been inflated with a can of *Cheez Whiz*.

Me or her? Could he do it? It had come down to that. He had to do it. He thought about holding her under water. Could he really do it? He thought about drowning his sister's cat and how it struggled until it died and thought of making love with Neddy, of sipping champagne, and of her perfumes. Me or her? It was *Exitus acta Probat*, the end justifies the means. This must have been how Julius Caesar felt.

Before Manor Boudreaux's dahlias and peonies, which fluoresced in summer splendor, paying weak homage to the peacocks that spread their showy feathers, he trembled. It was a stinking hot day, well into the nineties, and there she was at the pool. They'd swim together for the last time, and he'd hold her head under water and leave. He sorrowed.

She looked like a daffodil, relaxing in her yellow, polka-dot bikini, so unaware of what would happen. The bikini was the same one she wore when they first met. The lyric sprang into his mind:

Now she's afraid to come out of the water,
And I wonder what she's gonna do.
Now she's afraid to come out of the water,
And the poor little girl's turning blue.

Primping away, unaware of her future, she looked up at him smiling, wads of white cotton between her toes and the acetone smell of nail polish in the air. He walked towards her, but before he could speak, there came that familiar grrrrrr.

"You love birds having a niiiizzze afternoon?" It was Cheez Whiz Calamari. Nedda tied up her top as he leveled a black, 9 mm at them.

"Chaim!" she cried out.

"Both of you, on your knees," he snarled, waving them to the ground, facing the pool. "Scared, Putz? This won't take long. I don't trust you, Putz."

Calamari snapped the slide, and the bullet clicked into the chamber. Chaim thought about turning and lunging at him. Who would be first? Calamari breathed heavily through his deviated nasal septum, and Chaim became nauseated with the Squid's rancid BO. Chaim turned his eyes to Nedda.

A shot ripped the afternoon's poolside calm and strawberry spray coated them. That was the end of Johnny "The Squid" Calamari.

Donny Fiasco and his FBI marksman had done did their job well.

***

"Chaim!" she screamed. "Look what happened!" They sat in her bedroom. "I told you!" She shook the evening edition of the *Philadelphia Inquirer*: Gangster Toppled. He'd never seen Stella so furious. It was titillating.

"You went over there and fucked her? Chaim, what about us?"

"How do you know?"

"I knew something wasn't right. I had to see her."

He blanched and felt weak. "You *saw* her?"

"I left just before you arrived. She told me everything; lots of stuff that wasn't in the paper, Chaim; the meat cleaver, the hand, the FBI, everything.

Jesus Christ, you're a big shit… and we're in big shit." He'd never heard her swear like that. "Johnny's death is just the beginning."

Through their *sturm und drang* Stella had transformed into a different woman and, for them, this hurricane was such an aphrodisiac. They made breathless love until, completely sated, they parted and he sighed, "Stella, we're leaving in a week. We'll be away from all of this. When we get to California, it'll all be different," he said and, when she kissed him, he believed it all to be true.

***

Calamari's demise was offal thrown into a pod of great whites, and that vacuum set off a cannibalistic feeding frenzy within the disorganized crime syndicates from Bangor, Maine to Key West. Stella, Neddy, and he, like moths, had already singed their wings getting perilously close to the flames. They stayed far from the madding crowd.

In what turned out to be his last visit with Nedda, in her bedroom, the last time he saw her, she amplified the New Year's story.

"Here's what really happened. Calamari and I *were* lovers. That was *his* baby. Harry surprised us. Harry'd come to kill *me*," said Nedda.

"But why?"

"I had to tell him about us, about you. He was insane."

"Nedda! Why would you do that?"

"He found the closet, and he knew I'd ratted him out to Johnny, but he wanted, really wanted to possess me, to control me. We fought all the time."

"*Oy vey*," said Chaim, holding his chin in his hands.

"Then it all got crazy. You know how big Uncle Johnny was; a big, big man. Harry and Johnny were like lions fighting. Johnny whacked off Harry's hand with the meat cleaver and then shot him. That's what happened. I wanted to die after it was all over. I took too many pills. I couldn't ask Ping to clean it up… three can keep a secret, you unnerstan'."

Chaim was breathless. "So *you* didn't shoot him?"

"I could have. I should have."

"The hand in his truck?"

"Johnny wanted to show the guys. His wife had kicked him out and he was coming back to get the rest of Harry out of here, but that's when he found you. He wanted to kill *you* when he left."

None of this made sense. "But why didn't he…?"

"Kill you? You did those deliveries. They were very dangerous. He knew the FBI and BNDD guys were watching. He needed you, and they'd never suspect you," she revealed. "You were very brave."

She passed her hookah mouthpiece. "Try this," she offered, and he did. "It's better than opium. We're chasing the dragon."

"Nedda, I know I am pretty loaded, but try it again."

She started over. "This is the honest to God's truth. Harry deserved what he got, but, no, it wasn't me who killed him. It was Johnny. Christ, I tried to whack at him with the cleaver but I only got him on the shoulder. That's when Johnny got in on it. Jeez, Harry was strong."

"So you were the victim but Calamari got to him?" he asked. "This is strong stuff," referring to their smoke. "Long before I actually turned over those books?"

She assented, nodding her head. "Like it?"

He held her. "Yeahhhh," he said, his words and thoughts were elongated, like bubbles from a kid's bottle of bubbles. "But, nothing I did."

She shook her head "no." She cried. "I can't believe that you'll be gone."

"What are you going to do? Stay here?"

Chaim exhaled. Everything seemed so velvety. "You have meant everything to me," she said. "He would have killed me without you. I'm going to live with Vladimir and Wanda."

"Did you ever really tell Harry about us?"

"No... but Ping did. They were lovers." She laughed.

Chaim gulped. "What's funny?"

"Vladimir always says, 'there are Jewish pianists, homosexual pianists, and bad pianists.' I am going to find out which one of those I am."

He had to make sense of this but he wanted to sleep. "So Harry the Bee, with all his toughness, was a fag?"

"C'mon, Chaim. I need you one more time," she said, ignoring the Harry slur, then running her hands across his sculpted abdomen. "Let me play for you... one last time." And she played *Moonlight Sonata*. Who knew what it really sounded like, they were both righteously stoned, but to him she produced musical ambrosia.

"Why are *you* crying?" she asked, her words seeming so slow.

"Oh, Nedda, I'm going to miss you," he said, his knees and heart weakening as he stood beside the *Bechstein*, running his hand across the swan wing. The carvings on the piano reminded him of the talons on that claw-footed tub. "I'll miss your," he groped for a word, "grandeur," he managed. "You'll be okay?"

"Chaim, I am cream. I like it on top, you know that. There're lots of lucky little girls for you at college," she said, emotionally pulling away, and that stung him.

"But they are *little* girls, and I don't want them anymore." She passed the pipe again. He waved her off and noticed a new bauble on her gold necklace. "What's that?"

"It's a bee... from the tiny bit of gold from Harry's ring." They snuggled on her day bed.

He was shocked. "After he treated you so badly?"

"Honey, Sugar Pie. You floated like a butterfly, he stung like a bee. I'll always *love* him."

"Ddddidn't you love me?" He was heart-sick and very stoned.

"Oh, yes... yes... Christ," she said. "Yes, I did. You're built like a brick shithouse," she said. "Oh, and your hands and lips are fabulous," she moaned, and with that she took him in her mouth, holding him firm with her right hand, then encircling and rubbing him with her left. He gazed down into her blue eyes and watched her lips on him, and in his dream he closed his eyes. "My special backrub," she said. "Now," she demanded, and turned over. "Do it hard."

They woke a while later and, as they began to part, she said, "You gotta understand what really happened. You were brave, but you knew too damn much. Anyone who knows too damn much is a threat. Promise me you'll never tell anyone about this?"

"The sex?"

"No, dummy... the heroin, the everything... all that you know. People could get killed."

"It's between us," he assured. "I promise. Omertà."

She had another thought. "I have a little more to say."

"The real, real truth, this time?" He laughed at her mendacity.

"I want you to know what really happened. Really."

"Go on. I'll have to write a whole novel about you one day, Nedda."

"What really happened was that Johnny pulled him off me. Harry was raping me."

"And the meat cleaver?"

"Harry's a little rough. They hated each other and they were both fucking me and it... it got a little, well, out of hand. I had to stop Johnny's struggle with Harry. *I* chopped off that hand. That was the end of our marriage. I'd had it."

"Some people just accept a ring back, Nedda."

"Then, I lost control."

"And hacked off his hand?"

"I went crazy once I saw all the blood. Johnny made me stop, Chaim. Honest."

"The reason his body was so hacked up at the wake."

"Johnny shot him in the head at the end... like putting down a horse."

"Then Johnny left you."

"And I was so alone, and I felt so awful. I'd just hacked up my husband."

"And swallowed the pills."

"I don't *know* what happened," she wailed though torrential tears.

It was preposterous, all of it. He'd never know what went on. "Nedda, Calamari killed Harry the Bee?"

"Yes." She answered stone cold.

"And Fiasco killed Calamari? That we know."

She assented. He puzzled. "Wwhy... did... Calamari come to visit you? He was here before I got here, so he didn't follow me. How did he *know* to come here... after messing with me... after I went to Dr. Nick?" Then he paused as the facts tumbled like lock works into place. "Nick. Nick's the rat. Then, Nedda, you baited Calamari to come here, didn't you? You knew what would happen."

She sobbed.

"Here's what I think really happened. You and Harry got into some sex thing on New Year's. He stayed too long... because you expected Johnny... then Johnny showed up, and the three of you got into it. You whacked Harry, Johnny finished the job... and when I went to Dr. Nick's, he called you; you called Johnny."

She lay on her bed and stopped crying. "Jesus Christ, Nedda, I have to know the truth!"

"Johnny wanted to kill you because you... you were the one who knew everything. And you were a smart-ass shit, and he knew, we all knew, that if the cops got to you, we'd all go down. You're a good kid and, Chaim, you know I love you, so don't take this wrong but, Christ, you do have a big mouth."

"I got Harry's money," said Nedda.

"Which belonged to Johnny."

"And Johnny was going to kill me? Or was it you? You were going to kill me or have me killed? Because I knew about the sex dungeon and the fortune?"

"I couldn't take the chance. It was you or Johnny."

"Or both, Nedda, how...?" He stopped abruptly and began to cry. Through his tears he asked her, "Nedda, how did Fiasco know to come here?"

Both wept uncontrollably, Chaim was so wounded, they cradled each other. "I told him," she said. "We were lovers... and..."

"You were fucking all *three* of them— and me?"

"I told you, Chaim," she said, then composed. "We own the cops. I get whatever I want."

"So, it's true. Three can keep a secret if two are dead. My god, Nedda, I'd been drinking with that devil Johnny, but Nedda! You *are* the devil and you're fucking... me!"

"I made these for you," she said and with his gift, her wrapped box of cookies, he left Manor Boudreaux... forever. That was how it ended between them.

***

Chaim was grateful that Fiasco was an expert marksman. However it came to pass, he was safe yet, he spelunked into the worst funk for several days. He twisted the black volume dial on the Philco TV as the world watched President Johnson sign the Civil Rights Act. Things would be better for Jews, too, for all people. Against this background, years later, when he went to bury his mother, he recalled his turbulent summer of 1964.

Along with his coming of age, his America seemed to have split apart at its seams like a worn pair of Levi's, and then President Johnson did what was right and America, and the world changed.

He turned off the TV and sought solace in his dark room. They'd gotten air conditioning, and he enjoyed the cool. He never wanted to see Nedda again, but he missed her.

And so it came to pass that on the fourteenth day of August 1964, the sixth day of *Elul* 5724, at 7:53 PM, the Shabbat began, a mere ten days after Mississippi searchers discovered the remains of the three civil rights workers. The next day he would leave for Los Angeles.

He filled his trunk, his father's portmanteau with the paisley lining from which such troubles flew. In his acceptance materials, Culley sent him a decorative decal with the college's seal in black and orange along with three books he was to read in preparation for History of Civilization.

He was so proud over the sticker and of the sense of belonging that it conferred, that he stuck it right in the middle of the cover's rectangle. He'd become an authentic college boy. The door opened, and his mother entered, her cigarette tip aglow. "Honey, here's your train ticket," she said, tears flowing. "I can't believe you're leaving... so, so, soon," she said, his tickets quaking like turning maple leaves. She tried to kiss him, but he turned away.

"It's been seventeen years, Mom." On his Victrola, he sat on his bed listening to Mahler disaster music, mulling the discordant tragedies he'd withstood in his last year of high school, and he pushed her away. "Mom, no!"

"Don't push me away. I can kiss you. I'm your mother." With that, infuriated at his rebuff, she turned and stormed out. She bored deeply into his soul, like a treponema, and he was glad that he'd hurt her. He was so angry at her indecent liberties, her violations, like what Jeffrey had done.

He pulled out his giant-sized, leather bound Rand McNally atlas of the United States. The route took him through small town America. Like Thomas Wolfe's journey to the Great West, he'd stride to the limitless Pacific from Trenton, to Pittsburgh, Detroit, and Chicago. Then, Madison, Minneapolis, Omaha, and then Wichita. The itinerary after Chicago followed the "Route 66" song: St. Louis, Joplin, Oklahoma City, Amarillo, Gallup, Flagstaff, Kingman, Barstow, and San Bernardino.

What an adventure it would be, he thought, fingering the route in the book. He envisioned crossing the valley of the shadow of death, Death Valley, wondering how hot it would be, and then to the promised land, Los Angeles, California. At Union Passenger Terminal, 800 North Alameda Street, Uncle Phil would meet him. He would be like James Bond meeting a foreign agent.

One final question came. "Dad, what was it about all those famous authors?"

"I forget," he answered, but Chaim pushed him.

"Tell me."

"I had something to say, then. I thought I'd write." He seemed pensive, sullen. "But then I realized that I had nothing to say, and your mother would say whatever it was that I needed to say. So, now, I say nothing. I have nothing to say."

"Were you friends with Hemingway?" Chaim asked.

"He was magnetic. I met him in Alexandria, and I knew he was great. I wanted to become him," said the father. "He was an author who had something to say." And that was how they left it. Chaim would never again revisit his father's brushes with Hemingway or hear more of his inchoate passions about writing. At one time his father desired greatness. What a puzzle.

In his desk rubble he found Anna's funeral program and began to place it, as a memento, into the trunk. Then he recapitulated, crumpled it, and threw it into the garbage can. She was dead, and he was leaving Levittown, all of it, behind, opting for shorts and tee-shirts.

His mother re-entered his room, and he wanted to tell her how sorry he was for all that had happened, but managed only, "I'm gonna miss you, Mom."

"I'm gonna miss you too, Honey. Your hair is so curly. Get a haircut in L.A.," she said, running her hands through his red locks while kissing his forehead.

Then it came, but as a trickle. "Can you forgive me for being such a bad son?"

"You weren't a bad son. You just grew up."

"You don't have to worry about Stella and I, you know. We'll be so far from each other." Deception was better than the truth because he wanted to make his mother feel better.

Finally, finally, finally, he overcame his shame and made amends with his father. "Dad, I'm so sorry for my *Schadenfreude*."

Artie sat on his reading chair in the living room. "What?" he grunted.

"*Schadenfreude*? Isn't that what it was?"

"Where did you ever learn such a word?"

"I'm sorry," he said and hugged his dad and they wept together. His dad knew what he meant. "I'm sorry about so much, Dad."

"It'll be all right. Don't worry," his father said. "My father never spoke to me. My mother never kissed me... ever." He teared up, wiped his eyes. "Never."

"Tell me more," he questioned, but Artie waved him away.

"I have forgotten all of it," he said, and it was then that Chaim realized that WW-I Poland, in the ghetto, was just too painful a reminiscence for his father.

His dad handed him a small, green jewelry box, with Rolex, in gold print, on its top. "Your mother and I want you to have this." His mother had come into the room. He opened the box and there was a gold, Rolex, Perpetual Date-Just President with alligator wrist straps. On the back, it was engraved with his initials and the date of high school graduation: CBG June 27, 1964. The trio hugged, and Chaim knew that all was forgiven.

Then came his final night with Stella. Wearing his new Rolex, they infiltrated the Country Club through a hole in the fence at the fourth green, where he'd watched Poe dissect that rabbit. She said, "I don't want to cry, but I can't hold it back."

"What a year. I'll always think of you," he whispered in her ear. They intertwined like the wisteria vines, hugged and kissed softly, tenderly, and all seemed so well. "We'll be together in California... soon," he said, and this certainty soothed his spirit. If there was anything he could depend upon, it was that.

In the heat of the night, lighted by fireflies in the moist, unhurried air, they swam in mercury moonlight. "Stella, oh, Stella," he swooned. He sang *Stella by Starlight* as he kissed her neck, bubbled water into her neck, humming their song. She whispered in his ear. "You were so good when we thought of having our baby. You didn't leave me. My mother said that you'd dump me, but I knew how good you are."

"And with my crazy family, you didn't leave me," he whispered, clutching her. "I'd never leave you." His words were as delicate as bees wings fluttering into the nape of her neck.

"I have to tell you more," she whispered. He wrapped her in his cocoon. "My father was drunk when Judas died, raging like Mr. Boudreaux. I was so scared at Nedda's. He stumbled lighting our bar-b-cue with gasoline and the can spilled over, onto little Judas. The garage exploded and there was nothing any of us could do. I pulled him from the fire and got burned. I nearly died, too. He burned up like Harry. My dad left us, and my mother never forgave him. I've never seen him again."

Stella was so sad, so pummeled. "Chaim, Judas and I were twins. I still hear his heart beat."

"Oh, Stella," he cried and drew her to him.

"I need you so, Chaim. Be with me always."

"Yes, yes, always."

He'd recall this moment many times over his long life, how it scared him, how close he felt with her, soul to soul. They cried together until he said, "I have no more tears. When I feel like a *schmendrik*, a *putz*, you make me feel like a *tzaddik*."

She laughed through her soft sobs. "You are my daffodil," she said, and he kissed her eyelids, and they made love. They had come together the way that crayons melt in the warm summer sun, and their colors had become one form.

He did not know that this was his last night with her for all time.

***

327

Decades later, at his mother's graveside, as if looking through gauze, he recalled those moments at 22 Turnhill Lane when Evalyn asked, "When do you want to go?" There was a finality to it but, even then, there remained one more confrontation. The venue? In her kitchen.

"Mom, we've been over this. Stella's taking me to the station. I'm a big boy now. Let's not fight about this." Exasperated and impatient, he opened the hollow-core Levitt door and entered his childhood bedroom.

There was his baseball card collection stowed in shoe boxes, his mother had already pruned away his books, but there were remnants of science projects and his childhood microscope. "I'll get a binocular one when I get to medical school," he said, holding the toy scope. The right angle book case was gone. They'd sold it. The roll-away bed where Jeffrey violated him remained. He never forgot that memory of swallowing that mouthful of salty ejaculate.

His parents stood behind him. He felt as if he were visiting his own museum. "Maybe your cousin Eddy will give you his," Arthur said, referring to Aunt Claire's son. "He's at medical school at USC," his father extolled Eddy, setting the benchmark. "You should be so good as Eddy to get in there." Always the jab, always the put-down.

He walked to the far wall, clutched and petted his signed, Hank Greenberg, first baseman's mitt, while thinking about whacking his dad with his Louisville Slugger, thinking about Nedda and what she did to Harry the Bee. He recognized that his anger had actually abated. It wasn't the way it had once been.

He scooped Uncle Elijah's red transistor radio from his desk, tucked the gold pocket watch into his Bermudas along with Captain Bliss's parallel bars, furtively concealed his stash of rubbers, which he had yet to use, hidden in a wood 3x5 card box. Then, heart heavy, closing the door, he returned through the portal into the kitchen, recalling as he walked that macabre, bacchanalic *Seder* which went so awry and Uncle Elijah's bank robbery.

Chaim looked at his father, feeling his dirk stabbing him in his chest, recalling his painful graduation remark. "Dad, do you really feel that I'll never amount to anything?"

Arthur sat in his reading chair in the living room and looked so low, so tired. Maybe it was the light, but he had deep fatigue lines around his eyes. "You almost killed yourself in that car crash, and then what you did at the *Seder*, but then... then... you..."

Arthur faltered, reaching for more words. "The awards, the backhoe, all of your talents, playing the trumpet. I have never done anything, and here you are. You'll do well. We're very proud." Tears splashed onto his dad's loose-fitting Italian net tee shirt. "I'm sorry I couldn't have been a better father. It was all I could do to stay alive. I thought about ending it all. It was all I could do."

His father cradled him and said, "You're the best son... ever." At first, the comment felt as if it came from watching *Ozzie and Harriet*. But his father cried, and those were real tears on his freckled cheeks and for that moment the centrifugal forces threatened to tear everything apart. Then, the forces relented, and they drew together as a father and son.

Chaim was Biff talking to Willy Loman. He'd bested his father. He'd won. They embraced, and Chaim kissed the sad man, and he felt his father's thin lips on his neck as he kissed his son. "You've grown up, *Boychick*," his father said, and they parted, both crying.

"But cccan I come home for Christmas?" he asked with tears. Arthur turned away as if shunning him. He embraced his father and hung on him. "Dad, Dad, I am so sorry," and he sobbed.

Arthur hugged him, pulling him so close. "It's okay, my son. I understand," he said, his cheeks soggy.

Then, after a few moments, both became self-conscious. Chaim reverted to Bogey and said, "I got a train to catch," which sounded rough enough, then, kissing his fingertips, he touched the mezuzah for the last time, and passed from the portal at Manor Goldberg into his Diaspora.

He hugged his mom for what seemed a long while and then said, "Bless me father, for I have sinned," stunning his mother yet again. "Hope to Christ," he said, savoring his blasphemy, laughing at his irreverence.

Startled, in tears, unable to speak, she laughed, raising her hand in a mock attack. She wiggled her fingers, beckoning him again, pulled him to her. She gave him the most gentle and loving maternal kiss and handed him a wrapped package. "*Hammantaschen*," she managed through her tears.

Stella honked, bah, bah, bah, baaahhhh, then bahhhhh, bahhhhh, bahhhhh, baaahhhh. Closing all open issues between them, then, in Mahler finale, he'd become a man.

***

Futures in flux like melded summer crayons, they nestled together, sitting on the hard oak train-station bench, like the pews at Anna's funeral. They fit so well together. He felt alone within the crowd of others going places. These benches had that characteristic dark patina on the top rail, shined with the polish of body oils and tears from all those good-byes, from folks, who, like them, had nervously burnished the top rails with their fretting, moist palms. Each person endured their wait for their train, knowing how its arrival would insert change into their life.

"That was a *real* barnburner, wasn't it?" he asked, trying to joke, to make small talk. Stella laughed, as she always did, and punched his arm, but she was morose, drenching her pink, seersucker blouse with her tears. As she toyed with his hand he sensed a reticence, as if something remained unsaid.

With an anticipatory burst of industrial pungency, two locomotives pulled the gleaming stainless steel cars into the station, fuming and blowing diesel smoke. The train rested.

Chaim and Stella gingerly shared what would be their final bag of peanut M&M's. They nibbled the colored buttons one at a time, as if to slow the future by making the candy last as long as possible. He was fearful setting out to the unknown, and a newspaper page blew across the platform. *The Trenton Times* headline announced carnage: **USS Maddox Attacked in Tonkin Gulf.** He felt a stick into his right thigh from the pin on the back of the captain's bars.

Two boys his age stepped onto the platform, seeing the couple in emotional throes, and looked at them. One smiled and asked, "You comin' to boot camp with us at Fort Dix with us?"

Chaim didn't answer, but repositioned the bars, grateful that he'd be 2-S.

The mustachioed stationmaster, a tall, slender distinguished fellow, with his Jack Russell at his side, in blue suit, held his folio, snapped open his pocket watch and, noting the time, called out, "Chicago, an' all points weeeest! Allll ab-o-ard!"

"That's it. That's your train," she said, as if he didn't know.

As cool evening air mingled with the moist afternoon mass, fog rolled in just as it was in *Casablanca* and, through his tears, he had to say it. "Here's lookin' at you, kid," but it didn't come out the way it did with Bogey. "I'll see you in L.A.," he softly whispered in her ear and licked her ear lobe for the last time.

"C'mon, you two," chided the stationmaster, "if'n youse goin' West." And once again the Negro announced, "All Abooooooard... American... Royal... Zephyr; Pitts-burgh; Chica-ca-ca-aaago; all poooooints weeeessssst!" Enjoying his theater, he bit the stainless steel whistle and tweeted shrill triplets followed by one, elongated whole note: Mahler.

"Passengers, ticket-holders, only," announced the conductor as he stepped up the stairs. Chaim's heart tore along with his ticket stub as he boarded, then raced to his couchette where he dropped the window. On the platform, she lifted her crushed penny, wagging it to and fro on the necklace chain, her cross bouncing alongside at each cycle.

Half of his body stretched out of the window, as he called to her, "I had no idea what was going on, Stella. I thought it was all a game. I'm sorry for all of this. Stella! Stella! I love you! Forever." His penny bounced against his mezuzah as he held it forward.

The leviathan budged and grew into life, banging car-after-car-after-car as the train gained speed. He experienced an emotional upheaval, like the vomiting from his first night with Nedda, like what his mother experienced when she exhorted him not to marry a *shiksa*. He felt his parents ripping from his insides, like the tearing of cloth when Anna died. Then, it was as if the spirits exited his being... and there was calm.

Ambivalent, then, as if he could still catch her, he ran through the Pullmans, to the last one, where he stepped through its door, and stood in the wind. The wind battered him and he watched the station and Stella turn to specks, as if peering through the wrong end of the Zeiss binoculars. Levittown, Trenton, Bucks County, Pennsylvania, and Calamari's ilk all shrank away.

Overwhelmed, back in his room, massaged by the vibrations and repetitive rhythms of the heavy wheels beneath him, he smelled the clean, ironed sheets, and took solace and refuge in a coma-like nap.

***

When he woke the next morning, a new conductor strode down the thin corridor, calling out, "Next stop, Caaan-ton. Can-ton. Fooooot-baaaall Hall-of-Fame! Yeah!" He looked Canton up in his Rand McNally and watched cornfields, thinking of Stella and him in their cornfield and of their loving blanket. "Home of Hank Williams," sang the troubadour on his return trip down the narrow aisle. Canton 60 miles, said the sign.

America's guts flitted past his couchette window: her wrecking yards, her cows and sheep, her junkyards and smashed up car lots and laundry drying on clotheslines, her collision shops, her welding factories, and her worn out, for-sale Caterpillar and John Deere heavy equipment. It was like looking into America's colon.

Before breakfast, he comforted his loneliness with thoughts of his beloved Stella and opened her Hallmark card, knowing that she'd say something sexy and wonderful. A puppy with a pink tongue licked out at him. A bulge in his shorts reminded him of how much he anticipated one of her warm erotic notes that she'd perfected.

"Dear Chaim," she began, in her flowing penmanship. "My mother..." He skimmed. "Vassar." He was unable to read further and crammed the letter into the cushion cover. Going to Vassar, like her mother... an ice pick into his heart.

"Stella! Stella!" he cried out the window into the wind. Crushed like a beer can. No more. He envisioned her body hitting the tracks. Fuck her, he thought and sliced her out of his life with his obliterator. She could not make him bleed.

Distraught, he ran to the end of the train and thought about jumping into the tracks, but the harsh consequences deterred him. He would not end that way. Frustrated. Angry. Nedda had given him some marijuana soaked in opium. Huddled in his couchette, he lighted one, felt his muscles relax and fell asleep.

When he woke, just past Merrillville, east of Chicago, he realized that he'd missed the Canton stop and the Chicago one, too, where he could have had a shower in the station. He hadn't eaten since Trenton and was famished. Once in the dining car he plucked up the New York Times from an abandoned table and centered on a large article about President Johnson slugging it out with Goldwater over the Gulf of Tonkin resolution. Stocks plummeted.

Another article about the U.S. bombing in North Vietnam was followed by an Op-Ed on draft resistance. Grateful that he wasn't on the way to boot camp, he realized that he wasn't eighteen yet. Until December, he didn't have to register. It would all be over by then, he convinced himself. How long can a war go on?

The next morning, a painfully thin Latina, maybe thirty, not as cute a Nedda, in a sleek, figure-hugging, pink silk dress faced him at an adjacent table. She watched him eat. Famished, he confronted what the handwritten menu described as *huevos rancheros, con cuatro salchichas y refritos, arroz especial, y dos tortillas de maiz.* His studies paid off in that he could understand the Spanish!

He pulled out the bottle of Cholula Original Mexican Hot Sauce with Wooden Stopper Top # 5 and, without tasting it, dumped it all over his eggs, *estrellas*, sunny-side up. After his first forkful, he startled with quite a surprise. Eyes flaring, he looked up, grabbing for water.

The watchful woman asked, amused at his exuberance, "Are you okay?"

"I've never tasted anything this hot before," he said.

"Try *me*," she said and winked, showing off mal-positioned teeth, like pickets in a fence needing some work. She was Nedda's age, had lovely breasts, and removed her lace, cream-colored *mantilla* head-scarf.

A grizzled man wearing a greasy fedora leaned over from another table and offered his two cents. *"Es major con tequila."*

"I have a Parcheesi game. Wanna play?" she enticed in a seductive manner similar to Nedda's come-hither voice. Within moments they had roll-around, industrial-level fucking in her compartment. She moaned and gasped. Following the Kenosha stop, she was gone. She said her name was *Habanera*.

He hoped she wasn't a train whore like Dr. Nick warned him about. She didn't ask for money... and seemed delighted, but it was arduous fucking with so much food in his tummy.

By lunch he'd recovered from Stella's bomb and sliced her surgically from his thoughts. They no longer existed. Fuck Stella. At Madison, Wisconsin a beautiful hippy girl, hugging a fresh copy of *Vogue*, attracted him. She could have been Miss Wisconsin, she was that pretty and very white. She was brunette and smelled of sandalwood incense with hair down to her hips. She softly sang:

Rows and flows of angel hair
And ice cream castles in the air
And feather canyons everywhere
I've looked at clouds that way...

"I graduated from Wellesley," she said in the dining car. "Elizabeth Alice McGaw," she introduced herself extending her hand to him, "but I like Ali." She wore a necklace made from polished chestnuts, and hadn't shaved her legs.

They fucked between Eau Claire and St. Paul. She wasn't as good as Nedda, but better than Stella and, once he got over her hairy armpits and her BO, she was sexually fun. "Great opium. Peace," were her parting words, kissing him on the cheeks and handed him a fifth of vodka and a copy of *The Book of Mormon*. "I'm going to see relatives. They're Mormons, but I can't stand all that crap." Her chestnuts reminded him of Anna's dead eyes, and he couldn't get that image out of his mind. He tossed her book out the window. He'd never met a Mormon.

The hunt was on. Hunting like a lion, emboldened by successes, crossing through Iowa, he approached an athletic woman a few years his senior whose raw sexual passion seeped through her skin with her musky perfume. How little could he do to get laid?

She was a CIA grad, a private chef for a family in Shaker Heights, on her way to a family funeral. Her mother had died, crushed in a combine at their corn farm in Sioux Falls. She looked like a parochial school advertisement, wearing black and white Buster Brown saddle shoes, pleated, khaki shorts, and a tight, pink Chemise Lacoste shirt which showed off her nipples and titties like Mrs. Bliss' kitty titties. A fraternity lavaliere and a genteel gold cross like Stella's adorned her neck. A modest ring touted that she was trothed. She, too, was on the hunt and enticed him towards her couchette with, "Are you hungry?" He knew what she meant.

"Would you like to have your ass fucked?" he replied politely, as innocently as possible, wanting to experiment with how intrusive and aggressive he could become.

She blushed and giggled. "That's the nicest thing anyone's said to me in weeks." He'd read her right. Clothes slipped away. Afterwards, she brought him a warm washcloth and fed him a beef tongue sandwich with cranberry sauce on a crunchy Italian roll that she'd made for her journey. "I sliced that myself," she said, feeding him and licking his cheeks like a mamma lioness.

He looked out at the countryside as he pulled on his pants, taking a bite. "I like the pepper," he commented, devoured the snack, and left with a grin and her kiss, and closing her door, suggested, "Let's meet for dinner." When he returned at 6 PM, in her room an elderly couple snored.

Her name was Marianne Forrest and he'd remember her always.

Stella and Nedda memories faded like color photos left in the sun within a few stops. His heart pitter-pattered, his mood improved. He headed west. This was a working train, hauling America's hod: coal and tractors and steel and cars and grain and cattle and steak and sheep and lambs and pigs and ham hocks for market, sheets of tin and pipes and culvert and sailboats and trucks and mail and those who mailed the mail.

Everyone in America was on this train ride, and he recalled Stella and her cupcake breasts and the engineer tooting the train horn the previous August. Car-after-car-after-car-after-car-after-car-after-car-after-car-after-car-after-car-after-car... and on they sped... and she became imaginary mist.

Marveling at the wildflower assortment festooning the meadows, in his flower guide he could see many of the specimens: Western sweetvetch, Sitka valerian, arnica, blanketflower, bitterroot, white pasque. He tried to memorize the Latin names, but there were so many. The sight would have made Monet come... paintbrush, goldenaster, and bergamot.

The food was great, and he packed down great servings of *cioppino*, *paella*, and *bouillabaisse* and, on his inclusive ticket, they served him all the booze he could put away. He felt like Brer Rabbit in the briar patch and laughed himself sick over his ironic good fortune, making a mental note to write his dad when he arrived in the Promised Land. The train was a champion idea.

He exhausted himself at the sexual buffet, including a surfeit of indulgent, anonymous, married and single women of many colors, those with blue or black eyes, and then, as the West neared, he expanded his taste for Mexican women and the inevitable food they brought along.

He loved tamales and discovered tacos in Flagstaff, laughing himself silly when a Mexican girl, *Conchita*, told him what the street vernacular for *taco* meant. They squealed, and she loved his *salchicha*. He examined her straight pubic hairs and noticed how dark were her labia compared to Nedda or Stella. She bought him several Coronas and a Don Julio and gave herself as his erotic *postre*. The *Latinas* found alluring his porcelain white skin, freckles, and red hair.

Muy chevre, said his *belleza*, and he loved the Spanish language, and she schooled him in Mexican vulgarities. *"Chupa mi verga,"* is a good one, she told him. "Suck my dick," she translated and demonstrated.

He felt saucy, *muy guapo*, like Mr. Fox, sleek and triumphant in this briar patch, making a transition into a society he knew he'd love. He snapped open Uncle Elijah's watch. The Zephyr sped along through the high countryside, and he watched wild horses galloping on the vast prairies, their sweat-sheened coats reflecting the sun. He remembered Aku and his horses, his mother in embrace with Aku, and the barn fire. Zzzziiiip. Gone. Mountains erupted from the land, and he recalled Thomas Wolfe's descriptions of these great square states without boundaries. He had never imagined such grandeur, and on went the train.

What a mythic figure was Uncle Elijah. The absurdity of it all, he thought and laughed. Imagine robbing a bank with a violin case filled with herring and whitefish. What a disappointment he became, what arrogance, what a fraudster. Not-his-uncle was a Wizard of Oz figure, a fake, a bumbler, an imposter of the worst order, a failure; a phony. Zzzzziiiip.

He opened Mrs. Bliss's gift: Roget's Thesaurus. He flipped through it, seeking synonyms to describe his outrageous mother. Pettifog– that was a good one. There were, he counted, fifty more words that applied.

His anger dwindled and dissipated. Tired, he rested there in the couchette, watching the dramatic mountains pass, and his past seeped in like water into a dank basement. He tumbled Nedda's kaleidoscope, moving one finger against the other, looking out of one eye while looking into the kaleidoscope, enjoying the parallax and the crazy monocular images. Her calumny made Lady Macbeth look like Florence Nightingale. Forget her. Zzzziiiip.

His rabbity father had given him Sartre's *No Exit*, which, after he took one look at it, he decided he'd never read—far too dense. He opened the window and threw it out into wind. The book tore to pieces as it landed. Exhilarated, he laughed as it metaphorically joined up with The Book of Mormon. Zzzziiiip.

Then he came to Stella's gift, *Leaves of Grass*. Fuck her, he thought and threw that out the window. Zzzzziiiip. It bounced into the siding gravel at seventy miles per hour and flew apart, pages fluttering behind the train.

On his red transistor radio came Vera Lynn's song, Anna's favorite:

We'll meet again. We'll meet again,
Don't know where, don't know when,
But I know we'll meet again, some sunny day.
Chaim teared up.

What if Stella met another boy at college? She would. He anguished. Zzzziiip, zzzzziiip. Watching the peaks swell from the earth, he squirmed, thinking of his mouth on cousin Jeffrey, about Jeffrey's salty taste, about the humiliation. He muddled over what had happened with Steve. Zzzzziiip. How could he ever extirpate such memories? They were like carbuncles in his soul.

He fanned out like playing cards the handful of photos his mother gave him. "Here, Honey," she'd said. "These are from this year." The photos were of her friends, her parties, and all the people he hated. He took great joy in flinging them out the window of the speeding train, watching them flutter helplessly. "Fuck you!" he yelled into the wind.

He'd smoked too much marijuana and opium, but it was not enough to quell his morose feelings. Who loved him? He felt so unloved, so uncared for, so alone. He writhed and tried to get it all out of his mind. Even fucking all these women hadn't erased his hurts.

These men whom he admired and wanted to emulate, they disappointed him so. And the women he loved, why did they always have to be so painful? Holding *Look Homeward, Angel*, he tried to obliterate his childhood from his mind and think only of what was to come in the West. He was pretty stoned, all right, and it seemed as if thoughts came simultaneously slowly and quickly and pulsing and confused and jumbling, like the thunder of the train wheels. *Teki'ah, shva'rim, teruah, teki'ah gedolah*, came the blasts, jerking him back to reality, like his mother's slaps.

Okay, so you don't like your name, *perico*, using his new Spanish slang. What name do you prefer? Do you really want to be Wolfe's Eugene Grant? That boring? That generic? Chaim Goldberg wasn't so bad, he concluded, and he returned to Stella and his sorrow at losing her, as massive an upheaval in his life as were the mountains in the West.

Then dripped acids of remorse like those in his mother's stomach when she hunched into the toilet, bleeding. How badly he'd treated his father, too, and his apoplectic explosion. He was a pig on a spit at a country fair, his fats dripping away, flames searing his skin.

Gallup-to-Holbrook-to-Flagstaff-to-Kingman-to-Barstow-to-L.A.... He recited the final route mantra, but ghastly thoughts, like a dybuk, returned and infused and haunted him. Beelzebub stowed away in his luggage and would not leave. The vodka went down so well with the opium and marijuana... and off in the distance he heard Anna's caution, "Chaimy, whaddafuck d'you think you're doing? Doan do dat."

Dodge City, read the next sign as the train grunted up a long hill. Whistles blasted. The train hiccupped and halted with cars bashing against one another hard, couplings snapping. Something had happened, and when he exited the train along with all the passengers, the sight was appalling.

The newly risen sun shone at his back as he approached the head of four yellow BNSF locomotives. A wag in cowboy regalia said, "I guess we're havin' steaks tonight." It looked like an abattoir, with bull parts all over. The head and shoulders, complete with broken off horns, lay in the rail bed, its eyes, like Anna's, staring at Chaim, its hind quarters laying open, intestines, liver, lungs...

"Welcome to the west, city boy," sneered the cow puncher.

"Doan look at it, *mijo*," said an old Taos woman clutching her basket of apricots. "*Malo suerte!*" Then she offered, "*Albaricoques, quiere*? Fity-cent." He was unable to avert the gore, drawn into it with the same intense curiosity that he experienced at Harry's wake. Sirens, police, firemen, and hospital workers decorated the scene. He was agitated as the drugs wore off and he had to get back to his cabin.

The sorry train lumbered away, gaining speed, and on the way back to his compartment he purloined a bottle of Courvoisier from the train's larder in the club car, defiantly yanking its neck as if entitled to have one on the BNSF tab. He retreated to his couchette, drank about half of it without the formality of a glass, and smoked two more marijuana joints laced with heroin, inhaling deeply, holding the poison as long as possible. Had he taken a lethal dose?

He picked up Stella's letter again. "Chaim, you have lied so much that I just can't be with you." He sighed and gave in. The demons won. He was in such despair that he was ready to go. It was okay if he didn't wake up. He'd given up to his fire and ice.

He needed anesthesia. But what he got was not anesthesia. Intoxicated, malicious spirits plagued him. They were Macbeth's witches, and in his opiate spell they plucked away his blockades that he'd created with his obliterator and pizza cutter. As he nodded along, the demons tore at him like jackals on a kudu in a Hemingway mental free-for-all.

Through his obtundation, Eva appeared like Cerberus. How old she looked, face puttied with make-up. She wore a rubber over her body... her truth stretched like a rubber... with reservoir tip.

Nedda was Lady Macbeth adorned in burgundy and mauve silk robes. Stella was Cinderella. Calamari and his tentacles insinuated themselves into everyone.

Truths melded into fantasies. How had he gotten into this mess? Yes, he was a heretic, but he'd been a kid, fer Chris' sake, only wanting to graduate high school and go to college. Mr. Phillippo hired him for the Club. He jus' wanted a job, and he made some money... and with Calamari, a lot of money.

In this dream state he'd seen it all so clearly... and then this bull collision... with a huge pile of... "Bullshit!" he cried out, pulling upright in bed and looking directly into the mirror... and he gave back all the money.

Why did he hate the *goyim*?

They made him feel so inadequate, so powerless, so imperfect... and that was the reason he lied and fabricated when he was around them, to feel more than what he was. The *goyim* made him feel as if he were the untouched, and he rejected their leftovers at the Club which he slid into... the garbage. They made him feel like garbage.

NEEDLES, ARIZONA-CALIFORNIA, ELEV. 495, GATEWAY TO THE MOJAVE DESERT: LOS ANGELES: 260 MILES, read the sign. He thought he could smell salt air. He was getting close, but it was a little boy pissing on the track bed, his mother holding him by his hips, as the train ambled through town. How lovingly she held him, he thought, and he recalled the last time his mother whopped him across the face.

TOO GOOD... TOO BE... TRUE... BURMA SHAVE... proclaimed the red, white, and blue signs on a junk yard's t-posts and Chiam laughed at the usage error...like lynch and lunch. A thermometer on a telephone pole registered 115°F.

The train cars bashed together when they halted at Badwater Basin in Death Valley to spray the livestock and water some horses. An electric reader board said: 132°F. Alongside the tracks was a fine-looking, aluminum Air-Stream Duchess travel trailer which had a sign: Bottom of the Barrel: 282 feet below sea level: Ice, Cold Beer, Sodas, *y Chicharrones*. He had no idea what *chicharrones* were, but he bought some, and a Mexican woman splashed *Cholula* sauce all over them.

"*Gracias,*" he said.

"*Cervezita?*" she asked, and he replied, "*Si!*" then savoring sips from his first sweating bottle of *Dos Equis*. Many more would follow. Within moments, though, at that heat, the bottle and the label dried. He loved this place, the language, and felt at home.

As he re-boarded the train he realized that Fiasco and LaGuardia played him like a *gefilte* fish. Omertà! LaGuardia was FBI... both of them were. Christ, they save his life. He had remembered what he was s'pposed to forget and blabbed everything. Jeez, it was life or death. He was just doing his job. What else could he have done?

If the Squid's affiliates found him, he'd be chum, fulfilling Calamari's New Year's prediction. He had to be very careful in his new life. He'd become a mob sinner, and he recalled Harry the Bee's mutilated corpse. He looked over his shoulder as the train started up and noticed no *ladrones*.

At some point, there would always be some bean counter somewhere in the organization who would put two and two together, and Chaim Goldberg's name would come up. He ran his hand against his face and realized that in all ways, he needed a close shave... get this scum off.

Anna's death, nearly shooting and killing his mother, agreeing to participate in the murder of Nedda's husband and, though unwillingly, agreeing to kill his lover, Nedda, and then participating in luring mob boss Johnny Calamari to the FBI where they executed him... all of this lay at his feet. What would be his future? And how would he end? Were these events the sum certain from his hamartia, the proceeds of his lying and misdeeds? How far would he descend?

Nedda's cookie box smelled more of her designer shoes than brownies and chocolate chips, so it didn't come as a great surprise when he sliced away the red wrapping paper and pulled off the top of the shoebox that he found two packets of heroin wrapped in butcher paper with graphic hearts drawn in red lipstick and kiss marks and X's and O's... and a brick of $50 bills with her underpants beneath the band... but no cookies. Nedda hadn't a clue how to bake anything more than hashish.

He paused. He'd stopped calling them Grants. Stella was right about that.

343

He had loved her deeply, or whatever it was that he felt do deeply about her. On Manor Boudreaux note paper, embossed with her name, she wrote:

My darling, these are better than cookies,
don't you think?
It's your commission for a job well done,
for the happiness you brought me.

A dramatic lip print followed with her initials... and he thought about her lips all over him again. This was a financial relief package. He could sell the drugs in LA for a fortune. He knew how to do that, having learned from the masters... and the money... $5,000... exceeded his entire first year college bill... and he needed a car... and he could come home for Christmas. Wouldn't they be surprised?

"Shiiit!" He yelled. He liked the money... but did he like what it meant? Could he love money more than a good life? Look at what the money cost. Joe Zubarsky, Ann Zubarsky, Pippo, Harry the Bee, the Squid, and Dr. Palumbo, found in his own incinerator.

And the lying and cheating, and double dealing? And never being able to rest. And Fiasco and LaGuardia. And Dr. Palumbo, a *gutta nishumah*? And those hideous reflections in the carni mirrors? Was it worth that?

He had to do this, or he'd be sucking Jeffrey's, or Johnny Calamari's, or someone's dick the rest of his life. He liked the money, sure, but what else did he like? What else was more important?

He broke the spell as he raised up the window in Death Valley, in the valley of the shadows of death, where he tore open all the papers and let fly the best Asian heroin ever... and a whole slab of 50's... all, out the window... and her *Gianmarco Lorenzi* shoe box... all of it.

He had to be able to look at a mirror and see an honorable image. How could he create and save lives when he was killing himself?

When his frenzy ended, he dreamed deeply. It was as if a *maestro* had raised a baton and he was the soloist. It was time for his cadenza. He raised his trumpet, and the orchestra hushed. All audience eyes riveted on him, and he played as he'd never played before. Low, brooding notes came at first.

He took Nedda's meat cleaver and bore his breast. He had to get clean! He doused himself in Clorox. He had to do this to purify his incorrigible soul, to tear his fetid flesh apart.

Nedda, you exploited me! Dad, I was your inconvenience! Mom, I was an errant and defiant son! The notes came faster, but still in a minor key... and Stella, oh, how I adored you... but I lied to you. This part was *dolce*. And you Calamari, and to all of your distorted vermin, to you, hear my defiant song! And he played his trumpet into a major key, more brilliant and higher than he'd ever played.

He opened the window, tossed out the cognac bottle along with the rest of the Thai stick and marijuana, and watched it burst as it hit the track bed. He was alive as never before, vibrant with optimism.

As the Pacific came into sight just at the crest of the final pass, he'd keep on going and with renewed zeal, never to give up, never to be like that pussy Hemingway.

He exalted. He would live, and he breathed the fresh western air. He'd made it to his West. And then he smelled the salt air for real. The Pacific Ocean.

A polite knock came at his couchette, and a new porter slid open the door. Chaim, awash in his thoughts, huddled with his pillow and kaleidoscope. "Ooooh, man. You don't look so good."

Chaim looked at the porter. "What you got dere, *amigo*?" asked an elderly, husky Indian, face, swarthy from far too much southwestern sun.

"It's a kaleidoscope." Chaim focused and asked, "Are you an Indian?"

"I am hundred percent Sioux: Bear, Running-Eagle. My great, great, granddad died fighting Custer in 1875."

"At Little Bighorn?" Chaim asked, incredulous, like meeting someone who could have seen Lincoln shot.

"You know your history. So, what're you lookin' at?"

Chaim chuckled and answered, "It would take a while to explain, sir."

He passed it to the Indian, like a peace pipe, and the old man looked into it. "Whoa! Yeah, that's sumptin'. But you can't see nuttin' wit it," he said, pulling the eyepiece back from his right eye.

"Yeah, you can. You just have to know what to look at."

"You can see stuff wit' dat?"

"Yep."

"Man, you sure is smart," he said, wrinkling his eyes, trying to make some sense of the instrument.

"I'm going to college. I'm gonna to be a doctor," he said, cotton-mouthed, hung over.

"A medicine man! Wow! Now that's sumptin', too." The Indian placed his hand onto Chaim's forehead and withdrew it quickly. "Ohhh... you are a strong spirit! You'll be a powerful medicine man; help a lot of sick people." Then he surprised him with, "*Mazel tov.*"

On Chaim's radio came, "Howlin' at a quarter-million watts... down here with the donkeys, heee-haw, Wolfman Jack, here. XERB, Tijuana, 1090 AM. It's six in the AM," the Wolfman pattered and then the time tone, eeeeeeeeeeeee.

The porter pulled out the stem on his pocket watch and synchronized his time. "Yeah, dat's right," he agreed with the Wolfman and snapped the case shut. "Welcome to da' West, *amigo.*"

Chaim liked the ring of becoming a *medicine man*. He wanted to heal. With his torrid past behind him, nothing mattered except his future and the good he would do. He felt like Albert Schweitzer, elated, feeling as if he'd outrun his lies. He had one hell of a headache after his Death Valley binge and searched for some cool, clear, water.

"Los An-ge-leeeees, Union Passen-ger Ter-min-al. Last stop. Union Passenger Terminal," cried the porter. "Los An-ge-leeeees. Da laaaaast stoooop!"

The porter walked past his open door. "Twenty-minutes, Mistah Medicine Man." When he clicked the lock shut, Chaim shivered, the sound still reminding him of that distinctive cocking snap from Calamari's pistol at Nedda's pool.

There was one final order of business he had to settle. He pulled out the Luger. He'd brought it along "just in case"... just in case he would kill himself. He'd rehearsed how he'd do it. Put the muzzle into his mouth... and he'd blow off the top of his head, like Hemingway. After all of this indulgent, simpering, and whining self-torture, for that was what this all was, Jesus F., Fucking Christ, he would live, no matter what... *teki'ah gedolah*.

He tossed out the shells and each exploded on the tracks as they percussed into the rip-rap. Then he launched the pistol out the window. The train was going very fast then, and the gun hit a large sandstone formation, then caromed into a block of desert granite, exploding into a million parts.

He felt bright, shiny, new, and clean.

That was the last of his demons. It was more purging than his mother's *Reinigung mit Bleichmittel* tantrum.

The train slowed on the outskirts of L.A., and he changed into clean Madras Bermudas, which he'd saved for this disembarkation. He realized that he'd read none of the required college books. "Too busy fuckin' around," he heard Anna Zubarsky joke. Yes, she would have joked.

Henderson the Rain King fell out of his bag along with a New York Times article headlined: *Boris Pasternak's Nobel Prize*. His father scratched through Pasternak's name and wrote above it: Chaim Goldberg. Yes, his father did love him and he felt blessed. He adjusted his Rolex to Pacific Daylight Savings Time and kept the book. He'd read it someday.

Packing up his couchette, he sat on the leather bench, fondling Captain Bliss' bars— he'd keep those— and he looked into his kaleidoscope. His retina had become a make-believe ballroom and, as he gazed, he looked at love from many sides, like the song. The year had been a lot of noise and then, after this long trip, in the still of the night, he heard it no more. Finally he rode along in the sound of silence, in disbelief that he'd arrived.

There was a stunning moment, a glistening space where everything became clear, where he stumbled no more. He recalled Anna's sage advice: fuck 'em! He vowed to be like The Pennsy Line, relentless, unstoppable, on his journey. Can you really get a whore in Trenton? he puzzled. He'd made a terrible mess, but he'd cry no longer for those *treponema* girls. He had to cease all thoughts of his life in the East. A whole continent, three thousand miles, protected him.

He looked into the mirror in his couchette one last time. What had he learned through all of this struggle, this *sturm und drang*? If he hadn't learned something profound, then all of these novels and all of these films were only so much meaningless humbuggery. Who was his hero? Was he Lon Chaney or Hemingway? Or Steinbeck? Would he be like Spencer Tracey and transform so unpredictably between Dr. Jekyl and his lunatic alter ego, Mr. Hyde?

This was his final question, his final analysis. Who was he after all of this turmoil? Into what sort of a person had he evolved? Such a profound question for such a young man, wasn't it? He was overwhelmed.

Like Knauss?

...or Aku or Calamari...

...or like Father Barzack? He was a good guy, and how he rued those moments when he hurt people so unnecessarily.

And... would he, like his father, spend a life reading the world's literature, but his soles would never stride the earth?

The train wheels, each at 300 kilograms, squealed and shrieked: Tell us, tell us who you are! Tell-us-who-you-are! Tell-us-who-you-are! Tell-us-who-you-are! Tell-us-who-you-are!

The train cars clattered, We-must-know! We-must-know! We-must-know! The engines grunted for him but he had to do-his-part, do-his-part, do-his-part. And as he approached the station, three thousand miles west of his Gomorrah, he drew in a breath of the sea air, free of all drugs, and in the mirror, as he wiped lather from his face, he saw his answer. The vision was clear. He was young and handsome, shaven, and could stand alone. He was the young man before the sea. He was himself. He needed no one else. He, alone, had become enough.

He would have to look before leaping, breathe before speaking, but he was Chaim Goldberg, man of the earth, a man of goodness, and he'd arrived in L.A. to heal the suffering and to become that medicine man.

Los Angeles, August 1964, stretched before him. On the platform in L.A., he smelled a toasty, comfy, corn scent and noticed *El Gallo* and *Quintanaroo*, the food kiosks. In the breeze he caught familiar scents. Chanel Number 5. Stella? Another woman's scent hung in L.A.'s sea breezes, *L'Heure Bleue*, but there was no Nedda.

In the train station, the cacophony of *Los Colores*, a mariachi band of twelve trumpets, drums, trombones, violins, guitars, basses, and *vihuelas*, embraced him and brightened his spirits as he walked amidst the droves.

Where was Uncle Phil? A *Coca Cola* ad, brilliant red and white on a gigantic billboard, proclaimed, *Refresca Mejor*!

"Let's get outta here," came a familiar male voice from deeply tanned, mostly bald, Uncle Phil, his real uncle, and they drove off in his black 1965 Caddy convertible. He puffed his huge, dark brown Cuban cigar. He always had a brand new car, and Chaim liked the familiar cigar aroma.

Uncle Phil seemed to know everything about the town. "That's the Civic Center at Alameda and Los Angeles Streets; the Ziggurat tower from the 1928 City Hall, the 1940 Federal Building and Post Office," he narrated.

Chaim was energized, astonished. "It's so huge!"

"You like movies?"

"Oh, yes!"

"Then that's where they filmed Dragnet, the Los Angeles Police Department. They shoot movies all the time here." Then, he asked, "Hungry? Let's go to Santa Monica and get some tacos," Uncle Phil said, his real uncle. It felt so good to be with real family. Uncle Phil smiled and snapped on the radio.

"93 KHJ, Rock radio, L.A. with 'Surfin' USA,' Danny Siegel here."

"Want the top down?" his uncle asked rhetorically, pressing the button. "You don't even have to get out anymore with these new models." Uncle Phil glimpsed at Chaim's Rolex. "That's a doozie," he said. "They must love you a lot."

Uncle Phil's notice boosted Chaim's spirits, and he replied, "Yes. Yes, they do. My parents gave it to me for graduation."

He remarked, "Your dad tells me you're pretty good with a backhoe."

Then, Chaim Goldberg's sorrows from the East evaporated in the warm California sun along with the lifting beach fog, and before him lay all of Lyndon Johnson's Great Society. "This is going to be so good!"

Discussion Questions:

Q. You call this genre autobiographical fiction or memoir fiction. Is this really "you?"

A. This is the first question everyone asks a novelist. Of course, it is "I," in the same way that anything one does is that person. The story is fiction, but the emotions I portray approach feelings I encountered and learned from.

Q. Is the picture of Bucks County accurate?

A. I have used literary license, but the union struggles, the Mill, the local economy's reliance on the Mill, all of that is true.

Q. Is Johnny Calamari "true"?

A. I saw a lot of mob influence as I grew up around Trenton and Southeast Pennsylvania...a lot. There were shady figures like Johnny "The Squid," but he and all of the murky characters I portray are fictional. There were various violent events which were similar.

Q. Did the Rintala's exist?

A. They were family friends, although in no way as distorted as I have portrayed them.

Q. Did you work at the Club?

A. I did work for a golf club, and the anti-Semitism I portrayed is fairly accurate.

Q. Chubby's? For real?

A. No; a composite of a local creamery and too much imagination.

Q. Good, evil, and ethics?

A. It was a challenge finding my ethical and moral path, and this story portrays that struggle.

www.ingramcontent.com/pod-product-compliance
Lightning Source LLC
Chambersburg PA
CBHW022349020726
47500CB00002B/190